GILLIAN BRADSHAW

Kingdom of Summer

METHUEN

A Methuen Paperback

KINGDOM OF SUMMER
ISBN 0 417 06750 X

First published in Great Britain 1981
by Eyre Methuen Ltd

Methuen Paperback edition published 1982
and reprinted 1984
by Methuen London Ltd
11 New Fetter Lane, London EC4P 4EE

Printed and bound in Great Britain by
Cox & Wyman Ltd, Reading

In Memoriam
Lt Col and Mrs H. R. R. Rouquette

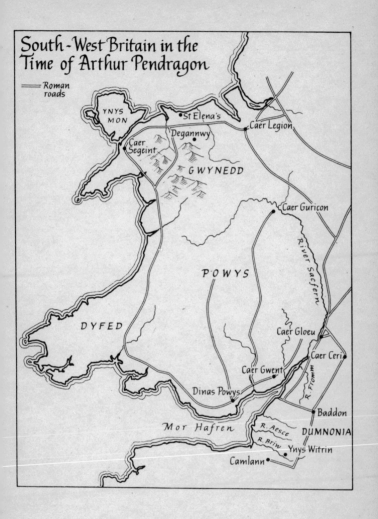

South-West Britain in the Time of Arthur Pendragon

— Roman roads

YNYS MON

St Elena's

Caer Legion

Degannwy

Caer Segeint

GWYNEDD

Caer Guricon

River Sacfern

POWYS

DYFED

Caer Gloeu

Caer Ceri

Caer Gwent

R. Fromm

Dinas Powys

Baddon

Mor Hafren

R. Aesce

DUMNONIA

R. Briw

Ynys Witrin

Camlann

One

Dumnonia is the most civilized kingdom in Britain, but in the north-east, in January, it looks no tamer than the wilds of Caledonia. The fields are swallowed by the snow, with only the stubble tips showing pale above the drifts, and the sky is drained of colour and seems to weigh upon the heavens. Beyond the cultivated lands – in the case of my family, beyond the river Fromm – lies the forest, dark branches and white snow mingling to form a lead-grey cloud along the horizon, mile upon mile of silence and the panting of wolves. In the summer, men and women ignore the forest. Fields are tended and the produce is brought to market, the oxen draw the plough, the horses the carts – but in the winter the wilderness hanging beyond the river looms large in the mind. Life is quieter, and a ghost story which a man laughed at in the harvest season suddenly seems horribly probable, for humanity and civilization look very small and light against that ocean of the cold.

My cousin Goronwy and I had no love for going out to the forest in January, but it happened that our householding needed more wood. That meant a trip across the ford with the cart, and two grown men to make it, so we had gone, and spent the noon-tide hacking away at the loose brush, only occasionally pausing to glance over our shoulders. We were glad when we could turn back with the cart piled high. We crossed the river again, and paused on the home bank to let the oxen drink. Goronwy sat holding the goad, looking on the sleek backs of the beasts, who, since we were impatient, must needs take their time.

I looked back across the river. The water of the stream was dark with the winter, and the afternoon sun lay upon it and upon the heaped snow banks, casting horizontal beams that shone like warm bronze but gave no heat. The only sound in the world was the water whispering on the banks and the grunting of the oxen. It was three miles home, back to our householding, three miles back to the cow-byres and hearth-fires and the faces of men. The thought left my heart hungry for it, but I let my eyes drift slowly down the black river and along the trees of the opposite bank. And because of that, I saw the horseman there before he saw me. A glimpse of crimson drew my eyes from the water, and then, a mounted warrior rode openly out onto the river bank in the heavy sunlight.

He had a red cloak wrapped tightly round him, one hand half-extended through its fold to hold the reins. Gold gleamed from his hand, from the fastening of his cloak and the rim of the shield slung over his back; the spears tied to the saddle, and the bridle of his great white stallion caught the light like stars. He reined in his horse by the stream, and together they stood a moment as still as the trees behind them, white and crimson and gold. I felt as if I had just opened my eyes and seen a being from a song I had loved all my life, or a figure from a dream. Then the rider turned his gaze along the river, and met my own stare, and I came back to myself, and knew enough to become afraid.

'Goronwy!' I seized my cousin's arm.

'Well, and what is it . . .?' He followed my stare and froze.

The rider turned his horse and came up the far bank towards us, the stallion stepping carefully, with a light, clean stride, delicate as a cat's.

'Eeeeh.' Goronwy nudged the oxen with the goad and jumped out of the cart. The beasts snorted, backed up, breath steaming.

'Do you think we can outrun him?' I asked, annoyed with Goronwy and trying to prevent all the wood falling off with the jolts. 'Oxen, against a horse like that one?'

'Perhaps he cannot cross the water.' Goronwy's voice was low.

'You've laughed at tales of the Fair Ones before this.'

'I laughed at home. Sweet Jesu preserve us now!'

'Oh come! He must be a traveller. If he's no bandit, he will only ask the way. And if he's a bandit, there are two of us, and we've nothing more than death to fear.'

'I fear that enough, without the other.' The oxen shambled away from the bank, and Goronwy leapt back into the cart. 'But who'd travel in winter? This far from a road?'

The rider reached the ford and turned his horse to the water. The stream was not deep, and came no higher than the animal's knees, though the horse tossed its head at the coldness. Goronwy gave a little hiss and sat still again. If the rider could cross the water, perhaps he was not a spirit. Or perhaps he was. Either way, we could not outrun him.

He reached the home bank and rode up beside us and, as he did so, the sun dropped below the tree-line and covered us with criss-crossing shadows. I saw more clearly as the dazzle and glitter vanished, and could have cried for disappointment after such a shining vision. The horse, though splendid, had a long, raw gash across its chest, its bones showed through the hide, and its legs and shoulders were streaked with mud. The rider's clothes were very worn, the red cloak tattered and dirty, the hand on the reins purple with cold. His black hair and beard were matted and untrimmed, and he had clearly not washed for a long time. He might be a lost traveller, he might well be a bandit, but . . .

I met his eyes, and was shaken again. Those eyes were dark as the sea at midnight, and there was something to their look that set the short hairs upright on my neck. I crossed myself, wondering whether Goronwy might be right. My father always said that the tales of the People of the Hills were so many lies, and yet I had never seen a look like that on a human face.

The rider smiled at my gesture, a bitter smile, and leaned over to speak to us. He had drawn his sword, and rested it across his knees so that we could look at it as he spoke. It looked a fine, sharp sword.

'My greetings to you,' said the rider. His voice was hoarse, hardly above a whisper. 'What land is this?'

I saw Goronwy's hand relax a little on the ox-goad, and then he, too, crossed himself before replying, 'Dumnonia, Lord. Near Mor Hafren. Do you ask because you have lost your road?' He was eager to give directions.

The stranger said nothing to the question, only looked at the fields beyond us. 'Dumnonia. What is that river, then?'

'The Fromm. It joins Mor Hafren a bit beyond two miles from here. Lord, there is a Roman road some twelve miles eastwards of here . . .'

'I do not know of your river. Is the land beyond close-settled?'

'Closely enough.' Goronwy paused. 'Baddon is not far

from here. There is a strong lord there, and his warband.'

The rider smiled bitterly again. 'I am not a bandit, that you must threaten me with kings and warbands.' He looked at us, considering. 'What is your name, man?'

Goronwy rubbed his wrist, looked at the oxen, glanced back at the sword. 'Goronwy ap Cynydd,' he admitted at last.

'So. And you?'

'Rhys ap Sion,' I answered. It might be unwise to offer names, but we could hardly avoid it. I again met the man's eyes, and again I felt cold, and wondered if we were endangering our souls. But I thought the man human. He must be.

'So then, Goronwy ap Cynydd and Rhys ap Sion, I have need of lodgings tonight, for myself and for my horse. How far is it to your householding?'

'My lord, our householding is poor...' Goronwy began, a trifle untruthfully, since we are one of the first clans about Mor Hafren.

'I can pay. How far is it?'

'Three miles,' I said. Goronwy glared at me. 'We are not so poor that we must be inhospitable, Chieftain.' Goronwy stepped on my foot, as though I were too stupid to understand what I was saying, but goaded the oxen, turning them back onto the rough track home. The stranger urged his horse beside us at a slow walk, his drawn sword still ready. The hilt gleamed gold, and a jewel smouldered on it redly.

I looked at that jewel and wondered what would come next. The man might yet be a bandit, but would a bandit have a splendid horse and a jewelled sword? He must be a member of some warband, the servant of either our own king, Constantius of Dumnonia, or of one of the other kings and nobles of Britain. If he was Constantius's man, he probably would leave us in peace, and might even pay us, but if he served anyone else he'd be worse than a bandit. He had said, 'I can pay', but that didn't mean that he would. Still, if he intended violence, there were enough men in the clan to deal with him, even armed as he was and largely unarmed as we were. If he were human. No, he must be human. And he hadn't tried to kill us outright for the price of the cart and oxen, so perhaps he did only want a place to rest for the night. Perhaps he was a messenger, or on some special errand for his own clan, and had left the main road in his haste and become lost. Or perhaps he was recently out-lawed. If he was a warrior . . . I wondered if we could get him to talk about it. An old longing took hold of me, a thing most clansmen leave behind with their childhood, and which I had tried to leave behind and been unable to, some-thing to do with gold and crimson and the glint of weapons.

'Lord,' I said, after a long silence, 'what road would you wish to be taking, come tomorrow?' It was as good a way as any to ask where he was from and where he was going.

He eyed me suspiciously, but I refused to be frightened. 'That is of no matter,' he said.

'Well, Lord, if you're in need of lodgings, we could tell you something of the roads hence.' Goronwy again kicked me quietly, not daring to tell me openly to be quiet and leave matters be.

'The roads do not matter to me.'

'Well, but they might to your horse.' Goronwy's kick had only made me angry. 'I seek only to be of service, Lord, but it seems your horse would walk the easier for a good feeding.'

He looked down at me, cold and proud, then looked at the arched, white neck of his stallion. He drew the hand that held the reins down the horse's crest, and the animal flicked its ears. 'My horse has strength enough for a charge,' the rider suggested meaningfully, and looked back to me. I thought, though, he seemed rather anxious for the animal. 'But tell me then, Rhys ap Sion, who seeks only to be of service, what way do you think the finest for horses?'

I was uncertain a moment, but recovered myself. 'There is the Roman road, the one from Baddon to Ynys Witrin, past Camlann – and the one eastward, if the road doesn't matter, to the land of the West Saxons, joins the first road to the south. Do you have no lord, Chieftain, to whom you are travelling?'

He smiled his bitter smile again. 'I am the Pendragon's man.'

Goronwy looked up at him sharply, catching his breath. The Pendragon was Arthur ab Uther, 'Imperator Britan-niae', in the old title, 'Emperor of Britain'. His warband was said to be the finest west of Constantinople. Not two years before, the Saxon invaders had been stopped, their

13

strength shattered for some generations to come, at the great battle of Baddon. This had been worked by the Pendragon and his warband, then and in the years before. Since that time, some members of the great warband had gone back to their own lands, some had been set by their king to fighting the hordes of bandits in the west of the country, and some had gone over to Gaul to aid Arthur's allies there, while many stayed with the Emperor at his fortress of Camlann. All the members of the warband were nobles, able to speak their mind to any king in the island, to command their share from the tribute paid to Arthur by the other rulers of Britain. Some of them were rulers in their own right. It was unexpected to have one of these men turn up in our own land, and that in mid-winter. I thought of what I had felt when I first saw this man, that he could have come from a favourite song. If he was of Arthur's Family he probably did.

'May the due honour be yours, then, Lord,' I said. 'And I am not one to withhold it.'

He looked at me keenly. 'You feel no anger, then, for the Pendragon who raised your taxes?'

'None, Lord, for the Emperor who broke the power of the Saxons.'

He smiled with a little less bitterness.

'If you are indeed the Pendragon's man, what brings you here?' Goronwy demanded, glaring both at me and at the other.

The rider glared back, cold and proud again. 'It is not yours to question, man. Mind your oxen.' He turned his eyes on the track ahead of us. Inwardly I cursed Goronwy, and I kicked him surreptitiously for his pains. He had shut the man up just when he seemed to be relaxing a little. I knew better than to suppose the direction about oxen was meant solely for Goronwy. Yet Goronwy surely had no more authority than I. My father, not Goronwy's, was head of the householding, and my father was generally inclined to support the Emperor, if with some reservations. Perhaps, if we gave him hospitality, the stranger would feel himself among friends and speak more freely. I wanted to hear him talk. Like a boy, I wanted to hear about Arthur's warband, the Family; about battles and kings and the struggle against the barbarian darkness. I wanted it like any

14

child or like a man too stupid to know the difference between a pretty tale and the grasping, violent men whom kings and warriors are most like to really be. I had always wanted to hear about those things, even when I knew myself a fool for wanting to, even when I was good at everything a farmer and clansman should be good at, and was too old to want such things, and had no call in my life for wanting. I had even wanted to be a warrior. But men must be trained in that trade from their early boyhood, and they not infrequently begin fighting while no more than children of fourteen. Yes, and they die before they are twenty. But once I had thought that death might be worth it, and still, this man had but to ride across a river and I wanted it all again.

It would probably be better if this stranger said nothing. I had had trouble enough with my wantings before, and surely I was settling down now, with time. There was no call to stir the old demon up again. I was twenty-one, not old, but too much of an adult to run mad with the fancies of children.

The rest of our three miles passed in silence. The sun set in clouds, and the stars were clouding over. The wind was cold in our faces, stinging the eyes to tears. The warrior huddled in his cloak, finally sheathing his sword, though I noticed he kept one hand on it. My teeth were chattering when we reached the long, low-lying buildings of home and smelt the warm fires and food.

I jumped out of the cart at my own family's house, telling Goronwy to wait. He agreed with a grunt, though he looked at our guest nervously. The stranger merely held his horse steady and looked at Goronwy and at the door.

My mother and the elder of my sisters were by the fire, cooking. My younger brother Dafydd sat playing with the dog, while my grandfather talked to him. They all looked up as I opened the door.

My mother smiled. 'Well, then, Rhys. We had thought the forest swallowed you. But we've kept dinner despite that. Was it good wood you found?'

'Good enough. But we found more than wood, Mother. Where is my father?'

'In the barn. But what is it?'

'You'll know soon enough. Stay indoors.' At this suggestive statement, my brother jumped up and began demanding, and two cousins ran up from some corner to see what about, but I grinned and ducked back out.

When I came into the barn my father was brushing down our little brown mare, the one that draws the cart in summer. He was humming softly, his thick hands quick and sure and gentle. I paused a moment, hand on the door, looking at his thick-set figure and wondering what he would do. My father is the head of our householding, of our family: all the descendants, to the fourth generation, of Huw ap Celyn, some thirty-seven people in all. Our clan is not a high-ranking one, but we are prosperous enough, and recognized over the land south of Mor Hafren in Dumnonia. My father could speak in any quarrel and be heard, and men from other clans and householdings would come to ask his advice on crops and taxes and what to do about their neighbours' habits. He had always supported the policy of the Pendragon, and whenever others talked about refusing to pay the higher tribute which Arthur's warband required, he'd defend the Empire – but that was a different matter from taking a member of that warband as a guest, under constraint. My father never liked doing anything under constraint, and we were strong enough to dispose of one warrior. Still, we were a Christian householding, and my father was a Christian man, and believed in hospitality (within reason) and in courtesy. I shut the door quietly and walked towards him across the beaten earth floor.

'Well, Rhys, and have you stored the wood?' my father asked, without turning around.

'Never mind the wood. Father, Goronwy and I met up with a warrior. He says he's of Arthur's Family, and he wants lodgings for tonight. For himself and for his war-horse.'

My father set down the straw he was using as a brush, straightened and turned deliberately, meeting my eyes. 'Indeed. Where did you meet him?'

'At the ford. He crossed the river shortly after us.'

'From the forest? Alone?'

'Yes. But he is not equipped like a bandit.'

'Armed?'

'Well armed, I think. And I've never seen a horse as fine as his.'

16

'Where is he?'

'In front of the house, with Goronwy and the cart.'

My father caught up his lantern and walked out of the barn. I followed him.

The warrior was still sitting on his stallion, waiting, and Goronwy still looked uneasy. As we came up, I noticed that the door was open a crack, the firelight bright in it. My family was watching.

My father lifted the lantern high, trying to see the face of the dark, mounted figure. He was tense, I could feel it, but his face in the lamplight was calm and steady. The light made his red hair, grey-streaked as it was, look dark, and it cast his bright blue eyes into shadow. He looked young and strong, firm in his authority.

The warrior stared at him, eyes glinting through his tangled black hair. Then, slowly, he dismounted, steadied himself with one hand on his horse's shoulder. He half raised the other hand.

'Sion ap Rhys.' He named my father in his hoarse voice.

'Gwalchmai ap Lot,' said my father. 'Ach, I did not think you would remember.'

'I told you I would. This is your householding, then?'

'I am the head of it.' My father slowly walked closer to the other, stopped. 'And such as it is, Lord Gwalchmai, you're free and welcome to the use of it; indeed, the family is honoured. Rhys!' He half turned to me. 'You and Goronwy get the wood unloaded and the oxen stalled. Lord Gwalchmai,' he turned back to the other. 'Come into the house and rest.'

'My horse,' said the other. 'I must see to my horse first.'

'Rhys can . . .'

'I look after him myself.'

'Oh, very well. The barn is this way, Lord. Rhys, first tell your mother to get something special on for dinner – some of the ham, at least, and eggs, certainly eggs, and some of the apples – ach, she'll know better than I. But some hot water? Yes, hot water. Well, go on then!' He started back to the barn, and the other followed, leading his horse, limping a little.

I hesitated, then ran to the house, gasped out my father's message – unnecessarily, since the eavesdroppers had heard it themselves – ran back to the cart, leapt in, and told

Goronwy to hurry up.

'But I don't understand it,' complained Goronwy as he goaded the oxen, and then began to shamble towards the wood pile. 'My uncle Sion knows that warrior?'

I shook my head, in astonishment rather than in denial. My father had said many things about the Pendragon, his warband and his policies, but the strangest was that once, as he was taking some wheat down to Camlann to sell it there, he'd given a ride in the cart to a young man whom he later discovered to be Gwalchmai, son of Lot, king of the Ynysoedd Erch, those islands north of Caledonia. The two had talked somewhat on the way, and my father had paid the other's lodgings for a night, ignorant of the other's identity. Afterwards he discovered that the youth had just escaped from the Saxons, and was on his way to Camlann to join the Family. 'I knew, talking to him, that he would be a great warrior,' my father would say when he told the story. 'And I asked him to remember me. And that is pure pride, wanting to be known by a famous and glorious lord. But see, he is a great warrior. He was a good lad when I met him. Quiet, courteous, generous – perhaps a little uncanny, but . . . I wonder if he does remember me. I doubt it.'

It was nine years since my father first told that tale. Then he had just returned from the journey, and Gwalchmai ap Lot was still an unknown. By the end of that same summer he was spoken and sung of over all Britain. Numerous tales, of varying probability, were told of him. He was said to have tamed one of the horses of the Fair Folk, an immortal animal faster than the wind, that none could ride but he alone. He was said to have an enchanted sword, and to triple his strength in battle. He could, it was said, cut down three men with one blow; nothing could stand before him. He was a favoured ambassador of the Emperor, because of his courtesy and eloquence: they said he could charm honey from the bees or water from a stone. Whatever one chose to believe, he was one of the finest, probably the very finest, of Arthur's Family, which meant the best warrior in Britain, and, though it was generally agreed that there was something 'a little uncanny' about him, he was admired from Caledonia to Gaul. But he remembered my father Sion, and he would be staying in our own householding as a guest.

'You've heard my father's tale,' I told Goronwy. 'That is

the lord Gwalchmai ap Lot.'

Goronwy eyed me and muttered something. I didn't ask what. I knew well enough he thought me rather mad, and likely he was right, but I was too excited to care. I do not think wood was ever unloaded faster than I unloaded it then, and when the cart was empty, I left it and the oxen to Goronwy. They were, after all, his father's oxen, not mine. I ran back to the house and, finding that my father and the lord Gwalchmai were still at the barn, I ran there, ostensibly to see if they needed help.

Our brown mare had been moved, and the white stallion had her place. My father had poured out some grain and the horse was eating this as his master rubbed him down, slowly and stiffly as though the man were very tired. As I came up, he stopped, and asked me quietly if I could bring some hot water from the house.

'You don't need to bathe the beast,' my father commented.

'He has been hurt. I need to keep the wound clean,' Gwalchmai replied. 'Softly, Ceincaled, *mo chroidh*...' he spoke soothingly to the horse in a language which I guessed was Irish. The men of the Ynysoedd Erch came from Ireland a generation or so ago.

I brought the hot water from the house and he cleaned the slash across the horse's chest with it, still speaking to the animal in Irish. I wondered if it did understand, if it was truly one of the horses of the Fair Folk. It looked large and strong and swift enough.

'The cut is recent,' observed my father.

'We were fighting but yesterday afternoon.' The lord Gwalchmai finished with the horse's wound and began checking and cleaning the animal's hooves.

My father fidgeted. 'You did not have the horse when I met you.'

The warrior looked up, and suddenly looked less uncanny. Almost, he smiled. 'I had forgotten that. Yes, I let him go after I escaped from the Saxons with him. But he was a fool and came back to me at Camlann.'

'A fool?'

'Well, he is not a horse from this earth. He is a fool to stay here and have spears thrust into him for my sake.' He picked up the stallion's off hind foot and frowned at the rim

19

of the hoof, checking the shoe. Even I could see that the metal was worn. The horse lifted its head from the manger, glanced back, then resumed eating. Gwalchmai sighed and, setting the hoof down, stood up. 'He is overworn.' He slapped the stallion's rump. 'Perhaps I should stay here with him tonight.'

My father was offended. 'You'll do no such thing. Haven't I just told my wife to cook a special meal, and all because we've you as a guest? The horse will be fine. I think, my lord Gwalchmai, you're more overworn than he is.'

The lord Gwalchmai stared at him.

'By all the saints in heaven!' said my father. 'Are you grown too proud to accept my hospitality?'

Gwalchmai made an averting gesture. 'Not so, Sion ap Rhys, indeed! It is only...' He stopped abruptly, then went on, 'Well, the horse will be fine, then, and I thank you for your hospitality.' He patted the horse again, said something else to it in Irish, picked up some saddle-bags, and the three of us walked up the hill to the house.

My mother had the meal nearly ready: fresh bread with sweet butter; apples, cheese and strong, dark ale were already on the table. A pot of ham and barley stew was cooking over the fire, and I could smell the honey cakes baking. Everyone in the house was waiting around the hearth: my aunt, with her three children (her husband had died some six years before); my two sisters, my brother, my grandfather and my mother. The rest of the clan, in the two other houses of our holding, were going to have to do without ham and barley stew, and come and see the guest in the morning.

My father introduced everyone, and the lord Gwalchmai bowed politely. There was silence and an uneasy shuffling of feet, and then my mother asked Gwalchmai if he wished to put his cloak aside, or wash before dinner. There was time, she said, before the stew was done. Gwalchmai stepped back a little, stiffly, shaking his head, so my sister Morfudd brought him some ale, and a place was made for him by the fire. My father seized a piece of the bread, smeared it with butter, and sat down, eating it enthusiastically.

'It's best while it's warm,' he told Gwalchmai. The warrior nodded, and leaned sideways against the roof-tree.

After a little while, he loosed the brooch that held his cloak, as though he felt the heat. 'More overworn than the horse,' my father had said. It was true: the man looked near to dropping. 'We were fighting but yesterday afternoon' – it was not good weather to be fighting in, nor to travel in, for that matter. I wondered whom he had fought. There are plenty of bandits about to the north-west. Even in the summer I would take a spear if I had to go up the north road very far.

The stew had finished cooking and, when my father had asked the blessing, we crossed ourselves and set to. The stew was delicious, the honey cakes as good as they smelled, and everyone except the guest ate eagerly. Gwalchmai, though he complimented my mother very nicely and asked courteous questions about the holding, ate very little, and that slowly.

When we were finished, and the meal had been cleared away, my mother looked at the lord Gwalchmai and shook her head. 'My lord, do give me that cloak a moment,' she pleaded. 'That's a great tear you have in it. I'll mend it for you.' As he shook his head and began a refusal, she wrinkled her nose and added, 'And the rest of your things could stand some mending and a good wash, my lord. Rhys, why don't you get some of your other clothes, so I can wash the lord Gwalchmai's?'

I was a bit shocked by my mother's forwardness, but the lord Gwalchmai only said, 'There would not be time for them to dry. I must leave tomorrow morning.'

'Tomorrow morning? Well, if I hang them by the fire, they can dry by midmorning, and certainly you can stay till then. But you must stay longer, indeed you must. You are not well enough to travel in such weather.'

'I am well enough. I must leave early. Just show me where I can sleep.'

'Let me mend the tear in your cloak, then, at the very least. Come, it lets in the wind to chill you, and the snow to drench you, and I can mend it in no time.'

When Gwalchmai began another polite refusal, my mother, exasperated, seized the cloak by the front, unpinned it, and took it away from him. He stood back, hand dropping to the gold hilt of his sword. I noticed the glint of his chain mail under the woollen over-tunic – then noticed that the tunic was slashed and unravelling across the

21

ribs, and that the edges of the tear were stained a darker red. My father also noticed it.

'So-o-o,' he said, surprised. 'Your horse wasn't the only one to take a spear thrust.'

Gwalchmai backed quickly to the roof-tree and drew his sword half out of the sheath. The blade gleamed with an unnatural brightness in the flickering light.

My father stood where he was, the blood slowly rising to his face, making it dark with anger. My mother looked at him, not at Gwalchmai, the cloak still in her hands. I looked around for a weapon.

'You have your hand on your sword,' my father pointed out in a level voice. I knew that voice: when I was a boy, it had usually preceded a thrashing for me.

Gwalchmai made no reply. Only his eyes moved, quickly checking the room, fixing on my father.

'You can put the thing away,' said my father. 'I knew you for two days, nine years ago, but I believe that in that time you consecrated the thing at Ynys Witrin. You should not be so ready to let blood with a consecrated weapon. Especially the blood of your host.'

Gwalchmai flushed slightly, and stared at my father for a long moment. Then, abruptly, he sheathed the sword. His hand dropped from its hilt and hung loosely by his side.

My father hurried over to him. 'Let me see this wound of yours.'

The warrior looked at him a moment, then made a helpless gesture and began unfastening the tunic. My mother, lips pressed firmly together in disapproval, put some water over the fire to heat.

It was a painful-looking wound, a slash across the ribs on his right side. Gwalchmai drew his under-tunic off over it carefully, and set the garment on top of the mail-coat. His torso was criss-crossed with old scars already, more than I cared to think about receiving, mostly on the right side of his body. My mother shook her head, took a clean cloth and began cleaning the cut. She paused a moment, and he sat down by the fire. He was thin, and shivered a little. The look on his face was terrible: exhaustion and humiliation and, almost, despair.

'Why did you try to hide it?' my father demanded angrily. 'You can't go travelling with that. You will have to stay here.'

Gwalchmai shrugged, winced at the movement. 'I have already travelled with it. Most of today. I . . . well, most . . . farmers would . . . kill a man of Arthur's, if they knew it were safe to try. Ach, almost everyone this side of Britain hates the High King.'

My father's face again grew dark with anger. 'I would not kill a guest of mine if he were my worst enemy, even if he were fit and strong and ready to do me injury, and not sick and wounded. I am not like to kill a man I met as a friend, no matter who his lord is. And I support the Emperor.'

Gwalchmai looked up at him steadily, then, very slowly, he smiled. 'Forgive me. I did not even think, nor pause to look at you. You would not.' He drew a deep, sobbing breath. 'It has been a long, long time.'

'Since I met you?'

'I was not even a warrior then. One forgets how people act. Ah God, Sion, I am weary.'

'Stay here, then, till you are rested.'

'I will pay you.'

'Sweet Jesu be merciful! When a guest of mine pays me, I will sow my fields with salt, so witness me Almighty God, and all the saints and angels.'

Gwalchmai smiled again, and a light seemed to touch his dark eyes. 'I had forgotten such people,' he said, very softly, to himself more than to us. 'And I deserve nothing of it. Sweet Jesus is indeed merciful.'

I sat and looked at him as he sat cross-legged in the red light of the fire, with my mother bandaging the wound. Not what I'd expected for so glorious a warrior. I realized, as I looked, that he could not be too much older than myself. His face, under the dirt and matted hair, was still young and very good-looking. But it was already marked by pain and disappointment. He seemed so much older, so suspicious and controlled until now. I looked about at my family, a close circle in half-light and warm shadow. Yes, it was good. I could afford to be young; I had one place, a good place, a place worthy of love.

But yet something in my heart felt like a sparrow caught in a house, which flutters about the eaves, looking for the clear sky and the wind.

Two

The lord Gwalchmai slept very late the next morning. When he woke, he bathed, washed and trimmed his hair and beard, and put on some of my clothing to go and look at his horse. My trousers and tunic were loose on him, and just a bit long as well, but my mother had confiscated his own things and was working on them, shaking her head over their condition as she worked.

The white stallion stood comfortably in our barn, devouring our grain and ignoring all the other animals there except our brown mare. Gwalchmai argued with my father about the grain.

'The cost of the grain must fall to me, Sion. Warhorses are costly to keep, a luxury for their owner. No host is obliged to provide luxuries for his guest.'

'A warhorse is no luxury for a warrior who fights from horseback. I have the grain; let him eat it.' And my father kept his stand, despite the other's persuasive arguments.

The warrior also checked his mount's hooves again, and again looked concerned over the shoes. 'Is there any blacksmith nearby?' he asked, hopefully.

'None professionally, at this time of year. Some come by when the weather's warmer, and set up their stalls on market days. But we could shoe your horse for you. My nephew Goronwy's a fair hand at that.'

'It would be well if he could. And could he also, perhaps, mend my coat of mail?'

'Ah, that's harder. Very hard, I should think.'

'It need not be a complete repair just now. Simply a few links worked in sideways to keep the rest together, on the line where the spear broke it.'

'You can tell Goronwy what you want, and see.'

Gwalchmai nodded, and we started back to the house. My father excused himself outside the barn and went to check on the cattle in the byres.

'How did the spear break the mail?' I found myself asking, as we trudged up the hill. 'I thought chain mail would keep a man safe.'

'It was a thrusting spear.' I must have looked blank, because Gwalchmai suddenly smiled and explained. 'Chain mail will keep off throwing spears, provided you're not too close to the thrower of them, and it can turn the edge of a sword or knife if the blow is shallow. But a thrusting spear, or the point of a sword, or a hard straight blow with a good sword, will cut mail like leather. You'd expect more of the stuff, knowing the price of it, wouldn't you? Still, it's a deal better than the next best.'

'How much did you pay for yours?' I asked, curious.

'I didn't buy it. I took it from a Saxon chieftain.'

After killing him, of course. A hard, straight blow with a good sword? I looked at the jewelled hilt of Gwalchmai's sword, glowing against the grey of my second-best over-tunic. The gear of war has a beauty which had spun a glitter of steel and bronze and bright banners over all my thoughts of it, ever since I first saw a party of warriors ride down the south road from Caer Legion to Camlann one summer morning. But, after all, that gear and glitter were only the tools of a trade, and that trade was killing or being killed. Why should I consider it glorious? I was old enough to know better.

The sword was still very beautiful.

Gwalchmai ate somewhat more that evening than he had the night before. He thanked my mother for the meal, very courteously. The hoarseness was gone from his voice, but he still spoke softly. Morfudd, the elder of my sisters, was very quick to notice anything he might need, and watched him, demurely but with a glint in her eyes. I knew she would discuss him with my other sister later. I could see why a woman would. I suddenly thought of my own face in contrast. Not the sort, I feared, to inspire that kind of look from women. More the kind that evokes sisterly confi-dences, and from women other than my sisters. No, not ugly, but big-boned, red-headed and blue-eyed like my father, and irregularly freckled in summer. Everyone always observed that I looked honest. An honest farmer, of a reasonably prosperous clan, of an age to settle down with some honest wife and continue the clan. Gwalchmai's face was fine-featured, with high cheek bones and dark eyes, his beard, now trimmed down close to the jaw, making his face look even narrower. He looked like what he was, a warrior

25

and twice royal. Why should I feel that that was so much more than what I was? Britain could do without warriors more easily than without farmers, and kings and their clans come and go, while my clan had farmed the land around Mor Hafren before the Romans came.

But with Britain as it was now, if the warriors had not fought, the only farmers about Mor Hafren would be Saxons, and I and my clan, if we lived and stayed free, would be looking for land among the mountains of Gwynedd, or across the sea in Less Britain. The Pendragon had saved us, and the man who sat across the table from me refusing the ale Morfudd was offering him, he had fought against the darkness. . . .

I was the one who ate only a little at that meal. My mother gave me a hard look as she took away my plate, a 'come-and-tell-me-about-it-later' look. I wondered if I could. 'Mother, when this warrior goes off again, I want to go with him. I want to see Camlann and Saxons and war; I want to abandon my family for the sort of thing this Gwalchmai has embittered himself with.' No, it would not do. It was a child's plea, an absurdity, and it was impossible anyway. It was just as unlikely that Gwalchmai would be willing to take me as that my mother would be willing to let me go.

We sat down by the hearth fire, and Gwalchmai asked my father polite questions about the householding and the clan, and the land around Mor Hafren, and the last harvest, and listened very attentively to the answers. It took my father a while to work the talk about to his own questions. He eventually did it, though.

'. . . set them out to pasture when the snow isn't too deep, even in the mid-winter. But now, well, too cold for anything of the kind, and they won't leave the byre. Cleverer than humans that way. Or than some humans.'

'I am not clever, then?' Gwalchmai looked serious, but his eyes were a trifle too bright.

'You are travelling at a time when sensible men sit by the fire.'

'I am sitting by the fire now.'

'But what we had to do to put you there! Truly, lord Gwalchmai, when did you set out, and why?'

'As to the when at the beginning of November; as to the

why – I am looking for a woman. She may have come this way, eight years ago, in the late autumn. A fair-haired woman, who rode a brown mare and was followed by two servants, one of them an old man with half an ear missing. She had blue eyes, may have worn blue, and spoke with a northern accent.'

'A noblewoman?' asked my father. 'No, I've not seen nor heard of such a woman. But why are you looking for her?'

'I . . . owe her something. I have not had the opportunity of repaying her, while the war lasted, and now that we have peace in Britain, I am trying to find her again.'

'In the middle of winter? Who is she?'

Gwalchmai looked down. 'Sion, it is a complicated tale, and a long one, and one not greatly to my credit.'

My father shrugged, fumbled at the foot of his stool, and picked up a piece of wood he had been carving into a cup. 'As you please. But, if the tale is long, we've this night and the next, and on till that wound of yours is healed, my lord.' He stopped, his eyes meeting Gwalchmai's. 'Why does it trouble you so?'

Gwalchmai smiled. 'Because it is a bitter memory.' We were quiet for a moment, and then he went on abruptly. 'I loved that woman once, and wronged her.'

My father eyed his cup, and began to whittle at the rim, studiously avoiding Gwalchmai's eyes. 'And you still love her?'

'As God witnesses me, yes. But I must seek her forgiveness at the least. I did not ask it when we parted, and I had brought great suffering onto her.' There was another long silence. Gwalchmai looked at his hands, the long fingers twined together on his knees. 'You've a right to hear the tale, Sion ap Rhys, if you wish it. I've no right to conceal the matter to save my pride, or to preserve an honour which I forfeited to her. And I also owe you a debt.'

'Mm. Of trust,' said my father, beginning to carve properly. The knife made a soft *chk*-ing sound. 'I should like to hear the tale.'

Gwalchmai looked up and into the fire, as men do when they summon their memories of an event, and wonder how to set the words to it. He rubbed the palm of his sword hand against his knee, slowly, as though something clung to it.

'I suppose, then, that it began in the spring, eight years

27

ago,' he said. The wind rustled in the thatch, and my mother's needle glinted as she sewed. Gwalchmai straightened and sat motionless, eyes still fixed on the fire. 'Eight years ago, in the spring of the year, my lord Arthur sent me on an embassy to Caer Ebrauc. The old king, Caradoc, had died, and his nephew Bran ap Caw, the eldest of the twelve sons of Caw, succeeded him. All the sons of Caw were enemies of Arthur over some blood feud begun when my lord seized the High Kingship, so my lord feared that Bran might begin a rebellion. This was during our northern campaign against the Saxons of Deira and Bernicia and the other northern kingdoms. The campaign had till then gone well, and the Saxons were feeling the force of our raids, but to no greater degree than that which made them determined to have revenge on us. They were as much stronger than us as they ever were, especially when they leagued together, but we had moved about, striking where they least expected it, and raided until they had had to go hungry a bit that winter. It would take another year at least, though, before they would have to make and keep terms, and a rebellion by one of the British kingdoms at that point could be fatal to us. My lord had to send an ambassador to Bran to try his mind, and to conciliate him. He chose me.'

'You were fairly young at the time.' My father gave him a sharp look. 'That was only a year after I met you.'

'I was just eighteen.' Gwalchmai smiled. 'But my lord had to send one of his best warriors, or Bran would be insulted. He couldn't send Cei or Gereint or my brother Agravain, because they'd be liable to throw wine in Bran's face the moment he hinted any insult to Arthur, which would hardly conciliate the man. He couldn't send Bedwyr, because he is a Breton and only moderately well-born – though a nobler man never breathed upon the earth – and Bran could be insulted at that, if he chose to be. He told me all this when I pointed out that I was too young. He sent me.'

'Gwalchmai the Golden-tongued,' murmured Morfudd coyly.

He laughed, glancing at her. 'Cei first called me that as a joke. Well, I set out for Caer Ebrauc from King Urien's fortress in Rheged, I, and two others from Arthur's Family. The roads were bad, and it took us some seven days, though we all had fine horses. The apple trees were beginning to blossom, though, and the woods were becoming green. My horse Ceincaled ran like the sun on the waves. I thought it very good to be alive, to be young, to be Arthur's warrior – the last was still new to me. I had no great concern for Bran of Llys Ebrauc. I could not in my heart see how any man in Britain could oppose Arthur and his Family. There is no one like my lord Arthur the High King, and no war-leader so great in all Britain.

'But, when we reached Caer Ebrauc, I began to see that Bran might be a danger after all. The city is one that the Romans built to keep their legions in, and it has a great wall, still strongly fortified, and a great deal of room for war-riors, while the land about it is rich and well populated. The town behind the wall is more than half abandoned, like any other town this age, but it is prosperous enough. The king's warband stays in one of the old Roman barracks, instead of in a feast hall or their own houses. It is a large warband. Mostly foot fighters, not cavalry, but still, some five hundred trained, well-armed warriors. And Ebrauc could also raise an army from the subject clans, while Arthur had to rely on his subject kings for that, and they are not easily to be relied upon. I rode into Caer Ebrauc with greater care than that with which I had ridden up to it.

'Bran lived in the palace of some ancient Roman com-mander, which had last been repaired by some vicar of the north a century or so ago. I and the others would stay with him, as fitted our rank. We stopped in front of this palace, gave our horses to the grooms, and tried to see that our luggage was put somewhere safe before we went in to see Bran. While we were busy arguing with the servants, a girl came out of the palace and went over to the grooms to see that the horses were stabled.'

He fell silent for a moment, then shook his head. 'The sunlight was as clear as spring water over clean sand, and the doves were cooing on the broken tiles of the roof. She walked like the shadow of a bird on a clear stream. Her hair was the colour of broom flowers. When she reached the horses, she felt my eyes on her, and turned around, and blushed when she saw me watching. Then, the servants had the luggage, and we were being shown in to the king.

'I felt like a harp-string which has just been plucked. I

29

wanted to make a song about the way she moved. I think my blood was singing. But I had to still myself to speak with Bran.'

'Was she very beautiful?' asked Morfudd eagerly. My mother looked at her sharply. Gwalchmai stared a moment, then looked away and shrugged.

'She seemed so to me. Others have told me, no.' He paused, and added harshly, 'Her nose was too long, her teeth too big, and she was thin as a fence post.'

'But you said . . .'

'I said! Well, but there was the way she moved, the way she lifted her skirts to run a little, and turned her head, and the light that slid across her face when she smiled. Let her stand still, and you might call her plain; but when she moved, or spoke, she was like a skylark above the hills. She it was that made herself beautiful, not the beauty given by nature.'

He looked back at the fire, clenching his fists, and spoke as though it caused pain – which, for a man such as he, it doubtless did. 'And that was all. I wanted to see her again, and thought that I desired her, but I didn't particularly care if I knew her name. It was the way we talk of such things. I had never . . . well, she made me feel a great thing, but I had no thought that she could feel, too. God forgive me, but I wanted to enjoy myself and give nothing.'

Gwalchmai gave my father a straight, fierce look, then unclenched his hands, rubbed them together and went on. 'I went and talked to Bran of Llys Ebrauc. It was a fine combat of words. He kept suggesting or hinting deadly insults, and I kept twisting them about into straightforward questions or harmless comments, and both of us hinted at the political implications unceasingly. In the end, Bran asked me how long I intended to stay. My lord had told me, "Stay there as long as the situation requires", and it was plain to me that the situation required me to watch Bran constantly. So I replied, "By your leave, I will stay until my lord enjoins my return." Bran didn't like it. He knew that he couldn't prepare any rebellion while I remained in Ebrauc, and he did not dare to order me killed, for fear of my lord's vengeance. I could see him trying to think of some way he could say that I had insulted him, so that he could command me to leave; but he had no reasonable pretext. So he told me he would give a feast that night, to welcome me, and that all of his were mine for the using, and so on. I was glad to get away from him. But, when I lay down to rest before the feast, I thought again of the girl. It seemed to me that she must be one of Bran's servants: she had been plainly dressed, and had seen to the horses. Bran had made an offer of hospitality, and I thought, "If we must stay a while, perhaps I will take him up on it." I fell asleep wondering what she would look like when she smiled.

'She was, indeed, at the feast. She came in on the left side of the hall, to pour the wine for the high table, and she wore a dress of blue silk fastened with gold, and more gold in her hair. Bran smiled at her, and said, half-laughing, "Why, the moon is rising!" and she smiled back and filled his glass. The man next to me whispered, "That is Elidan, daughter of Caw, the king's sister."

'And that, I told myself, is that. I could spend my time with serving girls, if I pleased, but Elidan, daughter of Caw, the king's sister, was not to be touched, and most especially not to be touched by her brother's enemy.

'She poured the wine, and sat down beside Bran, taking the queen's part, since his own wife was dead in childbirth. After a little while, she rose again to refill the glasses, and when she came to pour for me, some of the wine spilled. She gave a little gasp and nearly dropped the jug. I caught the side of it to steady it, and my hand touched hers, my eyes meeting hers as I looked up. She blushed again, and I could feel the trembling in her hand. The wine shivered, light and dark rippling on its surface.

'I let go the jug. After a moment, she filled my glass, curt-seyed and went on down the table. I watched her as she went, and my blood was singing again.

'We stayed at Ebrauc, and Bran and Bran's people by and large ignored us. Some tried to quarrel, but both the men I had chosen to come with me knew how to pretend they hadn't heard, or even that they didn't care. Still, it was no pleasant place for us, and I wished fiercely to be back with my lord Arthur, fighting. I knew that the Family had been gathered, and had raised the standard and ridden off to war. They were all there, my brother Agravain, my friends Cei, Bedwyr and the rest; and I sat about at Llys Ebrauc, a dead weight on the earth. I knew that Arthur wanted me where I was, and that it was an honour to be trusted with such a task – but it was early May! I could have killed from sheer frustration.

'And then I had a chance meeting with Elidan, and forgot all else.

'About a week after my arrival, I went to the stables to see to my horse, and she was there, looking at the horse. I had not seen her since the feast. When I came up, she blushed again, and backed off from the stall.

'"You needn't be afraid," I told her, "he won't hurt you." She looked at me, gave a little bow with her head, and stood still. I went into the stall and caught Ceincaled's halter, and he snorted and nuzzled my wrist. "See?" I told the girl. "He is very gentle." Still she said nothing. "Would you like to come and see him?"

'She edged closer slowly, coming into the stall on the opposite side of the horse. Very carefully, she put out a hand to pat his neck. He eyed her and flicked his ears forward, and she smiled. I thought it was the first time my eyes opened, when I saw her smile.

'"Is this Ceincaled?" she asked, in a low voice like the sound of a soft note on the pipes. "Is it true that he is of no mortal breed?"

'I told her yes, it was true, and, when she questioned me and smiled again, I told her the whole story. I am not in the habit of telling it, and certainly not as I told it then, to impress. But it had charm enough for her, and she listened with her eyes shining and her lips slightly parted.

'"So I am blessed with the finest of horses," I told her, when I finished the tale, and, before I myself knew what I was saying, I went on, "Though he needs exercising, as any other. Do you know of a good place to ride, my lady?" "There's Herfydd's Wood," she replied. "A very lovely place. There are open meadows in it, too, where horses can run." And then she paused, and added, "I am taking my mare there this afternoon, if you wish me to point out the way." "I would indeed wish it, and would be grateful," I said. "And grateful also if you would show me this wood." She stammered an assent.

'There was nothing in this beyond courtesy, nothing to make anyone suspect. She had her servants with her the while. But we could talk. It was a glorious ride. I have no recollection of what we spoke of, merely that I talked a great deal and made her laugh. Her laugh was like the flutter of a bird's wing, and it set my mind flying. When we returned to Ebrauc, I asked her if she knew of other good places to ride in, for, though I had enjoyed Herfydd's Wood, variety is a pleasure. She said yes, there was Bryn Nerth, which she could show me, if I wished. Thus we rode together the next day, and the next, and the next as well. The world seemed to me like the laughter of sunlight in the trees, all shimmer and light dancing.

'But after five days of this, at the time we had set for our ride, she appeared with a set, chilled face and told me that she could not take her mare out that day. I argued with her, and she made excuses and left. I went out alone in the end, very angry, and rode at a full gallop until Ceincaled was sweating and eager to stop, and that is a long way. It was plain enough why she had not come. Bran had begun to suspect – not remarkably – that this riding together was not just courtesy; and he had spoken to Elidan, had warned her or commanded her against me. I told myself that I shouldn't have asked her to come with me in the first place. It was madness to desire her, and to cherish the hopes I did. Her brother was very fond of her – and she was fond of Bran, if it came to that. Even if my interest had been in anything permanent, which it was not, still it would have been impossible. One cannot contract marriage alliances with one's lord's enemies. And if it were not a marriage, Bran would have good reasons in his rebellion. I owed it to my lord Arthur, to my honour as a guest and an emissary and her respect as a Christian noblewoman to leave the girl alone.

'I resolved to be no more than courteous, and I kept my resolve, too – for a week or so. But I held her at night in my dreams, and when I played the harp alone I found myself singing of her, and I began to wonder how we could fool Bran; and I could think of many ways. And then one day I saw her in a corridor in the palace, alone, and without thinking I seized her wrist and said, "I will be riding in Herfydd's Wood tomorrow after lunch," very softly into her ear. I let her go and walked on, feeling her eyes on me as I went. I cursed myself afterwards for saying that, and resolved that I would not go to the wood the next day. But I went. I spent an hour or so riding about the wood, alone, then turned back in disgust – and met her near the wood's edge. She had only one servant with her, an old man with half an ear missing, and he wore a look of great reluctance.

'I leapt from my horse and ran over to catch her mare's bridle. "You came," I said: it was all I could say. She looked down at me gravely and nodded, then let go the reins, kicked one foot from the stirrup and jumped from her horse. I caught her as she jumped. The wind touched her hair, but her eyes were still, stiller than the sky and as deep. I felt as though the force that drives life itself had touched us, that we stood between earth and heaven. I could feel her heart beating through her ribs as I held her, like the heart of a wild swallow, and I was filled with the wonder of it. All was astonishment. We stood and looked at one another, and it was as though we looked into a gulf of light, a fire burning beyond the deep places of the world, or gazed at each other through the blur-edged reality of some vision. But she was there, and in my arms, a thin, strong body and solemn blue eyes and straight fair hair. "You came," I said again, and I kissed her.

'"Yes," she said. "I came." She turned to the servant and said, "Hywel, could you stay here and watch the horses?"

'The old man nodded unhappily, and we walked off together into the green silence of the forest.'

Gwalchmai fell silent, and sat resting his head on his arms, leaning forward to stare at the low fire on the hearth. My father was motionless, his carving knife a still line of brightness in his hand. Only the wind still made its hollow sound in the thatch.

Morfudd stirred first. 'I think that is beautiful,' she said dreamily. 'Beautiful.'

Gwalchmai straightened abruptly, throwing his head up and giving her a fierce dark stare. 'Beautiful! Och, King of Heaven, beautiful? Woman, it was a very terrible thing.'

'You loved her very badly,' said my mother matter-of-factly, beginning to sew again. 'And it seems that she loved you. You were both young. Such things are terrible enough.'

'It was badly that I loved her,' he replied bitterly. 'And the worse because she did love me, while I, what did I love? A beautiful feeling! Dear God, I didn't care if it destroyed her, and, if it came out, it would. I took advantage of my

34

position as a guest in Bran's house, I betrayed my lord's trust, I betrayed her and I betrayed my own honour. I treated a king's sister like a common whore, and it was the worse because she loved me. Afterwards, that first time, she cried. She wouldn't tell me why until much later, and then she said, "It was because I knew I loved you so much more than you loved me, and because of my honour." She risked everything for me, and I . . . beautiful! Lord of Light, have mercy.'

'You're overstating it,' my father said.

'I wronged her greatly.'

'You wronged her, yes. But there was no need for her to come and meet you. Any girl would know what you meant, and any girl of sense would not have gone.'

Gwalchmai looked back at the fire, linking his hands together and only replying with silence.

'If you feel that way, why didn't you marry her?' asked my mother.

A shrug. 'Later I wanted to. Much later. Too much later. After I had killed her brother.'

'So there was a rebellion?' asked my father.

He looked up at us. 'I thought all the world knew of that. Well, the north must be more aware of these things than Dumnonia.'

'I have heard that you killed Bran of Llys Ebrauc,' I volunteered. He gave me a questioning look. 'There was a song,' I explained.

'Trust Rhys to listen to songs,' muttered my father. 'Well, so Bran found out?'

Gwalchmai leaned forward again, his elbows on his knees. He still spoke carefully, anxious that we should see the worst of it. 'No. The rebellion had nothing to do with it. We were very discreet. After the first time, we didn't see one another for a while. I was angry with her for crying, and because the thing we had was so much more solid and mortal than the vision of it I had at the first. But, after a little while, when I had been thinking of it and of her for a time, I sent her a message through her servant Hywel, the old man. He had been with her since she was born, and didn't like the business at all, but she'd told him she'd go alone if he didn't come, and I gather he wished to protect her reputation as much as he was able to. She was accustomed to go riding

35

with only one or two servants – Ebrauc is safe enough that a woman can do that, near the fortress – and we would ride out in different directions at different times, meet at a set place, and then return, again at different times. We were very careful. We spent most of the summer in this, until about the middle of July. Then one of Bran's men successfully picked a quarrel with my companion Morfran. He is a fine man, brave and steady and quick with his tongue, but has no looks at all and is well-used to hearing of this, which is the reason I chose him for this mission: I knew he would not fight over every trivial slur. But some insult was offered which no nobleman could ignore, and there was a fight. Bran's man was killed. Bran summoned me to see him – summoned me, as though I were his own man and sworn to obey him. He demanded reparation, and by that he meant not a blood-price, but Morfran's life. I refused, of course, and Bran then had the excuse to command me to leave Ebrauc. He added to this command some Roman sentence of exile, by which I and my companions could be killed if we returned. I knew very well that, as soon as we had gone, he would summon his warband, equip it, and raise his army for a rebellion.

'I spent a great deal of time wondering whether I could have prevented it by closer attention to Morfran and the other. I had not precisely ignored them, but I hadn't known of the fight until it was done with and Bran's man was dead. There was nothing to say, "This you should have attended to; thus it could have been prevented", and yet I do not know, and cannot know, whether I could have managed it better if it had not been for Elidan. I was angry about Bran's order, and angry with myself when I left. I was angry with Elidan on both accounts, and yet I longed to see her to say farewell. But our departure was hurried, and though I looked for her until I almost forgot discretion and went about asking for her, I could not find her, and rode out of Llys Ebrauc angrier than before. And I was thus angry when I met her on the road.

'She rode out of the wood beyond the wall, on her brown mare, with Hywel after her. She was wearing blue, and the wind caught at her hair so that she looked like a feather blown on a bright gale. My companions stared at her. I had not told them about her, afraid that they might make jokes, and that to the wrong people.

'She drew rein on the road, and her mare champed at the bit and sidled towards the bank. She patted its shoulder with one thin hand.

'"So you are going," she said.

'"I am going," I replied, angrier than ever because she was so beautiful and so daring. "By your brother's order."

'She looked down and fidgeted with the reins; looked up again. "God go with you, then, my falcon," she said.

'It hurt me that she should call me that. I had once asked her not to. Though my name means "hawk", my mother used to call me by it, and the memory of that is most bitter. She is very terrible and dreadful, my mother Morgawse. "God may well go with me," I said, "for certainly he will not stay with the injustice of Ebrauc."

'At that, she too flushed with anger. Morfran looked at her and suggested that we take her hostage, which made her straighten and glare at all of us; but I shook my head.

'"Oh, indeed," said Elidan, "I am not to be a hostage, by your mercy, my lord. Come, I know that there will be war, Gwalchmai ap Lot. My brother wants it. It would be better if I could, as a hostage, prevent it; but no one can prevent a warrior from killing. You care for blood too much." I did not know where such words came from, and I stared at her in astonishment. She urged her horse closer, and then leaned over to catch my hand and press it to her forehead. "But I love you, and I love my brother, Gwalchmai. Do not you fight him. Promise me that you won't hurt him. Promise me that you will speak to your lord the Emperor about him, and tell Arthur that if Bran ap Caw swears a peace, he will keep it. But promise me that you won't kill Bran, most of all promise me that."

'I snatched my hand away. I was thoroughly enraged by this slavish pleading for her brother. "If your brother wishes to play the treacherous fool, that is his affair, and he must be prepared for whatever consequences my lord imposes," I said. "My lord knows far better than I how to deal with rebels." But when she turned white, and looked at me with a strange, chill look, I had to add, "But for my part, I will not kill him. I swear by the sun and the wind, I swear the oath of my people I will not. And . . . my lord Arthur is merciful."

37

'She pressed one hand to her forehead, drawing the hair aside, as though her head ached, and she nodded. "God and his saints preserve you then, Gwalchmai." We looked at each other for another long moment, and I tried to find words that would make it a sweet parting, but I could think of none. So I nodded and urged Ceincaled on, and he started into a canter and left her there. At the first bend of the road I looked back at her, a quiet figure in blue on a quiet brown horse, and I thought of what it meant for a woman to hazard herself thus to say farewell, and wished I had been kinder.

'"And what was all that?" asked Morfran, driving his horse next to mine. I shook my head, and he smiled at me knowingly. "Her falcon, she calls you? The daughter of Caw, the king's sister. Well, well, and that should be a thorn in the shoes of our friend Bran. You golden-tongued goshawk, why didn't you tell us? I'd like to make a song for the beauty of it all. A song about the hospitality of King Bran of Ebrauc!" And he began to make jokes about Elidan. I felt awkward, angry, and, after a while, I laughed.'

Gwalchmai had been playing with a piece of kindling: he threw this suddenly into the fire, and drove the heel of his hands against his eyes. My father set down the cup and his carving knife and stood, took a step towards our guest, then stopped again. 'Lord Gwalchmai,' he said gently, 'you need not tell us this tale.'

Gwalchmai looked up again. 'It is well that I should tell it. It is right that the shame of it should be known.'

'Say nothing further tonight, then. It is late, and you are tired.'

'I am. And I thank you for your hospitality, Sion.'

'What we have, you are welcome to. Sleep well, my lord.'

'Sleep well.'

Three

The next day my father again sent me out across the river, this time to cut down saplings to repair the cow byres. I did not think they needed repair, but I went, this time with my brother Dafydd. I thought about our guest and his tale all the day, and hardly glanced at the forest. I tried to picture this Elidan riding out of the wood, dressed in blue silk and looking like the Queen of the Fair Folk in the songs; and then I remembered that she was thin and a bit plain, and the nonsense became impossible to believe in. No, it was nonsense, the whole of it, and Gwalchmai was making a deal too much trouble over it all. My father had always said that, if a wrong action can be repaired, one should go about repairing it at once; if not, trust it to God. Gwalchmai seemed to be far too fierce about it either way. But warriors had to be fierce. I recalled all the tales I had heard about their violence, cruelty and licentiousness, and decided that our guest's scruples were exaggerated and absurd for a man in his position, since that position doubtless included murder and pillage on a wide scale. I managed to feel fairly detached about his presence by the time I returned home, worn out and chilled to the marrow of my bones.

I went to the barn to look after the animals, and found Gwalchmai there. To my astonishment, he was rubbing down our mare. I stood frozen, pitchfork in hand, until he turned and smiled at me. Then I closed my gaping jaw, leaned the pitchfork against the wall and said, 'You shouldn't be doing that, my lord.'

'Och, I know well enough how to look after horses. I will not hurt yours. She is a fine little mare.'

'I didn't mean that! You're ... well, you're sick, and a guest.'

'This would be no trouble to a newly weaned child. But I cannot look after the bulls. You must do that; I know nothing about cattle. Well, perhaps a very little about sheep.' He turned back to the mare, humming softly to himself. She snorted and closed her eyes. His war stallion tossed his proud head and nickered, and his master laughed and spoke to him in Irish. After watching a minute or so, I picked up my pitchfork and went to look after the cattle. Gwalchmai's scruples no longer seemed quite so absurd.

I was tired after supper, and my mother suggested that I go straight to bed, but I would have to be much more tired than a single day's work could make me before I would do such a thing. I sat down at the right of the hearth and scratched the ears of our hound-bitch while the talk began. The dog occasionally grunted with delight, and licked me furiously every instant that I stopped.

'I've been thinking of what you said last night,' my father told Gwalchmai, 'and I can see why you didn't wish to tell the tale, and also why you did. Did you kill Bran, then?'

'I did. Deliberately, and when I might have spared him.' The warrior's voice was very level.

'In battle?' asked my father, his voice equally level.

Gwalchmai nodded. 'Yes, but I might have spared him just the same.'

'I've heard that you go mad in battle.'

Gwalchmai paused. 'Yes. But I was not mad then; or at least, not mad as I usually am . . . I will tell you the rest, as I said I would.

'The rebellion did not begin until September. We had some hard fighting before that, not pitched battles, but ceaseless raiding. Raiding is a sad business, and hard on the horses – but my lord's wars are always hard on the horses, since we must move at least twice as fast as our enemies. My lord gave me work, enough so that I had no time to think about Ebrauc and Elidan. Indeed, I did not think much at all, except to wonder when next I could rest.

'Then, in September, my lord called me aside for a private conference. We were at a holding near Gwyntolant on the Dyrwente, a clan headed by a man named Gogyrfan – yes, the Queen Gwynhwyfar's father. The clan supported us, and we had used the holding as a hospital for most of the northern campaign, and the lady Gwynhwyfar had attended our wounded better than a doctor. Arthur married her before the campaign was out, but he never, for that, failed in his attention to the war.

'My lord called me to the private room he had been loaned, and sat down at the table. There was a map there – there always is, with Arthur – and he began checking over the roads. I wondered why it was that he always seemed to have more energy than I, when I knew that he worked harder.

'"Bran of Ebrauc has rebelled," Arthur said, "or will do shortly."

'I dropped into the chair opposite him, again wondering, out loud, if I could have prevented it.

'My lord looked back up from his map and told me, "Enough of that; it wasn't your fault. The question is rather, how to stop Bran without the Saxons finding out that he's rebelled. We're a good hundred miles from Caer Ebrauc; still, with the south road we could do it in four days, or three if we pushed hard . . . though we'd be in no condition to fight then. Bran is still raising his armies now. He hoped to catch us off-guard by rebelling at the harvest season, but he has the disadvantage that it will take him longer to gather his forces, and they'll disperse more quickly if the war is drawn out. He won't have all his forces yet, and I think we could risk a pitched battle." I shifted in my seat, and Arthur grinned at me. "I could wish I was so eager for it. Very well, I plan to ride to Ebrauc tomorrow, force a battle, and be back north in two weeks, which shouldn't give the Saxons time to do more than realize we were gone. We can leave King Urien to make some raids on his own to confuse them – but only if Bran hasn't found too many allies. He's been gathering supplies all summer, but allies . . .' Arthur frowned at the map, and began discussing all the kingdoms that neighbour Ebrauc, asking me how the various kings and nobles were disposed towards Bran and towards himself – I had been ambassador to most of them by then. They none of them seemed to me the sorts to risk their crowns on an uncertain rebellion, though we'd have cause to worry if Bran had some success. There were other kings, of course, like Maelgwn Gwynedd, who would be only too eager to rebel, but they were far away from Ebrauc, and, if we moved quickly enough, should be unable to help.

'"Then we will force a battle," Arthur concluded. "But, Yffern! Bran would choose now as the time to rebel. Aldwulf might have decided on battle, and it only takes one more defeat for him and he's broken. Bran must have thought I'd be unwilling to leave the campaign just now."

He sighed, and began tracing a line on the map with his finger, thoughtfully looking into nothing with a wide grey stare. I waited.

'"I want you to leave this afternoon," he said at last. "The Family can't be ready to leave before noon tomorrow, but you leave now and take Bran my terms. Give him the impression that the rest of us are still north of the Wall, and waiting for his reply before we act; hint that the Family is scattered, and will be unable to assemble for at least a week. But see if you can talk him round: unlikely as it may be, it's worth the trial. Bran is an honourable man, and unlikely to dismiss a herald with violence, unless – there's no truth in the rumour about you and his sister, is there?' His eyes focused on me for an instant. I did not meet them. I stared at my hands, and at the scarred wooden table. I had asked Morfran and the other to keep the matter quiet, but it had come out despite that. When it came up, I would laugh, make a joke of it, and change the subject as though it were only a mad harper's tale, but I could not lie to my lord. "There isn't, is there?" he demanded again, impatiently. I was silent. He put both hands flat on the table and looked at me. "Before Heaven, there is." I did meet his eyes then, knowing it would be worse if I did not. The shame of it cut deeper than a spear point. I had dishonoured him in Ebrauc, since I was his emissary and ambassador, sent in his name; I had betrayed his trust. "There is," I said.

'"Why didn't you tell me?" my lord asked, his face very calm.

'I shrugged, not knowing what to say. "You have kept me busy. The matter did not arise. But if you wish I will go as your herald to Bran."

'"I do not want you killed," snapped Arthur. "I will send Rhuawn."

'"There is no need to send anyone else. Bran had no idea of this when I left, and he should have none now. The girl is not so foolish as to tell him."

'Arthur studied me, his face still so calm; I have seen it look like that when they tell him, after a battle, who of his men are dead. I could no longer look at him, and so pretended to study the map, furious and ashamed because he was disappointed. "Was she very beautiful?" he asked at last, and I looked up and saw that the set look had softened. I opened my mouth to say no, and instead said, "As a birch tree is, with the west wind blowing; as a lark singing." And as I said it, I wanted to see her again. I would have given the bright world, all of it, though it were an unequal bargain.

'At this Arthur smiled. "Is she?" He folded the map slowly, thinking of something else – of Gwynhwyfar? "Then you are fortunate. You believe that Bran does not know?"

'"My lord, I am certain that he does not. Even in the Family most people do not believe it, and I doubt that Bran has even heard the tale."

'"Then I will send you," Arthur said, and told me what terms he was willing to offer Bran for peace. I went out from the room, saddled Ceincaled, and turned him south-ward, my heart full of Elidan.

'But when I came to Caer Ebrauc, I had not even a glimpse of her. Bran kept me at the gates of the fortress, waiting until he came down from the palace to meet me there. He listened to the terms Arthur had proposed with a cold lack of interest, and when I had done, said only, "You were exiled from this land. I could have you put to death for coming here." I felt for my sword, but he continued, "You came from the north very quickly. See if you can do better going back, and tell Arthur ab Uther, that bastard who lays claim to the imperium of Britain, that Ebrauc has her own king, that Bran ap Caw has more title to the Pendragonship than he, and that we will bow our heads to no yoke, least of all to his. Go, and tell him!" He shouted it with a kind of delight, and, drawing his sword, struck my horse with the flat of the blade. Ceincaled reared up, but I checked him, drew my own sword and saluted Bran with it. The light that dwells in the blade kindled, and it burned like lightning – it is not an ordinary sword – and Bran's men fell back. "I will tell these things to my lord the High King," I said. "And may the end be to your account, Bran of Llys Ebrauc." I turned Ceincaled and set my heels to him, and we were off down the road like a falcon swooping. I was angry enough to weep, and all my thoughts turned on Elidan.

'I rode north until I met the Family on its way south, and told Arthur that Bran had turned me back from the city gates with boasting and insults. My lord was not surprised, and only sighed and shook his head, and told me to ride in the van. We rode in silence. No one liked leaving the northern campaign for this rebellion. We were worn by a summer's fighting, and not eager for a pitched battle.

'We reached Caer Ebrauc some three days after I left it. Bran had had no more than a few hours' warning of our approach, but he had room enough in the city for armies larger than his, and time enough to bar the gates and set a watch on the walls. We spent the night camped before these, wondering what to do. We could not support a siege without forfeiting the northern campaign, but no one knew how to take a city. Whatever the Romans may have done, no one fights from a city now.

'In the morning, Arthur came out of his tent in the grey dawn, and walked about the walls, looking at them. Then, while the camp was breakfasting, he returned and gave orders that, as soon as we were done, we were to move off and burn and plunder western Ebrauc. The corn stood in the fields then, thick and white for the harvest, and all the men were with Bran since the army had been called up. There were none to stop us.

'It was barely two days before Bran left the city, with his warband of three hundred cavalry and two hundred infantry, and an army of some fifteen hundred: as Arthur had thought, he could not afford to lose the harvest. At that time the Family numbered under six hundred, since some of us had been raiding far afield when Arthur assembled the warband, and many were dead or wounded from the summer's campaign. About half of us were cavalry: the odds were not bad. But Arthur called a parley first.

'We held it in the middle of a field we had burned, with untouched fields across a pasturage shimmering in the wind to remind Bran of the cost of war. We did not dismount, and Bran looked at nothing with a hot blue stare while Arthur talked. Arthur's terms were generous: he offered to return the plunder we had taken and provide transport for grain from other parts of Ebrauc to the region we had pillaged, if Bran would swear submission and agree to pay the tribute. But Bran didn't even wait for Arthur to finish before saying, "So you will return the goods which you stole from me. Will you return me my sister?"

'Arthur did not look at me at all. "Speak plainly."

'"My sister, I say, my sister Elidan, the brightest, the purest woman in all Britain until your whore-mongering sorcerer corrupted her. Can you redeem that wrong, Imperator Britanniae? I will make terms with you if you give me the man you sent upon that mission, so that I can . . ."

'"Enough!" Arthur said. "As before, when you set your men to quarrel with mine, you dredge up excuses, and fasten on a private grievance as the pretext for rebellion."

'"A private grievance, a pretext? When your emissary makes a whore of his host's sister? I know that there is no faith in you, or any of yours. Truly, I will be protecting my women if I make peace with you!"

'"Enough," Arthur said again, and Bran stopped. "Your mind has been set on this, King Bran, since first you came to power; and when you turned my emissary from your gates with insults a week ago, you had no such pretensions."

'"If I had known then," Bran cried, 'then I would have given him the edge of my sword, and not insults!" He looked directly at me for the first time, where I sat my horse at Arthur's right. "You witch's bastard, I will see to you before the day is out. Mark me in the battle."

'I could answer him at last, but I did not answer him, only asked, "Where is your sister?"

'He glared at me and said, "I have shut her up where you cannot defile her again. For all your sorceries, you will die today, if my sword hand has any strength."

'"I may, if mine has none," I said. I felt completely calm, and I knew that I would kill him that same day. I studied him carefully: the brown hair, beard cleft by an old scar, eyes the colour of Elidan's, the grey stallion and the purple-edged cloak. I was sure I would know him in the battle. It seemed to me entirely reasonable and necessary to kill him, not because he had insulted me, but because he was Elidan's brother and determined to keep me from what was mine.

'We rode back to our own lines. Arthur had already settled the dispositions. But as he dismissed Bedwyr – who was in charge of the cavalry, as always – and me to our places, he caught Ceincaled's bridle and said in a low voice, "Do not kill Bran unless you have to." I said nothing. Arthur shook the bridle a little, leaning over in his saddle and forcing me to look at his face. Then he let go, turned his horse, and raised his voice to encourage the men to fight well.

'It was a battle like most of our battles. Arthur had chosen hilly ground, which scatters a charge, and makes numbers of less weight. Our foot faced Bran's centre, where he had stationed the infantry of his warband, flanked on each wing by the irregular forces of his army, and, on the right wing, by his cavalry opposed to the drawn-out line of our own. Our foot charged before Bran was quite ready, and forced his centre to retreat. The army was thrown into confusion, some of the men trying to encircle us, the rest, afraid of a flank attack from the cavalry, trying to retreat with the centre. When Bran's warband managed to slow its retreat, the army was further confused, and our cavalry charged, caught Bran's cavalry – which had been trying to outflank our foot – and struck through them into the right wing.

'I go mad in battle, and this is a gift of sorts, and not a frenzy such as berserkers have. Everything seems as clear as spring water over sand, and everyone around me seems to move under water, slowly and without force. If I am wounded I cannot feel it, for I feel nothing but a sweet joy, and I can never remember killing, though I know I must have. My memories are fragmentary, once the charge has begun, and so I remember the first part of this battle. From the time I threw my first spear it is like the memory of a dream. And yet some of the fragments remain. I remember seeing a brown-haired man on a grey horse fighting his way towards me, but in the madness it meant nothing, though something in me seemed to remember him. And then I was face to face with him, fighting, still as in a dream. I remember striking at his hand, and that he cried and dropped his sword, then turned his horse and rode off at a gallop, clutching his hand to his chest.

'But something of the madness was gone from me, and, though I still scarcely knew what I was doing, I drove Cein-caled after him. Others crossed my path and I cut them down, but after striking, again looked for Bran.

'It was late afternoon. Later I found that the cavalry charge had shattered both Bran's cavalry and his army, and that the warband surrendered after their king had fled the field. At the time I saw only the purple-bordered cloak retreating over a hill, and a black thirst came over me to see

46

it dark with blood. He had a good start, but there is no horse like my Ceincaled, and I gained on him quickly.

'The afternoon sun lay richly over the autumn trees, and the din of the battle blurred behind us as we left it behind a hill; the loudest sound became the pounding of our horses' hooves and the jingle of harness and gasp of breath. He had a good horse. It kept running after most beasts would have dropped, but it could not keep running for ever. It stumbled, stumbled again, and Bran drew rein before I reached him and leapt down, his shield on his right arm, gripping a spear in his shield hand. He grinned at me, all teeth. His face was a mask of blood and sweat and dirt.

'"Well, sorcerer," he said. "Your sword isn't burning now. Does the magic fail before human courage?"

'I didn't understand a word of it then. I reined in Ceincaled and slid to the ground, my sword in my hand. I cared only to kill Bran. I was mad, but it was not my accustomed madness: nothing was clear, there was a red mist over my eyes and a salt taste in my mouth. I cried out, howling like a dog, and rushed at him.

'He blocked my first thrust with his shield, clumsily, turning as I circled him and tried to get to his right, wounded side. I struck at him again and again, and once or twice shallow blows went past his guard, but he fought. By Heaven, he fought bravely, and never dropped his savage grin. "I . . . am not afraid . . . of your magic," he told me, working hard to get the words out. He must have wanted very badly to say them. "I am a king, a king, may Yffern . . . take you . . ." His shield drooped a little, and I saw my chance and thrust forward, driving the sword through his ribs to the heart, so that he fell forward onto me and died, and was silent, his words unsaid. I stepped back and let him fall to the earth. The fine linen of his cloak began to darken with his blood. I kicked the body twice, hard, then left it for the plunderers and went back to Arthur and the Family. And that was how I committed murder.'

Gwalchmai was silent for a very long time, looking at nothing at all. In his eyes was an old, weary pain that I did not want to think about, and he rubbed the side of his sword hand with the thumb of the other hand, leaning forward above the fire. My hand was frozen in the neck fur of our hound-bitch.

After a little, the dog whined and nudged my hand, and Gwalchmai straightened and looked up at the smoke hole. 'And no one in the Family said anything about it,' he said, as if he had not stopped. 'Arthur asked me where Bran was, and I told him that the man was dead. He said nothing, only looked at me. Not angrily, only . . . I do not know. He has trusted me no less since that time. I swear the oath of my people, he is the greatest of all lords on the green earth, and I do not deserve him.

'The day after the battle we rode to Caer Ebrauc and the people there opened the gates for us. Bran's half-brother Ergyriad ap Caw had been chosen as his successor by the royal clan. Bran had designated his full brother Heuil for that position, but Hueil was a trouble-maker, and Ebrauc apparently wanted no more wars with Arthur. Ergyriad was too pleased to be king to risk his position by greater ambitions, and swore submission to Arthur without trouble. Arthur returned all the plunder we had taken, re-leased all our prisoners without ransom, and helped arrange for provisioning the regions we had pillaged, and Ebrauc was reconciled to us. So the rebellion ended. My lord planned to leave for the north the next day, and raid in southern Deira on the way. I went to look for Elidan.

'Bran had said that she was shut up somewhere, but I knew that she must be in the city, and roamed about the place threatening the servants until one of them, an old woman, told me where she was. I ran there desperately, getting lost twice on the way through very eagerness. Since I had killed Bran, it had seemed as though all the world were stricken and bloodless, and I was broken with weariness and sickness of heart. I could only think of Elidan.

'Bran had locked her up in a little room above one of the palace stables. She knew nothing of the battle until she saw me. The old woman in the palace, the one who told me where she was, had brought her food once a day, and otherwise she had been left alone.

'I cut the bolt from the door with one blow of my sword and burst into the room without even calling to see if she was there. She was standing in one corner of the bare room, her back to the wall, ready to fight – until she saw that it was me. Then her face lit up, like the sunlight flooding through a lake, turning everything to shining colour. She cried,

"Gwalchmai!" and ran across the room into my arms. I held her and held her, kissing her hair and neck, and something of the black ache went out of my soul.

'But finally she pushed herself away from me a little and looked up at me, her hands against my shoulders, and began asking me questions. "How are you here?" she asked. "Was there a battle? Is my brother safe? Has he sworn fealty? Where is he, and where is the Emperor?"

'And I had no answers. I tried to pull her close again, but she kept her hands braced against my shoulders, smiling with shining eyes. "When was the battle?" she asked. "My brother found out, and he was very angry. That is why he shut me up here. I fainted when I heard how he sent you away from the gates, and he noticed . . . is he safe?"

'"What does it matter?" I asked.

'She frowned. "He is my full brother; how could that not matter? Where is he?"

'There was nothing I could say. She stared at me, her eyes widening. "He's not . . . hurt . . . is he?"

'I could not look at her. "He is dead," I told her.

'"No, oh no. He can't be. You promised; he can't be."

'Then I remembered that I had promised, and I was horrified. I had broken my sworn word, and, until that moment, had not even thought of it. I became furious with her for binding me with that oath, and, as I thought, making me forsworn. "Promises like that are meaningless," I said. "They are impossible to keep in a battle. Your brother came at me to kill me. What was I to do? Offer him my sword?"

'"Gwalchmai," she said, and something in her tone made me look back at her. Her eyes had become very large and dark in her face, a face grown pale and stricken as the whole world. Something in me twisted and grasped desperately at the edge of an inner abyss. "Gwalchmai, *you* didn't kill him?"

'I was quiet for a long instant, and then I was enraged, desperate. "Yes, I killed him," I shouted at her. "And every inch of the steel was deserved: he was a traitor and a rebel, a brute who would lock you up and part us and insult me, yes, and I did kill him!"

'"You perjured, murdering liar." Her voice was even and savagely cold. "You . . . sorcerer. You are just what

49

Bran said you were. Oh, my brother, oh, Bran, Bran." She turned from me and walked abruptly to the wall and leaned her head against it, pressing one hand against her mouth. Her shoulders shook beneath the thin dress. In the stable beneath us the horses shifted in their stalls, and the doves cooed in the thatch. I stood in the middle of the room, and the light was black in my eyes.

'"Elidan," I said. She did not move. "Marry me." I had not till that moment thought to ask it, but as I did, I saw that I desired it with my heart's blood.

'She whirled on me, her face twisted, but her eyes bitterly cold, like Bran's. "Marry you?" she said. "Marry the man who murdered my brother, while the blood is still hot on his hands? Marry the perjurer, the liar . . . I wish I had died the day I saw you first! Leave me!"

'I crossed the room in two strides and caught her by the shoulders. "Don't command that. Tell me anything else. I swear the oath of my people, Elidan, anything else and I will do it."

'"Go away! Let me mourn in peace. Go! I never want to see you living again. You warriors are all the same, all thinking of nothing but your own fame and glory. You care nothing for the pain you cause, if you get what you want and make a name in a song. Well, you won't get me. For all your skill at murdering, and all your looks and your noble blood, you can find another whore to worship you; I've been whore enough . . ."

'"Don't call yourself that!"

'"Go!" she screamed, and tore one arm loose to strike me, then lashed out again with the same furious determination. I let go.

'"Go away," she repeated. "If you come near me again, I swear I will kill myself, and I do not break my oaths."

'I stood back and looked at her, and she stood still, straight and proud, her lips parted for breath, eyes too bright, face wet with tears. I felt that if my eyes parted from her, my soul would part from me as well. But in honour there was nothing else which I could do. So I did the hardest thing of all I have ever done, and walked back across the room and out of it, closing the door very quietly behind me. As I left the stable I heard her begin the keen for the dead and quickened my step. I have not seen her from that hour to this.'

Gwalchmai stopped. I had ceased to scratch our dog's ears, and she whined and nudged me several times hopefully, until I slapped her. Gwalchmai suddenly stretched out his hand and called her, and she came over, sniffed the hand politely, then settled at his feet while he began scratching her ears as I had.

My father was frowning. 'You did nothing more for the girl?'

The warrior shrugged. 'I sought out the old man, Hywel, and gave him all the money I had with me, and borrowed more from the other members of the Family, and told him to let her use it for whatever she wanted. I don't imagine he told her where it came from, or she would not have accepted it, but I know she received it. I went to her half-brother Ergyriad, the new king, and virtually begged him to let her do all that she pleased. I had to give him presents; I borrowed from Arthur for that. When we left, I had someone watch to tell me what she did. It seems she left the city the same day we did, that afternoon. She took her brown mare, Hywel and another servant and a mule laden with goods. No one knows where she went, except that she turned south. I had had a large enough share of the plunder in that campaign, so she could have bought some land, and had men to work it for her. I do not think she would go to another king, for she was not overfond of the court and its plottings.'

'Then why are you looking for her?' my father asked. 'Seeing that she is probably settled and happy?'

'To ask her forgiveness. I did not even admit to her that I had done any wrong.'

'In the middle of winter?' My father looked at him. 'My lord, it's a noble enough objective, and I can see how a man such as yourself might think it needful, but couldn't you have sought her in the summer?'

Gwalchmai smiled again, and began rubbing the dog's ears with both hands. 'There was never time. Before Baddon there was the war; since Baddon, I have been trying to get away from my lord for this task, and first he sent me to Deira, and then to Gwynedd, and then to Caledon. I was on my way back from my embassy to Aengus MacErc of the Dalriada up in Caledon when I stopped for the night at

51

Caer Ebrauc. When I was seeing to my horse I began talking with one of the servants at the court, and this man said he thought that she had gone to eastern Gwynedd, away from the road in the Arfon mountains. I considered the matter, and decided that I would have time to look for her. I wrote my lord a letter, and sent it to Camlann with the man who was accompanying me, and myself set off for Gwynedd with the servant who had told me of it.'

'I have heard that King Maelgwn Gwynedd is Arthur's enemy,' my father pointed out.

'It is true that Gwynedd is no friend to the Pendragon. But there was no reason to see Maelgwn the king, and I am not wholly helpless. But the servant from Caer Ebrauc was wrong: she was not there.'

'Hmm. The man probably only wanted protection on his journey.'

'It is possible. He needed protection, for he was from Gwynedd, but had killed his cousin years before and fled. His clan took him back when he appeared, though. But he had worked in the stable at Caer Ebrauc, and had heard one of her servants say that they rode to Gwynedd. And she did pass through Caer Legion, for I met a man there who remembered her. But in Arfon there was no trace of her. I looked, from near Castel Degannwy to the springs of the Saefern, and no one had seen or heard tell of any such person. So I returned to Caer Legion, and tried to discover where else she might have gone, and . . . well, I have been looking since.'

'I do not see why it was so important,' said Morfudd. She had grown increasingly restless as Gwalchmai spoke, and now she gave Gwalchmai a smiling, light-hearted look. 'So, this woman was offended at you; well, you provided for her. I don't see why you should go running after her any longer, unless you still want to marry her.'

Gwalchmai looked away from her. 'It is possible,' he said. 'Though I do not think she would. She is not a light-minded woman, but proud, willing to do all in love and no less serious in hate. But can you truly not see that this was a terrible thing?'

'What was so very terrible about it?' asked Morfudd, tossing her hair. 'You were in love. Oh, I'd be very angry if someone had killed Rhys here, or even Dafydd, but you did kill this Bran in battle, and he was a rebel, and had tried to kill you first. If Rhys had done all that, and had even shut me up in a stable for a week, I'd be perfectly willing to forgive you for killing him.'

'Thank you,' I said. 'It would do you good to be shut up in a stable.' But I muttered it.

Gwalchmai did not smile. 'I was a guest, an emissary, and I betrayed my host and my lord. I dishonoured her, broke my word to her, and murdered her brother. I disobeyed my own lord and broke faith with God. By the Sun and the Wind! I deserve to die for it.' Gwalchmai's hand was hard on his sword-hilt, suddenly, the knuckles white. 'I have forfeited my own honour, and I must go to her, and admit as much. I have not acted for the Light, but I must at least deny Darkness or I will never be free of it. Even if she is justly angry, I must; and if she is angry, it is so much the better, for her anger is deserved.'

'You are too fierce with yourself,' said my father levelly.

'I cannot be.'

Their eyes met. The dog whined and crept over to my father, seeking reassurance. 'You are too fierce with yourself,' my father repeated. 'It is the nature of men to commit sin, and it is only in God's mercy that any are forgiven.' He crossed himself quickly and went on, 'You killed a man in battle whom you should not have killed, but it was not murder: you did not creep up upon him, but killed in combat, in the heat of passion. Very few men would have done otherwise, and very many have done the same and lived peaceful lives after.'

'That does not make it right.'

'Your lord, from what you've said, does not see fit to blame you.'

'That is my lord's mercy.'

'Your lord Arthur's mercy, as I have heard the tale, extends only so far as is safe for Britain. I do not believe he would be so quick to trust you after this if you were so blameworthy as you think yourself. I wonder how serious his order not to kill Bran ap Caw was, and for whose sake he said it. You said that you deserved to die for what you had done. You didn't, by any chance, think of administering that justice yourself, did you?'

Gwalchmai flushed and raised his hands in a gesture of

helplessness, suddenly smiling again. 'You are a shrewd man, Sion ap Rhys. The night after she told me to go away I walked about the walls of the city all night and wished never to see the morning. But I know and knew that my life was owing to my lord and to Heaven, and if I could still be of use to either, it was not mine to escape so easily.'

'Indeed. You might apply the same notion to your guilt. Do what you can to make reparation, and by all means go and ask the girl's forgiveness, but do not make yourself sick with self-hatred over it, and travel in the winter. It will not do you, or her, or your lords one bit of good.'

Gwalchmai smiled sadly rubbing the palm of his hand again. 'Perhaps.' He looked up, the lines of weariness, pain and tension for an instant leaving his face, as his eyes followed the smoke from the fire. 'Perhaps.' Abruptly, 'I would sell my sword to see her once more, Sion. She was like an aspen, standing caught in the brilliance of its shadowing leaves. I have thought of her so often since we defeated the Saxons at Baddon.'

'Have you no knowledge where she might be now?' I asked.

He shook his head. 'There are a few roads I might ride down yet. But they are not truly possibilities, only safeguards.' He was silent another minute then said, softly, 'It would be better for me to go back to Camlann now. My lord the High King has had no news of me since November, and he may need me. I know I will not find her on this journey; I will have to wait, and try again. Tomorrow I will leave for Camlann.'

'Not for at least a week,' my father said. 'Stay with us as long as you desire.'

Gwalchmai again shook his head. 'I am near well enough to travel now, and it is not far.'

My father began to argue, and Gwalchmai argued back, eloquently and interspersing deep thanks to all of us. He and my father both stood up, the better to express themselves. My father seemed solid, his stocky frame unshakeable. Gwalchmai was thin and dark and graceful and equally inflexible. The thought suddenly occurred to me, as I looked at the warrior, that it would not be intolerable to be his servant. When I had been younger, the idea of serving was the one thing that kept me from running off to join a warband, and when I had day-dreamed about it, I had always had to devise some improbable means of escape from that humiliation necessary to a farmer. But Gwalchmai had a kind of a humility, an outlook that saw nothing worthy of scorn in farming, or, I suspected, in service. If only ... but why not? The thought chilled me. He might not want a servant, but I could offer to be one. It was possible; it actually was possible. I had only to speak a few slight words to him alone, and I might be off and away. Did I want it? It was absurd at my age, but ... would Gwalchmai take me? Even if he didn't, he might know someone at Camlann who would ... should I?

In spite of my tiredness, I lay awake a long time that night.

Four

My father persuaded our guest to remain for three more
days and, for the same three days, contrived errands to keep
me away from the householding. I was certain that he did it
deliberately. He first sent me out to check on the sheep and,
as soon as I had done with that, my mother sent me down to
the river to fetch sand for the oven. When the sand had been
fetched she found that she needed some clay, and so on and
off away from the house, and I had no chance to talk to
Gwalchmai. I wondered if my parents knew the question I
kept rephrasing in my mind or if they were simply determined to restrain my talk of war and the affairs of Britain.
As Gwalchmai had said, my father was a shrewd man.

The rest of my family busied itself with Gwalchmai's
gear. My mother mended his cloak, and as much of the rest
of his clothing that she considered worth mending. Some
she simply tore apart and replaced from ours. She tried to
make him accept some spare clothing and a new cloak as
well, but he adamantly refused this with the warmest expressions of gratitude. My father and Goronwy set up a
forge and Goronwy shod Gwalchmai's stallion – and our
mare, for good measure – and patched up the mail-shirt
with a few flattened iron rings. The rest of the houses of our
holding approved of the warrior and discussed him with
great interest and curiosity, and recounted to me how courteous he was, how little the sort of man one would expect the
Pendragon's nephew to be.

Gwalchmai himself was busy, cleaning and sharpening
his weapons, and offering assistance with any work, his or
ours. For myself, I slunk in and out of the house on my
errands, and said barely five words to him in a day. And
then it was the afternoon of the day before he was to leave,
and the man had scarcely met me. I was horrified at it.
Almost I decided not to talk to him after all – but I knew that
I would have no second chance, if I let this one pass me by. I
could stay with my clan, and perhaps be head of our householding after my father; I could marry, and would soon
enough, no doubt, if I could find a girl to take me; I could

farm the land by Mor Hafren, as though the world were as it had been in my grandfather's time. As though Rome had not fallen, and in the time of my grandchildren all would be the same. As though all these things were life itself, and not just a way of life. I had to go. I knew that I had to go to Camlann, though why my heart had seized me thus I could not say, and to go to Camlann I had to talk to Gwalchmai. So, when I came back from one errand I did not even go into the house, but instead went down to the stable, hoping.

He was there, cleaning his horse's harness and singing in Irish. He had a fine singing voice, a strong, clear tenor, and sang well. But he stopped when I came in and stood quickly, catching up a rag and drying the soap from his hands.

'Greetings to you, Rhys ap Sion,' he said politely, and waited for me to get what I wanted from the stable. I came over a little closer to him, looked at him, and felt my heart settle like a wine-skin with a puncture. I did not see how I, Rhys ap Sion ap Rhys, could ask him to take me. But I shuffled my feet, looked at the horse in the stall behind him, and blurted out, 'There is a thing I wish to ask of you, Lord.'

Without looking at him, I knew that he smiled. 'That is well indeed! Any service I can render to your family, after the grace you have shown me, I will do most gladly.'

I shuffled my feet again. The horse was fine-looking, and much easier to watch than this chieftain. 'Lord,' I said again, and there was no hope for it, I had to go on, 'I have had all my life a great hunger for . . . for the world of kings and emperors,' and finally I had to meet his eyes, 'and I would like to go with you to Camlann.'

He was shocked. The black brows contracted. 'You do not know what you are saying,' he told me. I did not reply. 'Ach, most boys want to be warriors, I think: yet it is not the way of life you may think it to be.'

'I am not a boy,' I pointed out. 'Farmers may not age as quickly as warriors do, but I'm twenty-one, and no silly child. And I think, Lord, I can see what your life must be from the way it has used you. I still want to go.'

He looked at me carefully, then leaned against the horse's stall, shaking his head. After a moment he began to laugh quietly.

At this I grew angry. 'I'm not as ridiculous as that! I know how to ride, and how to look after horses, as well as other cattle. I can throw straight, so I think I could protect myself if you gave me a spear. I can't read, but I know Latin as well as British, and no one's ever got the better of me in a market place. I'm no fool, whatever you think.'.

'I did not think you were.' Gwalchmai was abruptly serious again. 'Only . . . I am sure that you are an excellent farmer. But being a warrior is a hard task, and a bitter one, and I should think that serving warriors is worse still.'

'But all warriors, especially when they go on embassies, have servants.'

'I never have. And there is too much fighting I must do to take a servant with me, and if I travel more to look for her it will be worse.'

'I can fight,' I said. 'I've not been trained at it, but I can hold my own against any clansman from Baddon to Caer Gloeu.'

Gwalchmai shook his head again. 'Can you throw a spear?'

I looked at the throwing spears that leant against the wall with the rest of his gear, ready for the morning. They were made of light, straight ash wood with leaf-shaped heads of fine steel, the butt ends sheathed with bronze. They did not look particularly difficult to hurl, unless one was on horseback. I picked one up and hefted it: it weighed a bit more than I had expected, but it seemed well balanced for throwing. Gwalchmai considered me, then pointed to the wall of the barn.

'That plank with the double knot-hole in the middle. Hit that,' he told me.

I shifted my weight, brought my arm back and threw the spear. It wobbled unevenly through the air and struck near the base of a different plank, sticking out sideways. Gwalchmai said nothing. I picked up another spear, and threw that with no better results. I threw the third, then went and pulled all of them out and tried again.

'Stand with your weight on your left leg,' Gwalchmai said, after a while, 'and shift it to your right as you throw. That's it. But stop trying to throw with your arm. The force comes from the shoulder. Don't move your wrist at all; it only makes the spear wobble . . . there.' My hurled spear finally flew levelly and struck straight into the wall. I felt elated until I noticed how far it was from the designated plank. Gwalchmai went and drew it out, came back, and then sent all three spears into the plank, just by the knot hole, with really astonishing speed. He collected them again and set them against the wall before turning back to me. I knew that my face was red, and I said nothing.

'You really do know how to throw things,' the warrior said. 'It took me months before I could throw that well. I was a slow learner – though I can throw spears from horse-back as well, which may compensate. If you'd been properly trained, you'd've made an excellent warrior.'

I looked at the plank I had hit. 'How much training does it take?'

Gwalchmai shrugged. 'In the Orcades – the Ynysoedd Erch, that is – we start when we are seven. The training lasts until we are fourteen or so, and then boys of high rank can begin to go raiding, though they still need some practice for the rest of their lives. And then, fighting from horse-back is another matter entirely.'

I'd heard it before, of course. Warriors begin training at seven, fighting at fourteen or fifteen, and, usually, die before they are twenty-five. Gwalchmai was over that. I was too old to begin. I had known it, but I had never really realized how much that training meant without that accursed plank staring at me. I glared at it.

'I never said I was a warrior,' I told him. 'And perhaps I would get skewered in a battle. But I know that warriors have servants, and their servants do not fight, and other warriors do not harm the servants.'

'No, they don't. Servants are valuable property, if sold to the right buyer,' Gwalchmai observed dryly, then, in a serious, tired voice, added, 'You are your own man, and of a free and prosperous clan. Your family can only be called a gift from Heaven. Why, by all the saints, would you wish to cast all that aside, be subject to another man's will, and wander about Britain with every man's hand against you?'

'I know it is mad, I know.' I stood there, groping for words. 'I know. I only . . . Lord, Rome has fallen, and the Emperor in the east left us to defend ourselves. My grand-father told me of it when I was a child. I . . . ' I struggled with myself, trying to explain something I didn't understand myself. 'And your lord is defending us. Yes, and we are the last Christian land in the West, the last fragment of the Empire – and the Church does nothing, and the kings of Britain do nothing but pretend that the world will go on for ever as it is now, when already it has changed so that the last Emperors would not be able to recognize it.' At this something seemed to give, and I found that I could speak quickly. 'Lord, the West is in Darkness. The Emperor Arthur has given the Saxons one great defeat, but still we are fighting a war, the battle is still continuing, isn't it? Is Britain at peace, Lord? Is the world?'

'The world never will be,' murmured Gwalchmai. But he watched me with a quiet intensity.

'Ach, no, of course not. But now less then ever. Now we have a war between the law and chaos, between Light itself and Darkness. And perhaps Arthur is, as they say, a violent man, but even if he were as corrupt as the king of Gwynedd paints him, it is something to go out and fight against death and ruin, better than sitting up in Arfon like a vulture waiting for the end, or working on a farm near Mor Hafren and pretending that the world's at peace!'

Gwalchmai's face was expressionless. I drew a deep breath, not really knowing what I'd said and feeling weak and exhausted. 'Well,' I said, trying to calm myself, 'is it a reason?'

'It is. You sounded exactly like my lord the Pendragon.' He sighed and ran a hand through his hair while I gaped. 'It is a good reason. Something of that was my reason, as well.' He sat down on the straw and gestured for me to sit next to him. I sat.

'You have reason to join with the Family, Rhys ap Sion.' Gwalchmai laid one arm across his knees, the hand limp. Chain mail glinted at his wrist where the mail-shirt projected from under the tunic. 'Though I suppose it is for every man to fight for my lord the Light in some way, still it is true that my lord and the Family fight in a way special to this age. If you cannot be a warrior, then, you must be someone's servant. I have never wanted a servant, but there is sure to be someone else who will, someone who knows that he fights for the Light of Heaven. There is only one matter that is against you.'

'My family,' I said. I was trembling. He had agreed, I was

going.

'I owe them a great deal.' Gwalchmai picked up a piece of straw and began splitting it. 'I am indebted to your father for more than a few nights' lodging, I think. He is a wise man, your father. It would not be just of me to steal his son. And I think he does not want you to go.'

'I think the same. But if he agrees to let me go, you will take me?'

'If he agrees, and willingly lets you come, I have no choice.'

I put out my hand and, after a moment's hesitation, Gwalchmai took it.

When I went to look for my father I felt neither exalted nor utterly lost.

My whole family was by the hearth, with dinner nearly ready.

'There you are, Rhys,' said my mother. 'Did you bring the salt?' (That had been her latest errand.) 'You did take your time at it!'

I gave her the salt without comment and turned to my father, who was sitting by the hearth. 'Father, I need to talk to you.'

Something in my voice made both my parents go still and glance at each other.

'If you have need to talk, I must have need to listen.' My father walked to the room he and my mother shared with the youngest children and opened the door. I went in and he shut it behind me and sat on the bed, looking at me expectantly. I felt even less inclined to speak than I had under Gwalchmai's eyes.

'Well, what is it?' asked my father.

It was best to say it quickly. If I delayed, I did not know that I could say it at all. It is a terrible thing to part from one's own clan, and worse when it is plain that the parting is not a light one. 'I have asked the lord Gwalchmai to take me with him when he leaves here. I told him that I wanted to be servant to some man of the Pendragon's. Gwalchmai has agreed to take me with him, if you will freely let me go.' My father's hands clenched into fists, and I added, 'Father, he didn't want me to come at first. He tried to talk me out of it. He said he didn't want to "steal your son".'

The fists relaxed. My father looked at me for a long

moment, then, suddenly, put his hands to his face and turned his head away. 'How could he steal what I had already lost? You went to ask him.'

There was a horrible roughness to his voice, and it cut me as nothing had done before.

'I am asking you,' I said, 'to let me go freely.'

'Is there something more you wanted here?' he asked, in a quiet voice unlike his own. 'Is there anything we should have given you and held back?'

'Father,' I said, and I was shaking with the hurt of it, 'you've given me more than I needed, you know that as well as I. But it's that I myself wish to give more.'

'There is the land, and the clan. You can give all of yourself to them, and they need more. It is no easy thing to run a householding, especially in these times, and it is no small thing to run one well.'

'But I want to go to Camlann,' I said. 'That is a bigger thing. It is the greatest thing in all Britain, and I want to be part of it. I want to serve God . . .'

'You can do that anywhere.'

'But in a special way at Camlann.'

'They will fail,' my father said, his voice shaking, but still quiet, angry. 'They are trying to fight darkness when they have too much darkness in themselves. Not so much Gwalchmai, nor the Pendragon, either, but do you think the Family is made up of such men? Warbands in general care nothing for the fight to preserve civilization or for the Light – oh yes, I know what you're after, I've felt the pull myself – but warbands care for plunder and for glory. Civilization is here, in the order and peace of this householding, and not at Camlann. Look at Gwalchmai. He is a fine man, sensitive and honourable, and even in so pure a warband as Arthur's he's dragged into a crime and made to wear himself away with suspicion and doubt. If he had given himself to land and a clan, and kept them in order, and if the Pendragon had done that, they could have made a place where the crime could never have occurred.'

'Which the Saxons would have destroyed,' I said. 'Father, I must go. Maybe you are right, but still, I must go.'

He jumped up, caught my shoulders and shook me. 'Do we mean so little to you?'

'Oh no, no.' I could barely speak, and I was appalled that

despite it all I still wanted just as much to go. 'You mean so much. But I must go. Give me your blessing on it.'

He looked at my face, and I looked at his. It was a strong face, as I remembered. But there were lines about it, and the blue eyes were tired. He was getting older. I had not noticed.

'If I did not let you go willingly, you would run off on your own, wouldn't you?' he asked.

It made me grow cold. I had not even thought of that. But I nodded. He was quite right. Once I had explained why I must go, it had become impossible to avoid.

'Well, then. Go, with my blessing. You are a good man, Rhys, and the desire is, in the end, honourable and just. Perhaps you are right. Perhaps we are not strong enough here. Perhaps the sun rises at Camlann.' He put his arms around me and gave me one of his bear hugs. 'But remember that we are here,' he whispered, 'and if ever you can, come back.'

He let me go and strode abruptly to the door to call my mother.

My family was astonished and appalled. They clamoured with questions which I didn't know how to answer. Gwalchmai arrived from the stable into the midst of it, and they clamoured at him as well. All through supper, all the evening it was the same – 'But why, Rhys?' and 'What will you do, Rhys?' I couldn't say to them the fine words I'd said to Gwalchmai, nor could they understand without my saying anything, as my father had.

My mother cried quietly. I think she did understand my reasons, though, because she asked me no questions, only went about the house packing things for me. She did it quickly and deftly, not missing a thing I might need, and carefully considering space and weight, all the while brushing away the tears. My sisters were anxious and plaintive, my cousins vociferous, with a tendency – restrained by my father – to be accusing. My brother Dafydd was unhelpfully thrilled, grabbing a broom and threatening to spear everyone about him.

I don't think anyone slept well that night. I know that for my part I lay awake long after even the rest of the house had settled. I listened to the logs drop in the fireplace, the wind in the thatch, and to my brother's even breaths beside me. I thought of my whole life, and wondered if I would ever come home again. I prayed a bit, as one does. But I did not cry. There were no tears in me for that departure, greatly though it hurt; and that I had no tears perhaps hurt most of all.

The next day was damp and cold. The clouds hung low, pale and swollen, and in the distance the hills looked like ledges of grey stone. The sun was not fully up when we left, and the earth was hushed. The entire holding huddled outside the barn to see us off. My father saddled our mare's three-year-old foal Llwyd, a shaggy little grey gelding, and handed me the animal's bridle without comment on the gift. Gwalchmai bound most of our baggage behind Ceincaled's saddle, and readjusted the strap that held the shield across his own back. He wore his crimson cloak again, and in the early light looked as strange and otherworldly as he had at that first moment by the river. He turned to my father.

'I am sorely in your debt, Sion ap Rhys,' he said in his soft voice. 'Any thanks I may offer you are shallow and useless indeed.'

My father shrugged, scratched his beard. 'I've done no more, Lord, than provide common hospitality.'

'You have done a very great deal more than that.' Gwalchmai hesitated, then, drawing his sword, dropped to one knee in the snow, graceful as a hawk swooping. He held out the sword, hilt first, to my father. 'If ever this sword may be of any use to you and yours, Sion ap Rhys, if I should then refuse it, may the sky break and fall upon me, may the sea rise up and overwhelm me, may the earth gape and swallow me. Witness it.'

My father, staring at him, slowly lifted his right hand and let his fingertips rest upon the ruby in the sword's pommel. The blade glowed as though some bright light were reflected from it – but there was no light. And that picture took hold of my mind, so that now it sometimes leaps before me at things that have nothing to do with either Gwalchmai or my father: the warrior in his gold and crimson, kneeling, and my father in his grey homespun accepting the pledged trust, half in embarrassment, and half in assurance; a proud humility and a humble pride, and the sword burning with light between their hands.

Then my father dropped his hand, and Gwalchmai stood and sheathed the sword. 'Use it to protect my son,' my father said, a little hoarsely. Gwalchmai nodded and mounted his stallion. He began adjusting the spears tied alongside the horse, checking that they were in easy reach. I swallowed and tried to say goodbye to my family. I did a sad job of it, and was glad to scramble onto my horse. It had all taken too long, I thought, this farewell. Such things should be done as quickly as one is able to say the words.

Gwalchmai gave one final half bow from the saddle, turned Ceincaled's head, and rode down the hill and away from the holding. I gave Llwyd a kick, and the horse started, shied, and trotted after the stallion. I did not look back at my family. Not until we had gone over the next hill and left the house out of sight did I look back. Then I turned just long enough to take it in: the slope of the pasture land, the pale stubble of the snow-covered field, the grey of the forest beyond the river under the leaden sky, and the streaks of smoke hanging motionless on the damp air. Smoke I had seen so many times before, coming home from a day's labour, eager for the hearth. I turned my eyes to the grey morning ahead of me. Gwalchmai's cloak was a splash of crimson against the heavy sky.

'Makes himself damnably conspicuous,' I muttered, to distract the gloom from my heart.

The warrior stayed silent. We rode on towards the old Roman road that leads southwards, to Ynys Witrin, and beyond that, runs onward past Camlann.

Five

We reached the Roman road about mid-morning. Gwalch-mai drew rein as we turned onto it, and looked down the length of it. Ceincaled tossed his head, breath steaming about him, and then was still. I stopped Llwyd and looked down the road as well. I had seen it before, and it seemed even less worthy of observation than usual. It followed a straight line through the curve of the hills, and had once had a cleared space around it which was now grown over with scrub. It looked cold and deserted, and there were no tracks in the snow that covered it, but it was a good road. Gwalch-mai, however, continued to look at it.

The wind was cold, and I saw no reason simply to sit in it and suffer. 'Lord,' I said, after a while, 'this is the road.'

He glanced at me quickly. 'Oh. Indeed, it is. Only . . . would you object to making another day's journey north, before turning to Camlann? It would be good to check one more road she might have taken.'

I looked southward down the road and rubbed my hands together, understanding why no one travelled in the winter. 'We go where you want to, my lord.'

'I am not your lord. You are a free man yet. Only . . .' He looked to the north.

I looked south again. 'We'll go north then, lord.'

He turned Ceincaled north and urged the horse into a trot, eagerly, and I followed with a great deal more reluctance.

We rode north for some fifteen miles with no other occurrence worthy of note except that it began to snow. I had a good warm cloak and warm clothing, but my ears and feet and fingers froze. Llwyd, who was used to better treatment than this, became stubborn and bad-tempered, shying at nothing and trying to slip away and go back home. I had my hands full to control him. Gwalchmai seemed not to notice the cold and rode easily, setting a fast pace despite the snow.

We reached Caer Ceri in the early afternoon. It is an old Roman town, walled, one I had been to once or twice before when our holding had some trading to do and the market at

Baddon was closed because of the Saxons. Caer Ceri was deserted when we came to it, though, and the market square was occupied only by a flock of sheep. I expected that we would stop and buy a meal by some warm hearthside. I had been looking forward to it for the last five miles, to getting off the horse I hadn't ridden since autumn, and sitting down by a warm fire to eat warm food and drink hot ale. But Gwalchmai rode straight through the town without pausing, and turned left onto the west road to Powys. When the walls fell away behind us and he urged Ceincaled into a trot again, I realized that he had no intention of acting in a rational fashion, and I must resign myself to the cold sausage and oat cakes my mother had supplied for lunch. These were half frozen. I offered some to Gwalchmai, who took them with thanks and some surprise, and we chewed the food slowly as we rode.

Llwyd was growing tired, since he was as much out of the habit of being ridden as I was of riding, and, while it made him less troublesome, I began to worry. If he went lame or grew overworn, where could I get another horse?

'Lord,' I said to Gwalchmai, 'how much further do you want to go today?'

'To Caer Gloeu, above Saefern Hafren. It's another ten miles or so, I think.'

That was quite a distance for a short winter day. It would be nearly dark by the time we reached the town. We had done some twenty miles already, by my reckoning. I remembered all the songs I had heard of Arthur's campaigns sweeping from one end of Britain to the other. Hard on the horses, Gwalchmai had said. Very hard, I thought, and hard on the warriors as well.

'Lord, my horse is unused to so much travel. He has not been ridden this winter since the snows began.'

Gwalchmai stopped, dismounted, and looked at Llwyd. He checked the gelding's legs and hooves, then straightened, chafing his hands together. 'He needs the exercise, that is true,' he commented. 'But he will not go lame or be overworked – though he may consider himself such. He has a strain of the pony in him, hasn't he?'

I admitted it, and Gwalchmai nodded and remounted his war stallion. Ceincaled seemed as rested as he had been that morning. We rode on, and I felt as thoroughly outclassed by the warrior as Llwyd was by his mount. I had always considered myself a good horseman.

Caer Gloeu was more twelve miles distant than ten, and the sun was setting when we reached it, a dim copper disc half-smothered by clouds. It was still snowing, in fits. I was chilled through and ached all over. Llwyd plodded with his head drooping, not caring where he was. I cared: I still wanted the hot ale.

Caer Gloeu was slightly larger than Caer Ceri, but equally deserted. It might almost have been the same flock of sheep milling in the market square. Gwalchmai stopped Ceincaled in a street opening to one side of that square and sat motionless, as though waiting. I huddled my shoulders and felt wretched and angry, too tired to care whether we were standing about for some purpose or just looking at another road.

After a few minutes, however, the door of one of the old houses opened, and a man came out, carrying a spear and pulling a threadbare cloak around his shoulders. He stood on his door step and gave us a steady, hostile stare. This, apparently, was what Gwalchmai had expected, for he dismounted and walked over near the man, keeping both hands up at shoulder height in plain view.

'I need a place to stay the night, for myself, my servant, and our horses.' His voice was quiet, but clear enough to carry across the square. The townsman continued to stare, holding his spear ready to thrust. He was a tall, pudgy man with thin brown hair and no beard. He glanced towards me with narrow eyes.

'Your servant?' he said to Gwalchmai. I suddenly realized that it should have been my task to ask for hospitality. Too late. I already looked a dolt, and Gwalchmai was going on.

'My servant and our horses; the horses will need grain. I can pay, man.'

At this, the man spat, but he lowered the spear and nodded. 'For the one night?'

'For this one night only.' The man nodded again, and Gwalchmai walked back to the horses and caught Ceincaled's bridle. The townsman gestured for us to follow, and we went back down the street, through an alley, and back up a smaller street to what I supposed was the back door of his own house. There we were led into a ramshackle stable, very draughty and dirty, with a small donkey and a cow, a few chickens and a pig occupying what space was not filled with wood and rubble. Gwalchmai looked about it and asked the man to move the cow, so as to make room in the stall for the horses. Our host argued a bit, swore some, and complied. Then Gwalchmai silently began to clean out the stall while the townsman stood about watching him suspiciously. I was furious. Any decent man would bring his guests inside by the fire and give them some hot ale, not make them clean his own filthy stable.

Deciding that I had better behave like a servant, I dismounted, stiffly. My legs shook when they touched the ground and I had to steady myself against Llwyd's shoulder before going to a corner of the stable to get fresh straw and the grain. Our host tried to give us less grain than the horses needed, and I had to argue with him. He claimed that we were being extortionate and trusting in our strength of arms to get away with it. 'But this is a town,' he told me. 'We have a civic government, a Roman government, and we enforce the laws. You can't rob citizens here.' I supposed his Roman government consisted of the levy of all the able-bodied citizens, ready to perform whatever extortion they could agree on. I felt revolted by the man, and then thought to wonder if he would have acted in the same way if I had come as a farmer, and not as the servant of a warrior.

We settled the horses and left them hungrily chomping the grain. Llwyd rarely got such food at home, but if he was to do more travelling he would need it.

Our host's house was nearly as dirty as his stable, and, besides wife and numerous children, it also contained chickens. No householder that I knew would have tolerated such a place, but things are different in the towns. Few people live in them any more, since only the very rich and the craftsmen can afford it. Our host's house was filled with drying pottery and wet clay, so plainly he was a potter. I picked up one of the plates and examined it. He was not a very skilled potter. Nonetheless, he snarled at me and told me to leave his valuable ware alone. Well, it was probably valuable enough. Potters can usually make a living.

The potter's wife had apparently begun to make porridge as soon as her husband had agreed to let us stay the night, and she now set this before us. It was lumpy, badly cooked, and had neither meat nor eggs in it. I put down the bowl after my first spoonful. This was too much for my temper.

'Since we're paying you might give us some meat,' I suggested to the potter's wife, quietly. She looked as surprised to find me speadking to her as she would if one of her chickens addressed her. 'Or an egg,' I added.

Gwalchmai looked up from his porridge, also in surprise. He had apparently been willing to eat the lumpy porridge without a word. But I was in no mood to let anyone cheat me of a much-desired meal. 'Bring us some bread, with butter, mind you, and some cheese!' I ordered, slamming my bowl down. 'And if you have some ham, bring that. And ale. Hot ale. My lord and I have been riding all day, and if you think we'll settle for poor porridge at the end of it, you are much mistaken.'

The woman glanced nervously at her husband. One of her children snickered. Gwalchmai coughed behind his hand, not looking at me, and the potter became red in the face. 'I've no need to offer you hospitality!' snarled our host, 'Any mongrel warrior thinks he rules the earth. Well, you don't, and you're no warrior even, servant. I take no talk from servants. I . . .'

'My lord, though, is a warrior, and no mongrel about it,' I said, and was going to tell the man that this was Gwalchmai ap Lot, the Pendragon's nephew, son of the king of the Ynysoedd Erch and so on, when I noticed Gwalchmai's look of alarm, and recollected that he had not mentioned any names at all to the potter. He knew more about it than I, and I would do well to tread carefully. But I was not going to give up my hot ale and ham. 'My lord happens to be a very good warrior, as you may hope you will not discover,' I finished. It seemed so easy to threaten the man.

'We're a town here! We have a government here!' said the potter. But he looked uneasy.

'Of course. And you are our host, even if you're paid for it,' I replied. 'And since you're a civilized man, and a host, you might give us some civilized food.'

The woman suddenly ran off and fetched the food, good wheat bread, butter, cheese and ham, and began to heat the ale. Her husband swore at us for a while, then grumbled into silence. Gwalchmai gave me a look I could not read – irony? annoyance? amusement? But the food was delicious

70

and worth the effort, and I didn't care who was offended.

When he had finished his bread and ham, Gwalchmai began asking whether the potter and his family had lived in Caer Gloeu long. Yes, the man admitted sullenly, he had. Had he been there eight years before?

'I've been in Caer Gloeu all my life,' said the potter. 'What of it?'

'Only this: some time in mid-autumn, eight years ago, a woman may have come this way, a thin, fair woman, probably riding a brown horse and perhaps wearing blue. She had two servants, one an old man with half an ear missing.'

The potter listened attentively, then shook his head. 'Never seen any such woman. What kind of a whore was she, travelling like that? Must have been good.'

'She is not a whore.' Gwalchmai's voice was still quiet, but there was a chilling edge to it. The potter looked at him, and suddenly crossed himself. The dark warrior looked dangerous and completely uncanny, though he sat very quietly with his emptied plate on his knee. 'She is a lady of high family.'

'Well, I never seen her. Never heard anyone tell of her, either.'

'Neither here in town, nor on the road north, nor from the west, across the Saefern?'

'If she went by there, I never heard of her.'

Gwalchmai looked at him a moment steadily, then sighed. The whole journey suddenly made sense to me. Caer Gloeu stands between Powys, Dumnonia, and the southern wilds of Elmet. Anyone who travelled to any of these lands was likely to stop for the night at Caer Gloeu, and a woman travelling alone, with only a few servants, would probably have been remembered. Our host did not seem to be lying, so it was plain that Elidan had not come to Caer Gloeu, and we could turn back to Camlann in the morning. I was relieved; Gwalchmai was plainly disappointed. He took another drink of his hot ale, then set the mug down.

'I thank you.' He actually did say it, and I was amazed. So was the potter, who blinked at us as though he had heard a ghost. Gwalchmai continued matter-of-factly, 'My servant and I will sleep in the stable, by our horses. Have you any extra blankets?'

'You can sleep in here by the hearth,' said the potter. 'Won't need many blankets. A good fire, there.'

The warrior glanced at the smokey fire and said, 'We will sleep in the stables.'

I wanted vehemently to protest. The thought of going out into that draughty and filthy building, just when I was beginning to get warm, made me want to hit someone. But I couldn't, so I worked on getting good blankets from the potter. In the end I managed to make him give us a rug, though he wasn't happy about it.

When Gwalchmai had said we would sleep by our horses, he had meant it, and we settled for the night in the very stall, near the manger. It wasn't too cold, after all. Gwalchmai began to unfasten his baldric, so as to set the sword where he could reach it in the night.

'Why couldn't we stay in the house?' I asked.

'I do not trust them.' He said it simply. He frowned, loosening the fastenings of his chain mail, but not taking it off. 'This way we can guard ourselves and the horses at once.'

It made sense, if one could conceive of the potter slipping a knife into his guests for the sake of two horses and some valuable weapons. But who would do that? Or would he? If he thought we might leave without paying him, since he hated us so much as it was? The thought frightened me, not even so much for the danger, as for the appalling amount of suspicion and mistrust it demanded. But the potter . . . just might.

'Should I have said those things?' I asked, suddenly aware that it might have been an activity of questionable worth.

The warrior laughed. 'You know better than I.' We lay down and drew our cloaks and the rug over us. 'I would not have said such things,' my companion added after a moment. 'But the ale was very good on a night like this. Sleep well.' The straw rustled as he felt for his sword, and a horse shifted its weight in the dark above us. I knew that Gwalchmai would wake instantly if anyone came into the stable. It was safe here. Not comfortable, though: the floor was hard and cold even through the straw, and I ached quite enough as it was. Probably, I thought, I will sleep badly . . . and fell asleep on the thought. I slept the whole night without so much as a dream. Too much riding in bad weather will do that.

When I woke the next morning, dim sunlight was filtering through a crack in the roof, making a patch on the staw near my head. I lay awake for a while trying to determine what I was doing in a barn, then remembered that I had left home and sat bolt upright. My head cracked against the manger above me, and the two horses paused a moment and looked down at me, then began to munch their grain again.

I sat up again, more cautiously, and straightened my cloak and tunic. Gwalchmai was not there. I picked up the rug and blanket and began folding them to take them back to our host. Just as I stood up, Gwalchmai came out of the back door of the house.

'Good morning,' he said, smiling. 'You are a sound sleeper, Rhys. Our hostess has made breakfast, and it is inside.'

I was ready for breakfast. My bones ached from the damp and chill of the stable and from the previous day' riding, and warm food by a fire seemed a provision from Heaven. 'I am glad of that,' I said feelingly. I picked up the rug and draped it over my arm.

Gwalchmai was fidgeting with his cloak. 'Have you a spare brooch?' he asked.

I had one, at the bottom of my pack, a plain bronze clasp identical to the one that fastened my own cloak. I went and dug it out. The warrior thanked me and pinned his cloak with it. He seemed to have lost his own brooch, and I wondered at it: I'd noticed the clasp, and it was a valuable one if I was any judge of the thing. It seemed hard that he needed mine, which wasn't worth a tenth of the other, but was valuable enough to me. But he was doing me a great favour, I reminded myself, in taking me to Camlann, and I ought to be generous with my possessions.

Morning apparently improved our potter's temper, for he was almost pleasant, and his wife had produced bread with egg and sausage for breakfast. Gwalchmai had eaten already, and stayed in the stable to tend to his horse, so I settled down to my eggs alone, but with enthusiasm nonetheless. The potter leaned against the wall opposite, actually humming, and turning something in his hand. I was nearly done with my meal before I realized that what he held was Gwalchmai's brooch.

I knew the potter could not have taken the brooch. That

meant that Gwalchmai had given it to him as payment, but it was a vast over-payment, especially given the potter's sullenness. No wonder the man was cheerful now. He'd made a very fine bargain indeed. But I didn't like the thought of a pudgy-faced townsman profiting from his extortion. I finished my eggs thoughtfully and put the plate down. 'I see my lord gave you his brooch.'

The potter smirked.

'You can give me the change from the payment,' I said. He eyed me, pretending not to understand what I meant. 'Well, you don't think my lord meant you to grow fat off what he won on the field of battle against the Saxons, do you?'

'He gave it to me.' But there was a defensive whine in the man's tone. He didn't believe for an instant that Gwalchmai had meant him to keep the brooch.

'Of course. He gave it to you, and you can give me more goods to make up the value of it. Or, if you prefer, you can give me the brooch back and I'll give you the value of your hospitality – or rather, the value of a night's hospitality, since I wouldn't give a sick chicken for yours.'

'But this is a small brooch. It's not worth a hen.'

'Not worth a hen!' I wondered if the man thought me an imbecile. 'Man, you could buy an ox with that, and easily. Irish gold work! And those are garnets, not your Gaulish enamel.'

'Well, there was grain for the horses. That warhorse is a waster of grain, my expensive grain.'

'Not that expensive. All that you gave us and the horses together is worth no more than a scrawny capon.'

'It's worth a pig at the least!'

'Well, the brooch is worth an ox, and you yourself admit that your goods are not worth that. Give it to me.'

·A crafty look came into his pale eyes. 'Stealing it from your lord?'

I tired to look unconcerned, though the man turned my stomach with his suppositions. 'If you think that, I'll call him and you can tell him that.'

The gleam faded from his eyes, and reluctantly he set the brooch down on the table. 'What'll you give me, then?'

I hadn't thought of it. I looked down at the clasp for a moment, then unfastened my own bronze brooch and set it down beside the other. 'That.'

'That? I wouldn't give a dozen eggs for it.'

We bargained for a while, and eventually the man accepted my bronze pin and a bronze ring, and gave me the brooch and a flask of his ale. I collected my gains, and fastened my cloak with Gwalchmai's brooch.

'May you prosper,' I said to the potter, standing up.

'*Vale*,' he returned, speaking, like a true townsman, in Latin. Then he added, 'You're a farmer, aren't you?'

I paused at the door 'I was that.'

'I knew it. Only farmers, and of them only householding clansmen, drive a bargain like that. God deliver Britain from such!'

I grinned and went out into the stable. The potter knew he'd got the worst of the bargain.

Gwalchmai had already saddled both horses and was waiting, and we mounted and were moving out of the town in short order. The sun was still low, and it glittered off the new snowfall with a jewelled brilliance. There were more clouds in the west, however and I judged we'd have more snow before long. I ached with every step Llwyd took, but I felt cheerful despite it all. I waited for Gwalchmai to notice the fruits of my bargain.

He did, before too long. Soon after we had reached the road to Caer Ceri, just beyond the walls of Caer Gloeu, he suddenly frowned and reined in his horse. His eyes were fixed on the brooch.

I grinned inwardly, but put a serious look on my face. 'Would you like your brooch back, Lord? I found it for you this morning.'

'Where did you . . . I gave that to the potter.'

'That I know. I'm wondering why. He could have bought an ox with it, and he deserved a thrashing.'

Gwalchmai rubbed his chin. 'Could he? I didn't know it was worth so much. Oh, I know I overpaid him, but what else? I am the Pendragon's servant, and it is honourable to be free of what I own, and I haven't any more gold, except what's on my Ceincaled.'

'You didn't know it was worth so much? Then how did you get it?'

'From a Saxon I killed a few years ago – now this potter will be confirmed in his opinion of warriors. Did you tell him I would kill him unless he gave it to you? That is a wrong.'

So much thanks I had for saving his money. 'Threaten him? Well, God knows, the man deserved it. But no, I gave him my brooch and a ring, and he gave me this and a flask of ale. I have the best of the bargain, and the man is busy thinking how warriors are cleverer than he thought them to be, or, at least, have clever servants.'

'You bargained?'

'How else does one buy things?'

Gwalchmai looked at me. No, I realized, he would never bargain. He would give, mostly, if he starved himself to do it, and from his lord's allies or enemies, take without payment.

'Well,' I said, sighing a bit because men are so different, 'well, for those who are not warriors, bargaining is the only way to buy, and those who do not bargain are fools. I told our potter that I was collecting the change from your payment, and have this,' and I lifted the flask of ale, 'as well as the brooch to show for it, and our host is cursing the bargaining of farmers. Is it wrong?'

Gwalchmai shook his head. 'You did not threaten him, but still left him cursing?'

'I left him a plucked goose. All that food, and the grain for the horses, for one bronze pin and a ring not worth half a dozen eggs!'

Gwalchmai gave me the same ambiguous look he had given me the night before, then suddenly burst out laughing. 'Ach, *righ rearach!* It is wonderful, it is a miracle! A flask of ale as well? I do not see how it was done, but Rhys, it was done well.'

I grinned back. I thought so too. 'So,' I said, 'here is your pin back, and you can give me mine.'

He shook his head, throwing up one narrow hand, palm out. 'Not so. You made a fine bargain for it; it is yours.'

I looked at the pin, glittering red and gold against my plain woollen cloak. An ox would be a low price to pay for it. I could not think of myself casually wearing something worth so much, it seemed almost scandalous. 'That would not be proper, my lord. You won it in battle; I merely talked to a fool. You take it back.'

But Gwalchmai shook his head again. 'I will not. Yours

76

will hold my cloak, and if someone takes exception to it, I can get another at Camlann.' He touched Ceincaled's sides with his heels and the horse broke into a flowing trot, and I kicked Llwyd until he jolted into the same gait. 'I have never seen a townsman bettered in my life, except when it is a matter of making them pay the tribute at sword's point, and that is no sweet thing. When we reach Camlann I will give you a ring to replace yours, and, by the sun, the tale is worth more than that.'

A ring, I thought, I did not want. I did not want the brooch, either, but I had it now. Well, I could always trade it for some less flashy gear. Or, if I found someone I could trust going that way I could send it home. Or even . . . sometimes my father himself brought grain to Camlann to sell, and I could give it to him, perhaps with some gifts for the rest of them. A good thought, that.

We rode no fewer miles that day than we had the day before, going all the way to Maeldyfi and the monastery there (Gwalchmai would, I think, have gone to Baddon if he had been alone, but Llwyd was tired and could not keep the pace of the war stallion). It was even colder than the day before, and it began to snow around noon, when we again ate as we rode, and, what's more, I ached more than I had the day before. But my heart was a deal lighter. I was not an utter dead weight on my lord – my lord until we reached Camlann, at least, when I'd have to find some other master. I could get the better of townsmen, which my lord couldn't, and provide ale to go with the sausage and oat cakes we had for lunch. I could not only go to Camlann, but I could provide something there.

The monks at Maeldyfi where we stayed the night were in the custom of providing food and shelter for travellers, though they asked for a 'donation', by which they meant as much as they could get from the travellers. Too many monasteries in Britain are thus. I have heard that the Irish monasteries are different, and have been since Patricius brought the Faith there. I have met one or two Irish monks who have come to Britain in voluntary exile, desiring, for their love of Christ, to be parted from all that is familiar and secure and devote their lives to God. Most British monks seem to want to devote their lives to the prosperity of their community, and ignore God as much as possible. My father used to shake his head over them and try doubly hard to out-bargain them – for their own good, he would say – relieve them of some excess possessions, and explain to me that the fault was not of the Church, but of the man who ran it. Whatever the fault may be, monks will try to take more from their guests for a night's hospitality than either towns-men or farmers. Some people, awed by the candles and chanting, will pay it. I saw to it that in Maeldyfi we did not – for their own good, of course. I had to give them my spare tunic, but I got in return some bread and cheese for the next day's lunch, as well as the night's lodging and grain for the horses. Gwalchmai, to his own keenly felt shame, had no spare tunic to give (my mother had thought it not worth mending), and awkwardly promised me a better one than the old, when we reached Camlann.

The monks were hungry for news of the world, since they had few visitors in winter, and treated us much more hospitably than the potter, but Gwalchmai was as sus-picious of them as he had been of the townsman, and again insisted on sleeping by the horses. I remembered that the Pendragon was generally unpopular with the monasteries. He had insisted that they help the war either by paying tribute or by converting the Saxons. Being unwilling to take the risks involved in converting the Saxons, they paid, and hated. Gwalchmai, I noticed, again avoided mention of his name or loyalties.

We left Maeldyfi early next morning and took the road on southwards towards Baddon, which is some eighteen miles from Maeldyfi. My family's lands lie some fifteen miles west of the road, and about as far north of Baddon. I began looking for the familiar turning onto the rough track that led home, and was overcome by the strangeness of passing back down the same road only a few days after leaving home, and this time, truly knowing that it was all changed, that I was not turning my horse onto that side road.

Gwalchmai began singing, primarily in Irish, after leaving Maeldyfi. After a little, however, he stopped his verses and slowed his horse until it walked beside mine. He said nothing about this, and I was busy enough with my own thoughts to let it pass without question. But late in the morning, about the time I first began thinking of lunch, Gwalchmai suddenly touched his horse to a full gallop and

tore off towards the wood at the side of the road. I reined in
Llwyd in astonishment, looking after him, and only then
saw the arrow sticking upright in the snow that covered the
road. For a moment I could not understand where it had
come from; and then I thought 'bandits', and looked back
up to Gwalchmai.

The scrub there had been cleared back from the road and
Gwalchmai was half-way to the line of trees, his white
stallion running like a falcon swooping on a swallow,
weaving back and forth to throw off the archer's aim, a
dazzle of speed, mane tossed like light off water. Someone
screamed, and then a body staggered out of the woods and
fell with a spear – Gwalchmai's spear – jutting from it. I
think I cried out. I know I must have clapped my heels to
Llwyd's sides and started towards the struggle, not
knowing what to do, but somehow thinking that I must
stop it, as though it were only a quarrel between my
cousins. But now there were other men running from the
wood, yelling, men in tattered cloaks, carrying thrusting
spears and bows. One more staggered back, spitted on a
spear; and then there was a flash like lighting sweeping from
the horizon, only holding, holding: Gwalchmai had drawn
his sword, and it was incandescent with light.

There was more yelling. I think some of the bandits must
have tried to flee, but they had no chance to. Some were
trying to fight, at any rate, and it was useless.

Llwyd ran like a horse in a nightmare, crawling across the
snow, but finally I reached the edge of the wood and did not
know what to do. There seemed to be blood and dying men
everywhere. Their eyes stared up at me, reflecting the
morning sun. I later realized that there were only six bandits
in the group, but at that instant there seemed to be fifty at
least, and the shadows swung wild across the snow, cast by
the burning sword.

One man backed up against a tree, holding his spear
ready. I had time to look at him. His face was white above
his brown beard, but his eyes were terrible and dark, and
they were fixed on the sword. Gwalchmai swung his horse
about, and the stallion reared, splendid as fire and wind,
plunging towards the bandit.

'Don't!' I shouted, unable to bear it. 'My lord, don't!' and
somehow I drove my horse up against his and caught his

sword arm.

His head whipped about when I shouted, and our eyes met when I caught his wrist. Looking at him, I became terrified. 'I go mad in battle', he had said. Despite what he had added, I had thought of berserkers, men who foam at the mouth and rage like dogs when they fight, and had thought he had meant that – but Gwalchmai was not berserk. He was smiling, not with savagery or irony, but with a kind of ecstatic joy or even love, and there was a light, an exaltation in his face that should not be discovered on any human face. His hand was raised to bring down the sword, and I knew that it was nothing to him whether or not he killed, because in that madness, the difference between death and life was finer even than the sword's edge. He could kill me where I stood and not even notice. Somehow, it was not the threat of death that was terrifying, but the total foreignness of his eyes. I knew, meeting them, why those who saw angels were so afraid.

'Gwalchmai,' I said. His sword hand under mine did not move, but his lips parted as though he would speak. 'My lord,' I repeated.

Slowly, the glory began to fade from his eyes, and a kind of bewilderment crept into them. He dropped his gaze, the smile falling from his face, and looked down. His arm relaxed, and I released his hand. The light was gone from the sword, leaving it a mere piece of edged metal, cold in the winter sun.

Gwalchmai lowered the sword until it pointed to the ground, and drew away towards the bandit without looking at me. The robber stared at him, holding his spear level; then abruptly threw the weapon aside and flung himself on his face in the snow and began to beg for mercy, gabbling his pleas. I looked around and saw that around us were only corpses, lying on the snow. Five corpses.

'Sit up,' said my lord levelly. The bandit grovelled. 'Come, sit up.' The man rose to his knees and stared at us, his lips trembling, blue with cold. 'Why did you seek to kill us on the road just now?'

The man licked his lips. 'For money,' I said. The man bobbed his head in agreement. 'Arglwyd Mawr, Great Lord,' he said, 'I have no land.'

'Have you not? Then you should choose another craft

80

than this. What is your clan?'

He licked his lips. 'I have none.'

'Because you have been disowned by it, kin-wrecked, for the murder of a kinsman?'

He stared, then bobbed his head again. Most robbers are kin-wrecked.

Gwalchmai sighed. 'Is there any reason why I should not kill you?'

'Great Chieftain, I am a poor wretch and helpless, and you, you are the lord Gwalchmai ... yes, yes, I heard your servant say so, and who else has such a sword, and such a horse, and fights so? Is it fitting, Great Lord, Master, that a falcon strike at gadflies?'

'If the gadflies strike at him. Get up. Come, get up. I will not kill you now.' The robber stood, shaking. 'Your companions here are dead. Have you others in your band?'

'One other, Chieftain. He is sick.'

'Then take what goods you have, and what you will from these bodies and buy oxen. There is land enough lying vacant; and if you will not farm, set up in a trade, you and this other. The Saxons have been defeated, man, and my lord the Pendragon is already sending men out to hunt down wolves such as yourself who prowl these roads. Do you hear me?'

'I hear you, Great Lord.'

'Then give thanks to God that you live yet, and take steps to avoid another encounter like this one where the numbers as well as the skill will be against you, and there will be no mercy shown.' Gwalchmai turned Ceincaled and rode off at a gallop. I followed, silently, wondering. I had begun to think that I knew Gwalchmai. I had put him down as a gentle, over-sensitive man, brave, honourable, over-conscientious. I had forgotten the first thing I knew about him: that he was the deadliest cavalry fighter in all Britain, Arthur's sword hand on almost numberless battlefields. I told myself, as I rode behind him and looked at his crimson-cloaked back, that the deadliness made his gentleness and self-control all the greater. But I felt sick. For all the songs I had heard, I had never understood what it means to see men killed, and the eyes of those five corpses still burned in my brain like glowing coals.

We rode thus for another half hour, and then Gwalchmai

drew his horse back beside mine. He still carried his naked sword, and there was blood on the blade. He lifted the hilt in a little gesture towards me. 'Rhys, have you anything I could use to clean this off?'

In silence I stopped, dismounted, and dug out of my pack a cloth my mother had meant for me to clean harness with. Gwalchmai also dismounted, rubbed his sword with snow, then dried the clean blade with my mother's cloth and slid the sword back into its sheath. The gold and ruby of the hilt glittered as he handed me the cloth back. There was only a little smudge of human blood on the material. I looked at the smudge for a moment, then put the cloth back in the pack and remounted. I gathered up Llwyd's reins, and saw Gwalchmai still standing, frowning a little.

'There is something the matter, then?' he asked. I tightened my grip on the reins, and Llwyd fidgeted and shied a little sideways. Gwalchmai caught his bridle, and the horse suddenly became very nervous, laying his ears back, rolling his eyes and snorting. I could see the reason.

'There is also some blood on your hand,' I told him. Gwalchmai glanced at his hand, and dropped it from the bridle so that the smell should cease to frighten my horse. He stooped and picked up some more snow to clean his hands. 'And that, also, is what is the matter with you?' he asked, without looking at me.

I did not know what to say. I looked at the reins, and Gwalchmai dried his hands on his cloak, then rubbed them together for warmth and wrapped them in some rags.

'My lord,' I said at last, 'I have never before seen a man killed, but I have just seen you kill five men. I am a fool, for I know that they would have killed us, and I knew from the beginning that you had killed many, but still, I am sick to see them dead, and you drying your sword and smiling.'

Gwalchmai looked at me thoughtfully a moment, then walked over to his horse and vaulted easily to the saddle. 'And they were poor wretches, too, were they not?' He straightened his cloak around him, the sword disappearing under its folds, and picked up the reins with firm hands. 'Outlaws, those, from Elmet, who starved in the north and so came south hoping to do better where the roads are more travelled but where they are not so much travelled as to be dangerous. Hardly equal opponents for me, hardly men with any chance of saving their own lives.'

I had heard of northerners coming south to practise robbery in the winter, so I nodded. If he did need to travel in the winter, my father always avoided the good roads. I had, in fact, heard of travellers killed by robbers on the south road, people in clans I knew. 'My lord, I know that they must have killed innocent men freely, and that they had no care for whether or not the fight was equal.'

'But we should care.' He touched Ceincaled's sides and started off at a walk. He stared down the road, looking tired. 'If I am to fight for my lord the Pendragon and for Britain and the Light, I ought to care.' He looked at me again, smiling a very little, almost questioning. 'And yet, it is not right to let them continue to kill when I can stop them. I let that man escape today. Perhaps this afternoon he will kill someone, because he did not die this morning.'

I looked at Llwyd's neck, and twisted my fingers in his coarse mane. If the bandit killed someone this afternoon, I was partly responsible, for I was the one who had prevented Gwalchmai from killing him. What if someone I knew, someone from a householding in the area, had to travel the road? What if someone from my family did? 'And yet, the man might buy some oxen. There's land enough that needs workers.'

'And he might not.' Gwalchmai looked back down the road. 'Well, I have killed the other five, and I frightened him, and it may be enough. But I do not see that I could have done anything but fight them.'

That was true. He could not have simply sat still and allowed the robbers to kill us both.

'I do not know,' Gwalchmai said abruptly 'I am used to the fighting and the killing now, and I do not think of it much, unless someone should ask me. And I do not remember killing. Only Bran; I remember killing him. But I killed him for myself, and the others I kill because I must. A servant of the Light gave me a sword, and it is meant to be wielded. If the Darkness is to be turned back, surely the sword is the means? I am ready to kill for my lord, to order and defend, and yet I do not know if it is wholly right. But there is no other way open to me, so I must fight, and trust Heaven for the rest.'

For some reason, I felt tremendously comforted. 'You

are right. If I wish to fight for civilization, I suppose I had better get used to it all. Forgive me, my lord.'

Gwalchmai gave me a strange look, then smiled. I smiled back. We rode on, under a clear sky. The sun stood in the middle of the blue arch, and the snow glistened around us. Gwalchmai began to sing a long, slow, melancholy song in Irish, his voice rich and clear in the silence which weighed over the forest about us. A strange world, I thought, and people the strangest thing in it. A complicated world, where to act might be to act wrongly, and not to act be even worse. It would take some getting used to.

Six

Gwalchmai was eager to reach Camlann, and from Maeldyfi wanted to press on as far as Ynys Witrin, a good fifty miles. At Ynys Witrin we could claim hospitality from the local lord, who would be bound to offer it freely to the Pendragon's nephew. But Llwyd was tired, and could not go fast, and the distance was too great – or so I said – and we eventually spent the night at a farm some ten miles south of Baddon. The farmer was a hard bargainer, unwilling to accept any of our goods until Gwalchmai took the gold-worked headstall from Ceincaled's bridle. Then he began to offer us more than we needed, eager for more gold. I took two bronze armlets and a silver ring in change (a better bargain than the other hoped for), and Gwalchmai knotted a rope to improvise a headstall, though he was not pleased with it. He would sooner have sold all his own gear than have touched the horse's.

The next day we rode on to Camlann, arriving at the fortress just after noon. At mid-morning we turned from the Roman road onto the raised track that goes through Ynys Witrin and the marshes, and made good speed towards the irregular hills that fill the horizon. The land about us was well settled, clear of forest, and the fields were well tended. It was another bright, clear day, and sheep and cattle were out in the pastures, giving the land a cheerful, in-habited look welcome after the long road and the forest. As we went west, Camlann slowly resolved itself from the sur-rounding hills, seeming to grow taller as we approached it. Gwalchmai urged his horse to a trot, then to a canter, and the stallion ran with a light step and pricked-up ears. He knew well enough where he was going. Llwyd had no such eagerness, but he followed the other horse. He had grown used to doing that.

The feast hall showed clear against the sky, crowning the great hill. Only after I had noticed that did I discern the walls and the ring and bank defences of the fortress. But the walls were large enough when we came to them, and had been strongly re-fortified, unlike the walls of any town I had ever seen. The gate we approached was also new, with a single guard tower set above it, and it was made of oak and iron. But it opened before we reached it, and Gwalchmai reined in just inside it to greet the guards, while his stallion danced in eagerness to be properly home. I drew in Llwyd, who was sweating from his run. Both the guards posted there came down from the guard tower and began shouting to Gwalchmai.

'A hundred thousand welcomes home!' said one of them. 'Man, we were wondering who we could send out to avenge your death. Your brother said no, it was like you to go travelling in winter – but he was the readiest of all of us to begin any revenging.'

Gwalchmai laughed. 'Was he? That is like my brother. He is well? And my lord Arthur? And the Queen?'

Yes, yes, they were all well, and there was news, and certain things had happened so, and Cei had said to Agravain – 'But you will hear all this soon enough,' the guard interrupted himself. 'And it is a cold day to stand about talking. I will see you at the feast tonight.'

'Is there a feast tonight?'

'There will be now. There's been no excuse for one these two weeks. Oh, and who is this fellow with you?'

'My servant. Rhys ap Sion.'

The guard cocked one eyebrow and looked at me as though I were someone's new horse. 'Gwalchmai the Golden-tongued has taken a servant? Do you plan to stay in one place, then?'

Gwalchmai simply laughed. I was ready to tell the guard that the job was not mine, and that I was to find another master in Camlann, but the man went on, 'Good for you, servant, and good luck! I hope you like to travel.'

Gwalchmai laughed again, wished the guard a happy watch, and started Ceincaled off up the steep hill at a canter.

Camlann is a huge fortress. There are seven hundred men in Arthur's Family; about four hundred of these sleep in the feast hall, while the rest have houses inside the fortress. Some of the men are married and have their families at Camlann. Besides these warriors, the servants and their families make their homes in the fortress, and the doctors, smiths, carpenters and masons, the grooms and the trainers and breeders of horses, and all the tradesmen who have settled in the fortress. There is also some farming done, since a number of cattle are pastured in the fields around, with flocks of sheep, while some pigs and chickens are kept in Camlann itself, and vegetables are grown there, but the rest of the food – all the grain, and much of the meat – has to be purchased. A fortress that size requires a great deal of grain, and warhorses must eat more grain in great amounts; it takes a good deal of care to keep the food coming in. There must be wealth, and a safe market, so that people can bring their goods in. There must be a steady flow of tribute from the other kings of Britain, who in turn take tribute from the clans subject to themselves, and this requires civil peace enforced by the authority and power of the Emperor. But this power and authority and peace existed, and Camlann was not only huge, but thriving. I looked at the people we passed as we rode up the hill. A girl stepped carefully through the snow, carrying a basket of eggs; some boys ran by hurling snowballs at one another with savage warcries; a man chopped wood; two women stood in a doorway, gossiping. Most of them waved or yelled at us cheerfully, and I thought of the dreariness and bitterness of Caer Ceri and Caer Gloeu, and knew that I was right, after all, to come to Camlann.

The stables at Camlann adjoin the feast hall, and it was to these that we rode first. Gwalchmai was again greeted with delight. There was a great deal of pounding one another on the back and joking when we dismounted. I did not know anyone, and everyone was too busy to pay attention to me, so I hung about, smiling to show that I sympathized with homecomings.

Gwalchmai handed Ceincaled's bridle to one of the grooms, saying, 'You can see to him just this once, Celli. I wish to go to greet my lord and my brothers. He has had some grain already this morning, but I have used him hard, these months, and more would not harm him. Ach, but you know your business – but he needs a new headstall, a good one, if there is one about.'

The groom took the horse's bridle as though it were set with diamonds, grinning. Gwalchmai caught up the saddle-bags and slung them over his shoulders, so I hastened to do the same with my gear. I stood for a moment, holding Llwyd's bridle and trying to think what to do with my mount, and then Gwalchmai remembered my existence, and again explained me as 'Rhys ap Sion. My servant.' I received more curious stares, but someone took my horse. Gwalchmai strode from the stable with a quick, eager step, limping only a little, and I had half to run to keep up with him, for all that he was carrying his spears and shield as well as his luggage, and wearing a mail-coat, which is no light burden.

The Hall at Camlann is high-roofed, and the swallows nest under the eaves in summer. Torches set in brackets along the walls burn even in the daytime, and in winter the fires in the hearth-pits down the centre of the Hall keep the place warm. It is always half-light, and usually glitters, since it is full of whitewashed shields hung against the wall, and spears, and warriors wearing jewellery. When we arrived the place was half full of men playing some board game or knucklebones, talking or listening to a harper. It had that sleepy, comfortable air peculiar to winter afternoons. No one really noticed us as we came in. Gwalchmai set his saddle-bags down by the door and leaned his spears carefully upright beside them. As he was unstrapping his shield, someone looked over, then leapt up crying, 'Gwalchmai!' and at once the whole place was up and crowding around us.

The enthusiasm of the welcome we had had from the guards and the grooms began to look rather dim. A few greetings stood out from the crowd here, however. One tall man with hot gold hair and beard and hot blue eyes thrust his way through the other warriors and flung his arms about Gwalchmai, shouting in Irish. My lord hugged him back, and began speaking in the same language. The one word I caught was the name 'Agravain', and I realized that this must be his brother. The two did not look very much alike. From what I had heard, they did not act much alike, either, and Agravain was renowned as an infantry fighter.

While Gwalchmai jabbered away at his brother in Irish, I hung about at the door, smiling to show that I still sympathized with homecomings, though in fact I was getting a bit tired of them, and wondering whether anyone would offer us food, which we'd had none of since dawn. After a little, I noticed a slight, dark, serious-looking man watching me. He was quietly dressed, only a silver chain around his neck proclaiming high rank for him. I smiled, and he smiled back and stepped over to join me.

'Greetings,' he said, courteously. 'Are you looking for someone, man?'

'Not yet, Lord. I am Gwalchmai ap Lot's new servant, and I am waiting for him to finish greeting everyone.'

The man looked at me with interest. 'Gwalchmai's servant. That is very unexpected, for Gwalchmai.'

'So I have been hearing. Actually, Lord, I'm only temporarily his servant. He said that he would find me a place at Camlann when I asked him to bring me here.'

'You asked him?'

I found myself grinning. 'Well, Lord, he was staying with my family, so I seized the opportunity. I have wanted to come here.'

'Indeed,' began the other, and would have asked something more, when Gwalchmai broke out of the crowd to clasp my companion's arm.

'Bedwyr,' he said, 'here you are, then. How is it with you?'

I stared at the man, trying to believe he was who he must be. Sure enough, his shield hand was missing at the wrist. Bedwyr, the man whom the Emperor had appointed his warleader after he had been his cavalry commander for years, his closest counsellor. I had not pictured him so plain and quiet.

He smiled at Gwalchmai, a deep, glad smile that filled his eyes. 'It is well. Camlann is much the same. But how is it with you? Did you find what you were seeking?'

My lord's smile stopped, and he shook his head. 'Not yet. It must be tried again.'

Bedwyr gave him a considering look. 'Then see that it is tried in summer. This winter quest has worn you, I think.'

Gwalchmai laughed. 'It is just being away from home. Where is my lord Arthur?'

'In his room, talking to a messenger from Gaul about the situation there, and about trade. If you wish to see him, it is not an urgent meeting.'

'I will wait for him. Where is Cei, then?'

'Out hunting. He has been bored.'

'I imagine. No one to fight.'

Agravain pushed back through the crowd to Gwalchmai

and caught his elbow. 'Since you will wait for Arthur, come have some wine with us and tell us where you have been.' He swept his brother off towards the nearest table, calling for the wine. Bedwyr, however, looked back to me.

'Why did you wish to come here, then, Gwalchmai's servant?' he asked.

I looked at him, quiet and calm and paying attention to me, and blurted out, 'Lord, I wished to serve the Light.'

He nodded, thoughtfully. 'A very good reason. Welcome to Camlann, then.' He turned and strolled over to the table where Gwalchmai was now seated with a glass of wine and a ring of friends, being talked to by his brother. I followed, hesitantly. Gwalchmai looked up to welcome Bedwyr, then noticed me and set his glass down hurriedly.

'Rhys! I had forgotten you. Agravain, this is my new servant, Rhys ap Sion.'

'A servant?' Agravain looked at me fiercely. 'Good. I've told you for years that you needed one. Can he look after horses?'

'I will not let him look after Ceincaled,' said Gwalchmai, smiling. 'No one will do that but I myself, whether or not it is dignified. But Rhys is a clever man, *mo chara*. He outbargains townsmen and leaves them cursing and admiring the astuteness and business sense of the Pendragon's warriors.'

'Mistakenly, in your case.' But the other seemed pleased at the thought of outbargained townsmen. 'Well, servant, go fetch your lord some food.'

I looked around, wondering which way to go to do this, and why Agravain should be the one to tell me to, but Gwalchmai whipped his feet off the bench and exclaimed, 'Ach, no. Come here, Rhys, and have some wine. Agravain, he's done a fair piece of riding, and that in bad weather, since he joined me. And he has never been to Camlann before; is he to go running about now?'

Agravain shrugged, bellowed for someone else to fetch the food, and I, after hesitating and looking around to the lord Bedwyr, came and sat down on the bench at Gwalchmai's left, feeling very out of place. A thin, long-faced warrior handed me a glass goblet of wine, and Agravain began talking again about what all the warriors in the Family had done since his brother left. I held the goblet gingerly, looking at it. Glass, like wine, is a great luxury, and neither are made much in Britain these days. The goblet was blue-green, with a sheen over its surface, and the red wine glinted through it with a purple colour. I sipped the stuff very carefully, trying to decide whether I liked it or not. I had never had any before, except for a little at Mass, and that had not been heated with spice and honey.

Agravain and the other warriors went on talking, prompted by eager questions from Gwalchmai. A servant came and set a platter of meat and bread before my lord; he broke off one edge of the bread, stabbed a bit of meat with his knife, and pushed the platter in my direction, nodding to what someone was saying. I glanced around, saw that no one was paying the slightest attention to me, and began eating. The meat was broiled venison, richer fare than I was used to, and very good.

After a while, Gwalchmai told his friends a little about his own journey. Most of it concerned his embassy to Caledon, and he managed to describe his wandering in search of Elidan very briefly and without mentioning the girl. But he did speak of my father. He had had a fight with some bandits, he said, and this had made him decide to seek shelter for the night. Before that, apparently, he had been sleeping in the open, and he would probably have continued to do so if I had not been there to be horrified at the hardship of sleeping in stables. 'So I went off through the forest, thinking that it would be safer if I reached Dumnonia, and by chance I found Rhys here by a ford. I had met his father before and found him a good man, so I stayed five days at the holding. They saw to it that my horse was shod, my cloak mended, and gave me such hospitality as travellers pray for, and Sion ap Rhys refused any payment, though I offered it him again and again.' This brought looks of astonishment. 'He is a man as generous as a king, and more generous than a king like Maelgwn.'

Agravain gave a snort at that. 'So you asked his son as a servant?'

Gwalchmai looked at me and smiled, as at a secret joke. 'Not so. His son asked me as a lord.'

'That sounds more like you,' Agravain commented, scowling. But his eyes rested on his brother with delighted pride. I wondered if Dafydd would look at me that way if I came home, and shivered.

'And you will treat your servant the same way you treat your horse,' Agravain concluded.

'I hope not. Rhys is not over-fond of oats, even in porridge.' Gwalchmai grinned at me.

Agravain shook his head and began to go on, and I was anxious for him to explain his remark, but just then someone at the front of the Hall shouted, 'Gwalchmai!', and my lord nearly tipped the bench over in his haste to get up.

'My lord,' said Gwalchmai. He went up the centre of the Hall, half running, to meet the man who had just entered it. When they met, the other clasped Gwalchmai's forearm, and Gwalchmai caught his hand, kissed it and pressed it to his forehead.

'Good indeed,' said the newcomer. 'A hundred thousand welcomes home, at long last. We have expected you since Christmas; where have you been? If you have told the others already, you will have to repeat it to me. Macsen –' to a servant – 'we must have a feast tonight. Go tell my lady that the lord Gwalchmai is back, and ask her to prepare it. And see if you can find Taliesin, and ask him whether he's finished that epic he was working on.' And to Gwalchmai, 'Did you find what you were seeking?'

Gwalchmai shook his head. 'It was a cold trail that vanished in the mountains of Arfon, a word I could not find again, and a bitter search after it. My lord, it is good to be home.'

'And yet, you will search again.' The voice was quiet, creating privacy in a public place, and not questioning.

'By your leave, my lord.'

'If you must. But not in winter, and not alone.'

At this, Gwalchmai smiled. 'If you are concerned that I travelled alone, my lord, it will please you to know I have found a servant.'

I had stood up as soon as I had heard Gwalchmai call the other 'my lord', and when the man followed Gwalchmai's gesture and looked at me, I did my best to bow. I was not very skilful at it. The other looked at me appraisingly, and I looked at him. He was tall, of average build, with light blond hair beginning to grey at the temples, and he wore his beard cropped close to the jawline, in the old Roman fashion. He had grey eyes, wide-set, and the kind of stare that seems to look beyond what it is fixed on. He wore a

92

gold collar about his neck, and his cloak was of the imperial purple. But he did not require the purple to proclaim him Emperor and Pendragon of Britain. He was the kind of man so accustomed to command that it is unconscious, the sort of man men obey without thinking.

'You are Gwalchmai's servant?' Arthur asked me. 'What is your name, man?'

'Rhys ap Sion, Great Lord, of the clan of Huw ap Celyn.'

'The clan of Huw ap Celyn. You live in Dumnonia, do you not? Up by Mor Hafren?'

'I . . . yes, Great Lord.' I was astonished that he should know. Arthur smiled, a quick instant of pleasure at my astonishment.

'I am also Dumnonian by birth,' he explained. 'And we have wheat from near Mor Hafren every harvest.'

I knew that, because my father took the cart up to Camlann every harvest, with some other holders from our area, and sold the wheat, but I had not expected the Emperor to know. 'My father, Sion ap Rhys, grows some of that wheat, Great Lord, and he is glad to sell it to the Pendragon, as I am glad to be here.'

Arthur grinned suddenly. 'Prettily said, man. You'll have no trouble when your lord takes you on an embassy.' He sat at the table, took a glass of wine, and nodded for the rest to sit as well. 'And, as regards embassies, I must see you,' he said, addressing Gwalchmai again, 'regarding that journey to Caledon, for there are a few things I wish you to explain further. Dear God, you need have no fear; I won't send you back there yet.'

'I thank you for that, for once. My horse needs a rest.'

'Less than you need one. Rejoice: till the spring comes I will give you nothing to do but write letters, confer with ambassadors, translate Irish into good Latin and *vice versa*, and look after your horse. My friend, you were a fool to swear your oath to me.'

'I consider it otherwise. Am I not to do accounts, copy your books, or give advice on the new building plans, then? How are the plans going?'

'If you wish, I will let you do all of those, except the accounts. Gwynhwyfar has taken to saying that everyone else makes chaos of them, and does them all herself. But the plans – well, we will begin the new store house after the thaw; I decided not to put it next to the old one, but down the hill . . .'

'Near Gereint's house?'

'No, eastwards . . .' After a few minutes of this, Arthur tired of trying to sketch the planned building on the table in wine lees, and leapt up offering to show what he meant. The idea of tramping about the fortress gave me no great pleasure just then, however, for my legs were sore from all the riding. I offered instead to carry our gear to wherever Gwalchmai wanted it carried. Agravain, rather surprisingly, offered to show me the house he and his brother shared with another prestigious warrior. So while Arthur, Gwalchmai and Bedwyr swept off to inspect the building site, I picked up the two sets of saddle-bags and began to collect spears.

Agravain watched me impatiently and finally exclaimed, 'My brother's servant, and you don't know how to carry a spear! Here.' He picked the spears up in a way that I could not see differed from my way in the slightest, and walked off briskly. I fumbled around to find the shield and ran after him, nearly dropping one of the saddle-bags as I hurried to catch up.

The house was a pleasant one, soundly built of mud and wattle, neatly whitewashed, and with a thick thatch. It stood to the east of the Hall, and from the doorway one could look out at the tor of Ynys Witrin standing like a watch tower against the marshy plain that leads to the Saxon kingdoms. Inside, however, it was a mess, with bedding and clothing and weapons strewn over everything. I later found out that Agravain had had a servant till the year before, when the man died of a fever, and no one had cleaned the place since. I set the saddle-bags down and wondered where to put things. Agravain leaned the spears against the wall with satisfaction.

'There,' he said. 'And now, Rhys, or whatever your name is . . .'

'It is Rhys.'

'Whatever it is, you are my brother's servant, and there are one or two things I will tell you.'

I wondered what. He looked at me, rubbing the knuckles of one hand.

'I gather you persuaded my brother into taking you on.

Well and good, for he needs a servant; he is always doing things a warrior ought not do, and takes no care for himself. But what he needs is a servant, one who will do as he is told and not give himself airs. You came into Camlann as though you thought yourself some kind of guest, and sat at the same table as the noblest warriors and the High King himself. My brother will not stop such behaviour. He will be inclined, if I know him, to treat you as he treats his horse – better than he treats himself – merely because you are dependent on him. It is a privilege to serve him, servant, remember that.'

I swallowed the anger that was rising in my throat and nodded, trying to look as though the privilege impressed me.

'And listen, servant.' Agravain stepped over and seized the front of my cloak, twisting it so that it choked me and forcing me against the wall. 'My brother will do nothing to punish you for insolence, but if you serve him badly, and let him do without while you live in luxury, and take advantage of his courtesy – I will see to it that you are beaten as much as you deserve. Do you hear me?'

'I hear you,' I croaked. I longed to tell him that I was a free-born clansman, a servant by choice only, and that I could throw his privileges in his face and leave; but the thought that I could stopped me, and made me hold my tongue. I had chosen, and I had had no expectation that all warriors would be like Gwalchmai or Bedwyr.

'Good,' said Agravain, and hit me across the face, just to show me what he meant. I had my fist up, ready to hit him back, before I remembered that if I did hit him, he might do anything, and he was a trained warrior. And also, I had chosen . . . I forced my hand to relax. Fortunately, Agravain had not noticed it. He hit me once more, with the flat of his hand this time, and let me go. I began to straighten my cloak.

'Where did you get that brooch?' Agravain demanded suddenly.

My hands froze. 'My lord gave it to me,' I said, trying to keep my voice deferential. 'He gave it to a townsman as payment for a night's lodgings, and I got it back by bargaining. Your brother told me to keep it.'

'That's no brooch for a servant. Give it here.'

I had not thought it a brooch for a servant, either, but I would not be told so by Agravain ap Lot. 'Lord, my lord told me to keep it. If I gave it away, I would be disobeying him.'

'You can give it to me. I'm his brother.'

'I will then – if he tells me to.'

Agravain grabbed one of the spears and held it upside down, by the neck like a cudgel. 'By the Sun! You will do as you're told.'

'I am, Lord. I was told to keep it.'

'Greedy fool.' Agravain glared at me a moment longer, and I braced myself for a thrashing with the spear. But he lowered the weapon. 'I will speak to my brother about this. He should not give such things away.' He tossed the spear aside. 'Get this place in order,' he flung at me, and strode from the house.

I sat down on one of the low beds, shaking with anger, and beat my fist against the mattress from sheer frustration.

'You should have expected this,' I told myself, out loud. But it did no good. I hadn't expected to feel like this. I had always been able to stand up for myself; for that matter, I usually won any fight I stood up in. But now any noble dog could treat me as he pleased, and I would have to smile and say 'Yes, Lord'. Gwalchmai and, it seemed, Bedwyr and the Emperor were pleased to treat me honourably, but I had a strong feeling that Agravains were more common. I slammed the bed once more, and hit my hand against the wooden frame.

I sucked my knuckles and looked at the frame, and then the pounded mattress, and had to laugh. Still laughing, I straightened the dented bedding, and got up and tried to set some order to the mess that filled the room.

By the time Gwalchmai arrived, at twilight, I had managed to put everything in a place. The wrong place, undoubtedly, but it was improbable that anything really had a right place. It was hard work, because I was no more used to it than the warriors were, but I was beginning to feel that I was winning the fight.

Gwalchmai opened the door quietly, looked around at the place in surprise, then shot me a questioning look.

'Your brother told me to put it in order,' I explained.

'Ah.' Gwalchmai closed the door, went over to the fire,

caught up a taper and lit a hanging lamp. A warm glow fell over the small room, and Gwalchmai blew out the taper. With the glowing end still raised, he turned and looked at me. His look was a little sad, his eyes attentive on my face.

'How many times did my brother hit you?' he asked quietly.

I stared.

'Oh come, you will not tell me you got that bruise across your face by running into a door, will you?'

I shrugged. 'Only once, hard.'

Gwalchmai sighed and sat down, twirling the taper with his fingers. The end made a little circle of red as it spun. 'Agravain came and told me I should not give servants valuable brooches, and warned me against insolence. I am sorry if I have got you into trouble.'

I looked at Gwalchmai as he stared at the end of his taper, his fine, thin face looking worn and worried, and suddenly, without thinking about his name and his troubles, I liked him very much.

'He only noticed the brooch after he hit me,' I said. 'My lord, some men talk with their fists, and I expected it when I asked to come with you.'

Gwalchmai shook his head. 'Agravain is a good man. He merely feels that he must ... maintain a position. And he doesn't know how to talk to people.'

I thought to myself that Agravain might be a good man to those he considered to be 'people', but I felt that that included only a small segment of humanity. However I nodded in reply to Gwalchmai's statement. 'My lord, it is nothing to worry about. I've had worse fights with my cousins.'

'But Agravain hits hard, and you couldn't hit him back.'

'He doesn't hit that hard.'

'Yes he does. I remember his thrashings. Vividly.'

At my look of surprise, Gwalchmai added, 'I wasn't always a good warrior, you know, and Agravain is more than three years older than me. And he knows how to humiliate. I hadn't thought of that when I agreed to let you come.'

'My lord,' I said, exasperated, 'the fact that one man feels that he must maintain his position at the expense of mine is no reason for me not to stay here.'

'But there are others who might feel the same way. There is Cei. I've known him to bully servants on principle. And he lives here, in this house.'

I'd heard of Cei. If Gwalchmai was famed as the finest warrior in Arthur's cavalry, Cei ap Cynyr was the finest in the infantry. There were nearly as many songs about him as there were about Gwalchmai, and most of them mentioned that he had a heavy hand and a hot temper. If I stayed with Gwalchmai at Camlann, to live in the same house as Cei and Agravain might be a bit tiresome. But then . . . 'My lord, if I won't be living here, what does it matter where Cei lives, or Agravain either for that matter?'

Gwalchmai looked up sharply from the taper, which had finally gone out. 'What? You're not going back home?'

'No. But you said you would find me another lord at Camlann.' Gwalchmai was silent. 'You told me you didn't want a servant.'

'Oh. So I did.' He tossed the taper in the fire, stood and leaned against the wall, watching it burn. 'I'd forgotten that.' His eyes lifted from the fire and met mine. 'Would you be willing not to go to another lord? To stay with me instead?'

I sucked in my breath and fidgeted with the cloak-pin. I knew my own wants well enough. For all that I had only known this man for a week or so, I knew I could trust him with my life and honour. I knew that, serving him, I would be required to do nothing demeaning or dishonourable, and that I would most certainly be able to work hard for the Light. And it would be hard, too, with more long journeys, and sleeping in stables – and probably in the open as well – and no food and long hours and plenty of enemies. But I wanted it, God knows. And besides the rest, I liked the man.

'My lord,' I said, 'I would be very willing to do that thing. But only if you want me to. I do not wish to do what your brother threatened to thrash me for, and take advantage of your courtesy. You are not responsible for me, just because you agreed to bring me here.'

'My courtesy! Man, this is scarcely courtesy. I am calling you to a hard life. If you served some other master, you would have an easier time of it. No, it is because you are a good servant and a good man to have at one's back.'

I wondered what, other than out-bargaining the towns-man, I had done to deserve that description. But I grinned. 'It is your courtesy, my lord, as far as I'm concerned. Is it settled, then? I stay with you?'

'It is settled.' He stepped quickly from the fireplace and put out his hand, and I clasped it. He smiled, and I grinned back. Agravain or no Agravain, I had a place for myself.

Seven

We stayed in Camlann about a month and a half before we set out again. I think it was probably the longest single period Gwalchmai had stayed there. The war and Arthur's embassies had kept him busy before. And, as Arthur had promised, he had work to do in that month and a half. Unlike most of the other warriors, Gwalchmai could read and write, his Latin was excellent, and he knew Saxon and Irish as well as British and was familiar enough with the web of British affairs that he could work a way into any tangle of alliances and enmities without offending the allied or hostile parties. All this was very useful to Arthur, who, I discovered, spared nothing that was useful to his ends, himself least of all. But he never asked more than his followers were willing to give. He was a man obsessed with a dream, a vision of the Empire arising again in Britain, and taking into itself all the barbarians, to create a new order, working with justice in peace; and to create it he worked with his whole life and the lives of those around him. He had the gift of making other men see what he meant, and the whole fortress assumed nothing else than that we were about restoring a Christian civilization to a world that was growing dark, though most of the people there would not have put it that way. It was an exhilarating assumption.

Not all the warriors were worked as hard as Gwalchmai, however. Most of them knew only how to fight and, when not fighting, played knucklebones, hunted, or were bored. Agravain and Cei were in this group, and, once I got to know them, I found them sometimes humiliating, frequently infuriating, but on the whole tolerable. Indeed, I quite liked Cei, though his temper was worse than Agravain's, and his tongue sharper. He was a very tall, heavy-muscled red-head with a thick red beard, and he wore more jewellery than any other man in the Family. His treatment of servants was all I had heard it would be, but he was not by nature a bully. He enjoyed being talked back to, though he might offer, and occasionally provide, a thrashing for it if one went too far. He liked arguing, and was a fine bargainer, and we had some grand disagreements about how I arranged matters in the house. He had an acid wit and a fine sense of sarcasm, but he knew how to laugh.

Agravain was completely different. He was indeed trying to 'maintain a position', and, seemingly, felt that he had to defend it at any cost. I wondered whether it might have something to do with his having come to Camlann originally as a hostage for his father's oath of peace. While there was little he would not do for his friends – and, more especially, for his brother – he would not lift a finger for anyone else, or stir by a quarter of a step from the lofty and glorious standing of warrior and first-born son of a king. On some days he was moody, and would fall into a rage at the imagined implications of a look – this with his inferiors, of course, not other warriors. The only way for us to handle him was to give him what he wanted, and that immediately. Still, after the first day he left me alone. I gather that Gwalchmai had had a serious talk with him, although neither Gwalchmai nor Agravain ever said so.

I was glad to be left to work, because I had more than enough work to keep me busy. The house had to be looked after: the fire kept burning, the place kept clean and orderly, the thatch repaired. Then, Agravain and Cei assumed that, since I was living there, I would naturally do all their personal work as well as Gwalchmai's. I had to see that their clothing was taken to a washerwoman, their small wants for this and that were satisfied, and that their weapons and armour were in good condition. (Another servant, Amren, showed me how to do this last.) The horses were looked after by grooms, which was a mercy, but I still had to exercise Llwyd, and sometimes Cei and Agravain's horses as well. Gwalchmai very rarely let anyone else near his Ceincaled, and, to tell the truth, was in other ways the least work of the three.

When I had finished looking after my lot of warriors, there was still much else to do in the fortress. Because the Family had for so long wandered over all of Britain, few of the warriors had personal servants, and the servants who worked at Camlann were adequate for a smaller community only. There were only about a hundred and fifty men and a hundred women for the whole fortress, and all of us were busy. The public places like the Hall and the guard tower and store-rooms had to be kept clean and ordered; the cattle had to be butchered, and the hides cured for leather; the kitchens had to be supplied, mead to be fermented, and so on and on. But I did not dislike the work, as I had thought I might. The pleasant thing about service is that, unlike farming work, it can be done in company and while talking. I found the other servants at Camlann good company. Perhaps two-thirds of them were either former townsfolk or descended from a long line of servants. But there were also a fair number of clansmen like myself, farmers who had lost their land to the Saxons, and had been unable or unwilling to find land and settle elsewhere. There were even a few Saxons, men who had been captured on a raid and had sworn to serve some lord or other in exchange for their lives. The others came from every part of Britain, and even from across the sea in Less Britain, and to hear their tales was as good as listening to a song.

The management of the household of Camlann was under the supervision of the Queen Gwynhwyfar. She was a thin, brown-eyed lady like a candle-flame, warm and shining, topped by masses of red hair. She never seemed to sit still, and always seemed to know where every man and woman in the household was and what they were doing. She never seemed to walk anywhere: she ran; some said she danced. She determined how much wool we had and how much we needed by buy and how much each person could take; she saw to it that the cattle were slaughtered in the right numbers and that we had enough grain; she ordered major repairs, like thatching, and kept all the accounts. Her instructions were administered by Gweir ap Cacwmri, who ran practically everything, and his wife, Tangwen, who ran everything, including Gweir.

Of the other servants – it would take weeks to tell. Amren, who showed me how to look after weapons, was Bedwyr's servant, and a Breton like his master. He had travelled in Gaul before he took service with Bedwyr, and could tell tales of the south, of Lugdunum and Massilia and the ships that leave for Rome and Carthage, tell them all night, if he was allowed to. And then there was Aegmund, a Saxon from Deira: he'd sworn to serve the lord Rhuawn at the beginning of the war with the Saxons, thirteen years and more before, when Rhuawn first went raiding. After the battle of Baddon, Rhuawn freed him and offered to help him return to a Saxon kingdom, but Aegmund had become a Christian, married, made a home, and wanted to stay. There were others – but enough of that. Suffice it that, by and large, despite Cei and Agravain and some others like them, Camlann was better than I had hoped it would be. I was sorry when Gwalchmai told me that we were to leave it again.

It was a day in mid-March, chill and rainy. I was in one of the store-rooms whitewashing a shield, and my lord sought me out there to tell me that we were to ride on the morrow.

I set my brush down in confusion. 'Where are we riding, then, my lord? And for how long?'

'Just to Gwynedd.' Gwalchmai dropped into a crouch beside me and studied the shield with interest. The months since our arrival had done him good, taking the gaunt, bitter look from his face, but leaving a kind of restlessness more plainly marked. He was wearing a gold collar, and the collar of his cloak was of embroidered leather, very fine, so that he looked more kingly than usual, and he could look fairly royal in a homespun tunic. Nonetheless, he picked up the whitewashing brush and frowned at the pot of lime. 'Whose shield is this?'

'Constans's,' I said automatically, wondering what next.

'You shouldn't be doing his.' Gwalchmai dipped the brush in the lime and began to dab it on the shield. 'I've told you, you're doing more than your share of work as it is.'

'Well, Macsen had to go and find some more thatch for the Hall today, and Constans wanted the shield done this week, so what's wrong in offering help? Don't you start doing it. Did you say we were going to Gwynedd?'

He nodded, painting carefully around the shield-boss.

'Just to Gwynedd.' Gwynedd was ruled by Arthur's greatest enemy, King Maelgwn ap Docmail, and the whole kingdom was a refuge for all who hated the Pendragon. 'Just' to Gwynedd.

'For how long?' I asked.

He shrugged. 'As long as is necessary.' The side of the brush grazed the shield-boss, leaving a white smear on it, and Gwalchmai looked about for something to clean it. I picked up a rag and rubbed the stain off myself. Gwalchmai leaned back on his heels. 'My lord had been planning to send someone to Maelgwn this spring; we had only about two-thirds of tribute due us from Gwynedd last year. As usual. It was necessary for us to deal with the man; and now there is this new matter of his reported guests, and the matter has become urgent. My lord wishes us to leave at once.'

'Guests? More outlaws?'

'No – at least, the reports do not seem to suggest that.' Gwalchmai smiled, but his right arm, resting across his knees, stretched out so that his fingers brushed his sword-hilt. 'One of my lord's men in Caer Segeint sent that some foreigner's came to the port, sailing in curraghs, which they were permitted to draw up high onto the beach. There were horses and wagons provided to convey them to Degannwy. The visitors spoke Irish.'

I let out my breath in a little hiss. 'Aengus of the Dalriada? Surely even Maelgwn would not make alliance with a king of Erin!'

'Why not? He hates Arthur even more than he hated the raiders. But Aengus is more likely. We will find out soon enough. My lord wishes to impress Maelgwn with the fact that he is watched, and that Arthur can move quickly.' Gwalchmai began painting the shield again. It was never any use telling him not to.

I stared at him, tightening and trying to relax my grip on the cleaning rag. 'Won't Maelgwn . . . isn't it dangerous?'

Gwalchmai paused a moment, then shook his head. 'Maelgwn will hardly have us killed, if that is what you mean.' He resumed painting. 'Such a killing would be sure to come out, and Arthur would break him for it. Maelgwn is cautious, a cunning fox of a man. He never takes un-necessary risks. He will try to find some way of outwitting us instead.'

I knew that Gwalchmai must be right. He knew a great deal about the ways of kings, far more than I did. But I had been raised on stories of border clashes with Gwynedd, and did not like the thought of living among enemies. But, I told myself, what else have you come for? You wanted to fight for the Light, and here is a chance. The Emperor's enemies plotting against him, and you and your lord ready to ride off into the midst of them, like Constantine in the songs . . . I still didn't like the sound of it. But I told myself that I should be eager for this chance to do something, and asked, 'What time tomorrow do you want to leave?'

'As early as possible. An hour or so before dawn would be good. I would like to reach Caer Gwent by nightfall.'

'But that's a good fifty miles away, and across Mor Hafren!'

'We will press the horses, and the ferry will run at evening. And if your horse is too tired, you can change horses at Caer Gwent.'

Yes, in such a case we could stay at a fortress. No sleeping in the open this journey. And the snow was over, though it was by no means warm. It wouldn't be unbearable.

Gwalchmai noticed my sour look and suggested, 'They will treat your horse well at Caer Gwent, and you can pick him up on the way back.'

He would think of worrying about something like that. I sighed. 'I'll do that, then. What will we need? Do you wish to travel light?'

'Light as we can, but take enough to impress. Is that shield of mine with the enamelled boss in good condition?'

'I cleaned it last week.'

'I'll take that, then. And my other shield, in case there is any fighting. Rhuawn is also coming: there must be at least two warriors on such an embassy as this. We'll take one pack-horse for the three of us, and change horses at Caer Gwent. You will need to talk to Rhuawn's servant Aegmund about that.'

'Is Aegmund coming?' I asked hopefully. I liked the man.

But my lord shook his head. 'No. One servant is enough. Besides, the man's a Saxon, and can't ride to save his life.' He painted over the last blank area of the shield with a flourish and leant back to consider it, then set the brush down and stood up.

I also stood, rubbing my hands with the cleaning rag, as though I'd done the work.

'If you need me, I am going to talk to Bedwyr, and then to my brother, and after that I will see to my horse,' Gwalchmai informed me. I nodded, and he slapped me on the shoulder and limped off.

I stood a moment, still clutching my cleaning rag, making a mental list of all that would have to be done. The first thing, I decided, would be to find Macsen and tell him that I couldn't fix any more of Constans's armour.

By that evening I had almost everything ready. Aegmund was a great help in it. He was horrified at the thought of riding from Camlann to Caer Gwent in one day, although his lord Rhuawn only nodded and said he thought it a fine idea. When the two of us began packing, we were a bit unsure of what to do: how is one to pack for three men, using one pack-horse which must be burdened lightly for a fast journey but still carry enough both to impress and to last out a stay of indefinite duration? In the end, though, we managed something, and I felt triumphant as I cinched down the last buckles on the pack.

'And an hour before dawn tomorrow,' Aegmund said gleefully, 'you will already be up and off. If I wake up, I will think of you.'

'If. Not likely, my friend, not likely. And we will not reach Caer Gwent until after nightfall. I wish you were coming.'

Aegmund shook his head. 'Though I will have much care for you, and for our lords. Well, God go with you.'

'He will have to, if I am to stay awake on this journey. But there, I wanted it.'

Aegmund grinned, and we slid the loaded pack up onto the wall of our pack-horse's stall, ready for the morning. We turned to leave the stable, then saw the Pendragon himself walking towards us, the dim light from our lamp glittering on his golden collar. We both bowed respectfully and stood aside for him, but he stopped when he came to us.

'Aegmund,' he said, smiling, 'I hoped you would still be here. I have a gift for Cynyr, lord of Caer Gwent. It is up in the Hall; ask the Queen for it. It is only a cup, man, you can easily fit it onto the top of the pack.'

Aegmund grinned, said, 'Yes, *myn kyning*,' using one of his rare phrases of Saxon, and was off to fetch the gift. I was ready to bow again and disappear too, but Arthur snapped his fingers for attention, and said, 'Rhys, I wish to speak with you a moment.'

'As you will, my lord,' I said, surprised.

Arthur walked on up the stable a little way, and, after a moment's hesitation, I followed him. He stopped at Ceincaled's stall and leaned over it, looking at the horse. 'Do you know,' he asked me, softly, 'where Degannwy is?'

'In the mountains of Arfon,' I said.

Arthur made a clucking sound to the horse, and Ceincaled came over and sniffed at his hand, scattering the dim lamplight. Arthur let his hand rest on the horse's withers. It was a strong, square, sensitive hand, an amethyst ring glowing purple on the ring finger. 'Has Gwalchmai told you the story of the daughter of Caw?'

I suddenly remembered why Arfon was significant. 'Yes, Great Lord,' I said, and, feeling that this needed some explanation, added, 'by way of penance, I think.'

Arthur smiled at that. 'He desires to do penance rather more than is good for him.' The hand dropped from the horse's shoulder and rested on the wall of the stall, the light dying in the amethyst as it parted from the lamplight. The emperor turned, and looked at me a moment. 'You have some liking for Gwalchmai, I think,' he told me.

'Great Lord . . .' I said, surprised again, then went on, 'he's a good man.'

'Then I will speak freely.' Arthur crossed his arms, leaning against the stall. 'I once commanded your lord not to kill Bran of Llys Ebrauc, not because I particularly cared to save Bran's life, but because I knew Gwalchmai, and knew him to be too proud to easily endure knowing that he had killed from hatred. If you know the tale, you know the outcome of that command. Gwalchmai is hard on himself, and will yet insist on seeking this woman. I cannot give him another command, to forget it and her, since there are some things that cannot be commanded. But no king ever had a better warrior than I have in Gwalchmai, and I do not want him to be too hard on himself. Nor do I want him to find the woman.'

He saw the question in my face, for he smiled. 'I only met that woman once, but from what I have heard, and from what I know of her brothers, I doubt that she will be willing to forgive. Their father, Caw, died fighting for the king his brother when I took the *imperium*. It was in the field of battle, yet, because I wished to have the good will of the royal clan of Ebrauc, I saw that Caw was buried with full honours, and returned all his goods to his clan, with praises of his courage and expressions of good will. It is reasonable that children should hate the man who caused their father's death, but the children of Caw went beyond the will of the royal clan, and returned to me many expressions of pride

107

and desire for revenge, saying that while the weak and cowards may forgive a wrong, the glory of the nobility is to avenge it. They were brave men, the sons of Caw, loyal to their friends, but implacable enemies; they are yet enemies, those that live, and for all that I do they will not be reconciled. I do not think that Elidan daughter of Caw will differ in this from her brothers.' He uncrossed his arms again, his eyes fixing on nothing, as they sometimes did when he was thinking. 'And if Gwalchmai finds her, and she accuses him again – it will be worse for him than before.'

'Wouldn't it still be better than uncertainty?' I asked.

Arthur's eyes fell on me again, and he smiled quickly. 'Possibly, and possibly not. I will not ask you to prevent him from seeing her, if she is indeed somewhere in Arfon. Only this: if your lord orders you to stay with Rhuawn or return to Camlann or Degannwy or any such place, while he goes questing for the daughter of Caw, do not obey him. Tell him that I have told you this, if he asks the reason. Do not let him see her alone, and take care for him. If he has someone with him, he will exercise some restraint on himself.'

I thought of my father telling Gwalchmai to use his sword to protect me, and here I was being told to protect Gwalchmai. I had to smile at it.

'Great Lord,' I said, then stopped, and decided that his Latin title would be more fitting: 'Imperator Arthurus, I would have had some inclination of my own to do as you say, at least as regards his not questing alone; I am glad to have a command for it.'

Arthur smiled slowly. 'A very insolent and insubordinate servant indeed! Excellent.' He gave the horse one more slap on the withers, and then we walked back down the darkened stables. The spring stars looked out through a wrack of cloud, and Aegmund was coming back down the hill with the golden cup and a lantern which cast a warm buttercup-yellow glow against the dark sky.

It was more than an hour before dawn when we left the next morning, and Camlann was eerily still under a faint moon. Everyone spoke in whispers as we saddled the horses and led them from the stable, their hooves loud in the silence, the jingle of their harness muffled by the moist air. The Emperor Arthur and the Queen Gwynhwyfar, half-seen forms in the dusk, bade us God speed and then we mounted and trotted off from the Hall, down the hill to the main gate, and out onto the road.

We did not take the usual path and ride down to Ynys Witrin to follow the Roman road north. Instead, we took one of the old, rough tracks across the hills directly north from Camlann, crossed the Briw river, and took a smaller Roman road up north to reach the ferry. The small Roman road does not go all the way there, but only up to the hills, where the Aesce river has its springs. The roads were thus bad all the way, but we had good horses, and to go by Ynys Witrin took us fifteen miles east, which we would have had to double by another fifteen miles back westward.

We set a fast pace, trotting steadily. I was half asleep, and slouched on Llwyd's back, thinking of my warm bed, cursing Aegmund in his, and vaguely wondering why it was necessary to go so far in one day.

We forded the Briw about seven miles downstream of Ynys Witrin. The water was cold and came up to the horses' bellies, so that we had nearly to sit on our legs to avoid drenching. It was still dark then, though the moon was low and the east grey. When we crossed the river, Ceincaled tossed his head and neighed, loud and clear and triumphant. Gwalchmai laughed. 'A fine day for a journey!'

I grunted.

As we went on up the winding track, the moon set, and the whole earth became grey, while the birds and animals of the land round about began to stir. Then the sun rose slowly, fiery and immense over the flat lowlands. I looked at it and thought, 'Bad weather coming,' but said nothing.

By the time we reached the Aesce, the birds were singing over the whole earth, and the wet grasses shone with amber and silver. Geese cried overhead, streaming towards the marshes, and before us lay the great mass of the hills, blue-grey and green.

'A fair country,' said Rhuawn. 'I wonder if the stories are true.'

Gwalchmai shrugged. This part of Dumnonia is called Gwlad yr Haf, Kingdom of Summer, which is also one of the commonest names we in the south have for the Other-world. It is said that men have found doors into the hills, and wandered through them into strange worlds, where the

Fair Ones feast in halls thatched with silver and the feathers of birds. There are the common tales of persons who are rescued from the hills, and the stories of those who spend a night there, and find that a hundred years have passed when they come out again, and so on.

'They say that the Kingdom of Summer is more beautiful than the earth,' Rhuawn murmured.

'It is,' said Gwalchmai. 'And yet I am not sure that it is wholly distinct from it.'

Rhuawn gave him a steady, serious look. Gwalchmai turned Ceincaled westward, following the Aesce to find the branch of it which would take us up its gorge into the hills. We walked the horses to give them a rest from the rapid trot which had taken us from Camlann, and their hooves sounded soft on the marshy ground, while the river gurgled beside us. Gwalchmai looked at the hills, his eyes very dark, but with a kind of light in them. After a few minutes, he began to sing, first in Irish and then, after a while, the same song in British. It was a strange song, and seemed to make a stillness about itself, almost frightening, though it was sweet and lovely.

'. . . The sheen of the sea you sail on,
The dazzling white of the sand
Extend in azure and saffron
As an airy and radiant land.

A sweeping plain for a countless host,
Where the colours glow into glory,
A fair stream of silver, plains of gold
Welcoming all to their bounty.

Along the leaves of a forest
Your curragh swims, and by hills
Where branches dip, fruit-laden
When your prow is parting the swell.

A wood shines with fruit and with flower
And the sweet wild scent of the vine,
Flawless, remote from death's power,
Gold-branching beyond touch of time . . .'

The sun touched the heaped hills northward, and the green glowed into emerald, while the blue-grey of the bare

110

trees shone with highlights of silver from the damp. Rhuawn shook his head thoughtfully.

'That is a strange song. What is it?'

Gwalchmai smiled, and a little of the glow went from his eyes. 'It is a song about a man who sailed to the Land of Youth, which is one of our names in the Orcades for the Kingdom of Summer. They say that if you sail far enough west, you will reach it. The song is called "The Voyage of Bran mac Febal".'

'I remember. You sang some of it once before.'

'That is so. This part comes later. When Bran had set sail, he met the son of Lir – whom they call a god, in Erin – riding across the sea in a chariot, and the son of Lir sang that song, to show that the sea was not a barren plain but a fertile kingdom, if one has the eyes to see it . . . We should turn right here, and we can follow the Aesce up to the hills.'

We forded the Aesce and started our horses to a trot again. The willows were yellow and green, and the air was almost warm. Almost. I thought about sailing the bitter salt plain of the sea, and finding then a fertile wood in the beauty of spring, and seeing the whole sensible world as another world. I shivered. A world as shining as a dream, more real than waking, which men might slip into in a moment's insight. Had Gwalchmai been there? I had heard some songs that said so, and which said that his horse and his sword had been brought from the Kingdom of Summer, the Island of Apples, the Land of Youth, or any of the other names of the Otherworld. A world which lay somehow beneath and behind our world, and which broke through upon us unexpectedly, yet was always there to those who had eyes for it.

I shivered again, but from cold, and thought to wonder if it could be warmer in the Otherworld. I snuggled my raw hands into my cloak, and checked the packhorse's lead-rein.

The Aesce enters the plain by a great gorge, flanked by jagged, sky-tearing cliffs. We had to dismount and walk the horses part of the way, for the river, swollen with its spring waters, had overflowed a section of the path. We were all drenched up to the knees by the freezing stream, and Rhuawn slipped and was soaked to his waist. We stopped at the head of the gorge to put our boots back on and to wring out our clothes, but then remounted and headed off at a fast trot, and soon reached our Roman road. We were some fifteen miles, as the crow flies, from Camlann.

We ate our lunch in the saddle, about as far north as the Ciw river, which joins the Afen west of Baddon. It was then beginning to cloud over, and in the afternoon it began to rain, while a fierce March wind battered the drops against our faces. We didn't really mind. Rhuawn told an exceedingly long and complicated tale about a man who caught the north wind in a fishing net, and what came of it, and had us all laughing.

We had to make the horses swim a few paces when we crossed the Afen, which was high with the spring floods, and this made us even wetter than the rain had. We trotted fast to keep the horses warm, and their sides steamed. We had lost our Roman road some time before, and the way was winding and muddy, but for all that we made good time, and reached the main west road from Baddon, not far beyond the Afen. This we followed direct to the inlet where one can take a ferry across Mor Hafren to the shore of Powys and to Caer Gwent.

We arrived at the ferry at evening, and dragged a boatman from his supper to take us across. The water was rough, and gleamed with white in the darkness, smelling strongly of salt. Our horses, except for Ceincaled, stood with drooping heads, too tired to be nervous. I felt quite seasick by the time we put in on the west bank in Powys, and made no argument when Gwalchmai gave the boatman the excessive payment of a gold armlet. Then it was remount, and drive our horses on another mile to Caer Gwent. But there were fires there, and hot baths and hot food, warm beds and a warm and courteous welcome.

The next morning we presented Cynyr, lord of Caer Gwent, with Arthur's gift, and he thanked us very prettily, and asked us to stay for a few days. Gwalchmai declined the invitation for us, and so we were provided with fresh horses – except for Gwalchmai, who wanted and needed none – and set out on the main west Roman road to Gwar Uisc. My fresh horse was inclined to be skittish. I had parted from Llwyd with only a twinge of regret. I knew that Cynyr would have him treated well, and he was welcome to any work he could wring from the lazy beast. I would pick the horse back up on the way home.

We did not go quite so far that day, since we would not change horses again until we reached Caer Legion in the north. We crossed the Uisc river on the bridge at Gwar Uisc, and then rode north through Powys. We spent that night at a farm near the river Dyweleis, and set out again early the next morning. Three days after leaving Caer Gwent, we reached Caer Guricon, just over the border of Gwynedd. Both Caer Gwent and Caer Guricon are old Roman towns, but the differences between them are astonishing. There were fewer people in Caer Guricon than in any Roman town I had seen, and those that did live there huddled close to the building which the local lord used as his feast hall. But the great difference was not this, but the hostility. The local lord gave us the hospitality we demanded, since it was our right as the Emperor's warriors; but he gave it glaring and grudgingly. No one in the town, from the lord's warriors to the Hall servants, would speak to us, and they had all a silent, vicious stare that set one's teeth to grinding. The lord wanted us to stay and sleep with his warband in the feast hall, but Gwalchmai insisted on a separate house. We were eventually given a small, narrow townhouse, with broken roof tiles, which had not been swept or cleaned for a long time.

Gwalchmai looked around it and laughed. 'Well, cousin,' he said to Rhuawn – members of Arthur's Family call each other cousin, when they aren't calling each other 'brother' – 'we are back in Gwynedd.'

'And a grief it is, too,' Rhuawn replied. 'Shall we keep watch?'

In the end we did not keep watch, but settled in the middle room of the house. Gwalchmai dragged his sleeping mat in front of one door, and Rhuawn pulled his over by the other, and no one slept in the middle of the room, in case anyone tried to drop things on us. If I had not been so tired from the journey I do not think I could have slept at all, and, as it was, it took me an hour to drift off, all the time expecting to hear stealthy footfalls creeping into the house. But nothing happened. Nothing was really expected to: it was simply wise to take precautions in Gwynedd.

We left as early as we could the next morning, and did a hard day's riding, reaching Caer Legion after nightfall. The town was a little more hospitable than Caer Guricon, and we changed horses there – again, except for Gwalchmai, who kept Ceincaled – and the next morning, our sixth day from Camlann, we rode westward into Arfon. The heights of the mountains were still white with the winter snow, while their flanks were green and grey. The sun struck their peaks, flashing from ice, glowing on mists, glittering on streams and cataracts. I could not keep my eyes from them. They tell the same kind of stories about Arfon as they do about Gwlad yr Haf, and it is easy to see why.

In the late afternoon we turned off our Roman road, pushing our horses hard, and followed a mountain track southward. It was the last step in our journey, the road to Degannwy itself. The sun began to set, turning the mountains rose and lavender. I was tired enough from the journey to be wide awake, but I felt like a rope that is drawn too tight, and quivers at a touch. At every bend in the road I half expected to ride clear out of the world, and find that the snows in Arfon were turning into apple blossom, and the trees to silver. Then, finally, we rounded a bend in the road and saw Degannwy far in the distance. There was nothing Roman about that fortress. It was built before Claudius came to conquer the east of Britain, before Julius Caesar ever invaded. The legions of Rome had never really conquered Arfon, for all their centuries and legions in Britain, for all their roads and towns and discipline. Looking at the green, twilit dark slopes around me, I could not think that anyone, even Arthur, could come into Arfon in war and bring his warband out intact and alive. No doubt the same thought had occurred to Maelgwn Gwynedd, and caused him to move his royal fortress from the Roman port town of Caer Segeint up to this small stronghold in the mountains.

It was fully dark when we reached Degannwy and demanded entrance at the gates. The guards kept us waiting, watching us with that vicious stare I was coming to expect in Gwynedd, while one of their number sauntered back to their feast hall to tell the king Maelgwn that some emissaries of the Pendragon had come. The stars were bright by the time the guard strolled back and told the others to open the gates and let us in, and we could ride our stumbling horses up the hill towards the Hall, with its lights and sound of music. The stables were a low-lying mass a short distance

114

down the hill from the Hall.

Gwalchmai swung down from Ceincaled in front of these stables, and caught the stallion's bridle while he began to talk to one of Maelgwn's grooms. Rhuawn and I also dismounted, stiffly, and I began to check the packs on the pony we had brought from Caer Legion. A group came down from the feast hall with torches, and I was glad of it, since I had light to see that everything was still in its place, strapped firmly down on the little beast's back. I looked back to Gwalchmai, awaiting directions.

He finished his interrogation of the groom, and turned to the party with the torches, ready to question and explain in his quiet, eloquent fashion. But he froze half-way through that turn, and stood moveless as a wild animal that has seen some predator. The torchlight glowed on his crimson cloak and gold jewellery, but the uncanniness suddenly filled his face so that he looked scarcely human. His eyes were very wide, lips half parted. One hand still held his mount's bridle, the other was raised, held forward in an arrested gesture.

I felt cold and shaken to see him so abstracted from himself, but I didn't want to look at what he was looking at. I glanced to Rhuawn, who looked puzzled, then over to the party with the torches, and finally at what Gwalchmai was staring at.

My first thought, looking at the woman who stood with the torch-glow red on her, was that she really did look very like Gwalchmai, as much as a woman can look like a man. The resemblance must have been even closer when he was younger. She had the same fine bones, the same high-bridged straight nose and thin, expressive mouth. Her hair, fastened behind her head and bound with gold, was the same deep black, and her eyes . . . but when I saw her eyes, I felt that she did not look much like him after all. Like his, they were black, but black in such a way that they seemed to drink all the light around them, and quench the colour in everything that surrounded her. Black enough to drink your life like a thirsty man gulping down a cup of water, and she would do it, and smile as she did it. She stood very straight, wearing a low-cut crimson gown which left her pale arms bare. She was extraordinarily beautiful, ageless, and she was smiling, but she looked at no one but Gwalchmai. Slowly, very slowly, she walked forward, and her shadow fluttered in the torchlight, and still my lord did not stir.

'So, my falcon,' she said in a low, soft voice. 'Are you then displeased to see your mother?'

He lowered his raised hand and straightened slowly, as though struggling to do so; and then he bowed, very gracefully. 'Lady, I had not expected to find you here.'

She gave a low laugh. 'Indeed not. But now we are a pleasant family party: you and your brother and your father and I.'

'My father? And my brother? Agravain is at Camlann.'

She laughed again. 'Agravain! Have you forgotten that you have two brothers? Your other brother has greatly wanted to see you again.'

'Medraut.' Gwalchmai's face was expressionless. 'So.' He raised his head a little and spoke in a different voice, proud and cold. 'I have come to Maelgwn ap Docmail, king of Gwynedd, as the emissary of Artorus Augustus Caesar, Imperator Britanniae, Insulae Draco.'

'Well, indeed. Maelgwn is in his Hall, feasting with your father. Do you wish to come and greet him now?' She took another step nearer, her eyes never leaving his face. 'Your father, for all that you have done, will still no doubt be glad to see you. I myself am glad to see you, my spring-tide falcon; very glad . . .' her voice grew lower. I could not think, nor move, and the torchlight seemed dim and colourless. She took one more step nearer, her eyes fixed as a cat's.

Then, suddenly, Ceincaled reared, screaming, and tore his bridle from his master's hand. The horse towered a moment, wild and white and shining, and descended, flinging himself towards the lady, ears back and teeth bared. She hurled herself to the side, and some of the men who had come with her drew their swords. Gwalchmai cried out and ran to catch his horse's bridle.

The lady picked herself up from the ground and turned and walked back towards the Hall without saying another word and without looking at her son once. Gwalchmai held Ceincaled's head, stroking the stallion's neck and speaking to him quietly in Irish. Both horse and man were trembling.

Rhuawn, after another moment's immobility, jerked his own mount's bridle and started into the stable. I took my

116

horse and the pack-pony, and Gwalchmai followed us with Ceincaled, still whispering to the horse.

We found stalls for the animals, rubbed them down and gave them some grain. Our horses fell to at once, but Ceincaled stirred uneasily. He nickered when Gwalchmai left him, and neighed loudly when we left the stable, so that Gwalchmai turned and called something in Irish which must have meant 'Be still'. We looked at the feast hall.

'I do not understand,' said Rhuawn at last, speaking in Latin so that Maelgwn's men would not understand. 'That woman is your mother, the Queen of the Orcades, the daughter of the Emperor Uther?'

'Illa'st,' Gwalchmai replied, tiredly, 'She is. And the King of Gwynedd is not plotting with Aengus of the Dalriada, or with any from Hibernia, but with Lot mac Cormac of Orcade, my father. Or rather, he plots something with my mother, for, when I left Dun Fionn, she governed most of the plotting, and I imagine that she is doing all of it now. My father is a strong man, but she is a subtle designer, and will outlast him.'

'I have heard, and now believe it,' Rhuawn said, very slowly. 'I have heard – but be gentle to me, and forgive me that I speak of it to you – that the Queen of Orcade is a great witch.'

Gwalchmai nodded. 'She is. By her skill in sorcery she has made herself a Queen of Darkness. And she hates my lord Arthur most bitterly, more bitterly than Maelgwn Gwynedd does.'

Rhuawn gave Gwalchmai a steady look. 'Although she is the Pendragon's sister?'

'Rather, I think, because she is the Pendragon's half sister than in despite of it, and because her mother was the wife of the Pendragon Uther, while Arthur's was some country girl. But it is no matter. We must find what it is that she and Maelgwn plot together, and tell Arthur, and stop them. They are more dangerous than Cerdic and the Saxons.'

Rhuawn nodded, very thoughtfully, and we began walking up the hill, accompanied by some of Maelgwn's servants, who had been waiting.

If the Hall had been friendly, it would have been a joy to enter. It was filled with music and light and warmth, and with a rich smell of roasting meat and strong, warm mead, triply welcome after the cold, wild air of the mountain twilight. It was a small Hall, and would seat no more than four hundred men, and he rarely had many guests. But it seemed both large and unfriendly when we walked up the length of it with all eyes fixed on us. The music stopped when we came in, and the only sound was the wind in the thatch, the crackling of the fires, and our own footfalls. Gwalchmai walked very straight and proud, his head held high, cloak thrown back from his left shoulder to show the hilt of his sword, and the shield with the enamelled boss gleaming over his other shoulder. He ignored the stares completely. Rhuawn also looked calm, but I was near enough to see how tightly his hand was clenched on his sword-hilt. I had no sword to clutch, and had no wish for these barbarian nobles to see how nervous I was, so I spent the walk up the Hall looking at the faces of the men at the high table.

Maelgwn held the centre of the table, of course, looking down the Hall at all his warband. He was a slight man, with gingery red hair and a thin beard. He wore a purple cloak, more than his status permitted him, and a gold circlet around his hair. The purple did not suit him. He pretended to talk to the man on his left, but something about the angle of his head told me that he was all the while looking at us. He seemed the sort for that, the kind of man I would not trust in a market place, or leave to guard my flock. But he looked lower than his reputation as a great enemy, a petty miserable little schemer who only chanced to be a king.

The man on his right was of another sort altogether. Though still not above average height, he had plainly been taller than Maelgwn, and something told me that once his hair had been like hot gold. It was grey now, and his face was lined and haggard, his eyes sunken. But those eyes were still a fierce, hot blue. They were like Agravain's eyes. I did not think that Agravain resembled his father quite so strongly as Gwalchmai did their mother, but there could be no doubt as to his paternity. I could just remember the days, more than twelve years before, when every movement of Lot mac Cormac, king of the Ynysoedd Erch, had been a source of gossip and debate in every kingdom in Britain; when many British kings would do nothing which had not been commanded by Lot at Dun Fionn. Those days had ended when Arthur seized the imperium in Britain, and compelled a Lot defeated in battle to swear peace and give hostages. It could still be seen that Lot had once been a great man. As we approached the high table, however, I thought how worn he looked now, and how much older than his wife.

We stopped before the high table, the main fire pit warm at our backs, and Gwalchmai saluted Maelgwn, drawing his sword and lifting it, hilt first. Maelgwn finally turned from his feigned conversation. As he did so, the man on his left also turned. This was a young warrior, a man about my age. His blond hair was lighter than Lot's, his first beard a soft, shining down on his cheeks, eyes a clear grey. He was very handsome, and smiled in welcome. It was a pleasant smile. I wondered who he was and what he was doing there, but only briefly. Gwalchmai was saying to Maelgwn, 'To Maelgwn ap Docmail of Gwynedd, greetings, in the name of the Pendragon Arthur ab Uther, High King of Britain and your king.'

Maelgwn drummed on the table with his fingers. After a deliberate, awkward moment's silence, he said smoothly, 'It gives me pleasure to greet the emissaries of my lord the Pendragon, especially when they are led by so illustrious a nobleman as yourself, Lord Gwalchmai. Be free, Lord, of anything that is mine.' He gestured to one of the servants, and additional places were made at the high table to his right and left. 'All that my hospitality can offer you is yours. You would be welcome to me, Lord Gwalchmai, for the sake of your royal family alone.'

Someone in the Hall laughed, but fell abruptly silent. Again there was silence in the Hall but for the crackle of the fire and the whine of a hound.

Gwalchmai bowed slightly, and said, with a smoothness excelling Maelgwn's, 'And I am welcome, I hope, for the sake of him who sent me here, by whose service I hold such honour as I possess. Though, indeed, it is a pleasure contrary to my expectations that I should meet my kin here. You, my lord father, I greet in my own name, and not in my lord Arthur's, and so also do I greet my cousins and my brother.'

Lot leaned forward, his hot eyes fixed on his son. He licked his lips nervously, but did not speak. The fair young man smiled again. Gwalchmai looked at him directly a moment and the smile faded, the eyes turned elsewhere. My lord lifted his sword-hilt and bowed once more, before sheathing the weapon and walking about the table to take his seat beside his father, on Maelgwn's right. Rhuawn drifted off to the left, and I followed him hurriedly, not wanting to stand in the centre an instant longer.

There were a few servants coming and going about the table and I grabbed a flagon of mead from one, and hurried to pour it for Rhuawn and Gwalchmai. The alternative was to go and sit down at the far end of the Hall with Maelgwn's servants, and the idea did not enrapture me. After the mead, I managed to grab a trencher of meat and offer that; Gwalchmai, however, ate nothing. I took the trencher back to a quiet corner on the right, and sat down with it and the remnants of the mead. The meat was lamb, cooked with plenty of mint and parsley, and was very good. I sat, eating it and watching my two warriors, plainly ready to serve their needs. I was close enough to hear what they spoke about, and I thought that, of the three of us, I was the most comfortable.

Maelgwn began the conversation by asking both Gwalchmai and Rhuawn about the health and plans of everyone at Camlann, listening attentively and offering encouraging comments, as though he were a great friend of Arthur's. Lot said nothing. The fair young warrior, who was now seated next to Rhuawn, attended him carefully, offering him water and salt and listening to whatever Rhuawn had to say, not looking at Gwalchmai at all.

After a while, Maelgwn ran out of questions, and the conversation at the high table slithered to a halt, though the rest of the Hall was still noisy enough. In the silence there, Lot leaned suddenly forward, shook his head as though to clear it, and asked Gwalchmai, 'And what of your brother Agravain?'

Gwalchmai lifted his mead horn and studied it. 'He too is at Camlann, and in good health.'

'He is happy there?'

My lord shrugged. 'Happy as he may be, while the weather keeps him still. You know that he does not like to sit idle. In another month or so, my lord Arthur will probably set him to chasing bandits, and then he will be happy.'

'Your lord Arthur.' Lot rested his chin on his hand,

looking to Gwalchmai; his face was also turned towards me as he did so, and I could see that his eyes were narrow and fierce. 'Your lord, Arthur. It is true that you have sworn that bastard warleader the Threefold Oath of allegiance?'

'It is true, yes.' Gwalchmai set down his mead horn on its stand, firmly, and looked up at Lot. 'For him, and for the cause we serve, I will live and die.'

Lot's mouth contracted, lips twisting as though in pain, but all he said was, 'And Agravain?'

'He has not sworn.' Gwalchmai hesitated, then added, 'And yet he too would fight and even die for my lord Arthur.'

Lot's hand clenched to a fist, then relaxed, and he laid his palm flat against the table. 'But still, he is not sworn to it. Well.' He gave Gwalchmai a long look, then smiled, a smile like the sun on a wave in summer. 'You have changed since you ... left Dun Fionn. They say that you are the finest warrior in Arthur's Family.'

Gwalchmai smiled back. 'Only on horseback. Agravain can still lecture me on where to put my spear when I fight on foot.'

Lot laughed. 'The horses, the horses! That has always been our downfall with Arthur. Oh, his men fight well on foot, but it is the cavalry charge that breaks armies: and I hear that these days you lead the charge.'

'Since we are at peace, no one leads the charge these days.'

'But you have been leading it, which I never expected of you. Well enough! Let us have a song about our shame and Arthur's glory, the High King's horsemen.'

One of Maelgwn's poets struck up a song on the harp, and began to sing of one of Arthur's battles, a song I am sure was not often sung in that Hall. For the rest of the evening mercifully little was said.

At some unreasonably late hour of the night the feast ended, and we were escorted to a small hut Maelgwn had allotted us, apologizing as he did so for the poverty of the accommodations. Degannwy, it seemed, was crowded, as well it might be with the King and Queen of the Ynysoedd Erch and their retinues packed into it. Our hut had but a single room with two low beds, but it was nonetheless both clean and warm, and had its own fire.

Gwalchmai dropped onto one bed and sat with his head

121

in his hands and his elbows on his knees. Rhuawn, after a moment's hesitation, took the other bed and began to untie his leggings. Since I, obviously, was to sleep on the floor, I began unpacking.

After a little while Gwalchmai sat up and began to build the fire up for the night. Rhuawn took off his mail-shirt, wrapped it in an oilskin, then pounded the bed a couple of times before lying down and arranging his sword by his head. 'Do we keep watch?' he asked Gwalchmai.

My lord shook his head. 'There is no point keeping watch against what we have to fear now. We must sleep, and trust God that we will wake again.'

'So there is danger.'

'Great danger.' Gwalchmai sat back down and began to untie his over-tunic. 'I . . . my mother tried to kill me when I left Dun Fionn.'

'Ah. I had heard that was the case.' Rhuawn rolled over onto his stomach and looked at his friend. 'Tell me, was it by sorcery?'

Gwalchmai drew off his over-tunic, then nodded, folding it.

'Well. I never thought to fight devils. I was told it was a privilege of the blessed angels.' He smiled. 'I don't qualify.'

Gwalchmai smiled and shook his head. 'Cousin, I am glad of you.' He looked around for another oilskin for his chain mail, and I handed him one from the pack.

'Will you go back to Camlann as soon as your horse is rested?' asked Rhuawn.

With his mail-shirt half off, Gwalchmai froze. 'Go back? Why should I?'

Rhuan shrugged. 'I would not care to fight against my own blood, and my own father. In all loyalty to our lord, a man cannot oppose his clan.'

Gwalchmai took the shirt off hurriedly. 'It is not like that.' Rhuàwn and I both looked at him, and he spread his hands. 'It is not a question of my family against Arthur's family. It is a question of Darkness against Light, and I am for Arthur.' When Rhuawn still said nothing, he went on, 'Don't you see that this is my mother's work? My father never visited Britain except when one of his allies summoned him to fight, and then he came at the head of an army. Otherwise, he plotted and dictated letters and listened to his spies. He would not of his own accord be here with a fox-faced schemer like Maelgwn. And because it is my mother's work . . .' He took a deep breath. 'Listen. The Saxons desire our lands. Well; and we try to prevent them from taking them. But the Saxons do not desire to see the lands empty, swallowed by wilderness, while the people flee and starve or go in fear. My mother does. If the Saxons put out the light in Britain, they may make some light of their own; but my mother wishes to see all drowned in Darkness, and revenge herself. Can one make peace with that?'

'Why should she desire such things?' I asked.

'Perhaps at first she did not desire them. But now she does. I know. No one knows her as well as I do. Perhaps my brother Medraut knows her well, but I think not as well. She taught me sorcery. That is my guilt, for I asked her to, when I was young, but from this I know that desire she has, the desire to drink up all the world into her own will, and to break all that will not be devoured. I know her . . . why do you think I speak British with a Dumnonian accent, while Agravain sounds as though he had just left Erin? I spent time with her.'

'Your brother Medraut speaks British with a Dumnonian accent,' observed Rhuawn softly. I realized that the fair young warrior must have been this Medraut. 'He seems a good enough man.'

'Ah God! Poor Medraut. I do not know how it is with him now, whether he has escaped her or not; but if he has not, she will use him up, as she has used up my father. We must fight her, Rhuawn.'

Rhuawn fondled his sword-hilt. 'In that case, brother, let us sleep with a calm mind, for we will need our strength when it comes to battle.'

'Good advice, my lord,' I suggested. 'You yourself have said that Maelgwn would be unlikely to kill us, and this is still his fortress. Go to sleep.'

Gwalchmai sighed and lay down, but left his hand resting on his sword-hilt, the sheathed blade lying beside him. I decided to leave the rest of the unpacking for the morning, and made myself comfortable in front of the hut's door, then blew out the lamp. With a few blankets under me the floor wasn't too hard, and I was, at all events, too tired to care if Morgawse of Orcade herself had dropped through the smoke hole with half a dozen demons in her train.

But I dreamed all that night, dreamed that I struggled in a vast, black ocean, thrashing desperately towards a light which receded endlessly away. After an aeon, it seemed that my feet hit solid stone, and I stood and staggered towards the light, which glowed brighter, like a star came to earth. But just before I reached it, it vanished with a sound like thunder, and I saw only Medraut ap Lot, holding a naked sword in his hand, and smiling.

Eight

Perhaps it was because of the nightmares, but I woke very early the next morning, feeling tired and depressed. The fire was low and the house very dark; both my warriors were still asleep. I dressed and went to the door. The morning was misty and cold. I looked back into the house. Rhuawn turned his head away from the light and muttered. I noticed that Gwalchmai's fingers were still curled about his sword, but he was smiling, as though his dreams were better than mine had been. I sighed and went out, closing the door behind me.

I wanted some hot water to wash in, and decided that it must be possible to get something to heat it in right in our own hut, so as not to compete with all of Maelgwn's warband in the Hall – if they washed, which I wasn't sure of. Breakfast could be eaten in the Hall, but it would be pleasanter to find some bread and bacon in the kitchen and bring it back. For both needs I'd have to take on Maelgwn's servants, and find the kitchens.

After getting lost three times in the mist and the unfamiliar stronghold, I finally found my goal, in the back of the Hall. A few servants were lounging about the low-roofed room, heating water and kneading bread, but there did not seem to be anyone who was in charge. Nor did anyone wish to pay any attention to me. Everyone I advanced on seemed suddenly to remember something which had to be done, and vanished, or else stared at me stupidly, as though they couldn't understand my Dumnonian accent. Exasperated, I sat down directly before the main fire, in everyone's way.

After a little while, a plumpish, rather pretty flaxen-haired girl marched up to the fire with a large copper dish held over her arm. There was water in it, and it looked about the right size. I eyed it appreciatively.

The girl halted in front of me and glared. 'Move over, if you please,' she ordered. I started: she had an Irish accent.

'Who's that kettle for?' I asked.

'The Queen,' she replied shortly.

Maelgwn was not married, so there was only one queen

125

in Degannwy. I reluctantly gave up my designs on the kettle, and moved over. 'Where did you get the kettle?' I asked her.

'A hen laid it in the rafters, having been affrighted in a coppersmith's shop,' said the girl. 'Who are you?'

'I, woman, am Rhys ap Sion, the lord Gwalchmai's servant. We need a kettle.'

'Indeed?' said the girl. She hung the kettle over the fire and stood back, her hands on her hips. 'And what do you want with a kettle?'

I grinned. 'I need to make a brood-nest for your hen. Come, who's in charge here? My lord will want some hot water for washing when he wakes up.'

She shrugged. 'There is an old man named Saidi ap Sugyn – you British have such strange names – whom I was told to mind about the kitchens.'

'Where is he, then?'

She tossed her head. 'Och ai, he is minding his bed. He will not rise until noon, and he goes to bed at nightfall, and all the while he is awake he complains that he is tired. It is not in my mind to mind him at all, and the rest of the servants are like minded.'

'I mind that he is not here when I want him. Where does he sleep?'

'His house is just behind the kitchen. But I would not wake him, or he will be angry, and stint you on bread.'

'He may try that as he pleases, but he will not succeed,' I boasted, and gave a slight bow to the girl before striding off through the kitchen. Only for an instant: my Irish servant girl shouted, 'Hai! Rhys ap Sean!'

I stopped. She was still standing at the fire, rocking on her heels a little. 'You are heading into the feast hall, Rhys ap Sean, lord Gwalchmai's servant. Saidi's house is behind the kitchen, the other way.' She gave me a self-delighted smile. 'Come, I'll show you myself.' She tripped off, and I followed, feeling ridiculous.

Saidi ap Sugyn was annoyed at being woken. He swore at me, complained about his age and general health, complained about southerners, the Irish, and the Pendragon, but eventually told me to take any kettle I wanted and go to Yffern with it. The serving girl giggled at me when we came back to the kitchen, so I made her go out of her way to show me where the kettles and the food were. I took an extra loaf of bread, beyond what we needed for breakfast, just in case.

As I walked back to our house I considered Degannwy. I suspected – and later knew for certain – that the place was badly run. The servants, from the steward on down, were overworked and underfed; and, from the steward on down, they made up for this by stealing and cheating whenever they could, and afterwards blackmailing each other with having done it. In consequence, everyone was ill-equipped and miserable. Eggs would disappear before they were needed in a cake; knives and pots vanished steadily, often reappearing, no one knew how, for sale on a market day. A woman would set out to weave a cloak, and when she was half-finished, discover there was no more wool to be had, and when she did get some more wool, there was no dye or the wrong dye for it. Maelgwn's warriors knew what was happening, and beat the servants freely, and the servants beat each other and the dogs, and cheated even more. And yet the place held together remarkably well, for everyone blamed their troubles on the high tribute demanded by Arthur, and held the Pendragon's wars against the Saxons to be the root of all their own wretched little difficulties; and everyone was afraid of his neighbour and his superior, and did not dare to carry his dishonesty to its extreme. So Degannwy was a strong fortress, but it was no joy to anyone. Its strength was of opposition only, as I saw it, without an instant's unity of mind or charity of thought to bind it into a civilized living place like Camlann.

I had more time to myself at Degannwy than I had had at Camlann. I was recognized as the Lord Gwalchmai's servant, and, as such, had no part in the life of the fortress. That left only two warriors and one house to worry about, with the horses from Caer Legion, and Rhuawn helped with those. Gwalchmai was at first very busy waiting upon Maelgwn, or, occasionally, talking to his father. He wrote Arthur a letter the afternoon of our first day in Degannwy, informing the Emperor about the situation. He rode from Degannwy with this sheet of parchment hidden under his shirt, telling the guards at the gate that he wished to exercise his horse. I am still not sure exactly how it reached Arthur. The Emperor has men in Gwynedd who report Maelgwn's movements to him, and Gwalchmai knew where to leave a message, though he could not speak directly to any of these men without endangering their lives. At any rate, he came back without the letter. He then spent his time talking to Maelgwn and Maelgwn's men, at least once a day. The matter of the tribute was settled – Maelgwn admitted he must have 'made a mistake', and would give an additional amount the next year to compensate – but very little more was learned of what Lot and Morgawse were saying to Maelgwn privately. There did not seem to be any preparations for a war: no messengers rushed to and from the Ynysoedd Erch or the various chieftains of Gwynedd; no one was gathering supplies; there were no long training expeditions of the warband into the countryside – but it was plain enough that two such kings would not be meeting unless they had something of the sort in mind.

In all his conversations with Maelgwn or with the warriors from the Islands, Gwalchmai avoided very thoroughly any encounter with his mother and his younger brother. When finished with his official work he usually rode out into the mountains and did not return until nightfall. When he was present, he was rather unnerving. While unfailingly courteous, remotely willing to oblige, and well able to be charming with Maelgwn, I could never feel that he was really there, caring about what anyone was saying. He had abstracted himself to some terribly silent place behind his eyes, and, from that first night on, refused to drop his guard with anyone. I could dimly see that his mother's presence at Degannwy might disturb him, but I didn't like it. And I could not see why he so avoided his brother. Rhuawn and I agreed that Medraut was a surprisingly likeable man.

On our second day at Degannwy I came into the stables to look after the horses, and found Rhuawn and Medraut hanging over the door of a stall and discussing one of Maelgwn's stock.

'These mountain horses are simply too small,' Rhuawn was saying. 'And they've no withers – look at this one! Nothing to hold onto in a battle. The first time your spear hits anything, off you fall; and even if you do not, you're too low to use a spear to any advantage. No, Maelgwn will never match any southern king for cavalry unless he buys some stock from Gaul.'

'On the other hand,' returned Medraut, smiling, 'those southern horses of yours, those Gaulish warsteeds, fall over their own feet in hilly country. This little mare could take you clear up Yr Widdfa in the middle of winter, or carry a charge downhill in the mud. Show me a southern cavalry band that could do that!'

'We've done it, in the Family.' Rhuawn stroked his moustache. 'It isn't easy, but we did it once, in the north. Once, in fact, we carried a charge downhill, across a river, and up the opposite bank into a Saxon shield-wall. Of course, your brother led that charge . . .'

Medraut laughed. 'Gwalchmai could saddle the North Wind, if he set his mind to it. He always could. He's the one who first taught me to ride, actually, though I'll never be as good as he is.'

'In cavalry charges there's no one on earth that good.'

Medraut smiled again. 'I am ready to believe you. Of course, when he . . . left . . . Dun Fionn, no one knew he was so much of a fighter, but I've heard the songs since. Strange, hearing that kind of song about a brother you haven't seen in years. Why doesn't Arthur let him command the cavalry?'

Rhuawn turned to lean against the stall, and noticed me. He interrupted the conversation to call, 'Oh, Rhys, I've already seen to that miserable beast of yours – Lord Medraut, this is Gwalchmai's servant, Rhys ap Sion, a good man.'

I bowed a little, and Medraut ap Lot straightened, smiled widely, and beckoned me over to join them. My dream flashed into my head for an instant, but dreams are ambiguous things, and usually mean nothing at all, so I came over and leaned against the stall.

'So,' Medraut began again, 'why doesn't the Pendragon give my brother command of his cavalry?'

Rhuawn yawned. 'Because he is so wild a fighter. Gwalchmai goes mad in battle, and will cut through anyone in front of him. If he is ever killed in battle, it will be because someone strikes him with a throwing spear from behind. No one will ever beat him, face to face. No one. But as for directing others in a struggle – once he's begun he doesn't understand plain British and can't recognize his best friends. Bedwyr, now, keeps his head in any circumstances. He is a philosopher, can hold the whole plan of battle in his mind, and see where everyone is and where everyone has to go. He can even direct Gwalchmai.'

Medraut looked thoughtful. 'He really does go mad, then? That might explain . . .' he stopped.

'What?' asked Rhuawn.

The other smiled. 'Oh, nothing. How does he go mad? I haven't had a chance to talk to him, and I don't know that I could ask him, anyway. It's hard to ask an older brother questions like that.'

'Mm. I imagine. Well, he just . . . goes mad. He pulls out his sword and rides down whatever is in front of him. He doesn't even feel it if he's wounded, until afterwards. Then he usually collapses. But during the battle he has the strength of three men, and moves faster than you can think.'

Medraut looked very intent. He nodded. 'Collapses afterwards. Yes . . .

'He isn't berserk,' I put in. Somehow, I thought Rhuawn was giving the wrong impression. 'I wouldn't even say that he was "mad", if that wasn't the word he uses himself.' I hesitated, groping for some way to communicate the ecstasy I had seen in his face during this battle madness. But Medraut nodded and said, 'Of course,' and began to talk about horses again. He was pleasant company, especially after the hostility of the rest of Degannwy, and I enjoyed listening.

Eventually the conversation turned to music, and he asked us to come to his house the next afternoon and listen to one of the Irish harpers, and both Rhuawn and I accepted willingly. I was flattered at being asked, and was glad that Rhuawn wasn't the sort to take offence at Medraut's asking me.

The lord Medraut was staying with a few other of the warriors from the Ynysoedd Erch, in a house a deal larger and finer than ours (though no less crowded), which adjoined another house where the Queen was staying, alone. Her husband did not share her room, which surprised me, but Medraut made no comment on the situation.

When we arrived, however, none of the other warriors were there, and Medraut explained that they were in Maelgwn's hall playing dice. 'And, alas, the harper is there too, playing songs to the rhythm of knucklebones clicking. But we have a harp here, if you can play it. I can, a little.'

Rhuawn also could, a bit (though I couldn't, not at all), and we settled by the fire. I sat off to the side, feeling awkward. Medraut rapped against the wall and, after a moment, the door to the adjoining house opened and the Irish serving girl from the kitchens appeared.

'Ah, there you are, Eivlin,' said Medraut. 'Does my mother still have any of that Gaulish wine lying about in there?'

'My lady does, but . . .'

'Then fetch it, like a good girl. Come, these are guests.'

She shrugged a little and turned to go, but, as she did, she lifted her eyebrows at me, plainly commenting, 'What are you doing as a warrior's guest?' But she came back with a jar of wine and three goblets, and poured for all of us. I was still not much of a judge of such things, but I thought it good wine. Eivlin apparently did too, for she didn't give me much of it, and left the jar with Medraut only very reluctantly.

Medraut took one swallow of his wine then set the goblet aside and began to tune the harp.

As members of noble clans, both Medraut and Rhuawn had of course learned harping, and both were good. Medraut sang a few songs about some highly favoured Irish hero named CuChulainn ('But Gwalchmai used to sing them better,' he commented); and Rhuawn responded with a song about Macsen Wledig, and an older song about Pryderi ap Pwyll. They began passing the harp back and forth, sipping the wine while they listened, and the damp afternoon was forgotten.

After a while, Medraut called Eivlin back, and asked her to fetch some bread and cheese from the kitchen. This brought a worried look, and I wondered if she had some work of her own we were distracting her from. I offered to go with her – I needed to clear my head a little by then, anyway – and she accepted the help with a surprised air.

We had a job to find the cheese. Someone had stolen the great round that morning, and Saidi ap Sugyn, who was up and about, did not want to cut a new one. I threatened him with Medraut, Rhuawn, Gwalchmai, the Queen of Orcade, and my fists, and he finally yielded. We exited triumphantly. Eivlin laughed.

'I am glad you came, Rhys ap Sean,' she said. 'Indeed, I would have threatened him with my lady and the lord Medraut, but that withered ram cares no more for them than he does for his own lord. You argue like a farmer.'

'I am one,' I said.

She raised her eyebrows again. 'In*deed*? Lost your land?'

I snorted. 'It would take a fine army indeed to take land from *my* clan. No, I'm here because . . .' I didn't think I could tell her my tangle of reasons. 'Because I support the Pendragon, and because I'm fond of my lord Gwalchmai.'

She looked very startled at this declaration of free choice, so I asked her whether she had been born a servant.

She tossed her head. 'In a manner. My father was kin-wrecked, and fled from Erin for his life, and took me with him. He's no kin in the Orcades, so there he went, and found service with King Lot.'

'What was he kin-wrecked for?' I asked, before I could think better.

'He killed his brother,' she said shortly. She took the cheese from me and opened the door of Medraut's house, before I could understand what she had said.

Medraut and Rhuawn had stopped singing and were talking. Eivlin set the bread and cheese down firmly and swept into the next room. I sat down, thinking about fratricide. They say that there is a curse on those who do such things, on them and on their descendants. Poor Eivlin. I wondered how old she had been.

Rhuawn absently cut himself a slice of bread and some cheese, and ate it, listening to Medraut, who was talking about harping.

'. . . twenty-three major songs, one has to learn, and the genealogies, which are worse . . .' Rhuawn snorted and nodded vigorously. 'All to be told in the bardic style, which is tedious as a summer afternoon and far less relaxing. Gwalchmai liked it, but he never sang in it. He used to sing me the stories straight, which was wonderful.'

'He's a good harper,' Rhuawn agreed.

Medraut laughed. 'I used to think he was good at everything. But then – well, do you have an older brother?'

Rhuawn shook his head. 'No.' He grinned. 'But I've a younger brother, so I can imagine.'

Medraut smiled, but the smile drooped suddenly with hurt. 'But then, of course, Gwalchmai . . . left. We thought for years that he was dead: not a word about him. And then reports that he was alive in Britain and fighting for Arthur, fighting brilliantly. We didn't believe them at first, but finally we had to. I don't know why he left, unless he . . . my poor mother was very worried.'

Rhuawn and I sat very still, awkwardly. Medraut looked at us sharply. 'Well, she was. Come, you don't believe all that nonsense about her being a witch, do you? She's simply a clever woman, and that makes men distrust her.'

I thought of her advancing on us that first night and shuddered. Rhuawn coughed and asked for the harp. After listening to the music for a while, Medraut cheered up.

When we returned to our own house it was growing dark, and Gwalchmai was sitting cross-legged on the floor, looking in the fire. He looked up and nodded to us when we came in, but that was all. Rhuawn seated himself on the bed.

'A very enjoyable afternoon. How was yours?'

Gwalchmai slowly traced designs on the ground before him with one long-fingered hand. 'Maelgwn says nothing more. The mountains are beautiful, in the spring.'

'Indeed?' Gwalchmai did not reply. 'We spent the afternoon with your brother, Rhys and I. You might join us next time, instead of riding about the mountains alone.'

Gwalchmai looked up sharply. 'With Medraut? What were you doing with Medraut?'

'Playing the harp, mainly. He talked a deal about you.' Rhuawn paused, then went on, carefully, 'Cousin, I do not think your brother knows much about the doings of the rest of your family, and he speaks as though you were once close. There is no reason to act as coldly towards him as you have done.'

'Medraut knows why I left Dun Fionn.'

'He said otherwise.'

'Did he? Then he was lying.'

'Cousin, he is not a bad man. I have found him very courteous, pleasant, and generous.'

Gwalchmai gave both of us a long, dark look, then shrugged. 'When I left Dun Fionn he had . . . taken certain steps in my mother's direction.'

'Couldn't he have changed his mind?' I asked. 'You say

that you did.'

Gwalchmai rubbed his face with his hands, tiredly. 'I don't know,' he said, after a long while. 'Perhaps. But he did know why I left . . . you think that I should talk to him?'

We told him he should.

'Then I will. Privately. But now I am going to see to my horse.' He rose and left us, vanishing into the cold twilight.

'He's just finished seeing to his horse,' muttered Rhuawn. 'He spends more time with that beast than with his friends and kinsmen.' He picked a straw from the mattress and tossed it angrily into the fire. It was true, and I too was annoyed, and said nothing.

The next few weeks proceeded in the same fashion. I saw a fair amount of Medraut ap Lot, and he and Rhuawn became friends and went hunting together. Gwalchmai, however, made no further mention of his brother until Rhuawn finally dragged the matter up again. Then he said, very coldly, 'I did talk with him. You are much mistaken if you think he has any love left for me, and I think he is also intimate in my mother's counsels.' And when Rhuawn shook his head and protested, Gwalchmai insisted: 'He does not seek you out either because he loves you or because he cares for the Light. I urge you, cousin, not to speak with him. I do not trust his motives.'

But neither Rhuawn nor I could believe this of Medraut. I decided that when my lord spoke with his brother they must have quarrelled, which was understandable after so much separation and reunion in such circumstances.

I had become somewhat busier than I had been. On another visit to Medraut's, the serving girl Eivlin had again had to drop her own work to fetch things for us, so I again had offered to help. While we were walking back from the feast hall with the jar of wine Medraut had asked for, she turned to me and said fiercely, 'And you are not afraid of the curse?'

'What curse?' I asked, though I was thinking about the curse on fratricides myself.

'Stars of the heavens! The curse that is on me from my father's deed; what other curses do you think I carry about?'

'Oh, that curse. I do not believe in curses.'

She stared at me, stopping in her tracks, and,

setting her hand on her hip, she put her head back and looked up at me. 'A fool, is it? You do not believe in the magic of blood and iron?'

I put my head back, too, and declaimed, 'I am a Christian man from a Christian kingdom, and if blood and iron can curse, blood and water atone. I'm afraid of no sorceries.'

'Not even my lady's?' she asked, very quietly. I felt cold, and was silent a moment. 'You believe, well enough.' She began walking again.

I hurried after her. 'Your lady is able to terrify, but that doesn't change what I believe, and no curse is stronger than Christ's power. It wouldn't trouble me if your father had killed all his brothers and his parents as well.'

She shivered. 'Your Christian sorceries are so powerful? I had heard they were . . . and you are really a Christian?' I nodded, and she stopped again, looking at me with a closed face. 'Is it true that you drink blood?'

I was shocked. I had known that the Ynysoedd Erch were a barbarian, pagan kingdom, but this idea passed belief. 'Holy angels, no. Where did you hear that?'

'Why, everyone says that. You mean it isn't true?'

'It is not. We Christians are not permitted any sorceries, let alone the drinking of blood or whatever.'

She shrugged. 'Well. I had heard that Christians had a rite where they killed babies, and ate their flesh and drank up their blood. All the servants at Dun Fionn say so. I had thought it a sorcery to match my lady's; and indeed, it seemed likely enough, for she has been trying for years to kill the Pendragon, and failed. But if Christians have no sorceries, it must just be that she cannot kill him because of the distance, unless someone else is protecting Arthur. Are you certain that there are no such rituals, and that you had heard nothing of them?'

In a flash of insight, I knew where the idea had come from. 'There is a mystery, a ritual I have taken part in,' I told her. 'But we use bread and wine, not flesh and blood. At least, it looks like bread and wine; my mother has baked the bread for it, sometimes. But we say that after the mystery, it is really flesh and blood.'

'Oh,' said Eivlin. 'And me thinking it was powerful. Well.'

'It *is* powerful,' I insisted. 'It is a mystery . . .'

'And it is because of this little dinner,' she snapped her fingers in contempt, 'because of this make-believe sorcery, that you sneer at curses? Indeed, you are a fool.'

'I am not afraid of curses,' I said, setting my teeth, and I tried to explain about the sacraments, and about Christ, and his victory over death and Hell. This led me into insisting that he was God and Man both, and I became confused, and thrashed about in the creeds. Eivlin eyed me sceptically and made acid comments, and I finally gave up in disgust, and retreated to reaffirming that I was not afraid of any curse.

'So you say, so you say,' she said. 'And yet you are afraid of my lady. Indeed, and you will be afraid of me, too, because I am accursed, and you will be certain to avoid me in the future.'

'I will not. Didn't I offer to help you today? As for your lady – did you say you had to turn the bed today? Well, I will help you with the heavy work.'

She raised her eyebrows, but assented in a meek tone. I helped her then, and afterwards had to help her some more to prove my lack of fear for curses. I was angry at first, then pleased that I was proving myself. It was not until the end of the afternoon that I noticed her smug smile and began to suspect that I was being made a fool of.

Nonetheless, over the next few weeks I helped her whenever she asked me to, to prove that I was not avoiding her, not afraid of curses, and not afraid of Morgawse of Orcade. I intended to back out eventually, but Eivlin, for all her plump fairness, was as cunning a bargainer as any I've encountered, a woman to fear in a market place. She was as convincing as a dealer in sick cattle, and twice as witty. The only thing that ever seemed to bridle her was her lady. I had occasionally also to see Morgawse, and I liked her no more on second glance than on first. She paid no attention to me at all, beyond the first sharp question to Eivlin, but Eivlin was subdued when the Queen was about, and always quiet for a time even after her lady had left.

And yet, when I had seen her room and helped to clean it, I could find no evidence that the Queen practised sorcery. She had a few books about, but nothing else, and I could not tell what the books were. Medraut insisted that she was no witch, and that her reputation was merely an envious legend, begun because she was beautiful and intelligent and

136

skilled at governing. 'And because she has a certain air about her. My brother has the same look, sometimes.' But I could not think that she and Gwalchmai were at all alike in their respective otherworldliness, and I knew that Medraut was wrong. Probably, I told myself, he says what he would like to believe.

As a few weeks passed, Rhuawn became determined that Gwalchmai and Medraut should speak to each other properly, and reconcile their differences. He asked Medraut over to our hut one afternoon, and kept him late, without warning Gwalchmai of what he did. Most of the afternoon was the usual pleasant, relaxed conversation; and then the door opened and Gwalchmai appeared. It was twilight behind him, and raining, and my lord's hair was plastered down from the wet, while he was dripping and tired looking. But he took one look at Medraut, and both froze. For a moment I thought Gwalchmai would back out into the rain again, giving some errand as an excuse. Rhuawn stood hastily, greeting Gwalchmai and offering him mead. Gwalchmai did not even look at him, but stood and stared at Medraut.

Medraut stared back. The two faces, the dark and the fair, were still as the sky, only their eyes brilliant and cold. Then, between one blink and the next, Gwalchmai strode across the room and stood above his brother looking down at him. The open door let in a wet night smell, and the rain dripped from his cloak onto the floor.

'What are you doing here?' Gwalchmai's voice was quiet, but something in his tone told me that here was danger.

Medraut uncurled himself from before the fire and stood, brushing wood ash from his shoulder, then smiling hesitantly. 'I was asked here, brother. If you don't want me, I will go.'

Gwalchmai glanced at Rhuawn, at me. 'Truly. You were asked. But what were you doing, Medraut?'

The other smiled, nervously, apologetically. 'I was playing the harp, the way you taught me once. What is wrong in that?'

'That is not what I meant.' Gwalchmai stared at his brother steadily. Some water ran from his hair and crawled down one cheek, shining like red bronze in the firelight. 'Medraut.' His voice had changed, become earnest. 'Once

137

you wished to be another CuChulainn for strength and skill, and for courage and honour, and I thought you might be such a one. Is it all nothing to you beside a whisper in the dark, and the hope of a purple cloak in the daylight?'

For just an instant I thought I glimpsed something strange in Medraut''s face, a chill, bitter darkness rushing behind his eyes. But that was only for an instant, and then he was smiling, ruefully and painfully, and I doubted whether I had seen anything. 'Still unyielding?' he asked Gwalchmai. 'Are we nothing to you, your family and your homeland, whom you loved once? Are we sold, for a white horse and a sword and a place behind the Pendragon?'

'I sold nothing, only gave it, and to the Light first, not to Arthur. And for all the grief, it is worth it. Is your bargain the same, Medraut?'

Medraut moved quickly to the door, caught it and stood with his hand on the latch. 'I can do nothing here.' He did not look at his brother, and his voice was strained by some inner pain. 'If you still wish, Rhuawn, we can go hunting tomorrow. Good night, Gwalchmai.' He slipped out, closing the door behind him.

Rhuawn stared at Gwalchmai angrily, but said nothing.

Gwalchmai sighed, unpinned his cloak, and stood a moment holding it, the crimson vivid against his thin, dark frame. Hesitantly he sat down, looked at Rhuawn, looked at me.

'You must not believe Medraut,' he said at last. 'Whatever he is planning, it is not to your good.'

Rhuawn said nothing. I did not know what to say. My lord had not treated his brother prettily. But after a while, I offered Gwalchmai some mead, simply to break the silence. I thought for a moment he would go on talking about Medraut, but he only took the mead, ran a narrow hand through his wet hair, and began to sip the hot drink slowly.

The following day, when I went to meet Eivlin and rapped on her door, she did not at once call out 'Come in!' I waited a moment, then rapped again. This time a voice did call, 'Come.'

I pushed the door open and stopped short. Morgawse of Orcade was sitting with her back to me, tying her black hair up with a strand of gold. She was wearing only a shift of crimson linen through which every line of her body was

138

visible, and she sat looking into a bronze mirror. I could see her face in the mirror, and the opened door with my own form reflected frozen there. Her imaged eyes met mine, and her mouth contracted. She turned. I let my eyes rest on her reflection, afraid – I will admit it – to look into her face.

'What are you doing here?' Her voice was softer than thistledown, but cold to freeze the marrow of my bones.

'Eivlin,' I gasped. 'I . . . I was going to help her mend the thatch.'

'Your help is unnecessary. Go – no, wait.' She rose and came towards me, and I had to look away from the mirror. I heartily wished myself elsewhere, and wondered why I had ever left my home. I cannot explain it, but this woman froze my blood. 'You are Gwalchmai's servant, aren't you?'

'Yes, Great Queen,' I mumbled.

She smiled sweetly. 'Then it is most generous of you to help us with our business. What is your name?'

I licked my lips, not wanting to speak of anything which might give her power over me and mine, but I had to say, 'Rhys ap Sion, Lady.'

'Rhys ap Sion.' She toyed with a gold pendant about her neck, her eyes fixed on mine. I felt dizzy, and squirmed inwardly, but I remembered my boasts to Eivlin, and just managed to stand straight and stare back.

She dropped the pendant. 'It is most generous. Does your lord, my son, know that you do this?'

I nodded, then shook my head.

'Perhaps he commanded you to,' she said, still smiling. 'I think that he did.' She reached out and rested one hand on my shoulder, then leaned forward, her lips slightly parted, still smiling. 'He is welcome to whatever you see. Tell him so. But be warned that I do not like to be spied upon, Rhys ap Sion, and those who do so . . . well.' She dropped her arm. 'Eivlin is in the kitchens for the day. Perhaps you can seek her there.'

I bowed deeply and left. As I stepped out of the door I nearly walked into Maelgwn of Gwynedd. He snarled at me and struck out, and I ducked, turning the movement into a bow and a muttered apology, and strode off as fast as I could. But behind me I heard him greet Morgawse, and I heard her low laugh, while a glance over my shoulder showed me that she was closing the door, and his arm was about her waist.

139

I walked half-way to the kitchens and stopped and stood on the clean grass with the clear sky over me. Gwalchmai had said that it was Morgawse who led the plotting, and truly, withered old King Lot did not look capable of it. Lot had worked in a world of armies and alliances, but Morgawse was more subtle. Morgawse would dominate her allies' minds and subjugate them not to a cause, but to herself, and she would start with Maelgwn. No matter who had invited whom, she was sleeping with the king of Gwynedd, and was going to dictate his counsels. The Ynysoedd Erch were simply too far away for her to work as she pleased, and so she had come to Gwynedd to hunt for a tool. Lot mac Cormac probably knew nothing about any of the plans, but there were probably others who did . . .

I turned from the kitchens towards the stables, hoping to find Gwalchmai.

As it happened, he was not there, but in the practice yard nearby, throwing spears at a target from horseback. Ceincaled swooped about the yard as lightly as a swallow darting about a barn, and Gwalchmai seemed to be a part of him, while the flung spears flew straight and steady. It was a fine sight, but I was in no temper to sit back and admire it.

'My lord!' I shouted. He glanced at me, then turned Ceincaled in an easy semi-circle and cantered over. He reined in before me and leaned over, elbow on knee, to listen to me.

'My lord,' I repeated, 'do you have any business in the next hour? There is a matter I need to talk to you about.'

He sighed. 'There is nothing urgent. Maelgwn is engaged this morning. Only . . . must you?'

I glared at him irritably. 'I must. And privately.'

He straightened. 'Och ai, in that case – does your horse need exercise?'

I soon had my wretched beast from Caer Legion saddled, and we rode out of the gates and into the mountains. It was early April, and the snow had melted. All the earth was green and misty, and sounded with streams. It made me think of the planting season and the green corn, and young lambs and calves to worry about at home. A deal of work, spring, but a good season.

Gwalchmai hummed abstractedly for a while, and sang a little in Irish. I tried to piece my thoughts together, and wondered how to communicate them. After all, she was

140

still his mother, and warriors kill men for making such suggestions.

'My lord,' I said at last.

'So,' replied Gwalchmai. 'You wish to talk about my brother.'

I was taken aback. 'Indeed not, my lord. About your mother.' And I told him what Morgawse had said to me that morning, and that I had seen Maelgwn going to her, 'to talk'.

Gwalchmai heard me out with patience, and when I ground to a halt he said, 'And you think she commits adultery with Maelgwn?'

'My lord,' I drew a deep breath, 'in due respect, I do.'

To my surprise he smiled a little, bitterly. 'She does, if you doubt it.'

I stopped my horse. 'You know?'

He nodded. gestured with open hands. 'I know my mother. I have been watching Maelgwn. The whole fortress knows, though they wouldn't mention it before us, of course. She has been quite open about it. I could almost be sorry for Maelgwn, only I so pity Lot.'

My face felt hot, and I looked between my horse's ears. To have come to my lord in such high haste, with such urgency, and such stale news! 'Lot knows too?' I asked.

'He probably knew before ever they set sail from the islands.' I looked up sharply, and he added, quickly, not looking at me, 'No. He is not indifferent to it. He would not assent – only he cannot any longer deny her any whim that enters her thoughts. He cannot decide anything for himself, Rhys. He still desires, and wills, but he cannot act. He . . .' Gwalchmai extended one hand vaguely in the air, 'he has withered away. He is only a shadow now, a ghost among his own warriors, who stares and cannot speak. I go to speak with him, and I tell him how things stand, with Agravain and with myself, and he is glad of this thing or that, but to act,' his hand clenched convulsively, 'he is like a dotard. And he is the one who was the shield of his people, the bulwark of the warband, leader of a thousand spears; the lord of Dun Fionn and the Orcades and all the islands to the north and the west of Caledon, ruler by his own strength and cunning and courage! Sweet heaven, how she has used him!' He brought his hand down against his thigh, half raised it again, then straightened the fingers with an effort. He rubbed the worn leather of the reins, looking off towards the mountains. Ceincaled tossed his head and walked on. The hooves of our horses made a steady rhythm against the earth.

I sat still, knowing that I couldn't say anything, and that it was best to leave him be for a while. It no longer surprised me that he spent so much time by himself, nor that he was remote when he was in Degannwy. He had quite enough worries as it was, without additional difficulties from Rhuawn and myself. Sweet Jesu, what a family! Except for Medraut, my lord could well afford the loss of the whole royal clan of the Ynysoedd Erch.

Except Medraut ... and Gwalchmai asserted that Medraut was as bad, close to the Queen and following in her road. Medraut, however, asserted – though never in so many words – that Gwalchmai was indifferent to his family and to natural affection, cruel, and concerned primarily with his own honour. Well, Medraut didn't properly understand the circumstances.

But could he, in his position, really not understand them?

I found myself weighing the two brothers in my mind. Gwalchmai, I knew, was accomplished in eloquence and courtesy, and, having seen him being persuasive with Maelgwn and his nobles, I knew that he could be very persuasive indeed when he set his mind to it. Medraut had a double measure of the same eloquence, and a graceful, amiable charm as well, a very real and forceful charm. I could not believe that he was what Gwalchmai asserted him to be, and yet I suddenly wished that I spoke Irish and could question Lot's servants about Medraut, to see if his deeds matched his words. No, I liked Medraut, I was sure there would be a good report of him ...

On the other hand, I was not quite as sure as all that. The manner in which he treated Eivlin leapt before my mind. No matter what task she was engaged in, he expected her to drop it at once if he told her to run and fetch something; indeed, I'd originally offered to help the girl precisely because of that. And I had a nagging awareness that he treated her better than he treated most servants. And yet, I argued, for a nobleman to be unaware of servants' feelings meant very little. Medraut was royally born and, unlike his brother, he had never left his privileged position. He could simply assume that servants were there to do things for him, and so be annoyed when they failed to, because that was what he had always known. I liked Medraut. There was some way, I was sure, in which it could be seen that both Gwalchmai and Medraut spoke the truth, and the whole problem was a misunderstanding.

But still, I might do well to ask Eivlin about Medraut, and perhaps even ask her to interpret what Lot's other servants had to say.

I looked back to Gwalchmai. He had settled somewhat after his outburst, leaning back in the saddle, one arm crossed under the other. I cleared my throat. 'My lord, since you know that Morgawse is . . . scheming with Maelgwn' (after all, that was the significant part) 'do we know what they're planning? At all?'

He sighed a little and shrugged. 'They have written letters, some of which were sent to the north. That much I know. But it is not likely to be open war, not now.' He hesitated, then said quietly, 'I should have told Rhuawn, and you, that we knew so much; and yet I could not. I fear I have been poor company, this last month. Forgive me. It has been a distraction to me, my family, and there has been this trouble about my brother.'

I nodded to indicate sympathy, and bit my tongue to stop myself asking more about Medraut. He straightened and tightened the reins a little, and Ceincaled pricked his ears forward.

'We've a fine hillside here,' said Gwalchmai. 'Why don't we gallop?' He touched his stallion and was off, and I kicked my own beast into following him.

We rode directly north from the fortress, heading towards the main east–west road, keeping the highest mountain peaks behind us and to our left. The land was wild, but much of it only seemed to be deserted, and in the summer was used for pasturage. It was a sweet country, if not a rich one, and it was a fine day to be away from Degannwy and out in the clean bright air. After a little while, Gwalchmai turned off the track we had followed, heading as though for a cleft between two large hills, and we slowed to a walk again. Gwalchmai glanced back at me,

143

smiled, and checked his mount until I caught up.

'Rhys,' he said. 'Can you climb trees?'

I opened my mouth, then closed it again like a fish. 'My lord? I mean, yes. Ordinary trees, that is, not ash trees. But . . .'

'That is well. I am not good at it myself. We do not have many trees in the islands.' He smiled again and explained, 'There is a tree where one of my lord's men here in Gwynedd leaves the letters and messages which my lord sends me. But one must climb to reach the place, and, as I said, I am not good at climbing trees.'

We rode on for a little way, then Gwalchmai stood in the saddle, peering at something, and then turned Ceincaled to the right. Soon we came to the edge of a wood, and there, huge and pre-eminent, stood a large oak tree. My lord reined in his horse and dismounted. 'This is the one,' He said, staring at one of the branches. 'And there is a message.'

I looked at the branch. It looked like a branch, to me. 'How can you tell?'

He glanced back to me. 'There was a sprig of holly back where we turned off the road. That means that I am to check the tree. If the message is urgent, there is a sprig of pine as well. When I have the message, I take the twigs away.' He placed one palm against the oak and looked up it again. 'Can you climb this?'

It had wide-spreading branches at some distance from the ground, but a large fork within grabbing distance. 'Certainly.' I jumped from my horse and clambered up. Just like the apple trees in my clan's orchards.

'Where do they put this letter, then?'

'There's a hollow where that big branch joins the larger fork, to your right . . . yes, there.'

I leaned over and searched the hollow with my hand. Something prickly. I pulled it out: it was a pine cone. I held it in my other hand and reached again: only rough oak bark and the sodden remains of last year's leaves.

'There's nothing here,' I told Gwalchmai.

'Nothing? What's that in your hand?'

'Only a pine cone.'

'That's the message. You're sure there's nothing more?'

I said I was sure, and he told me to climb down. When I reached him he took the pine cone and turned it in his fingers.

'Do you break it open?' I asked, intrigued by the ingenuity of the system.

He shook his head. 'No. It only means that Arthur received my last letter safely.' He sighed, tossed the pine cone into the wood and walked back to Ceincaled. 'I was hoping for more.'

I could see that, when a letter was sent for such a distance, there would have to be some sign that it had reached its destination, but it still seemed a complicated system. I said so.

'It has to be,' said Gwalchmai. 'any message passes through several hands on its journey, and any one of the men could be bought by Maelgwn or some other ruler, or be killed, and the message lost. As it is, those who bear the message do not know what it is they carry. The man who put the pine cone there was told only to do so much. There are a few other signs; Arthur and I agreed on them before we left.'

I suddenly realized that Gwalchmai was trusting me with a great deal. If I told Maelgwn, he could set watchers on the oak and capture the messenger, and perhaps through him find the rest of Arthur's supporters in Gwynedd. And even if I did not do that, it would be a simple matter for me to substitute any message I wanted. If Medraut told me to leave something there, I could drop his letter in that hollow, leave a sprig of holly by the track, and Gwalchmai could think that Arthur commanded him to be more charitable towards his brother.

But I could not. Gwalchmai must have known that, to trust me so far. While I thought it would be a fine thing if my lord were a little gentler with Medraut, I could not use trickery and deception to make him so. That would be the same as no gentleness at all. And then, even as I thought of it, I suddenly noticed that I did not quite trust Medraut. I would have to see about him. Truly, I would.

145

Nine

When I returned to Degannwy an hour or so later, I went to look for Rhuawn. It took some looking, but I eventually found him. He was with Medraut, and the two sat together in a quiet corner of the feast hall, near a fire, playing the harp in turns. Both looked up when I walked over to them, and Medraut smiled and indicated a place to sit. I sat, leaning against one of the benches. Rhuawn was singing a long song in praise of the spring, 'when warbands are splendid before a bold lord', and, while it was not exactly what I had been enjoying the season for, it was still a fine song.

When Rhuawn finished, Medraut took the harp. He began to pluck it idly, as men do before they've decided what to sing, bringing out light ripples of sound like the wind on a pool.

'We have songs such as that in Irish,' he told Rhuawn. 'There is one which is supposed to have been made by the greater warleader, Fionn mac Cumhail. It is the longest and dullest of the lot, so, of course, everyone has to memorize it.' He played a little more, the runs of music sliding into each other with a rush under his fingers, while he gazed dreamily into the fire. 'My brother was born in the spring,' he said, after a little. 'He will be twenty-seven this May.' A kind of tune began to grow out of the music, then faded again. 'I wonder if I could give him a present.'

Rhuawn snorted. 'I don't think you should; and I think, if you did, he would not receive it from you.'

'I might show him my care by it.'

'I don't think he'd pay any attention. He does not listen to me when I try to speak with him on your behalf. He keeps very much to himself.'

Medraut smiled warmly at Rhuawn. 'I thank you deeply for your efforts. It is good to have a friend in this ... but truly, I think he only misunderstands me. If I remain patient and generous, he will see that I at least am not his enemy.'

Rhuawn shrugged. 'Hawks may swim and salmon may fly.'

'My brother can swim, and his name means hawk. I wonder ...'

Rhuawn straightened and leaned forward, putting out his hand for emphasis. 'Your brother will remain obstinate. He's already made that plain to me, abundantly plain. I don't know why, but he's set against you and will never change his mind.'

I opened my mouth to say something in Gwalchmai's defence, but Medraut was already speaking. 'I can't simply give up his friendship. He is my brother.'

'He has abandoned you. He has sworn the Threefold Oath to Arthur, and he holds that above his own blood. He tells people that you and your mother are sorcerers, and he tramples your kinship. In your place, I'd have no qualms about letting him discover his own condemnation.'

I stared at Rhuawn, astonished. But Medraut was shaking his head. 'It isn't Gwalchmai's fault.' He stopped his harping for a moment, then began again with a different rhythm, and went on, 'Listen, Rhuawn. I will tell you a thing I have thought of.'

Rhuawn listened attentively. I shut my mouth tight and chewed on my lip, to remind myself to keep quiet.

'It is about this battle-madness of his which you have told me of.' Medraut's harp thrummed steadily. 'When my brother was young, and as I remember him, he had no such thing. He used to have fights with Agravain, and Agravain always beat him, and there was no sign of madness. The first time I heard of it was in songs, and in reports from Britain.

'Now, when Gwalchmai left Dun Fionn, he left suddenly. He took his horse from the fortress on a stormy night and rode off at a gallop across to the cliffs westward. He says – I have heard it, Rhuawn – that our mother tried to kill him that night. He has even said that I . . .' he hesitated, fighting with it, 'that I was with her, and assenting. But I know that no such thing happened. The idea is madness – me, to kill my brother? For a long time this confused me. I could not see why my brother, who had always been so close, should say such things. And yet, I think he truly believes them; and moreover, I have heard that he says he journeyed to the Otherworld after he departed Dun Fionn, and tells of many other impossibilities. What I think is that he had a fit of this madness you tell me of, for the first time, perhaps, and that he rode off in it, raving and seeing visions,

147

and that his mind has been warped by this demon ever since. So you see, it is not Gwalchmai's fault that he thinks of me as his enemy. It is only this disease.'

I had been searching for some way in which both brothers might be seen to be speaking the truth. Here, now, was a way. Madness and delusion, and it was undeniable that Gwalchmai did go mad in battle. It made sense, excellent sense, and neatly accounted for the situation.

And yet I was certain it was a lie.

But Medraut plainly believed his theory. He bowed his head over the harp, and the music went on.

Rhuawn rubbed his sword-hilt with one hand. 'Do you think so, truly?' he asked Medraut. 'If it is thus, this is a dreadful ill for him to suffer.'

'What other explanation is there?' asked Medraut.

'That something did happen that night,' I said. Both the warriors looked at me, and I looked back at Medraut. His harp-playing faltered a minute, almost became a tune, then resumed in a different, wilder key. It was an infernal distraction, that plunking. 'You wouldn't have had to know anything about it,' I admitted. 'Or, even, remember it.'

'But I would know,' Medraut said simply. His grey eyes were wide and grave.

'Of course he would,' snapped Rhuawn. 'Rhys, this makes a great deal of sense. I've never liked battle-madness, because it doesn't always happen in battle. Sometimes those Saxon berserkers go mad in the feast hall and murder half a dozen of their comrades. And if someone has the berserker-gang, I have heard that it gets worse with time.'

'My lord Gwalchmai is not mad,' I snapped back. 'You must have seen him fight. You know he's not a berserker.'

Rhuawn looked uncertain a moment. Medraut kept on playing the harp. 'I have seen Gwalchmai in battle,' Rhuawn spoke slowly. 'He is a very great warrior, but he is uncontrollable. And he collapses afterwards, just as the Saxon berserkers do.'

'I didn't say that Gwalchmai was mad,' Medraut added hurriedly. 'Only . . . touched, at times. Ill.'

'If you'd seen his face when it is on him, you couldn't believe that,' I insisted.

'Well, I have never seen his face at such a time, it is true . . .' began Medraut.

'I have watched him fight, and this is the only explanation for his treatment of Medraut. And when did you ever see his face when the madness was on him, Rhys? No one dares to meet his eyes then.'

'When we were coming down to Camlann we met some bandits on the road and he killed them. And even in the madness, he is still himself, only ... only ... ach, I can't say it. But your own servant, Aegmund, has told me tales of Saxon berserkers, how they foam at the mouth and howl like wolves. Gwalchmai is not like that at all.'

'But it must be the same kind of thing,' returned Rhuawn. 'We can't say what he sees in the madness.'

I couldn't answer this, and simply glared.

'It is a hard thing to believe of one's lord,' said Medraut, still hesitant. 'And, God knows, a hard thing to believe of one's brother. But I have no other explanation. I know that Gwalchmai desires glory and honour – as what warrior worth his mead does not? – but he would not, for that, spread lies about my mother and me. No, he has believed a thing proceeding from madness, and, having believed it, sought glory among foreigners instead of with his own kin. While one must honour the Pendragon,' Medraut nodded to Rhuawn, 'still, my brother forsook his own blood for Arthur's service, a thing no right-thinking man would do. And once he had given his oath to Arthur, whom political necessity had made our enemy, he could not but keep to the delusion. And now he thinks that my mother and I – and my father, too, I imagine – are fighting for some great darkness, while he and the Pendragon fight for some kind of light. But, in fact, all my father wanted and wants, is to have power in Britain, which is just what the Pendragon wanted, and has. And my father's rights are as good as the Pendragon's. He married the legitimate daughter of a Pendragon, and he is the legitimately born king of a royal clan, although he is Irish, while the Pendragon – and I say this not to disparage him, for, indeed, I greatly admire him for overcoming it – Arthur is only one of the Pendragon Uther's bastards, and legally clanless and unable to succeed to the High Kingship. Arthur is High King, as we know, and a great one: and that is a fact in the real world. It is not as though he stood for some pure light, while my father and my mother, who once with an equally good claim opposed

149

him, must perforce stand for darkness. Such notions are fine in a song, and lend elegance, but what have they to do with the world in which we live? My poor brother confounds Britain with the Land of Youth, the Kingdom of Summer. Och, by the sun, I have missed him, these years, and wondered, again and again, when I would see him: I see him, and find that he is still mad, and hates me. If only he were free of it, and could come home!'

Unable to command himself, Medraut turned his whole mind to the harp, and finally began playing some kind of tune, a weird thing in a minor key. I sat, bewildered, wondering where the bottom of my world had dropped to. It was true enough: Arthur had scant legal right to the imperium of Britain. Could the struggle I had seen so clearly, the struggle of Light and Darkness, be merely the clashings of dishonest kings? The idea was solid, easy to consider, without any vague indefinites and worlds within worlds depending upon it. And if it was true, then Medraut, and Morgawse, were quite innocent, and Gwalchmai was quite deluded, and I with him. Medraut's harp kept on steadily, and I thrashed about in his words, trying to find some way out.

'My friend,' said Rhuawn, 'you are right. This is a sickness which has come upon him. I wish to God that he were healed of it, for it is a dreadful thing for a man to be separated from his own clan and his own blood. I thought so at the first, and now that I am sure you are innocent . . . but what can be done? Are there treatments for madness?'

Medraut drew a deep breath, his eyes very bright. 'Yes. There are some treatments for madness.' His voice was soft. 'One can read of them in books, works written by learned Roman doctors. But I could not mention it to him. He would never trust me to help, though I have ached to try them.'

'These methods,' said Rhuawn slowly. 'Could I help?'

'Would you be willing?' asked Medraut in a surprised tone.

I struggled silently with Medraut's argument, trying to find the flaw in it. But my thoughts were confused, and all I could do was stare at the whole and think what sense, what excellent sense, it all made.

'Anything,' said Rhuawn. 'Gwalchmai saved my life in battle, once, and all my loyalty is due to him, together with the friendship I bear for him and for you, and, in honour, I will help him to a cure in any way which you show me.'

'He would not accept our aid,' said Medraut. 'We could never convince him that he is wrong, and probably he would think I devised some sorcery against his life. If we even suggested anything, he will write to his lord, and Arthur would listen to him.'

'Arthur trusts Gwalchmai above his own right hand,' said Rhuawn, 'and he does not understand the situation.'

'If I should give Gwalchmai some medicine, then, would you keep it secret from the High King?' Medraut asked, almost pleadingly. 'It would only take a little while.'

Rhuawn held out his hand. 'I will help you in any treatment you plan, and I will set Arthur's mind at rest that all is well with us.'

Medraut took his hand and clasped it gladly, then looked at me. 'Will you also, join us?' he asked.

I licked my lips, trying to find a way out, and looked at Medraut. He seemed humble and earnest and excited: no help. He must be wrong. He must be, but where?

'Perhaps Gwalchmai has spoken to you about me, or about this struggle he believes is going on. I know that he can be very convincing. But think carefully, and see if this does not seem more likely than those fantasies he spun for you.'

'Come, Rhys,' put in Rhuawn. 'We don't call him Gwalchmai the Golden-tongued for nothing. But Medraut is talking about real things.'

'Will you help us?' Medraut asked again.

I again licked my lips. Where, where, where?

Suddenly, there flashed before my mind the image of Gwalchmai kneeling to offer his sword to my father. There was no one to impress there, no advantage to be gained. The gesture was a pure gift, as Gwalchmai had given to Arthur and as Arthur gave to Britain: and it was real. The image was quickly followed by others: my lord laughing with admiration and telling me to keep the brooch; unthinkingly helping with a task unbefitting to his rank; talking earnestly with Arthur; singing that unearthly song in the marshes before Gwlad yr Haf. I dropped my half-lifted hand. There was really no question. Medraut was lying, and he had lied all along. While Gwalchmai's eloquence and courtesy were real things, expressions of his whole life, Medraut's came from words alone, fine paint over rotten timbers. Even without asking Lot's warriors, I realized that I had never actually seen him do anything courteous, noble or gentle unless he stood to benefit from it. I could weigh the two men together, and their two visions of the world, and there was no question whom I should believe.

'No,' I said. 'I will not.' And I stood abruptly and faced them both. 'I will not because my lord is not mad, nor deluded, and you, Rhuawn, you know that he is not, but you find it more likely and comfortable to believe Medraut. I will not have any part in certain un-named things done to "cure" him, things suggested by a reputed sorcerer who has made you swear not to tell his enemy and your lord, the Emperor Arthur, about any of this.'

Rhuawn leapt up in a rage. 'Do you accuse me of disloyalty to my lord Arthur?'

'That's as may be. You are disloyal to your friend Gwalchmai. A month ago he's cousin and brother to you, and now you're ready to forget this, and forget that he saved your life even as you speak of it, because of a few words from a man recently met, a man who openly admits that "political necessity" makes him your lord's enemy, whose father we came here to hinder in a plot, and whose mother is a famous witch. Tell me I lie!'

Rhuawn hit me across the face hard enough to make me stagger back. I stumbled into a bench, fell over it, and cracked my head against the floor. The world went black for a second, and then I scrambled around until I managed to stagger up into a crouching position, clasping my skull.

'You forget your place,' said Rhuawn. 'I should kill you for daring to speak so to a warrior. You need a thrashing to remind you that you are a servant, and that servants do what they are told, without back-talk. You have been honoured very much above your desserts as it is, and it has made you proud.' He took a step forward, drawing his sword so as to beat me with the flat of it. Medraut, who by now was also on his feet, caught his arm. 'Indeed, you must not thrash him, Rhuawn. He is Gwalchmai's servant, not yours.'

'Gwalchmai will not thrash him.' But Rhuawn halted. I rose to my feet, the feast hall wobbling about my ears. I was vaguely aware of some others down the other side of the room staring, but I was too angry to care. I wished that Rhuawn would come, even with his sword, so that I could hit him, just once.

'If Rhys chooses not to believe the truth, it comes from no evil nature, but only from a misplaced loyalty,' said Medraut, 'and it need not hinder us. If we can cure my brother, Rhys will be glad enough, I am sure. Come. Leave him be.'

I realized then that Medraut was making certain of Rhuawn for some scheme. He had hoped that I would have a part in it as well, but I was not essential. Rhuawn was . . . to reassure Arthur? I looked at Rhuawn. He was still fuming. I could not talk to him now. I glanced around the Hall, then turned and walked off, still holding the back of my head where I had hit the floor. Medraut and Rhuawn sat down again behind me, and I heard Medraut's voice begin again, softly.

One of Maelgwn's warriors jeered as I left the Hall: 'Oh, had enough of your betters' company?' and the rest laughed. I wanted to hit him, too, but I wanted more to find Gwalchmai, to find and warn him.

He was not at the house. Rather than run about looking for him I sat down and fingered the back of my head. A lovely lump I would have there. I had cut my mouth against my teeth, too, and I rinsed the blood with some stale, once-boiled water, then sat on the bed and waited for Gwalchmai.

I had not been sitting very long when there came a knock at the door. I called out 'Come in', and checked that I had a knife handy. But it was only Eivlin.

She looked about the room with some interest, then came and stood over me, hands on her hips. 'Truly, I hope the other man is worse off than you,' she said.

I glared and wiped my mouth. I supposed that my lip must be swollen, and there, it was bleeding. 'What do you want?' I asked her.

'Well, as though you had not promised to help me with the thatch today! "What do you want?" he says, bold as a bad dealer.'

'I went to your house, and your lady turned me out. I don't think she will want many people around today.'

Eivlin took her hands from her hips and crossed them before her. 'Perhaps she did,' she said in a different tone, then, 'indeed, I was working in the kitchen this morning like a common drudge. But she is finished now, and gone

153

out hawking with Maelgwn Gwynedd. I'd be glad of your help, Rhys.'

'Let the thatch wait. I must speak to my lord about a matter.'

'A matter of import?' she began lightly, and I cut her off: 'Yes, a matter of great urgency.'

She stood staring at me a moment, then suddenly sat down beside me and took my head in her hands. 'Och ai, you've had a blow here,' she said, touching the back of my head very gently. She looked about, saw the kettle of once-boiled water, and picked it up; then took a kerchief from her pocket and soaked it. 'Let me bind it up for you.'

I grunted, but let her. She did it deftly and gently. 'Now, I wonder who he was fighting,' she said. 'Saidi ap Sugyn?'

I had to smile at that. 'Sadly, no. More sadly, it was not a fight. It was nearly a beating.'

She hissed a little between her teeth. 'Not your lord? Is that why you must speak to him?'

'Not my lord, no, of course not Gwalchmai. Another warrior.'

'May they be damned, the lot of them, for their swords and heavy hands,' said Eivlin, bitterly and without a trace of mockery. I looked at her sharply.

'Do not be so easy with your damnings. Yffern is a heavy place to send a person ill-advisedly, and some do not deserve any such thing.'

'May they be damned nonetheless.' Eivlin dropped her hands to her lap and looked at me coldly. 'They've no thought for any but themselves and what pleasures them.'

'My lord is different,' I said. 'And I know others that are good enough men.'

She shrugged and sighed. 'I have never known them, then.'

I caught her wrist to get her attention and asked, 'What of Medraut, my lord's brother?'

'Him!' she said, then stopped abruptly, her face closing. 'Well, as you say, there is your lord's brother Medraut.' She stood, pulling away, and I let go her hand. 'So you are waiting for your lord here,' she said, her back still turned to me. I nodded, realized she couldn't see me, and said, 'Yes.'

'Well, do you expect him soon?'

There was the problem: I didn't. 'He will be back before

154

nightfall, if not before twilight.'

'And you would not be caring that he is at Medraut's now?'

'He is? What is he doing there?' I jumped to my feet, and my head twinged. Eivlin turned and caught my arm as I winced.

'Do not be touching that! The lord Gwalchmai is talking to the lord Ronan mac Suibhne, one of Lot's warriors, about some political matter. Ronan is a member of the royal clan, and so is staying with Medraut. It seems that your lord knew him before ever he came to Britain, and hopes to learn something of him now, since Medraut is not there.'

'Oh,' I said, 'That is all. Well, I will go and see him there, then – and maybe I will see how much thatching needs to be done, afterwards.'

'Don't do any thatching with that head,' advised Eivlin. 'You've a fine knock on the back of it, and thatching will make you dizzy.'

We set off across the stronghold, Eivlin walking beside me and chattering about the kitchens and the fools there. She made me laugh, which made my head ache, but I had to laugh even when it ached. When we finally reached the house, low and sprawling against the wall of the stronghold, rotten-thatched, Eivlin gave a little curtsey and opened the door. 'Do you go in first, since you have the headache,' she said.

I smiled at her, liking her a great deal, and stepped inside.

I heard only one soft movement from behind the door, and then, before I had time to turn my head, the world splintered in pain, went first red, then dark as I fell under the blow from the man behind the door.

I am not sure when I woke up. It could not have been too long, an hour at the most: but it does not make much difference, as I promptly fainted again when there was some jolt. My head hurt horribly, and I was sick to my stomach as well, and I heartily wished that the world would go black again and leave me alone. Instead, it swam in and out of my awareness as though I were on that thrice-damned ferry, come from Camlann to Caer Gwent and Degannwy. I could hear voices which my brain first understood and then didn't, and there was a good deal too much motion. When I

155

opened my eyes, I could see nothing.

But after what seemed a long time, the jolting stopped, was succeeded by a few jerks, and then I felt hands on my shoulders dragging me up. The dark was replaced by light, and I found myself standing, or sagging rather, between two men and staring stupidly at the horse they had just lifted me from. Someone behind me said, 'Take him inside,' and I was dragged off to a dimly-seen little hovel and dropped on a mattress. Then, thank God, everything was still and I could lie down and be quiet, closing my eyes so that my head hurt less.

After a little while longer, someone else came and looked at my head, and then began to give me a drink of water. I was thirsty and drank greedily, if slowly, until the face of the woman who was holding the cup registered somewhere. Eivlin. Yes.

And then I realiized that she had lied to me and betrayed me into some trap of Medraut's making. Of course, I told myself dully, you were a fool to believe her so quickly, a cursed fool to walk right into Medraut's house. You should have known that Medraut would have no intention of leaving you free to warn Gwalchmai. And yet, that Eivlin should . . . I stopped drinking and turned my head away from her.

She realized what I meant and said, 'Oh Rhys, I am sorry, I am sorry. I did not know that they would hurt you. Please, have something more to drink. It will make you feel better.'

But I wanted nothing from her, least of all her sympathy, and I gritted my teeth and did not look at her. After a while she went away.

It could not have been very much later when someone came over and dragged me up into a sitting position, and I found myself looking at Medraut ap Lot.

When he saw my eyes focus, he drew his hand away from my shoulder and smiled. 'So you are again to be numbered among the enemy,' he said lightly. 'Good. Mother has a use for you which I would like to see you serving.'

'Go away,' I moaned hopefully. I did not feel up to dealing with him.

He only laughed. 'Not feeling well? You'll recover.' Then his fine eyes narrowed, and he said savagely, 'I am glad it worked this way, whatever Mother says. I do not like having to be gracious to insolent servants.'

'And I don't like being smiled at by treacherous schemers,' I replied.

But he only smiled again. 'That conclusion is recent, I think. You thought me a fine nobleman until this morning. Admit it.'

'I thought so, until I started comparing you to your brother, yes,' I said.

That did hit him. He slapped me hard, and my head hit the wall. I promptly fainted again. After a few minutes I came groggily to myself, and Medraut was still there. I felt very ill, and leaned against the wall, wishing he would vanish.

'My brother is a fool,' hissed Medraut, 'and a traitor to the Queen our mother. He had the chance to win power offered him, by her, and he chose Arthur instead. He sold us all, scorned us, and ran away. He was not worthy of the honour she gave him. He is a fool, a deceiving, careless . . .' he stopped and stood abruptly. I looked up at him unenthusiastically and restrained myself from the comment I had sitting on my tongue.

'You, now,' Medraut went on in a different tone, smiling his pleasant, open smile, 'you are fortunate. Mother wishes to speak to you. I will tell her that you are recovered well enough to answer, and she will honour this place with the glory of her presence.'

I wished she would honour some other spot, but Medraut strode off, calling some order to another man who was sitting by a door. I looked about me for the first time. The place shortly to be glorified appeared to be one of those huts which shepherds use when their flocks are in the summer pasturage. Four walls of mud and wattle, a plain dirt floor with a fire pit in the centre and, for a bed, the heap of bracken I was sitting on. One of Lot's warriors sat on a three-legged stool by the door, watching me impassively.

'Do you speak British?' I asked him, without much hope. '*Loquerisne Latine?*' He simply stared. I groaned and lay down again.

My head throbbed, I still felt nauseous and generally confused. And Morgawse of Orcade was going to come and ask me questions. I could think of nothing to do except to pray for the grace to answer her fitly, and not yield; and so that much I did. As I prayed, I found myself wondering whether I could have avoided this. Well, there was Rhuawn. He was not a bad man. I knew that, in ordinary circumstances, he was as generous and even-tempered a warrior as any living. If I had spoken to him more gently, or at least spoken privately, he might very well have listened to me. Unless . . . I wondered again at Medraut's harping. Sorcery? Well, if so, it had not worked on me, and so should not have worked on Rhuawn.

But even if Rhuawn had supported Medraut, I began to think that I should have kept silent. Pretended to agree, and then gone and warned my lord when I knew the whole plot. More efficient and far less risky. If I'd used a little discretion, a little common sense! And common sense had always been supposed a strong point of mine. I groaned again, and resolved to be more careful in the future. If I had a future. Which was by no means certain.

Choices are strange things. Not three months before I had chosen to fight, actively, for the Light. I had asked a visiting stranger to take me to Camlann. And now here I lay waiting to be questioned, or God alone knew what, by a notorious witch, and wondering whether I would see another morning. The thought shook me. Never again to see the faces of my family, never again the warm hearth fire with my own place waiting there, or the fields white with the harvest or the oxen drawing the plough or the skylarks flying. To die in a strange land, with no one knowing of it.

But then, I had made the choice, and made it honestly, so it was no use thinking what might have happened. And everyone has to die some time, and it is good enough to die for the Light, keeping one's faith with a good man. Things might have been otherwise, I might have held my tongue with Medraut – but I hadn't, and, being who I am, I wasn't sure I could have. So I thrust all distractions from my mind and started praying again.

When I heard hoof beats outside, I pushed myself up to a sitting position and crossed myself, then waited. It had grown dark in the room, and I realized that it must be night outside, though whether it was the night of the same day that I was hit on the head I was not sure.

Medraut entered the room first, holding a lantern with a horn shield for the flame. He barely glanced at me, and raised the lantern high, standing aside from the door.

Morgawse entered the room like a flood. She wore a long, dark travelling cloak over her crimson gown, and to my still addled eyes it looked as though she trailed in the whole night after her. She stood very still inside the door, looking down at me. She was smiling a little, but her eyes froze my heart's blood. I braced myself and stared back.

'Light the fire,' she ordered, without moving her gaze.

I saw Eivlin creep from behind her back and slip to the fire, fumble about with the tinder. It made me sick to look at her, and I looked hard. She was very pale, and carefully avoided turning her eyes towards me.

The tinder caught, and a little more light flared up, making Eivlin's hair glow like ripe wheat fields in the wind. The shadows leapt, then steadied in the lamplight as the fire began to bite into the wood. Morgawse unclasped the silver brooch of her travelling cloak and let it fall from her shoulders. Medraut caught it and handed it to the guard, with a short order in Irish. The guard bowed slightly and left. The Queen looked neither at him, nor at Medraut, but only gestured slightly with her right hand. Medraut glanced about, and hung the lantern from the thatched roof, then picked up the three-legged stool the guard had used and moved it closer to the fire. He stepped over to me, caught my left arm and dragged me to my feet. My head swam, and I felt a wave of sickness, but I stumbled over to where Medraut pulled me, and flopped down on the stool, facing the Queen.

She crossed her arms. They were bare, free of her rich, dark crimson gown, and looked very white and strong. I would almost rather have looked at her eyes than her arms, but I tried to stare straight in front of myself and pay her no attention. Eivlin, I noticed from the corner of my eye, had crept back against the wall and huddled there, pale and dark-eyed and miserable.

'S-s-o-o,' said Morgawse at last, her voice very soft and cold. 'You do not believe that my son Gwalchmai is mad.'

I had not expected to hear that tale again. I shut my mouth more firmly and glared into space.

'Well, perhaps you are right.' The Queen's dress rustled as she moved. 'Now, perhaps, you are right. But tomorrow you may be wrong.'

I didn't like the sound of it. Did she plan to drive Gwalch-mai mad? Could she? He had said that she had tried to kill him by sorcery. Plainly enough, that attempt had failed. Perhaps she would simply fail again.

But perhaps she would not.

'Look at me, slave,' said Morgawse. I looked. Her eyes were even colder and blacker than I remembered, and I felt as though I were trying to swim at mid-winter. But I met them. I would not be afraid; especially, I would not let my betrayer Eivlin see how much afraid I was.

'You are going to help in the treatment Medraut will give my son for his madness,' Morgawse stated. .

I set my teeth. 'Lady, I will not.'

'Whether or not you will, by your help it is going to be done, and done tomorrow. Living or dead, you are going to help.'

I could feel my heart pounding very hard, and I felt sick again, but this time not from the blow on my head. I swallowed several times. I once heard a story about a man who fell into the hands of witches, but managed to slip away from them. Some time later he dreamed that they came, cut his throat and tore out his heart, draining away his blood and sealing the wound with a sponge. He dreamed that then they commanded him to do dreadful things, robbing the graves and churchyards, and that these things he did. He woke next morning in his own bed, shaking, and was glad it was only a dream, glad to travel on his way – and then, when he stopped at a spring to drink, a sponge fell from his throat and he fell over dead, 'with no more blood in him than a bled duck'. My sister Morfudd had told the story with relish, and I had laughed, but I could not imagine at what. Looking at Morgawse's eyes, I was certain that she could do, if not that, then something of the kind. Living or dead, she said, living or dead I would help her in whatever she and Medraut plotted against Gwalch-mai. Something in me, the very fabric of my flesh and blood, began to shriek at me to assent to whatever she asked. If I would betray my lord, living or dead, surely it was better to do it living? Then at least I might be of some help afterwards. Then she would not tear my heart out with that strong white hand, so that afterwards I fell over dead like that other . . .

'Lady,' I said, 'whatever you can compel my body to do, I will not help you in any scheme of yours. And don't think that you can terrify me into obeying you, for I know that, for all your sorcery, you cannot damn my soul any more than you can save your own.' And I put my head back and looked her in the eyes.

To my surprise, my words struck her. Her face flushed a very little, and her smile slipped only slightly, but some quaver seemed to pass behind her eyes, a horrible ravaging loneliness and a sick desire. She took a quick stride closer to me, and caught my hair, dragged my head back and stooped until her face was bare inches from mine.

'Bravely spoken!' her voice was almost a hiss. 'Keep your soul, then; but I will have your mind and your body for my purposes. And those I can have, slave, I can.' She thrust me violently away and snapped upright again. The thrust pushed me off the stool, and I scorched my leg in the fire before I managed to get onto my hands and knees and crawl away. Morgawse, Medraut and Eivlin watched me thrash about. The first two were scornful, almost amused, but a glance at Eivlin showed me that she sat against the wall with her knees drawn up, biting her lips and looking utterly wretched. I wondered what she was thinking.

I sat back on my heels, deciding that I was safer on the ground, and managed to look back at Morgawse. She still made my skin crawl with a black horror, but I no longer felt so afraid of her. I knew that her power was limited. More than that, I knew suddenly that I could die, and still keep the faith: and this knowledge was victory.

But her face was impassive again, deathly white except for those terrible eyes. She began speaking in her normal soft voice: 'You will go back to Degannwy tomorrow morning, and you will ask your lord to come and speak with you, away from the stronghold. You will bring him here, and say that there is something he must see here; and you will advise him to tie his horse securely outside. When you have him in this hovel, ask him for his sword. Tell him that you wish to swear on it. When he has given it to you, freely, you will throw it out the door as hard and as far as you are able, and you will then block the doorway if he tries to go out after it. Then Medraut and Rhuawn will come and bind him, and your part is done.'

161

'I couldn't do that, even if I were willing,' I said. 'Gwalchmai's sword is an otherworldly weapon, and they all say that it burns the hand of anyone else who tries to draw it. It even has some otherworldly name.'

'Its name is Caledfwlch,' Medraut broke in. 'May it soon be shattered! But it will not burn the hand that draws it when it is given freely. *You* will do as you are commanded.'

'Be silent,' Morgawse told him, very softly and sweetly. Medraut stopped as sharply as a fox when it hears a hound, and slunk back in silence towards the wall. I realized that he was terrified of the Queen, and felt bolder myself.

'It is no matter whether or not the sword burns my hand,' I told Morgawse. 'I will not help you. Try Rhuawn – but you can't be too sure of him, or you wouldn't be asking me. Is it that you have to keep him deluded? Well, try your sorceries on me, if you think they will work. But I say this, that I am a Christian man from a Christian kingdom, the servant of a good lord, of a great Emperor, and of the most high God: and I will not grovel to the mere Queen of Orcade.'

Medraut gave a slight jerk, as though about to rush forward and strike me, but he checked himself and looked at Morgawse. She merely smiled once more. 'Again, fine words. But say what you will, for all of your lords and gods I may do what I will with you now, and I will that these things be done, and I will make you do them. Medraut!' She languidly raised one arm and extended a forefinger, a thin, fine, strong finger like Gwalchmai's.

Medraut was only too ready. He rushed forward, grabbed me, set me back on the stool and began to tie my arms behind me. I looked at Eivlin out of the corner of my eye. She was huddled by the door, her hand pressed against her mouth, her blue eyes wide with misery. 'I didn't know they would hurt you,' she had said that afternoon. For the first time, my anger with her lapsed. She certainly wasn't pleased with the results of her treachery. Could I believe that she had not been lying to me all along, as Medraut had, but that she had merely obeyed her lady's orders without questioning them, because of her terror? My eyes had been sliding more and more fully upon her, and they met hers directly. She put her hand down and stared, stricken, her lips moving faintly. I looked away quickly. But I could believe that she had been merely a tool, frightened and ig-

162

norant. It was some comfort to know that such a person as Eivlin existed, and that she was not just a performance intended to deceive. And yet, she was still a tool.

And Morgawse wanted to make me a tool for betraying Gwalchmai, as Eivlin had betrayed me. Medraut finished with my hands and tied my legs to the legs of the stool. I set my teeth and waited.

Morgawse unfastened the gold bands that held her hair, and it fell over her shoulders and down her back. She ran her fingers through it, tossed her head. Very black, her hair looked.

'Pretty,' I commented, trying to ease my terror – and annoy Medraut – by being insolent. 'Do you pull out the grey hairs every morning?'

She did not trouble herself to reply, but spread her hands and chanted something to begin the rite.

I have never been able to tell anyone exactly what happened in the next few hours. It is not that it was so painful or so disgusting as to be unspeakable – it hurt to some extent, and was unpleasant, but no more than some sicknesses. Nor is it even that I found it shameful and revolting – though, God knows, I did, and still feel hot when I think of it. But my memory of it is blurred and, to tell the truth, I have never tried very hard to remember, since such things do no good to anyone, neither the sufferer, nor the hearer, nor, in fact, the performer. I fought Morgawse. She sang, and threw things on the fire, and made patterns, and tried to glare me into submission with her eyes. I set my teeth, knotted my fingers together behind my back, and fought her harder. She went on with the sorceries. I felt as I had in my dream, as though I were struggling in a black ocean, a numbingly cold force that drove down on me or tried to drag me under. I thought of my family and our farm, picturing them down to the cattle in the barn and the swallows in the thatch. I thought of Camlann. I thought a good deal of Gwalchmai, whom I could not betray. I thought of all of them at once, holding them like the words of a prayer: everything I knew of light and order and joy and love; and I looked back at Morgawse with my teeth set, and did not give in.

But she went on with it, on and on, and I began to feel that I was suffocating, and had to gasp for breath. My mind grew blurred about the edges, chilled. I twisted my fingers in the ropes around my hands, feeling my palms slick with sweat. The dim little hut swam in my eyes, and the fire blurred the way it does if you watch when you're half asleep. It all seemed unimportant and remote. I had trouble remembering names – who was the Emperor? my brother? my lord? I felt a great way away from all of it, and my life seemed the merest hair-line distinction from my death. Almost it seemed as though I could step out of that dim hut in Gwynedd into a whole bright and lovely universe, the Kingdom of Summer from Gwalchmai's song. I felt as though, if I looked, the wooden walls would burst into leaf, and the birds of Rhiannon begin to sing. But that feeling I fought as well. It was necessary (why?) that I resist, for someone (who?) would be hurt if I didn't. My head drooped; I raised it again and looked at Morgawse. Her eyes beat at me like waves beating against a cliff. A crumbling cliff. But her face was dripping with sweat, her hair wild and dishevelled. She held a long dagger with both hands, and the blade was smeared with blood. It was my blood, from some while before, but I looked at it indifferently. Nothing mattered. Only to hold . . . on . . .

'You will set the trap for him,' she said, for the thou-sandth time, 'and then, then, finally we will be revenged on him, Medraut and I. And when his mind has snapped we will give him back to Rhuawn, who will take him to Arthur. And Medraut will go too, very loving and con-cerned. And then! Rhuawn is ours in some measures, Gwalchmai will be a cruder sort of tool, and there will be others. Medraut will bring them. Just as others will join Maelgwn in his secret alliance, and wait until the Family is at war with itself. Then will the shield-wall be broken and the gate of the stronghold be battered down; then Arthur will die.'

She stood, radiant of darkness, horribly beautiful and appallingly certain. But nothing she said seemed to mean much beyond the confines of that hut. I stared at her and was unable to think or feel anything at all.

She began to smile, triumphantly, and raised the dagger. The walls flickered like a candle in the wind. I drove my heels against the floor and stared numbly back. Morgawse seemed to brush the ceiling, a black wave cresting and about to break.

'Medraut!' said the Queen. 'Now!' I leaned back, scarcely able to see her. 'Medraut!' The tide ebbed a little. Dimly, I was aware that Morgawse was glancing about. I slumped on the stool. 'Medraut! Where are you?' The Queen lowered her arm, only the dagger blade flashing as it moved. Then she turned away, crossed to the door, and left. I could not even think that she had gone to look for him. I could not think. The world before me was all dark, but I felt as though that other world lay under and around. I looked at nothing, waiting to see it flower around me.

The door opened again, but it was not Morgawse. It was Eivlin; somehow, even in the dimness, I recognized her. She darted across the hut, dropped to her knees behind me, and the next instant I felt her hard, desperate strokes against the ropes. I went on looking at the wall. I could neither understand nor care about what was happening – and yet I remember it very precisely.

She had my arms free, then my right leg. My right foot was asleep, and I curled my toes until they tingled painfully. The half-sensed music in the air seemed to grow dimmer, fading away. I shook my head.

The ropes holding my left leg gave, and Eivlin jumped to her feet, grabbed my right arm and pulled at me. I stood, wavering, beginning to wonder what was happening. Eivlin stooped and picked up something she had set down when she cut the ropes. It was a sword. She drew my right arm over her shoulder and half-dragged me over to the door and out of it. The moon was shining down on the threshold, and the night air was chill and damp. I stopped, looking at the sweet light.

'Come on!' hissed Eivlin, and dragged on my arm furiously. I began to stumble forward again. A little distance from the hovel a small pony was tied. There must have been horses, something told me, and there should have been a guard watching them; but there was only the one shaggy mountain pony. Eivlin rapidly untied its reins and caught the bridle.

'Come on!' she hissed again. 'Get on.'

Still not quite sure what was happening to me, I tried to mount, became dizzy, and had to stand leaning against the pony's side, pressing my hand over my eyes to clear them.

The little beast flicked its ears back and looked pleased, and I began to laugh. Eivlin exclaimed angrily in Irish and tried to pull me into the saddle by force, and, eventually, with her help, I managed to scramble up. Eivlin took the bridle, looped the reins under her arms, glanced hurriedly back over her shoulder – and froze. I looked back too, and saw Morgawse standing in front of the hut.

Something stirred in me, and I leaned dizzily from the pony, seizing the sword from Eivlin's motionless right hand. Eivlin shrank against the pony's side.

Morgawse began walking towards us, slowly.

I lifted the sword as though it were a cleaver, noticing for the first time that it was Medraut's. I would fight, I thought – and then noticed that I was not tied hand and foot this time. I grabbed Eivlin's hair and drove my heels into the pony's sides. He snorted, shied so that I nearly fell off, and started away. Eivlin was dragged along, abruptly coming to herself and staggering up against the pony, shivering like a scared rabbit.

'You will die!' Morgawse screamed from behind us. 'Both of you. You, vixen, you will die before the evening of this coming day. And he will die too, this lover of yours, soon enough!'

I kicked the pony into a trot, glancing back. Morgawse was not following us, only shouting, 'Do you think you can return to Degannwy? Maelgwn's men will keep you for me.' Her voice rose, climbing into a shriek of rage. 'Go, by all means! You have merely delayed his death, little fool, and caused your own. Go!' Eilvin jerked the pony's bridle and began running, and he started to trot a little faster.

I could feel the little animal warm between my legs, and the smooth-worn leather of saddle and harness. Eivlin's hair was pale in the moonlight. I looked up. The moon was softly blurred, a half-moon of spring, like a yellow apple, and the night sky was deep and soft, hazed with a little mist. The mountains lay about, silent black bulks, with only a few of the far peaks still ashimmer with the last snows. Over the smell of horse and leather I could catch the scent of wet grass, and the air told me that it wasn't long before dawn. And something in me leapt into heaven like a skylark as I realized that, contrary to all expectation and probability, I was actually alive and in possession of my own senses, headache and all. I wanted to sing, but the only song I could think of was Gwalchmai's song about the Otherworld, mixed up with hymns from home in a ludicrous fashion because I couldn't remember the words to it. It made me laugh, and once I began laughing, I couldn't stop. Eivlin looked at me sharply, her eyes gleaming in the dim light, and I laughed harder, which gave me shooting pains in my head.

'It is no matter,' I at last managed to gasp to her, by way of reassurance. 'Morgawse has not stolen my wits. Oh Eivlin, Eivlin, what did you do with Medraut? And what about the guard?'

'There is nothing to laugh at!' She was sharp and unhappy. 'Medraut went to see why I was so long in bringing wood for the fire, and I hit him on the head with a piece of firewood: I do not know whether he is alive or dead. As for Ronan, the guard, I first of all told him that my lady wished him to take the horses back to Degannwy and return at sunrise, but that he must leave one horse. Ach, I couldn't even think of what to say what the one horse was for – but he didn't ask, only left at once. He was unhappy to be there at all. Then I went back to the hut and waited behind the door until my lady came out, and I hit her on the head too, but I couldn't hit hard, because I was afraid of her.'

'Two horses, you should have said, and we could have ridden off like rulers of the world. Eivlin, you are the signet-ring on the hand of Daring, you adorn the earth as the moon adorns the night...' I wanted to quote more songs to her, but she only snapped, 'Enough of that. We must be far, far away from here by morning.'

I fumbled for the pony's reins, realized that Eivlin had them, and looped my hands in its mane instead. What with the headache, the sorcery and the escape, I was light-headed enough to want to try galloping. With Eivlin up on the saddle. As though the pony could gallop with both of us. 'Go where?' I asked, restraining myself.

'Caer Segeint! Caer Legion! Anywhere! But we must find the main road first, and then you must ride away as fast as you can.'

I was going to ask, 'And what about you?', when something else hit me and I asked, 'But what about my lord?'

She stopped, and the pony took another step, then halted,

tossing its head in disgust. Eivlin stared up at me. 'Your
lord? It isn't his life I'm selling my own to save. Let your
lord find his own way of escape.'

I frowned at her. 'I was in danger because I would not
betray Gwalchmai. How can I run off and abandon him to
Morgawse?'

'Och, Rhys, Morgawse cannot still have the same plan, if
you are gone, and Medraut is dead.'

'We don't know that Medraut is dead. I'd stake my head
he isn't. And they still have Rhuawn.'

'My lady has said that your lord no longer trusts Rhuawn
as he did. Come, he's in no more danger than you yourself,
and what's a lord? You can find plenty another man to
serve, or you can go back to your clan. Didn't you hear my
lady? We cannot go back to Degannwy. Maelgwn's guards
would not let us through the gate.'

My better sense told me that she was right about
Degannwy, though I felt ready to fight it single-handed,
and me too sick to walk far. But I knew one thing. 'I will not
let Morgawse do as she pleases with Gwalchmai. He must
be warned.'

'Man, man, you are mad! Do you throw away our lives
for this warrior, this man who only uses your service?'

'He is my lord, and I serve him because I chose to; and he
is worth my loyalty. I like Gwalchmai. I would even call
him my friend, if a lord can be called a friend. He must be
warned. And besides, I am his servant. If I flee when he
needs my service, where is my own good faith?'

Eivlin was shaking her head. 'Not so, not so. Rhys, my
lady is most terribly powerful. We must get very far away.
That is, you must, for I know that my lady will kill me by a
curse, before the evening of this coming day, just as she
said. By the sun, by the earth and the sky and the sea, by
your own god, Rhys, don't let it be that I die for nothing. If
we go back to Degannwy, you will die, he will not be
warned, and Morgawse will kill me when I have accomplished nothing. Let us hurry. Come, we must reach the
road before it is light. Morgawse will surely send Lot's men
after us, secretly.' She tugged on the bridle again, and the
pony moved forward.

I again fumbled for the rein, wanting to stop the animal.
'Eivlin, my lord must be warned. What do you mean,

Morgawse will kill you by a curse? She can't do that. We must get a message to my lord...' I stopped suddenly, remembering what I had seen – had it only been that morning?

Eivlin halted again, and the pony jerked impatiently on the bridle. 'But I will die!' she said, angrily and tearfully. 'And you will die too, and all for this warrior who cannot look after himself! But if we must...'

'We don't have to,' I said. 'Gwalchmai has a place he looks for messages sent to him from the Emperor. We can leave a message there. It is on the way to the main road.'

Eivlin looked at me, astonished, then hopeful. She began walking again, in silence.

The world was a pre-dawn grey when we reached the forked oak, and the first birds were beginning to give experimental chirrups. The exhilaration of the escape had worn off, and my head hurt a great deal, so much so that I felt sick. I was tired, too, tired enough to want to collapse under a tree and not get up for a week. I looked at the oak. I had told Eivlin to leave a sprig of pine by the track where we turned off. I thought that Gwalchmai had said pine for an urgent message. Yes, pine for an urgent message, holly for an ordinary one.

'The place is the hollow where that big branch joins the main trunk,' I told Eivlin. She dropped the reins and skipped over to the tree, then looked up it. 'Can you climb?' I asked hopefully.

She looked at me as though I had said, 'Can you fly?' Gwalchmai had said there weren't many trees in the islands, and what trees there were, I supposed, would be climbed by boys more than by girls. I wearily struggled off the pony and staggered over to the tree. I didn't know whether I could climb it. I could try.

'What will you write your message on?' asked Eivlin.

'Write?' I said, and suddenly I realized that I didn't know how to leave a message. 'I can't write,' I exclaimed.

'Och, indeed! He cannot write, but has come here out of the way to leave a message! I thought all Britons could write, all that speak Latin.'

'Maybe most townsmen can, but I'm a farmer,' I said. 'Where would I learn to write? Can you write?'

She only snorted. I gathered that writing was uncommon

169

in the Ynysoedd Erch.

I stared at the oak and dredged my aching head for ideas. I had never really wanted to write before, but I wanted it then. But it was no use wishing. A pine-cone meant that Gwalchmai's letter had been received; what would mean 'Beware of Rhuawn. Medraut and Morgawse tried to kill me, and will try to drive you mad"?

Gwalchmai would have to know that the message was from me; that meant I must leave something of mine. The brooch. He would remember that. I fumblingly unclasped it and balanced it in my palm. Medraut and Morgawse were the real danger; what did I have of theirs? Eivlin still had the sword.

'Eivlin, give me Medraut's sword.' She hesitated, looking at me questioningly, and I said, 'I don't know how to use it properly, and nor do you, so it's no use to us.'

'It's worth money. You'll need that.'

'This is worth more.' Eivlin reluctantly handed me the sword. I weighed the hilt of it. It was indeed a good sword, for as much as I knew about swords – which, after my time in Camlann, amounted to something. The blade was narrow, of fine-tempered steel. I looked at it, and at the brooch, then slid the sword blade over one side of the ring of the brooch, under the central pin, and over the other half of the ring. It bent the brooch a little, but I hoped I made my meaning evident. Now, how to warn him of Rhuawn? I felt about my belt, but I had nothing of Rhuawn's. Rhuawn was Dumnonian. Was there any way I could use something specifically Dumnonian? No, and I was Dumnonian too. Not that, then.

I stood, my feet growing wet from the dew, cold and sick and sleepy, trying to drag an answer out of a murky mind. The birds sang more loudly. The pony stamped.

Rhuawn was a member of the Family; the Family was ... was ...

Members of the Family sometimes wore a sprig of hawthorn through their cloak pins, to remind themselves of Baddon, where the hawthorn had bloomed when they drove back the Saxons. As plainly as if he stood there, I remembered Bedwyr's servant Amren telling me the tale of the hawthorn at Baddon. I looked around.

'Eivlin,' I said, 'I need a sprig of hawthorn.' She stared.

'It's part of the message.'

'I will bring it, then. You put the rest of your ... message in the place.'

'Give me a leg up, then. I do not think I can climb it.'

With some struggle and a great deal of dizziness, I managed to clamber into the fork of the tree, and Eivlin went off to find the hawthorn. I leant back against one branch to rest a minute.

'Rhys. Rhys. Wake up.' I opened my eyes and found that the east was touched with the palest rose. Eivlin stood under the oak with a branch of flowering hawthorn, white in her arms. She looked lovely as a day in spring. I muttered something, and she handed me the hawthorn. I twined it about the hilt of the sword and put the whole arrangement in the hollow of the branch. The sword stuck out a little, so I smeared some of the old leaves over it so that it would not shine, and jumped down. I collapsed when I hit the ground, and Eivlin helped me up.

'I need to sleep,' I told her.

'Indeed, if you fall asleep while I'm down to the end of the meadow and back, you do. But we must reach the main road first.' She helped me back onto the pony, and we continued on.

When we reached the main road it was nearly midmorning, and the sun had dried the dew. We found a hard bank and led the pony across it and into a brake, hidden from the road. Eivlin took some bracken and swept the bank, unnecessarily, I thought, so that anyone following would not be able to tell that we had left the road. She seemed certain that Morgawse would send some of Lot's warriors after us. I dragged myself off the pony and lay down. My head was throbbing but, for all my weariness, I no longer felt sleepy. Eivlin came back from sweeping and lay down beside me.

'We must not rest long,' she whispered. 'We must be away this afternoon. And do wake up before evening. Rhys, I want to talk to you before I die.'

'You're not going to die,' I said irritably. 'Why should you die?'

'My lady will send a demon to kill me,' she said simply. 'Ach, I know you will tell me that she tried to kill your lord and failed. Well, but your lord, perhaps, can fight demons.

They say his sword is magical. I cannot fight so. I was cursed before ever I was born, from my father's deed I was cursed.'

'You're not going to die,' I repeated. 'Morgawse is not the only power in this great world. Eivlin, if you are so sure you are going to die, why did you save me in the first place? Your lady is just as sure to kill me!'

'It was my fault you were in danger,' she said, in a very small voice. 'My lady told me to bring you to Medraut's house, and to tell you that your lord was there. I knew that she meant you no good, and yet I brought you there, and told you that, and then...' Her breath caught on itself. 'She wished to ... do dreadful ... things. And I was to help her. And when she was beginning, I said to myself, "Eivlin, here is the one man who has taken no notice of your curse. Here is a man, no warrior, but a servant like yourself, who has helped you freely, who can turn a phrase just so, and has just such a smile: and because of you, and his trusting you, he will be dead and damned."'

'But she couldn't damn me,' I broke in. 'Kill she can, but the other is beyond her.'

Eivlin shrugged a little: I felt the movement through the bracken. 'Well, I knew that she would kill you horribly. And I could not endure it. So I went and told Ronan to take the horses home, and I hit Medraut on the head and cut you loose. It is better to die honestly, at least. And you keep saying that you are a Christian and have your own magic, so hers cannot hurt you; I think you will escape her.'

I turned my head and looked full at her. There were tears on her cheeks, runnelling the smudges on her face. Her fair hair was limp, dirty and dishevelled. I thought her more beautiful than any woman on earth.

'You won't die,' I said, and hauled myself up on one elbow. 'As God in Heaven is just, you will not die. Believe me...' I put out my hand clumsily to touch her shoulder, just to comfort her, and suddenly she came into my arms and began to cry. I held her, and she put her head down on my shoulder and sobbed loudly while I stroked her hair and made soothing noises. For all the danger and weariness, for all my aches and sickness, that was one of the fullest moments of my life.

Ten

Eivlin fell asleep in my arms, still crying, and I was asleep very shortly afterwards. I had wanted to stay awake and just hold her for a while, but it was a matter of minutes before I was snoring. When I woke up the late afternoon sun was lying heavy on the brake and the road beyond it, and Eivlin was not beside me. I sat up and looked around. Neither Eivlin nor the pony were there. I had a moment of sick terror, thinking that Morgawse had sent a demon and that Eivlin was gone – but then I tried to imagine what a demon would do with the pony, and the bad minute passed.

I stood up carefully. My head still hurt, but not as badly. Gingerly, I fingered the back of my skull – there was one big lump, caked over with dried blood, which was exquisitely agonizing when I touched it. That must be the result of Medraut's blow, if Medraut had indeed been the one who hit me. Above it was a smaller lump, doubtless from hitting the floor after Rhuawn hit me. My sister Morfudd always used to say that I had a thick skull. Well, with such treatment I needed it. I wondered how Medraut's head felt.

There came a crackling noise in the bushes. I set my hand quickly to my knife and backed away out of sight. But it was Eivlin, leading the pony. I sighed with relief and stepped back into the open.

'You frightened me, when I woke and found you gone,' I told her.

'Did I indeed?' She brushed a strand of hair out of her eyes, smiling. She had washed her face and carefully straightened her hair, and had stuck a wild rose in the clasp of her dress. Very pretty she looked. 'I only wanted to find some water for the pony.'

'For us too, I hope.'

'Oh, to be sure. There is a stream just down the hill. Come, I can wash your head.'

I took a couple of hesitant steps forward, and she waited, holding out her hand. I took her hand, feeling at once embarrassed and very pleased, and we strolled down to the stream, leaving the pony tethered to a bush.

'You look very pretty,' I told Eivlin, remembering how my sister liked to have this commented upon.

'Do I?' she asked, in the tone that means 'So! You noticed.'

'Truly,' I responded. Eivlin smiled smugly and checked the rose to see if it was falling off.

The stream was fresh from the mountains, fast running over a rocky bed, and cold to make your teeth ache. After I drank from it Eivlin washed my head, which hurt and made me dizzy again, though she was gentle. When she finished, we sat a few minutes looking at the stream and listening to it gurgle.

Eivlin sighed and leaned against me. 'It is a fine day to die on,' she said softly. 'I could almost be glad. I am glad: I am away from her, at last, and I am with you, and it is a fine, honest way to die.'

'You're not still dreaming about that!' I said, irritated. 'I have told you, you're not going to die.'

She only laid her head on my shoulder and tickled the palm of my hand. I became a little more irritated.

'You won't die,' I repeated. 'Why do you think you should die?'

'My lady said I would.' She sat up straight again. I wished she hadn't.

'Well, your lady said I would die, too, but you don't seem to think I will.'

'You! Well, but you fought off her spells and her witch-craft for hours, right in her very presence. She thought it would be easy to govern you; she thought it would all be done in half an hour, but at the end she was so tired she could not even slay us both when she saw us escaping.'

'Maybe that means her spells aren't all that you think they are.'

'Not so! Rhys, I have seen her...' She stopped, then went on more quietly, 'And besides, I am cursed from my birth, and I have been her servant. For her to kill me is nothing, a snap of her fingers. And I do not have any of my own magic to protect me, as you have magic.'

I wondered what she meant for a moment, then understood. 'If you mean Christ, you can be protected too, if you believe. Here, we can stop at the first monastery or hermitage we come to, and you can be baptized, if that will stop your talk of dying.'

'What? What's that?'

'It's a . . .' I remembered my previous disastrous explanations of another sacrament. 'It's a kind of magic to free someone from past curses.'

Eivlin looked dubious. 'Is it a complicated spell? Can't you do it? Is there much blood?'

'I could do it, I suppose. I think it's allowed. But it's better if a priest does it.'

'One of your Christian druids?'

'No, a priest is . . . never mind. But there's no blood at all. All that is necessary is that you believe in Christ – I told you about him, didn't I – and they pour water on your head.'

'Where's the magic, then?'

'It's not exactly a spell, it's a . . . well, the water means that the curse is washed away. I had it done to me when I was a baby. My mother says I howled, but I can't remember it, of course, though I've seen it done for my cousins.'

Eivlin sighed and brushed a strand of hair away from her face. 'I do not see how it would help against my lady. But if you think it is a strong magic, perhaps it may.'

I thought of Morgawse, and for all my well-learned catechism I wondered whether Eivlin was right to be afraid. Sacraments are not magic spells, and, whatever they may mean to her spiritual state, could I be sure anything would alter the effect of Morgawse's very strong earthly magic? But firmly I told Eivlin, 'It's a magic against Morgawse. You won't die.'

Eivlin looked at me steadily, then sighed and stood up, brushing off her skirt. 'Ai, perhaps. But we must be gone, then, to find one of your priests, because it is late in the day.'

Reluctantly, I too stood up, and we went back to where we had left the pony. He was busily consuming every blade of grass within range, just as though he had not grazed most of the day.

'Your turn to ride,' I told Eivlin. 'I can walk.'

'"I can walk", says the man, and he with a lump on his head as big as my fist! Indeed, you will not walk; you will ride and try to get better.'

I protested, but not very convincingly. My head did ache, and the short walk up the hill had started it throbbing. The advantage of my sickness was that I didn't notice how hungry I was, although the last meal I had eaten was breakfast, the day before. But I wondered how Eivlin felt, and if she had had any supper. She was doing all the walking, and I could not think it good for her.

We started off down the road westward. 'We will go to Caer Segeint,' Eivlin said firmly. 'It is a big town, and a port, as I well know, having spent the night there when we first arrived in Gwynedd. If my lady has sent messages there, it is a good place to avoid messengers, and most of the men there spend their lives doing nothing else.'

I assented to the plan, though I would have preferred to go to Caer Legion, which I knew. But I could see Eivlin's point, and it was a good one. 'And after we reach Caer Segeint, what?' I asked.

She was quiet a moment. 'Perhaps we could sell the pony and take a boat down the coast?'

I groaned inwardly. 'How much would it cost?'

'What kind of boat are you used to using? For myself, I know a bit about curraghs, but that is all.'

'It is better than I can do. I was in a boat once in my life, crossing from Dumnonia to Caer Gwent, and I had no liking for it then. We'd have to hire a boatman as well as a boat, and, for myself, I know I have no way to afford it.'

'You have only once been in a boat? How . . .'

'I am not an islander. My family's holding is near the Mor Hafren, and the only water we need to cross is a river. I think we should take the pony on down the coast into Dyfed, and claim protection there in the Emperor's name. Dyfed isn't too friendly with Gwynedd, and they've fought invaders from Erin enough to hate anyone who speaks Irish – though they'll have to make an exception for you.'

Eivlin shook her head. 'We travel too slowly. The ones my lady has sent after us will certainly catch us if we try to go all the way to Dyfed with only one pony. Do we have enough for a horse?'

I checked my possessions. Three bronze arm-rings, one enamelled; and one gold ring Gwalchmai had given me at Camlann. Then there was my cloak – the weather might be warm enough to sell it. If we made the pony a rope bridle and sold the leather one, and rode bareback, we might have enough to buy one horse. But then we would have nothing to buy food with. I sighed. 'We can travel fast and not eat, or we can have our bread and ale and a slow journey.'

'Even so? Perhaps we can steal a horse.'

'Steal? We will do no such thing.'

'Och, Rhys, we need a horse. Come, if you will you can see that the horse's owner is paid afterwards.'

I didn't like the idea of stealing from some poor farmer, but she might be right. I struggled with my conscience a moment, and wondered what my father would say about it. If he were in my position, I decided, he would take the horse.

'Very well, if we pay him back. But don't you think we could avoid anyone Morgawse sent? If the south road's as empty as this one, we'll know someone's coming long before they reach us.'

'Unless Medraut comes.' Eivlin became very serious.

'You do not think he might be badly hurt, then?' I asked hopefully.

She shook her head. 'If he is sick, my lady will find some way to heal him quickly. And he can use sorceries to find us . . .'

It had the sound of truth. 'Then we will have to steal a horse. Or two horses, and leave the pony; and we can hope that they haven't passed us already.'

Eivlin nodded. 'Unless you only need one horse,' she added in an undertone.

'You are not going to die, remember? Come, let's hurry and see what we can find before dark.'

The afternoon was one of those long, slow afternoons of late spring that make one realize the summer is not far off. The mountains were all green, or blue with distance, with no snow to be seen anywhere. When the land to our right fell away we could see the Irish Sea, calm and blue-grey in the sunlight. Eivlin eyed it wistfully. She still preferred the idea of a boat.

It is a strange thing, but for all that we were flying for our lives in a foreign land, tired, hungry, sick in my case and afraid of imminent death in Eivlin's, we were cheerful as a pair of larks. The afternoon was beautiful, and it seemed as though it might well last for ever. We had escaped and were free and in love, so why not be happy? The sight of the sea started Eivlin telling stories about the Ynysoedd Erch, and I responded with tales about my family, and we laughed like a couple of idiots at a fair. The sun slipped down the sky only gradually, slanting into our eyes and lengthening the shadows behind us.

'And so,' Eivlin concluded one story, 'Eoghan fought a great and mighty and terrible fight against Ronan, to make up for the boat race, and he thrashed him thoroughly; for, except for Medraut, he's the finest fighter in Lot's warband.'

'Medraut's really a good fighter, then?'

'By the sun! From the time he first entered the Boys' House for training, he seemed a greyhound among housedogs, or so say all the warriors. And yet ... he does not fight much. Those he wishes to use, he charms, and through them he makes all the other warriors obey him. They are all afraid of him, because he can ruin a man's standing with a few words, and set all the others against anyone he wishes, and then there is the sorcery. Why once, to be sure, he ...'

Eivlin abruptly stopped, and also stopped walking, staring ahead of her.

'He what?' I asked.

'Rhys ...' she said. I looked ahead of us. I could see nothing but the empty road in the evening sun. I wondered if she'd forgotten something and left it in the brake where we slept.

'What's the matter?'

'What's the matter? Don't you see it?' Her stare was fixed, her head back so that the shadows trembled in the hollow of her throat.

I looked again. I could still see only the road. But Eivlin's hand was shaking, and the pony laid its ears back and began to shift its weight uneasily. It snorted.

'There's nothing there,' I said. 'Come on.'

Eivlin made a whimpering noise and took a step back. 'A shadow,' she whispered. 'There's something in the road.'

'There's nothing there. With this sun, all the shadows are behind us.'

'No! A shadow, another. By the green earth!' She spun about, letting go the pony' bridle. The animal sorted and half reared, and I grabbed the reins, tightening my knees. 'Rhys!' Eivlin screamed it. 'It is behind us, too!'

'Eivlin, there's nothing there. Eivlin!' She was not listening. I slid off the pony, seized her arm. 'There's nothing there.'

'My lady's curse. It has found us. Ahhh, it is coming nearer. Rhys, help me!'

I grabbed her shoulders. 'It is only a shadow. She's trying to frighten you.'

She suddenly flung her arms around my neck and pressed her face against my shoulder. 'Don't let them near me! Ai!' Her arms tightened till I could barely breathe, but I held her; and then she went rigid. She flung herself back from me and began to scream. I caught her arms. She tried to tear away from me. Her eyes stared horribly at nothing, so wide that the whites showed all about the blue, and her face was like that of a woman sick with a deadly fever. The pony neighed loudly, reared and jerked away, its eyes rolling. I let go of Eivlin with one hand and tried to grab its reins, but missed, and it bolted off down the road. Eivlin kept on screaming, an awful high rhythmic wailing. Foam flecked the corners of her mouth.

'Merciful, holy Christ!' I cried out loud. 'Eivlin, Eivlin, listen!'

She struggled harder, nearly wrenching free, striking at me with her free hand. It seemed to me that we were struggling in the midst of a choking black cloud, and I felt the same sick dizziness that I had meeting Morgawse's eyes. Eivlin kicked and clawed, and her scream shivered into short shrieks which frightened me even more.

'Eivlin!' I said again, but I knew that nothing I said reached her. A rage swept over me that Morgawse should be able to do this. I managed to grab Eivlin's other hand again. Morgawse had no right, not in Heaven or Earth, no right at all. I dragged Eivlin over to the edge of the road. Whatever I could do, I would.

There was some water in the ditch by the roadside, a shallow puddle from the spring rains. I dragged Eivlin over to it. She wrestled with me. I kicked her feet out from under her and we both went down. She splashed up, gasping and shrieking. I let go one of her arms, picked up some water in my palm, and poured it over Eivlin's head. 'Eivlin,' I said, 'I baptize you in the name of the Father, the Son and the Holy Spirit. And to Hell with you, Morgawse!'

Eivlin let out one long, high shriek and lashed out, hitting me on the side of the head. The world turned red a minute, and I let go of her altogether. She crawled off, collapsed, half lifted herself a few times, only to flop back into the water and lie still, face down.

I stumbled over and turned her right side up so that she could breathe. Her head fell back limply, eyes half-opened and glazed. I felt sick in the marrow of my bones. Shaking again, I realized that I must be sobbing.

I knelt in the puddle and drew her shoulders up onto my knees, resting her head against my arm. I was praying 'Lord God, don't let her be dead!' – over and over again. Very carefully, I set my fingers against the hollow where her jaw joined her throat. Her skin was cold and wet, and for an aeon I seemed to feel nothing . . . and then, very faintly, the pulse beat against my fingertips. I closed my eyes, feeling the course of her life throb slowly again, again, pause, again. Still alive. Thank God.

But she could die any minute. I had to find somewhere where there was warmth, fires and food and people who could care for her. I had to get away from the sunset and the empty road. I looked up the bank, prodded my memory. Yes, it seemed that the pony had bolted west. Good. If he had gone east, he would probably have continued all the way back to Degannwy and his own stall. As it was, he would probably stop and wait for his masters. Ponies are sociable beasts.

I dragged Eivlin's limp form up and pulled her over my shoulders like a sack of flour, then stood up. She was not light. She was also dripping wet and slippery with mud. Well, so was I. If only the pony had not gone too far. I staggered up the bank and onto the road.

By the time I had gone a hundred paces my head was throbbing violently and I felt faint. Clearly, I could not carry her far. Damn Medraut, or whatever that guard's name was; damn him for hitting so hard. But there was nothing for it but to keep on, and pray for strength.

I was lucky. It was not too long before I cam across the pony. He was standing in the middle of the road, trembling, his ears flat against his head. He shied away from me, but did not run. I set Eivlin down and walked over to him. He skittered off, eyeing me. I darted at him, and he shied.' I nearly fell and had to stand still, holding my head. 'Be calm,' I told myself, aloud. Animals are tense and afraid when humans are. I put out my hand and began to talk to the pony soothingly. Eventually the little beast let me take his bridle and pat his neck. He even pricked his ears forward a bit. I led him over to Eivlin, picked her up and piled her on his back. Her hair had come out of its fastening and fallen over her face. I stroked it back before starting on, holding the pony's bridle with one hand and balancing Eivlin on the saddle with the other.

The sun was almost down, though it was still light. Part of me was all rage at Morgawse, but I began to pray, for strength to keep walking, for somewhere to stop, praying mostly that Eivlin would not die. The pony's hooves clopped steadily.

The road faded into a blur just in front of me, a place to put my feet. My headache was nearly blinding. The tired pony was stubborn and nervous. I had to talk to it, both for its sake and for mine.

'Come along,' I said. 'Just a bit further, and we'll find you a place in a nice stall, with lots of grain and some bran mash for being such a good beast. Come along...' The sun sank, but the western sky was still bright. Eivlin looked ghastly in the half light. I wanted to stop and check her pulse, but I was afraid to stop. 'Come along...' I told the pony.

And then there came a swish, a flash and a thud, and a throwing spear was standing upright in the road before us.

I stopped, staring at it blankly. I felt as though I could cry like a child, from sheer anger. It was not just that Medraut should catch us now, after so much, it was not right. The pony snorted and set its ears back.

I turned and looked behind us. The road stretched empty, wild and desolate. The spear must have come from the side. They must have been waiting for us.

I clenched my teeth, rested Eivlin's head against the pony's neck so that she wouldn't fall off, and strode forward to pull up the spear. I clutched it hard to stop my hands shaking, and I shouted, 'If you want this back, come and take it from me!'

Silence. The mountains lay green and still all around.

Then, off on one hillside came a flash of motion. I pulled up the spear point. Best use it as a thrusting spear, so as not to waste it.

The movement came again, then resolved itself into a figure running down the slope through the trees. The

181

runner burst into the open at the foot of the slope, and hurried onto the road, and I wanted to sit down on the road and laugh, or, alternatively, weep. It was only a little boy, a white-blond child who could be no older than nine.

The boy ran out onto the road and looked at me with challenging eyes, startling dark eyes under the pale hair. 'Did I scare you?' he asked, hopefully.

I set the end of the spear against the ground, shaking my head. I did not dare to speak. The boy took a couple of steps nearer.

'Are you sick?' he asked anxiously. 'Is something wrong?'

'No, no, I'm not sick. But she is. Where do you live, lad?'

'Ohhh.' The boy stared at Eivlin. 'Did you fall in the river? You're drenched.'

'No, no. But this woman is very sick, and needs to be taken to a warm place quickly. Where do you live?'

'St Elena's Abbey, near Opergelei Monastery,' he replied quickly. 'My mother's a nun. The nuns know about sick people. I'll show you the way; I know all the quickest ways there.'

I remembered the sort of 'quickest ways' boys enjoy taking, and I hastily said, 'A way that won't be too hard on the pony, I hope. Or the woman. She is sick.'

He looked disappointed, but nodded. 'There's the way Father Gilla takes his mare. I'll show you, Lord.' I handed him his throwing spear, and he darted ahead of me. 'It's this way.'

'What's your name?' I asked, following him.

'They call me Gwyn. I don't have a father.'

'Gwyn' – 'fair', for his hair, of course. A nun's bastard. And he liked to practise throwing spears at travellers, thank God, and lived an an abbey where someone knew how to treat the sick. I could almost be overjoyed that his mother had defiled her vows to have a bastard, and raised him with the rest of the orphans which people would necessarily leave at an abbey.

My guide led me to a rough track which branched off from the main road towards the sea. 'This is a lovely way for horses,' he told me. 'Sometimes Father Gilla lets me exercise his mare, while he's saying Mass for the sisters. I can't go to Mass yet, you see. Are you a warrior, Lord?'

'Neither a lord nor a warrior,' I said, watching my feet.

Talk to the boy, ignore the headache. 'I'm only a servant. My name is Rhys ap Sion.'

'But you're not from here. You have an accent.'

'I'm from Dumnonia.'

'Oh! Have you been to Camlann? All the nuns at the abbey say that Camlann is a haunt of devils.'

They would. Monastics, and living in Gwynedd: they were doubly Arthur's enemies. 'I'm a servant at Camlann,' I said firmly. 'And there are no devils there. If you want devils, try Degannwy.'

He was pleased. 'I didn't think there were devils at Camlann. My mother says that all warriors are devils, but I think they're beautiful. I want to be a warrior when I grow up. Have you seen the Emperor?'

'Yes.'

'What's he like? The nuns say he's a devil and a traitor and has cloven feet, and that he will ruin everyone with his taxes.'

'No cloven feet, I'm afraid. The Emperor Arthur is – well, he's about as tall as me, with hair about the colour of yours, and . . .'

'Does he wear a purple cloak? And a diadem? Hywel made a picture of an emperor in a gospel, and he said you could tell it was an emperor, because only emperors can wear purple cloaks.'

'He has a purple cloak. I've never seen him wear the diadem. But he is a good man, courteous and just, and a very great king.'

Gwyn bit his lower lip, his odd dark eyes shining. 'I would like to see him. Have you seen all his Family? Sometimes bards come by and sing songs, and I ask them to sing songs about warriors. But my mother won't let them, and she gives me a thrashing when she finds I've asked the bards to sing.' He went on rather ashamedly, 'I know I'm wicked to disobey my mother – but have you really seen them? Gwalchmai and Bedwyr and Cei and . . .' the boy stopped suddenly, peering anxiously at my face. 'You're sick!'

I was. The 'lovely way for horses' was, as far as I could tell, composed entirely of vertical hills. It was dark, and I kept stumbling on things until my head felt ready to split.

'Is it much further?' I asked, my voice hoarse.

'Oh no, no. Let me take your pony, Rhys ap Sion. You lean against him and walk slow, and I won't ask you any more questions. Here.' He confidently took the reins, and I dropped back and leaned my forearm against the pony, supporting Eivlin's head on my shoulder. She was warm. I was glad: she could not be dead yet, for the night was chilly.

We walked on and on, and I could only set one foot before the other blindly, past thinking of the way. It did cross my mind to wonder that anyone would let a boy as young as Gwyn roam about alone in such wild country. But he was evidently familiar with the way, and it must be habitual with him. A nice little boy, for all his shocking parentage. He kept quiet so as not to disturb me, though he was plainly thrilled enough to want to shout questions. And he wanted to be a warrior when he grew up. Well, at that age I had wanted the same. A good lad. How far could this abbey be from the road?

Gwyn paused, and I nearly stumbled into him. Lifting my eyes, I saw a dark mass of buildings, with the amber of lamplight glowing before its gate and in two or three windows. I was too spent to feel anything much.

'Rhys ap Sion,' said Gwyn nervously, 'you see my throwing spear?'

'Yes.'

'Could you say it's yours? You see...' he paused, looked up at my face, and went on with a rush of candour, 'I'm not supposed to have it, and my mother would be very upset. I ran off after lessons today, so I'll get a thrashing anyway, but Mama would cry if she thought I had this!'

I almost grinned. So he liked to run off. 'Certainly. You can say that you're carrying it for me.' I thought of something else and added, 'And don't tell them that I'm a servant at Camlann. It might upset them.'

He nodded, began to lead the pony on, then paused again. "But you will give me the spear back again after, won't you?"

"Of course."

He nodded, reassured, and led us to the gate with excessive enthusiasm. After a minute or so, an upper panel opened, and I had a brief glimpse of a pale face; and then the whole gate swung open and a thin woman stalked out, eyes flashing.

'Gwyn!' she scolded. 'You've been gone since terce, and ... oh,' she added as she saw Eivlin, me and the pony. She

184

stopped, staring.

'This is Rhys ap Sion,' announced Gwyn proudly. 'He's very sick and the girl is even sicker. I met them on the big road. He let me carry his spear.' Gwyn gave me an in-on-the-secret look that the nun must have noticed if she hadn't been staring at me.

'Sister,' I said, trying to collect my splintered thoughts, 'the boy's speaking the truth. For the love of Christ, give us the hospitality of the abbey, or this woman may die.' She kept staring. 'I will give you all I have,' I added, desperately, 'and I serve a rich lord, who can give you more. But, as you would be saved, let us in and see that she is cared for!'

'Wh – why yes, yes. Sweet Jesu! Come in. Gwyn, run and fetch Sister Teleri – yes, and find your dear mother too. Oh, give me that spear!' Gwyn reluctantly surrendered the weapon. 'Your poor mother's been worried; go at once!' He darted off, and the woman ushered me into the abbey.

Things began happening quickly. The pony was led off to a stable, and I was led off to a kitchen, trailing along behind the women who were carrying Eivlin. A small, brown, middle-aged woman appeared from nowhere and began fussing over Eivlin. She shook her head.

'Not good,' she said, turning to another woman who appeared to be her assistant. 'She seems near drowned. You,' the woman rounded on me. 'What happened to this girl?'

'I . . . uh . . .'

'She's soaked through, poor child. Were you ship-wrecked?'

'No, she got wet when I baptized her.'

'You what! There was no need to be so thorough, and you should have asked a priest.'

'I couldn't! She was dying, and going mad, and I was afraid for her.'

'Going mad? She doesn't have a fever.'

'It was a curse.'

'What?' The woman eyed me. 'Well, leave it for now; you're sick yourself, and making no sense. Is this woman your wife?'

'My wife?' I blinked vaguely. 'No. I . . . I love her . . .'

'Indeed.' She said it a bit acidly. 'Well, behave with more respect in this house. You stay here, and this poor girl will have a hot bath and a warm bed – I think we can put her in

185

Myfanwy's cell. Yes, there's a fire there. Come along,' – to her assistant. She picked Eivlin up lightly in both arms.

'Wait!' I said. 'Who are you?'

'I am Sister Teleri, physician for this house, and I trust you will respect that.' She swept out of the room, her assistant following her with a lantern.

I sat down by the fire and leaned against the wall. Well, this Teleri seemed to know what she was doing, and there was nothing more I could do for Eivlin.

Someone shook my arm. I tried to push them away, then opened my eyes; realized that I had been asleep. Groggily, I looked around. Teleri was back.

'How is Eivlin?' I asked.

'If Eivlin is your ... friend's ... name – she is ill, and very weak. But she should recover. Now, what is the matter with you?'

'With me? I'm not very sick. I was just hit on the head a few days ago – no, it wasn't that long ago – it was ... yesterday afternoon?' I had to stop. It couldn't be only one day?

'Mm. Let me see. Oh, come.' Teleri caught my hair and pulled my head down, very gently examined the lumps. 'Hmmm. You're as sick as your friend. Look!' – this to her assistant. I looked at the other woman vaguely; she only looked at what Teleri was showing her. She was a tall, thin, long-faced blonde. 'Do you see his eyes?' Teleri asked. The other nodded. 'Pupils dilated and unfocused. You see that after head injuries. We'll clean him up, put him to bed and make him stay there. Come along.'

Teleri and the other woman hauled me to my feet. I wondered if the assistant were Gwyn's mother, the one the woman at the gate had also sent for. Their hair was near the same colour.

Teleri was very deft and gentle, and chattered cheerfully about head injuries the while, telling her assistant all the awful consequences she had seen. But I didn't care. They finally settled me in some quiet monastic cell, with lots of blankets, and told me to lie quiet.

'Look after Eivlin,' I told Teleri. 'She must not die.'

'I should think not! Come along,' she said to her assistant, 'let him sleep. They whisked themselves from the room, taking the lantern. I lay still in the warm, quiet dark. I must pray for Eivlin, I thought, and fell asleep thinking it.

Eleven

I woke up when the morning sun poured through the window onto my face, but I rolled over on my side and went back to sleep. I woke again when the abbey rang its bells for something or other, but resolutely kept my eyes shut. However, after a while I heard footsteps, and the door of the room creaked stealthily open, and I had to sigh, open my eyes, and sit up.

Gwyn stood frozen in the door, his dark eyes wide with remorse. 'Did I wake you up?' he asked mournfully.

'No. I was already awake.'

'Oh.' He closed the door behind him, smiled a little, shyly. 'Are you feeling better?'

'Very much so. Do you know how Eivlin is?'

'Who?'

'Eivlin. The woman who was so sick.'

'Oh! She's still asleep.' He thought a moment, added, 'Teleri told my mother she's never seen anything like it before, that the girl doesn't stir at all when there doesn't seem much wrong with her. Teleri says she hopes your friend wakes soon.'

'So do I,' I said, feelingly, 'so do I.'

Gwyn looked at me steadily and seriously. 'I'll pray for her,' he said at last. 'Father Carnedyr told me to pray when I'm doing my lessons, and I'll pray for her.'

'Thank you,' I said.

Gwyn shuffled his feet awkwardly. 'I should be at lessons soon,' he blurted out, 'but . . .'

'Come and sit down,' I told him, having to grin, despite everything. I would have done exactly the same thing.

He sat down next to me on the bed. 'Tell me about Camlann! Does everyone ride warhorses everywhere? Is the feast hall roofed with gold, like Tegid says?'

'The Hall is roofed like every other hall, with good thatching straw. No one rides warhorses all the time, and they certainly do not ride them everywhere. But . . .'

Gwyn smiled. '*That* would make a mess, if they rode them everywhere. Once I rode Father Gilla's mare into the refectory, pretending that it was a feast hall, and she knocked over the tables and broke a lot of crockery. I was thrashed for that three times – Oh. I'm sorry. Father Carnedyr says I always interrupt, and ought to be thrashed for it. But is the Queen very beautiful?'

He wanted to know everything, and could scarcely sit still to hear it. I could say barely three sentences before he would pour out more questions. It was not that he was without manners, but was simply quick-minded and excited. He wanted to be a warrior, he told me again in a confidential fashion, even though, 'My mother says I am going to be a priest.' But Hywel had given him the spear, and he practised with it every day; and had he really scared me on the road? I was glad he was there. I had no chance to think about Eivlin or the rest of the troubles, and he made me feel almost as if I were at home. I told him fine and splendid things about Camlann. I was still telling them when the door opened again and Teleri's assistant stood there, a tray of food in one hand.

Gwyn, who had been leaning eagerly forward, eyes shining, abruptly stood up. His face dropped. 'He was awake already, Mama,' he told the woman. 'Truly, I didn't wake him.'

The woman set down the tray. 'Indeed? But he's a sick man, my dearest, and you should not have come troubling him with your questions. And why aren't you at lessons?'

He shuffled his feet.

'He came to see how I was,' I put in, hurriedly. 'Since he was the one who found me, he felt responsible. And I've been glad of his company.' Gwyn shot me a grateful look.

The woman began to smile, but suppressed the smile, though her eyes glinted. 'It is good that you should worry about the poor man, my white heart. But you must remember that he needs rest – and you need lessons. Off with you. Father Carnedyr must be waiting.'

Gwyn did not look pleased at the thought of his schoolmaster waiting for him, but he brightened again when I said, 'Thank you for coming. If your mother doesn't mind, come again later.' He looked at the woman and she nodded assent, so he ran off cheerfully. The woman laughed when he was gone, and carefully closed the door.

'Gwyn is your son?' I asked her.

'Mine,' she said. 'Would you like something to eat?'

'I thank you. He's a very fine boy.'

She sighed, brushing a strand of yellow hair away from her blue eyes, the gesture as graceful as a willow tree. 'He is a fine boy, but a wild one. I hope he has not tired you.' I shook my head and she picked the tray up and brought it over. The food consisted of a bowl of porridge with honey, bread and butter, and fresh milk. The smell of it was magnificent. 'Gwyn is clever. He is good at his lessons, and sweeter-tempered than a day in June. But he is imaginative and too high-spirited, and is always running off. He will get himself into trouble.'

'He says that you want him to be a priest.'

'And so he should be. He is bright enough, and it is a noble vocation and much needed in this age. And it offers its own kind of honour and glory to those that follow it.'

I said nothing, but began eating the porridge. It was delicious.

'You dislike the idea,' she observed. 'Well, many men do. Gwyn, now, wants to be a warrior. If you will, do not encourage him in it, or tell him tales that might feed his desires.'

I looked back up at her, surprised, spoon in mid air. She stood straight and calm by the wall, smiling a little, plainly dressed, but her tone had something of command in it. I wondered where she was from. By her accent, she was not born in Gwynedd.

'All boys enjoy such tales,' I said. 'And there's no harm in a song. All they can do is make a boy want to be brave, and that's no evil.'

'That is no evil, no. But they can also make boys love war and conflict, and value gold and strength of body above virtue and honesty. They have much to say of the glitter of worldly power, and little of kindness, peace, and nobility of soul. I would not have my son listen to them. I tell you this because you were telling him about Camlann.'

I looked carefully at the porridge, embarrassed. 'Well . . . he asked me.'

'And you have been there?'

'I have been a servant there.'

She was quiet a moment, considering me, then said, 'Your own loyalties are your own affair, but I must ask you to keep silence about them to my son. I have trouble enough with Gwyn without having him admire – and perhaps run off to – the Family of a man I consider a usurper and a tyrant.'

'Arthur is a very great king,' I said, stung. 'A man given to the protection of his people, to the creation and defence of order and justice. And many of his warriors are good men.'

'Have you found them so? We differ then.'

I swallowed. 'You are very fierce, Lady.'

She did not notice my use of the title, but shook her head slowly, meeting my eyes. 'I have cause to be. Gwyn's father was – is – a warrior.'

'Oh,' I said. 'He . . . he didn't disgrace your vows?'

She shook her head again. 'No, at the time I had not made my vows. All I lost was my honour, though, God knows, that is loss enough.' She moved to the window and looked out. 'All I am asking is that you tell my son no stories about wars and warriors,' she said, more gently.

It was reasonable, since he was her son and responsibility, and anyway could be no more likely to become a warrior than I myself, so I agreed and ate my porridge in silence, wondering who she was.

When I finished, the woman turned from the window, smiled again, trying to lighten the air. 'Here, let me look at your head.'

I let her. She looked, then put on some salve and bandaged it. When she finished she stood back, wiping her hands.

'How is Eivlin?' I asked her. 'The woman I came with?'

'Still asleep. We are keeping her warm and comfortable.'

I was quiet a moment. 'Will she wake up?' I asked.

Instead of answering, she looked at me closely. 'Does it matter to you so very much?'

'Yes.' I had to say again what I had said the night before. 'I love her.'

She looked at me for a moment longer, then smiled in a way that made me realize that she had distrusted me before. It was an open, warm smile that made her face breathtakingly beautiful. 'You are speaking the truth,' she said. 'Forgive me – there is so much evil done to women in these dark days that one is inclined to suspect it when there is none. Your . . . friend is fortunate.' She picked the tray up

190

again. 'Now,' she said, briskly, 'you must stay in bed and
rest. Teleri says that that is the best treatment for head
injuries.'

'I'll stay in bed, then.' Though, without Gwyn, it would
be maddening for very long, and if Gwyn came I thought it
might be difficult to stay off the subject of Camlann. 'Are
you going to send a priest to give me the sacrament?'
Gwyn's 'Father Gilla' sounded sympathetic.

She smiled again at that. 'I'll speak to Father Carnedyr
when he has given the children their lessons. Teleri will
probably come by later, and you can talk to her as well, for
that is what you're wanting, is it not? You can tell Teleri
that I – that is, that Elidan – is seeing about the priest ...
what's the matter?'

Elidan.

After all my lord's searching, I was the one who had
found her, and quite by accident. But it had to be her. If she
had taken her vows after Gwyn was born, or just before he
was born, that made it eight years or so, the right time ...

And it meant that Gwyn was Gwalchmai's son, and it
explained how Bran had found out about Elidan's well-kept
secret. Dear God.

'Lady,' I said, 'I have heard your name before.'

She was startled, and for a moment, I thought, afraid; but
if she was afraid she hid it quickly. Only her eyes narrowed
a little as she said, 'It is possible. My name is not common,
but neither is it unknown. But I do not know where you
could have heard of me. I am only a sister at St Elena's.'

'Whose father's name was Caw, and whose brother was
once king of Ebrauc.'

Her face froze. 'That is nonsense,' she said at once,
making amends. 'You have heard of someone else.'

'Lady, I knew that you were thought to be somewhere in
Arfon, and your accent is northern, however much you
imitate the speech of Gwynedd. And you must have made
your vows at the right time. Why should you deny that you
are Elidan, daughter of Caw?'

She set the tray down again, hurriedly. 'Very well,' she
admitted, then bit her lip, straightened and went on more
quietly and with great dignity, 'I am Elidan, daughter of
Caw. But I have renounced the world and the things of the
world and ... I have enemies. You must not betray me.'

'There's no question of the world at large, Lady, but I fear I must tell my lord.'

'Your lord? Why, whose servant are you?'

'Gwalchmai ap Lot's. He has been looking for you, Lady.'

'No!' she cried, 'Not . . . no, I will never see him again. I swore to die first! You . . . listen, he deceived me, lied to me, perjured himself, murdered my brother, dishonoured me and my house. I swore never to see him again. Tell him I keep my oaths!'

Her anger and horror left me speechless for a moment. Then it struck me that, if Gwalchmai had been there, he would have knelt at her feet and agreed with her, and this made me angry in turn. 'He treated you badly,' I said, 'but not as badly as all that. There are two sides to every quarrel, and your dishonour was as much your fault as his.'

At this the vehemence vanished and she looked at me coldly. 'I forgot myself. Of course, you are only his servant. No doubt he told you some pretty story where I was all to blame. That was not the way of it . . .'

'He told me the story, but gave himself the blame. The only thing he couldn't claim was that he won you by force.'

'So I am to be blamed as a willing harlot? That was what they said in Caer Ebrauc. My brother was kinder: he believed I was ensorcelled.'

'You are no fool, Lady; you cannot believe he cast some spell on you. And if you thought him a sorcerer at the time, that makes it worse.'

'But he was so beautiful!' she cried, then stopped, pressing her hands to her mouth. I stared, and she lowered them again, looking at me with a return of the anger. 'Well, then, I have said it, and so he was. And he was nobly born, and famed, famed all over Britain though no older than myself. Every girl in Caer Ebrauc fell to sighing whenever his name was mentioned. But he looked only at me, as though I were more than the whole earth in his eyes. Dear God! He needed no other sorcery than his eyes and his words, I will confess it to you. I wished I could give him my soul. How could I refuse him anything in the bright world? But it was nothing to him. He took what he wanted, swore me an oath and rode off. Then he broke his oath and killed my brother. He used me. But I am of no ignoble family, and I will not be used again. He deserves to die!'

Her voice was sharp with pain, but her eyes were fierce, hurt but clear, tearless. I remembered what the Emperor Arthur had said of her, that she would not forgive.

'Lady,' I said helplessly, then, resolving to persevere, 'Lady, my lord nearly killed himself when he left you last, so he felt much the same. No, he didn't tell me that. He barely admitted it when he was charged with it. I first met him because he was searching for you over all Britain, alone, in the dead of winter, simply to beg your forgiveness.'

She stared at me in disbelief for a moment. 'To beg my forgiveness?' Her hands clenched, then relaxed. 'To beg *my* forgiveness? How . . . no. How can he expect such a thing of me? I am not so weak and frail as to fall on his neck again when next he beckons. I will not say to him, 'Very well, it was nothing, I will marry you.' He wanted to marry me. After he killed my brother. I should have died the first day I saw him come riding into Llys Ebrauc with the sun behind him: and may I die truly if ever I see him again and give him my "forgiveness".'

'But he has repented of it most bitterly!' I pleaded. 'And, in Christ's name, Gwyn is his son.'

At that her eyes froze me like the wind in January. 'Not Gwyn,' she said, evenly but with greater force than any she had used yet. 'Gwyn is my son. *He* will not take my child away. I will not let my Gwyn grow up a warrior in some fortress, to his own destruction. I will fight Gwalchmai with my bare hands if he tries to take Gwyn away from me.'

'You'd rather let your child be called a nun's bastard?' I demanded, trying to get out of bed to face her.

'Yes, yes, far better "nun's bastard" than "warrior's bastard"! You stupid fool of a servant, haven't you learned yet that courts are cruel, dangerous and cruel? As earth is under me, heaven over me and the sea round me, I will not let my son meet his father!'

As the words of her oath resounded in the small room, the door flew open and Teleri rushed in. She stopped in the doorway and looked from me to Elidan, then back to me. She came fully into the room and pushed me back into the bed with one hand. 'You,' she said. 'Sit down and be quiet. You should not go about shouting at your physicians.

193

Now, Elidan, just what is happening here?'

Elidan glared at her, then drew a deep breath, almost a sob, and shook her head. 'He . . . he is the servant of . . . of Gwyn's father.'

Teleri's eyebrows shot up and she stared at me in astonishment. 'Indeed?'

'And he says that his lord is searching for me.'

'It's true enough,' I said. Common sense was returning to me, and I saw, with a cold weight in my stomach, that they could very easily force me to leave. Which was all very well for me, but unthinkable for Eivlin. I realized, moreover, that the lady Elidan had some cause to fear discovery, and that my language had not been tactful. 'It's true that I'm his servant,' I said, 'but my lord was not as guilty in the matter as this lady may have thought. And he repented very bitterly of the way he treated her. I have just told her that he searched for her all over Britain, and that in mid-winter, all to ask her forgiveness. I could swear to it that he means no harm to her, and certainly none to this convent.'

'Oh, indeed?' said Teleri. 'Travel in mid-winter is a harsh penance for any man – but this is not to the point. I do not care, Elidan, whose servant this man may be. He is sick, and our task is to heal the sick. That is that, even if he does bring his lord down on us.'

'I am afraid for my son,' said Elidan.

'Ach. Your son. Yes.' Teleri's frown deepened. 'But, my dear, what is to be done? You cannot suggest that we throw this great ox out to die.'

Elidan flushed. 'I . . . but no, I do not make war on servants. Only . . . Rhys ap Sion, you owe us something for the care we have given you and your friend. Swear that you will not mention my name to your lord when you see him again. Swear as you hope for salvation.'

'How can I swear an oath such as that? My lord Gwalchmai will certainly continue to search for you.'

'What was your lord's name?' Teleri asked in a different tone.

'Gwalchmai ap Lot.'

Elidan turned away abruptly and went to the window. She held the sill, and I saw how the bones showed white with the force of her grip.

'You never told me your lover's name,' Teleri said to her.

'You never said that he was the Emperor's nephew.'

'There was no cause to,' Elidan said wearily. 'And I was afraid then that the sisters might reject me, if they knew how powerful my enemies were.'

'We would not have rejected you had your lover been the Emperor himself. But I see why you are afraid. Such a man might bring a whole warband to take you away, and to appeal to our king would be to ask the fox for shelter from the dragon.'

'Gwalchmai would never do such a thing,' I protested.

'I once thought that Gwalchmai would never break his oath,' returned Elidan. 'But he did, and my brother is dead. Now I do not know what he might do. If I went to my clan, to my half-brother Ergyriad, he would be pleased that the matter turned out so well. He would be honoured if Gwalchmai were to marry me. But I will not. I cannot forgive him. I will not fall so low as that.'

'Gwalchmai only wishes to speak with you,' I insisted. 'He is a good man, the best lord I could ask for. If you cannot find the Christian charity to forgive him, you ought at least tell him so to his face!'

'I have heard a great deal of Gwalchmai ap Lot – as who hasn't?' Teleri said cautiously. 'I have certainly heard, what with magic swords and horses and battle-madness, that he has more dealings with the Otherworld than is safe or fitting; but I have heard also that he is kind, a protector of the weak, and God-fearing. I do not know: it is hard to be certain of anything to do with the Emperor, here in Gwynedd, for there are men enough to tell evil tales to any who will listen. But if he were a common man, child,' and she went over to stand by Elidan, 'I would say, forgive him and forget him.'

Elidan said nothing, only stared out the window.

'I swear to you, my lord will do you no harm,' I repeated again. 'But if you disbelieve me – well, you will do what you wish anyway, and there's nothing I can do to stop you. But Eivlin, none of it reflects on Eivlin. She is a brave woman, and honourable. Nor have I dishonoured her, so you need not fear to keep her in this place. And if I haven't married her yet, there's nothing to say I won't.'

That last surprised me, for I hadn't thought about it before. And yet, I could do much worse for a wife, and not much better. I was quiet suddenly, considering the thought.

Teleri snorted, then laughed. 'Bravely spoken! But none of us are threatening your sweetheart. Of course she will stay until she is better, and you as well, for I can't answer even for a farmer's thick skull if you go running about as you have been. Elidan, did you look at his head this morning?'

Elidan pressed the heels of her hands against her eyes, nodded. Teleri checked again. I was sure that Teleri had been raised a farmer's daughter.

'It is better, a little,' Elidan said while Teleri examined the lumps. 'Or so I think. But you are right, he must stay and we can demand no oaths if he will not give them. We cannot punish him for another's crime.'

Teleri nodded, retying the bandage. 'Much better today. A good thick skull.'

'That is what my sister says,' I told her. 'How is Eivlin?'

Elidan walked over to the bed and sat down, looking exhausted. 'Her we could not have sent away. She ought to be well. She has no fever, is not chilled or shivering. She is not injured and has no signs of illness. But she feels nothing, responds to nothing, and her heart beats very slowly and unsteadily.'

Teleri pressed Elidan's hand a moment, smiling at her, and I looked at the woman, understanding why Gwalchmai had loved her. She would not let hatred cloud her sense of honour, and had the courage to risk a great deal for what she willed; and the strength of will and nobility showed through her like a stone under the current of a river, unyielding. But she would be unyielding, I thought, if Gwalchmai came and pleaded with her. Arthur had been right. The children of Caw accounted it a dishonour to forgive.

'Indeed, and we wished to ask you about that,' Teleri said briskly. 'What happened to this girl, to cause this? And no nonsense about curses.'

'But that is what caused it,' I said. Elidan's face stayed quiet and expressionless, but Teleri leaned back, thin black eyebrows again raised up on her forehead. 'It seems nonsense, and yet is true,' I insisted. 'My lord had nothing to do with it, though, do not think that. Eivlin was the serving maid of the Queen Morgawse of the Ynysoedd Erch. Morgawse, and King Lot, are at Degannwy, plotting with

196

Maelgwn Gwynedd, and my lord was sent there as an emissary by the Emperor. Morgawse had some plot against my lord, and wished to use me in it, but Eivlin helped me escape when I was captured, and for that the Queen cursed her.'

'You are saying strange things,' remarked Teleri. 'But well; a curse. And the baptizing you were babbling about?'

'Eivlin was never baptized. She was born in Erin and raised in the Islands. When she started screaming, and raving about shadows attacking her, I thought it might be some help. And she did stop screaming. She fainted, and became as she is now.'

'It is certainly less noisy.' Teleri studied my face carefully. 'But you believe this tale.'

'How could I not, when I suffered it?'

She looked thoughtful. 'I have never held much with ghost stories. And yet, I would not call you a fool, and I have never seen anything like this illness. But still . . .'

'But still, it rubs against the grain to believe it. Sister, I do not like believing it myself. When it comes to fighting, I prefer real things to shadows on an empty road. But Morgawse's power is real, and dangerous, as I have reason to know myself.'

'If there is sorcery about, it explains why Gwalchmai is here,' Elidan said bitterly.

'Lady, if you think Gwalchmai would worship devils, you do not remember him at all. But his mother, and his brother Medraut, and Maelgwn Gwynedd and all at Degannwy, all wish to destroy Gwalchmai as a part of some plot against the Emperor. And if they can, and if they do destroy the Emperor as well, how much longer do you think Britain will be safe? Merciful Christ, this is a struggle of Light against Darkness, not a tale to win your sympathy!'

'Stop!' commanded Teleri, holding her hand up. 'You go too deep. Now I,' she stood up, 'I am inclined to believe you when you say that the girl's trouble is a curse, though God help me for believing such a thing. I will have Father Gilla say a Mass for her, and we can all pray. It is not a means of healing I usually approve of, but it will at least do no harm. Beyond that, I do not know what to do. If she does not wake, she will die of thirst, since we cannot get her to swallow anything. But for the rest of your tale – your lord, and King Maelgwn and the Emperor and this famous witch Morgawse of Orcade – all this we will leave aside. The struggles of kingdoms are beyond us. Our task is to heal the sick, care for orphans, copy books and farm. So much our abbey has ever done, and so much we will ever do, God willing.'

I could say nothing to that. I nodded my head, thinking about Eivlin, and then about Gwalchmai. Had he got my message? Had he understood it? Could he do anything about it?

'Perhaps,' I said, slowly, 'perhaps my lord Gwalchmai might know what to do about Eivlin.'

'No!' cried Elidan. 'He must not come here. He must not know that Gwyn exists.'

'Elidan!' Teleri faced the other woman. She was a good five inches shorter and far less regal, but Elidan's firmness melted away. 'Elidan, if this tale is a true one, what has happened is beyond us. It would be a grave sin to let an innocent girl die for fear of this man who might heal her. If he can help, he must come.'

'But what of my son's life? What if he takes my son away?'

'Don't tell him about Gwyn. Keep the child a secret. If you cannot forgive the man, do not. But I do not believe he will force you to anything, and you must consider the girl's life.'

'Of course,' Elidan said after a long moment. 'May it be for the best. Rhys ap Sion, if you think Gwalchmai can help the girl, bring him here. I will speak with him. But, as you would be saved, do not tell him about my son.'

I hesitated. 'I do not know even that I can reach Gwalchmai,' I muttered, evading the issue. 'I can't go directly back to Degannwy. The guards would not let me through the gate. But if I do reach Gwalchmai . . .'

'Swear that you will not mention Gwyn to him. I will trust you with it, you must see that.'

I looked at her. If she did forgive Gwalchmai, she might release me from that oath. If she did not, or if she forgave him only in a form of words . . . It would probably be better, then, that Gwalchmai never knew of his son's existence. There would be nothing he could do about the child. He could hardly drag him away from Elidan. She had said

198

she would fight with her bare hands to protect the boy, and I believed her. And she was doing what she thought right. And if Gwalchmai knew that Gwyn was his son, and was unable to keep him, it would merely be another load of undeserved misery.

'I swear I won't mention Gwyn to Gwalchmai unless you yourself give me leave,' I told Elidan, looking into her solemn eyes. 'So help me God and all the saints and angels. As I hope to be saved, I will not.'

'Then tell Gwalchmai to come. I will speak to Abbess Maire and tell her the whole situation. I will ask her to support you, and give all the help she can, for I believe your tale of Morgawse's sorcery, and it is fitting to us to oppose it.'

'I thank you,' I said.

'Well!' Teleri put her hands on her hips. 'Well done! And now that you have decided to seek this lord's help, how is he to be reached?'

'I will go,' I said. 'I can try and climb the wall at Degannwy by night. It should not be impossible.'

'You will do no such thing,' declared Teleri. 'You will stay here and rest.'

'You can send a messenger with a letter,' Elidan suggested. 'He can enter by the gate, as though he would sell something to the fortress.'

'I don't know how to write,' I said.

She smiled. 'Then dictate it to one of us. This is an abbey. We do teach writing here. Father Gilla can take the message in, if he's willing; his little mare is the best horse we have. I will speak to him, and you can dictate the letter this afternoon.'

'But sleep now,' Teleri added. 'You look as though you could do with the rest.'

She swept from the room, pausing only to stoop upon the food tray and bear it off with her. Elidan followed without a backward glance.

I sighed and lay back, looking at the ceiling. There were too many things to think about, and I could not rest. Every time I managed to turn my mind from Eivlin, telling myself that worrying helped nothing, I found myself wondering about Gwalchmai. Perhaps it was absurd to ask him to help us; perhaps he needed help himself. He was surrounded by enemies, with only Rhuawn as a treacherous support. I knew that Rhuawn would side with Gwalchmai against Maelgwn, but Medraut's more subtle opposition had escaped him. He was a good man, Rhuawn, but deluded, and unlikely to come to his senses unless Medraut did something foolish. Unless Eivlin had hurt Medraut badly with that piece of firewood. That blow might delay Morgawse's schemes for a while. I trusted Eivlin to have hit hard, and thought that Medraut's headache might be worse than mine; and perhaps even Morgawse felt unwell. It was a cheering thought, and eventually I managed to relax and drift off to sleep.

Perhaps it was because of my head injuries, but I had nightmares.

It seemed to me that I saw Morgawse of Orcade, standing in a small, dark place, braiding her hair in a strange pattern and singing. After a while, beyond her singing, I could hear a keening, faintly at first, then louder, breaking into a dirge sung without measure in a foreign tongue. Morgawse stopped her song and laughed, her teeth showing white as she tossed back her head with pleasure. Her image faded, and the dirge grew louder. I saw a funeral procession, walking in the dark with smoky red torches wavering about. In the midst of the torches was carried a bier, with a still form lying on it, covered by a cloak. Of a sudden, the ring of mourners was broken, and Agravain ap Lot burst into the middle and flung himself down beside the bier, weeping. He buried his face in the cloak. The whole began to recede, the wailing growing fainter, and I struggled to go nearer, to know who it was on the bier because I was terribly afraid, deathly afraid that it was Gwalchmai. But the dirge faded until it was only a faint hum, like the wind, and the torch light seemed to recede back and back away. I sank into a black ocean, still struggling to follow. Then there came a crash like thunder, and I opened my eyes and saw Medraut. He was smiling.

'He appears well enough to me,' said Medraut smoothly. I looked behind him and saw that he was speaking to Teleri.

'You cannot take him,' said Teleri. Her hands were knotted together, her eyes too bright. 'For sweet mercy's sake, do you expect us to simply hand him over to you?'

'I expect that you will do what I tell you to, or else see

your abbey here burned to the ground. Get up!'

I sat up, impossibly confused. I was in the same room at St Elena's, and it was afternoon. The same rushes lay on the floor, the stone walls had the same chipped rocks. It was not a dream: Medraut was really standing before me.

He smiled again. I noticed that his head was bandaged. 'I told you to get up.'

I stood, gathering the bedclothes about me. I had only my underclothes on, since the nuns had taken my tunic and trousers.

Medraut laughed at me. 'Bring him his clothes, and hurry,' he ordered Teleri.

'In Christ's name, you cannot take him!' she said.

I was awake enough to know better. 'He can. And he will fire the abbey if you don't. Better go.'

Almost, she didn't. She stared at me for a long moment, twisting her hands together; but then she turned and ran from the room. Medraut laughed again, looked about and sat down comfortably on the bed.

'You've found excellent care here,' he commented. 'Not, perhaps, healing as rapid as my mother's: but then, no doubt the treatment is pleasanter. Where's the other slave, the one responsible for this?' He touched his bandage.

'She's dead,' I told him, praying that he couldn't tell otherwise. 'She died yesterday. Just before sundown. She started screaming, and fell down on the road, and she is dead.'

'I thought as much.' He drew one knee up and locked his arms around it. His fair hair caught the afternoon sun, and his soft new beard gleamed against his face. Gold shone on his brooch and collar. 'Mother defends her honour. The little vixen should never have dared defy her. I hope she suffered.'

I said nothing, hoping that Teleri had not mentioned Eivlin, hoping that Medraut neither knew nor was able to sense anything about Elidan and Gwyn. Teleri came back with my clothes, and I dressed rapidly and in silence.

Medraut stood, brushed off his cloak. One hand rested lightly on his sword, and I stared at the weapon. Either he had two swords with identical hilts or he had somehow recovered the one Eivlin took from him. He noticed the stare and flashed his easy smile.

'Yes. I have it back again.' He slapped the sword hilt. 'A useful thing. I could show you more of it.'

I had no particular wish to see more of it. I felt sick. Had he, or Morgawse, somehow trailed me and found the message before Gwalchmai? Or had that still form in my dream indeed been Gwalchmai?

It is no use to rely on dreams and guesses. Whatever had happened to my message, it did not change the fact that I had to leave quietly with Medraut, drawing no attention to anyone at the abbey, and be prepared to fight the whole fight over again. I was glad that the thought numbed me. If it had not, I do not think I could have left the room without falling down and begging him to spare me, which might have meant disaster. The final end, I told myself firmly, is not in our hands at all. We can only do what seems to be right, and trust God for the rest.

Medraut stood beside the door and gestured for Teleri and me to leave first. Teleri passed him proudly and briskly without looking at him. When I stepped after her, however, Medraut clouted me full on the ear. I stumbled against the door, hit the other side of my head on the frame, and fell to my knees on the floor. Teleri cried out. Medraut bent over and dragged me up by the front of my tunic.

'And that,' he said, his eyes savage, 'that is for running off and shaming my mother. I can't give you the full payment, slave, since that is her right, but it is not forgotten.'

The world was swirling about me in circles, so I closed my eyes, counted to ten, and managed to stand on my own feet. Medraut let go of me. 'Show us the way out,' he commanded Teleri, who stood, frozen, her hand lifted – whether to strike or help I was unsure. Her eyes flashed and she almost retorted, but managed to check herself. We walked out of the abbey.

Medraut had a dozen mounted warriors waiting in the yard. From the corner of my eye I noticed a huddle of nuns against the wall, and Gwyn, staring at the men wide-eyed with awe. My little pony was out and saddled, and at Medraut's order I mounted, wearily, and submitted to having my hands tied while someone else took the pony on a lead rein. Medraut swung up onto his own mount, a sleek, long-legged grey. He nodded to the nuns. 'It is good that you were sensible.' He gathered up his reins. 'As it is, all

202

you have lost is one insolent servant, and not your home and your lives.'

'What are you doing to Rhys?' bellowed Gwyn. Abruptly, the boy dashed from the wall and ran towards the horses. Someone shrieked. Medraut whipped out his sword.

'What's this brat?' demanded Medraut. 'One of your bastards?' he looked contemptuously at the nuns.

Elidan walked out of the huddle after her son. 'Mine,' she said, her voice calm and very clear.

'He showed me the way here,' I said, not daring to look at either of them. 'He's too young to have any sense.' I did not care to think what Medraut and Morgawse could do with the lad.

'Out of the way, brat, or I'll cut your ears off,' said Medraut in a pleasant tone.

Gwyn glared at him. 'What kind of warrior are you?' he demanded 'When I'm grown up I'll come and fight you. You can't take Rhys away like this: he's sick. Teleri and Mama both say so. Mama!' She had reached him and caught him by the ear. 'Mama, he can't!'

'He can,' said Elidan. 'And nun's bastards never become warriors, which is something to thank God for, for you will never be tempted to vulgar brutality.'

Medraut was too surprised to react, at first. Elidan dragged Gwyn out of his way. The boy protested, 'But Mama, he's . . .'

'He is a dog, but we have no power.' She thrust him out of the way.

Medraut drew his sword with a rasp of steel, and Elidan turned to him, graceful as a deer, her head lifting and her eyes clear and brilliant with contempt. I wished, wildly, to do something to distract Medraut: to laugh at her, or point out the ridiculousness of her gesture. But it was not ridiculous. She knew exactly what she was doing. She was making Medraut absurd by the purity of her own courage and honour; she was showing his act at its worst, and letting him see it too, and she smiled at his sword now, completely scornful of her danger. She was astonishingly beautiful.

Medraut swore, inarticulately, knowing what she had done; then clapped his heels to his horse and rode at her. He only used the flat of the sword, but the blow caught her on the head and she fell; and Medraut touched his horse to a canter and rode off without looking back. I risked one glance, as someone jerked the pony's lead rein and dragged me off after them. Gwyn was screaming, but Elidan had risen to her knees, her forehead streaming blood, and was putting her arms about her son and soothing him. Her eyes met mine over his shoulder, still brilliant, but now full of a profound grief and helplessness. Slowly, she shook her head.

The track up from the abbey seemed much shorter than the agonizing trip down to reach it. Medraut insisted on moving at a fast trot, which was about the best speed my pony could manage. When we reached the main road he ordered one of his men to ride ahead of us with some message. They spoke in Irish, and I understood nothing they said except for one word: *Riga*. I had already learned that this was the word the men of the Ynysoedd Erch used to refer to Morgawse. *Riga*, 'the Queen'. The messenger nodded to Medraut, called a greeting to his comrades, and touched his horse to a gallop, off to find Morgawse and tell her that Medraut had recaptured me. The rest of us followed him along the road at the same jolting trot. My head, which had been feeling better, began to throb again. I stared ahead blankly, trying not to see the men around me, trying not to feel. After so much, to be returning to Morgawse. After everything! If I thought of it, my hands began to shake and it became unbearable.

But at least Eivlin was safe – if she lived. Ach, Yffern take Morgawse, and Medraut and the lot of them, Eivlin had risked her life to save me. And now she was probably dying, but she wasn't Morgawse's tool. Nor would I be. And yet, I had been nearly spent when Eivlin had broken in to rescue me. Morgawse had very nearly succeeded. I remembered her smile of triumph.

But perhaps by now she did not need me for any plot against my lord. If Gwalchmai were dead, all that Morgawse would want with me would be to punish me for my presumption. If Gwalchmai were dead – I had no reason to believe that except a nightmare. A nightmare, and Medraut's sword, and the whole situation. What was Rhuawn doing? Still deluded? Ready to go back to Camlann with Medraut, leaving Morgawse with Maelgwn and . . . what had Morgawse said? 'Others will join Maelgwn in his alliance, and wait until the Family is at war with itself. Then will the shield-wall be broken and the gate of the stronghold be battered down; then Arthur will die.' All that order and unity, strength and laughter, all that Light, to fall and be broken. And there would be nothing, then, nothing but a wilderness which used to be a kingdom.

I looked down at the road. Could I throw myself off the pony head first and break my own neck? To kill oneself is a sin, but with nothing before me but a painful death, the act must be justifiable in God's eyes.

But I couldn't do it. It was sheer idiocy not to, but I couldn't even think of it seriously. I sat silent, clenching my hands against their bonds and looking at the mountains which stood calm and joyful in their spring green.

We did not ride to Degannwy, but headed off up another track, deeper into the mountains. Something in its curve touched my memory, and I recalled that I had ridden down it in the moonlight with Eivlin, laughing uncontrollably with the joy of our escape. Now Medraut sent half his men back to Degannwy, and the rest of us trotted up the narrow track in single file, riding in the last of the afternoon sun. We had made good time on the journey. My little pony was sweating from the pace. I was sweating too, but I felt cold, as cold as if it were February instead of late May.

We saw the shepherd's hut before us, and Medraut turned his grey steed over to the place down the hill where the horses had been tied before. There was a horse there now, a chestnut mare with fine trappings: Morgawse's horse. I closed my eyes, unwilling to keep on seeing it. We stopped.

'Get down,' Medraut commanded me. I slithered off, stood looking at my bound hands on the pony's thick mane. The beast tossed its head, sides heaving. Medraut gave some orders to his men, again in Irish, then turned back to me. 'Come,' he commanded. I took a deep breath, turned, and came.

All but one of the warriors remained by the horses. The one who came was that same Ronan who had stood guard before. It was almost more than I could bear, and I bit my tongue.

If the ride from St Elena's had seemed short, that march up the hill seemed to take years, and I was ready to scream by the time we reached the door. I bit my tongue harder, tasting my own blood. Medraut opened the door and shoved me in first.

Morgawse stood in the room, dark in gold and crimson, but there was someone else there as well, someone standing behind the door, because her eyes were fixed there. I saw that that was how it must be as I took another step in, as Medraut followed me; and then the door slammed in Ronan's face. Medraut whirled about, his hand on his sword, his face astonished, and I turned too.

Gwalchmai stood against the bare wooden door, his sword a streak of fire in his hand, mail-coat gleaming. His eyes were steady on Morgawse's eyes, his face without expression.

Ronan behind us pounded on the door, exclaiming angrily in Irish. Without moving, Gwalchmai gave some order in a low voice, in Irish. The pounding stopped, and Ronan queried.

Morgawse nodded, her eyes not stirring. She repeated what Gwalchmai had said. There was a long silence. Then I heard Ronan's footsteps retreating, and the air in the hut lay thick and still.

'So.' Gwalchmai spoke at last, his voice cool and detached. 'You had no notion where my servant might be.'

'Why is *he* here?' demanded Medraut, looking towards Morgawse. He eased his sword from its sheath, ready to attack. Morgawse said nothing, and, after another moment's hesitation, Medraut dropped back towards her.

Gwalchmai took a quick step forward and caught my shoulder, brought down his sword with a single swift stroke that cut my bonds in half. 'Rhys. Are you well?' His voice held expression again: concern. I was shaking. For one awful moment I had believed that Morgawse had carried out her first plan against Gwalchmai and succeeded. But this was clearly not the case, and I was too confused to think.

'I am fine,' I stammered. 'But you – you're not dead.'

'Of course not. Why should I be?' I shook my head, unable to explain, resolving never to trust a dream again. Gwalchmai gave my shoulder a soft shake and took another step forward so that I stood behind him.

'Lady,' he said to Morgawse, 'I have found my servant, and will not trouble you further. We will go.'

Incredibly, she smiled. It was a smile I had no liking for, an intimate, secret smile directed towards Gwalchmai alone. 'You have conquered, my falcon,' she said, very, very softly. 'Never would I have believed it, once. Always I thought you were a fool: first because you could be used, and then because you rejected power when it was offered to you. Now I see that you are wiser than I.' She stepped nearer. Medraut stared at her, bewildered. Gwalchmai stood motionless, just looking at her as he had that first night we came to Degannwy.

'It makes me like you the better,' the Queen went on. 'All the men I have known, and all my sons, they have always been weak. I am very glad, my spring-tide falcon, that you are stronger . . .'

'Mother!' said Medraut in an agonized whisper. She did not turn, but only took another step towards Gwalchmai, smiling that smile. It made my hair stand on end.

'My lord,' I said, 'let us leave.'

He didn't seem to hear. He kept looking at Morgawse. The point of his sword drooped, slowly, and she came closer.

'And yet I should have expected things of you, my second son. Born not to please Lot, nor for my plans, but for myself.'

Gwalchmai stepped back, almost stepping into me. I caught his arm. 'My lord, don't listen to her.'

She came nearer, lifting her arms as though she would embrace him. Her eyes were too dreadful to look at. Gwalchmai was shaking. He drew the sword up and sideways, the edge turning towards her.

He might kill her. He might not. If he killed her, his mother – what would it mean to him, what would it do to him, afterwards? I became very afraid. And if he did not kill her, she was coming to claim him, very plainly dragging up whatever dark memories she had left in his heart from his earliest years. Whatever he felt for her, he could not simply oppose her with his will. He was pulled by her into an unholy murder or a worse love, and I could see it all plainly when I looked at her.

Morgawse took one step nearer, and I looked away. Gwalchmai's sword gave a little lift, and I knew that he was going to strike.

'Mother!' said Medraut. She did not look at him, only at Gwalchmai. The sword swung back the merest hair, and I grabbed my lord's wrist with both hands.

He gave one heave that nearly tore his hand loose, but I was holding tightly. Morgawse did not move. Gwalchmai whirled and looked me in the face. His eyes were wide and furiously dark.

'Gwalchmai,' I said. 'My lord, let us leave. There is nothing more to do here.'

He spun back, looked at Morgawse.

'Come along,' I insisted. 'There are things to be done, and we must not waste our time.' I fumbled behind me for the latch of the door. Morgawse began to frown.

'What must be done?' asked Gwalchmai, like a man in a dream.

I risked it. 'I have found Elidan – and beyond that, there is the work your lord set you.'

His fingers went white on the sword hilt. 'Elidan?' he looked back at me.

'Stop,' said Morgawse.

'Lady,' Gwalchmai said, recovering himself, 'Rhys is right. There is nothing we must do here, and very much to do elsewhere.'

Morgawse, frowning, dropped back towards Medraut, not turning about. She lifted one thin, dark hand and held it palm up, fingers pointing at Gwalchmai.

'You will not leave,' she said. 'Medraut, assist me.'

Gwalchmai gave one long, sad look at Medraut, and looked back to Morgawse. Medraut dropped to one knee and held the hilt of his sword with both hands, the point slanting upwards before both his mother and himself. He did not look at Morgawse, but he was biting his lip in a kind of frenzy, so that it bled.

'Is that to be the way of it?' asked Gwalchmai, very quietly. He almost said something more, but checked himself. He drew himself up, raised his sword and held it point down, his right hand on the hilt and his left hand clasping the naked blade. He lifted it until the cross-piece was level with his eyes. A light stirred along the steel, and the ruby in the pommel began to glow with a deep radiance.

Medraut glanced at Morgawse, looked back at Gwalchmai, and seemed to brace himself. The Queen's face was taut, pale, her eyes fathomless and too wide. Slowly she raised her other hand and placed it, palm down, on top of the first.

I gripped the latch of the door, ready to fling it open. But Gwalchmai showed no signs of moving, so I merely held my place, waiting. The silence grew denser.

Morgawse spread her fingers, shifted her hands a very little. Her face was like a lightning bolt, vivid and inhuman with strain. As though with a great effort, she drew her hands apart a very little. I heard my own voice gasp: darkness boiled between her hands, seeped out to blacken the dimness of the room. I closed my eyes, opened them. The darkness still seethed between the Queen's thin hands. It trickled downward along the blade of Medraut's sword and flowed onto the floor, piled about Medraut's knees into a mass.

The sword in Gwalchmai's hands began to burn brighter, the deep crimson glow running from the hilt down the blade, paling to an almost white shade at its tip.

'Do you truly believe that will be sufficient?' whispered Morgawse. Her voice in that stillness was like the first breath of wind stirring the air before a thunderstorm: it made everything shiver. Her fingers arched about the darkness, curling with effort till they resembled claws. 'Behold! I am Queen and Ruler of Air and Darkness, and all Earth will be my domain, and all flesh obey me. Do you think that sliver of steel enough to restrain me? Fool!' She tossed her head back, and her hair swirled about the night, seeming to draw in the blackness, or to hurl it out.

I saw Gwalchmai tighten his grip on his sword, the bare blade cutting into his left hand. The radiance deepened. 'Darkness does not have sole dominion over Earth,' he said, his voice hoarse with effort. 'It is by Light that this sword was formed, and by Light it will hold, not as steel, but as the image of a will.'

Morgawse flung wide her arms, and utter blackness swallowed the hut and the very ground beneath our feet. I could no longer feel the latch of the door, and I could not tell where we were. It was as though we hung suspended, or fell through a huge gulf into which all light and life were pouring. I fumbled before myself and found Gwalchmai's shoulder. For all the blackness we could still see Morgawse, but as if she were the centre of that blackness, though she seemed ghastly pale, standing beyond the brink of that abyss before us, painfully near, appallingly remote. Gwalchmai's sword still burned, steady as a hearth fire on a winter night, or a candle standing before an altar: but his shoulder beneath my hand was knotted with effort, hard and cold as any stone.

'And what is Light?' asked Morgawse the Queen. Her voice was thin and cold, not a woman's voice, not a human voice. 'All things began in Darkness, and all things will return to Darkness, though you may struggle your brief moment on the edge of the abyss. All things are touched and shot through with Darkness. See how in this present age the darkness engulfs the world: Rome has fallen, and all the West has followed her. Can a little light hope to live in Camlann? Darkness has gripped the hearts of all who fight for Light. The heart of Rhuawn your friend has listened to it; Arthur your lord has obeyed its impulse; it holds its place in your own heart. All must fall back to the Darkness, break and return to where it began. Night comes, and there will be no day again. Light is illusion; Darkness alone is true and strong. Know this!'

For a moment the light from Gwalchmai's sword seemed to grow paler, fainter, seemed to illuminate nothing. I felt him stir, bracing himself. I wished to cry out to him, tell him to leave the struggle and flee, if there was anywhere we could flee to. But I could neither move nor speak. My body seemed locked in chains of ice, and my mind was full of darkness. Dear God, I thought, only let me see the sun before I die. Only let there be something besides the darkness.

'And God said, "Let there be light", and there was light,' replied Gwalchmai, his voice ringing clear and strong and glad. 'Though Rome has fallen, and though Camlann should fall; though I, and Arthur and Rhuawn have been shaken by Darkness to our souls, you cannot shake the stars, or call back the March winds when the spring breathes upon the orchards. Light is the first-born of Creation, by Light and in Light the world was formed, and Darkness is only that which Light illuminates, not force, but only its absence.'

Morgawse flung her arms above her head, the blackness

210

moving about her like water, her eyes distended and unnatural. Medraut's sword moved up like a wisp of shadow,
and I glimpsed him, saw that he knelt before Morgawse on
both knees now. In a high flat voice the Queen cried in a
strange language, syllables I had not thought a human
tongue could shape, sounds that made me want to cover my
ears. Gwalchmai staggered, dropped to his knees. His eyes
were shining in the light from the sword, his face streaked
with sweat or tears. I crouched behind him, afraid to stand,
to move, to breathe. I watched Gwalchmai's hands on the
sword shaking, saw the blood from his left hand trickling
across the blade. The light flickered.

Morgawse cried again. I saw that Medraut's head was
bowed as if in exhaustion, but still he held the sword up, his
arms shaking as though it were a terrible weight. At Morgawse's voice the night flowed upon us like a wave cresting,
breaking. For an eternal instant I could see nothing at all,
nothing but a faint glimmer where the sword had been,
dimming as though it were receding into the dark.

But the glimmer did not vanish. It brightened, faded
again, brightened and continued to brighten. I felt Gwalchmai tense, gather his strength, rise. The darkness ebbed,
fading, and with a shock I realized I could see the beaten
earth floor of the hut. I would not have exchanged that sight
for any rose garden on the green earth.

The Queen held her hands out, palms towards Gwalchmai, mouth framing words that came without sound. But
the light stirred again in the blade, grew bright, clearer, the
crimson brightening to rose, glowing almost white. The
Queen managed to cry out one last time, but the darkness
was fading. Medraut gave one sob and collapsed on the
ground at his mother's feet. His sword fell on the earth
before him, and the darkness vanished. The room was filled
with scintillating light from the sword, light that broke like
sunbeams through unquiet waters.

Gwalchmai drew his left hand away, his palm bloody
from clasping the blade, then lowered his right arm, the
sword swinging level again. The light faded to a ripple
along the steel.

Morgawse lowered her arms and stared at us over
Medraut's motionless body. Her crimson gown was
crumpled, and the corners of her lips and eyes drooped. For

the first time I saw lines in her face and white in her hair, and I knew that, like any other woman, she grew old. I turned away and unlatched the door. The mountain breeze was sliding along the heather, and the last of the sunset transfigured the mountains.

Gwalchmai's hand dropped to my arm a moment, fell away. 'Let us go,' he said, quietly, and, to Morgawse, 'Mother, much health.'

'No!' shrieked Morgawse. She stumbled forward, nearly tripped over Medraut. 'No!' in desperation. I turned my back and stepped out the door, and Gwalchmai followed silently. 'No, no!' she cried again, and began to sob. 'Do not leave me, I beg you! Still I am powerful, I can recover – give me time, a few days only . . .' And I thought she no longer spoke to us, but to some demon she had long served; but I did not look back. Behind me Gwalchmai gently closed the door.

Twelve

It was not as easy to leave as I had assumed. Beside Morgawse, Medraut's six mounted warriors had seemed an insignificant detail; but when we were outside and facing the road home I realized that six armed men are never insignificant. We went only a little way down the hill before Ronan saw us and began giving us orders in Irish, presumably to stop and go back. Gwalchmai gave a high, clear whistle, and Ceincaled cantered about the hill to him as he started to argue with the other. I should have expected that he had the stallion nearby. Medraut's men leapt onto their own horses, and Gwalchmai was fighting them before either of us had time to think about what was happening. The fight was not, however, fiercely contested. Medraut's men were nervous to begin with, and when Gwalchmai put a spear through Ronan, then drew his sword and cut down one other man, the rest turned their horses and fled. Too much had already happened for me to think or feel much about it. I simply caught Ronan's warhorse, mounted, and Gwalchmai and I set off. The first stars were kindling in the east.

'My lord,' I said, after a few minutes. 'We are taking the same path the Queen's warriors took. How far do you mean to follow them?'

He shook his head. He looked drained, haggard with weariness and strain – as he ought to, after what had happened in the hut. 'We do not follow them. They have friends in Degannwy. Let them hurry to reach the fortress. We must find a place to camp tonight.'

I nodded, then asked, 'How did you find me? What has happened in Degannwy?'

He raised his left hand in a gesture of protest, then frowned at the blood on it. 'Please,' he said, lowering the hand and staring at it. 'It is late tonight. There is too much to ask and to answer, for both of us, to do it now. The morning will come soon enough.'

We did not go very far that night. We turned north on the road to Degannwy, riding towards the main road since we did not trust our welcome at the fortress. But we turned aside shortly before the Roman road and found a good, sheltered camping place in a wood. There we built a fire and hobbled our horses, turning them loose to graze.

The air held a sharp chill, and it seemed damp in the wood. I did not anticipate sleeping well. But I could not consider looking for shelter at some farm holding nearby. Something of Gwalchmai's wariness had forced itself upon me, and I could not trust the world at large. I thought of my family, and suddenly felt horribly lonely. Morgawse was defeated, Gwalchmai still alive, and it was all too much for me. These vast conflicts were too absolute and lofty and remote from the texture of my life. I wanted home, the cow byres and the fields green with new grain, the warmth of the hearth fire and the voices and faces of my family: I was sick with the want of them. Sitting there in a wood in Gwynedd, with the huge mountains brooding around me, I thought of everything familiar and longed with all my being to go home.

Gwalchmai came over to the fire with his saddle-bags, and the hilt of his sword caught the light for an instant, as though about to burn of its own accord again. What, I wondered, did I have to do with him? There he was, royally born, Morgawse's son, perfectly accustomed both to dangerous battles and otherworldly conflicts. He belonged to all this. I did not, and I wanted to go home. Most simply put, I was tired.

Gwalchmai set down the pack and dropped beside the fire. 'I have some bread and cheese here,' he offered, softly. 'Also, some ale. I remembered how you liked it.' He opened the pack and handed me the ale.

I looked at the flask a moment, wanting either to laugh or sob. 'Thank you, my lord,' I said at last. He smiled and began to pull out the bread and cheese.

It was not much of a meal. I could have eaten good red meat, and the cheese was sad stuff. But I imagined Gwalchmai trying to coax it from Saidi ap Sugyn in the kitchens at Degannwy, and was amazed that he'd managed to get the ale. Saidi must have made him pay for it. If I had been there – well, but Gwalchmai was Gwalchmai, and I couldn't be annoyed with him for that. And I enjoyed the meal. Any food would have tasted delicious just then.

Despite my forebodings I slept soundly, though when I woke I found my neck stiff, my limbs aching from the damp, and my head giving the odd twinge now and then. Well, the way to cure that was to move about. I got up to find Gwalchmai saddling the horses. He gave me a smile and greeted me, and I managed to reply without being rude. The sun was just up, drawing the chill, damp mists out from the mountains, and I was glad to get on my horse and trot out onto the road. The motion at least was warming. Gwalchmai handed me the remainder of the bread and cheese, and I hacked off some of each and gave the rest back to him. I liked the food even less than I had the night before, but I was hungry. Gwalchmai apparently was too, for he finished what I'd given him, which I had not entirely expected.

We reached the main road very quickly and drew in our horses to stand for a moment, seeing how the line of it curled off into the mist. The morning sun was a brilliant blur eastward, and I thought the air should clear before too long.

Gwalchmai sighed and turned his eyes from the road over to me.

'Rhys,' he said, then stopped.

'My lord?'

'You said, yesterday, that you had found Elidan.'

So I had. I had forgotten about that. 'I have, my lord. She's at an abbey called St Elena's, the sister foundation of Opergelei monastery.'

'An abbey?'

'She's become a nun, my lord. I found her because Eivlin was struck by some curse from the Queen, and sick, and we could not go far, and this St Elena's was the nearest shelter.' I could not mention Gwyn, I reminded myself.

'Who is Eivlin?'

I realized that he must have been unaware that she existed. I thrashed about for a bit, trying to explain, and we turned down onto the road, following it westward at my direction. Then I simply told him all that had happened from the argument with Rhuawn until Eivlin had collapsed. I concluded by saying, 'I put her on the pony and went on until we met a person from this St Elena's, who showed us the way to the abbey. Elidan was working in the

215

infirmary there, with another sister. Eivlin was still asleep when Medraut came to bring me back to the Queen, and she wouldn't wake, whatever the healers did to her. I had intended, my lord, to send you a letter and ask you to come and see if there was any way you could help her.'

'Of course,' said Gwalchmai. He looked westward along the road eagerly, his eyes very bright. 'Opergelei is near the sea; and you say that St Elena's is near it?' He touched Ceincaled to a canter. 'Elidan! To see her once more! Did you speak to her?'

Kicking my beast savagely to make it keep up, I became angry. Elidan, Elidan, but it was Eivlin who was hurt, Eivlin who'd risked her life. 'I did. But can you help Eivlin?'

He shrugged, noticed my look, and slowed Ceincaled to a walk again. 'Och ai, this is a great burden to you.'

'And it ought to be, seeing that she saved my life and that I intend to marry her.'

His startled look slowly gave way to a delighted smile. 'So that is the way of it. I am glad for you, cousin.' He looked down the road again. 'It is probable that I can help her. Or rather, that she can be helped by my being there, with the sword. I do not know. I have never practised such things. But you can have hope, and I will do all that I can – but forbear me, Rhys, because I am sick to see her: what did she say to you, Elidan?'

He was saying nothing more than the truth, I knew, when he promised to do all he could for Eivlin. But he was wild for Elidan, and could pay attention to little else. It was a hard question to answer, and I sat a while, rubbing at a spot in the saddle. Eventually, I looked back up to him. He was watching me like the hawk of his name watching an intruder. It was best to meet his gaze evenly and say only the truth. 'She was . . . angry, afraid, when she found that I was your servant, though she did not hold me responsible for what you did nine years ago. But she has not forgiven you, and I think that she has made the thing worse, in imagination, than it actually was. She grieves over her honour, which she thinks she has lost. She says that she will not forgive you, but she will see you.'

'Ah.' he looked away. Even without repeating her bitter accusations, it was bad enough. After a while, 'Well, I will

ask her forgiveness, for all of that. And still it will be sweet
to see her again. Is she well? Does she seem happy?'

'She is in excellent health, and, if I read things correctly,
likely to be the next abbess of the place. I think she is content
with her life, and happy enough.'

It pleased him. 'I had feared that she would be reproached
all her life. It is a dreadful thing for a king's sister to be
known to have slept with the man who killed her brother.
Good. I am glad you found her.' He fell silent, beginning to
brood over what I had said.

Well content with her life, I thought, looking at him. I
remembered her suppressed smile at Gwyn when I had first
seen her. Well, she had success after a fashion, she was comfortable, and she plainly loved her son. Her life was less
ruined than Gwalchmai's, I thought. But then, she did not
really blame herself for it, and he did. I wondered how
Gwalchmai would like Gwyn, and how the boy would take
to his father. Very well, no doubt.

Perhaps Elidan would change her mind when she saw
Gwalchmai again. She had loved him very passionately
once.

Gwalchmai was rubbing his sword hand against his
thigh, and I was sure he was reconsidering all that he had
done in the light of what I had just told him, and I knew that
he would soon conclude, with Elidan, that his actions were
unforgivable. God preserve me from a conscience like his.
Partly to distract him and partly because I wanted to know,
I asked, 'How did it come about that you were with Morgawse when Medraut brought me back, my lord? Did you
find my message?'

He came back to the present, ready to be courteous.
'Your message? Oh, the sword and the brooch. Yes. Here.'
He fumbled under the collar of his own cloak and pulled out
the same brooch, still a little bent from having the sword
pushed through it. I took it, untied the knot I'd used to hold
my cloak, and secured the wool with the pin. Much better.

'Did you understand it all, then? Come, my lord, tell me
what happened at Degannwy.'

He shrugged, patted Ceincaled's neck and thought for a
moment before he began.

'I was concerned the evening when you first disap-
peared,' he said at last. 'Degannwy is a hard place, and many

things could have happened. I asked Rhuawn whether he had seen you, and he was affronted and uneasy. 'He was insolent to me,' he said, 'so I gave him a blow. Probably he has run off because of that.' And he told me that I should thrash you.' Gwalchmai smiled sadly. 'Ach, Rhuawn. He is a good man, brave and honourable and generous, but he is too much of a clansman and too much of a warrior, and it distorts his vision of things. Some other warriors of Maelgwn's told me that Rhuawn knocked you down in a quarrel, but no one had seen you since. I did not think you would have run off, but there was nothing to do. Yet I mistrusted Rhuawn. Medraut had lied to him and lied to him, and I no longer knew what Rhuawn might be thinking or feeling. Medraut lied to you, too, but I thought I could trust you further...' He noticed my look and added, 'Well, but you are not one to plot behind a mask or listen to fine justifications of what is not true. And perhaps, when a warrior is sent on many missions to foreign kings, even if he is honest in himself, he grows able to wear a face not his and suspect all his companions. So I mistrusted Rhuawn. I left the fortress early on the next morning, thinking you might have left the stronghold, and hoping you had left a message. And I found the message. The sword and the brooch were plain enough: Medraut had threatened you; but for a time I did not understand the hawthorn. I sat in that tree and fingered it and wondered what you could mean. And then I remembered the hawthorn flowering at Baddon, and the warcry and the Saxon shield-wall breaking, and I knew that you meant Rhuawn.' He looked at me, and I nodded. He went on. 'It darkened the sun for me. I have known Rhuawn very many years, and liked him well since the first day I joined the Family. Mistrust him as I did, I had not thought he would league with Medraut to kill or ensorcel you...'

'He didn't. I just wanted you to be wary of him.'

'So you say now. But at the time I thought he was plotting against us, with Medraut and my mother. I threw the hawthorn away and trod it into the ground, and rode back to Degannwy at a gallop, taking the brooch and the sword.

'I went to Rhuawn first; he was still in our house. I opened the door quietly and found him sitting on the bed, sharpening a spear. He gave me a greeting, cheerful but a bit forced. I only closed the door and looked at him until he asked what the matter was. Then I showed him the sword and the brooch, and told him how I had found them. He took the sword in his hands, turning it over, looking at the brooch. I said: 'There was a sprig of hawthorn bound to the sword, which I have taken to mean you. Do you claim to know nothing of this?' He set it down again, too quickly. 'I know nothing about it. Where is Medraut?' 'I do not know,' I replied, 'nor do I care: where is Rhys?' And then he accused me of not caring for my brother and for my own clan. And I said that my brother plotted against me, and Rhuawn had joined him, betraying Arthur and myself.' He paused, and added, 'I must ask his forgiveness for that word. But I was very angry. He became angry as well, but frightened. He said 'You *are* mad'; and I did not know what he meant . . .'

'It's what Medraut had been suggesting to us,' I said. I had not told him the details of the quarrel. He gave me a sharp look and I added, 'Medraut said that the Darkness was all a delusion of yours, born of the same madness that touches you in battle. He made it sound very plausible.'

'So that is it. Rhuawn refused to talk to me. I asked him about the hawthorn again, and he said that the whole message was two-edged nonsense and impossible to inter- pret, and that anyone might have stolen the brooch and left it. I do not think he believed it, but his honour was at stake because I had accused him of treachery. I finally told him that I would seek out Medraut. He angrily insisted on joining me.

'Medraut did not return until afternoon. I think my mother must have worked to heal his head and then left while it was still night, because she was already at the fortress, and he came back alone. We caught him before he could slink into his house, while he was still leading his horse into its stall in the stables. I gave him the sword, saying, 'This is yours, I think.' He took it, stared at it, and I think he was troubled, but then he smiled, trying to be charming. 'It is indeed,' he said. 'I lost it yesterday after- noon. I was looking for it; where did you find it?' I told him, and he shook his head. 'But Rhys was not there?' he asked me. 'Very strange.' He looked at Rhuawn and said, 'Rhys wanted to leave the fortress and had a quarrel with some of Maelgwn's men at the gate, and they followed him to stop him. I heard about it and went after, but the men thought he had been insolent to them and were stubborn and we came to blows. I was hit on the head, and I do not know what happened to Rhys after. Perhaps this was left by one of Maelgwn's men.'

'Rhuawn heard this tale with attention, and, after a moment's pause, nodded eagerly. I saw that he would accept it. But I asked Medraut which men of Maelgwn's had been responsible. He named names without hesitation, but he would not meet my eyes. And I knew that he lied, but that he could have the men he had named ready to join him in the lie within an hour, and that there was nothing I could do to stop him. So I let him keep the sword, and told him that I did not believe his tale, and left him there with Rhuawn. But Degannwy was unsafe for me, and I thought in my heart that I would leave as soon as I was able to without giving insult to Maelgwn.

'However, Agravain arrived from Camlann that night, and . . .'

'Agravain?' I asked in astonishment.

Gwalchmai nodded, tiredly. 'Agravain wanted to come when first my lord Arthur received news from me. He wanted to see our father. Arthur was reluctant to allow him to come, fearing that he would be forced into a position where his loyalties were divided; but eventually my lord yielded, and Agravain rode from Camlann to Degannwy as fast as his horses could take him. He arrived that night. The feast hall was very loud and ugly that night, with Maelgwn's men and my father's about to quarrel, and plenty of mead poured out to help them. But when Agravain burst into the hall it was like lighting a lamp in a dark place. Agravain was always popular with Lot's warband, and everyone murmured as he came up the hall. But my brother paid no attention to anyone but Lot. He walked directly to him, and they embraced the way friends do after a battle, when each has thought the other dead and devoured by wolves. But Lot and Agravain were always close: their wills held the same rhythm and they delighted in the same joys. When Arthur demanded Agravain as a hostage for my father's peace, it was a heavy grief to Lot, a thing that stole the colour from the earth.' Gwalchmai hesitated, then went on, 'My father always intended Agravain to be king of the Islands after him, and the royal clan and the warband had always favoured him, he was so plainly what a warrior should be. Now . . . I do not know. But after embracing our father he turned to me, and then greeted all the men in the warband with great delight. My father had him sit on his own right and called for a harper. It was very good to see my father so. He became more what he used to be. He began by asking Agravain about Arthur, and then about all our battles; and then they talked war and hunting and laughed together. But Medraut left shortly after Agravain arrived. He bowed to Lot, and said that his head ached from its pounding, and that he must lie down. I did not like the fact that he left, and I was sure he went to tell Morgawse that Agravain had come, if she didn't know already – but, on the other hand, it seemed likely that his head did ache, and I had no desire to leave the feast hall myself.

'My father and Agravain also left the hall early, to talk, my father with his hand on my brother's shoulder. Their gladness was as sharp and bright as a sword's edge, and it cut me to joy when I looked at them. I have never been able to be what my father wanted, but Agravain . . . well, it was very good. So I watched them go, and smiled as I watched them, and it was the last time I saw my father living.'

I stared at Gwalchmai in shock. I had not imagined that anything so huge could have happened to him. He looked down the road without turning, tapping the fingers of one thin, strong hand against his knee. 'My lord . . .' I said.

He shook his head. 'It is better so. Dear God, Lot could not go on thus. He was a proud, strong man, and he knew where he had fallen to. Better to have died now, than years from now; best to have died before this.' I looked away from him. Whether or not one was close to him, whether or not it was a good time, a father dead is a piece of one's universe missing. He couldn't feel what I would, if it were my father, but he felt something nonetheless, and I did not think he wanted me saying anything about it.

He began the tale again. 'Agravain was with him when it happened. He said Lot stopped in the midst of a sentence, clutched at his head, cried out and fell over. Agravain tried to help him, then ran back to the feast hall to fetch me, but there was nothing either of us could do. And there was a sense of Darkness in that room to chill the heart's blood, with my father lying stiff and grey by the hearth. I knew how he came to die so quickly.'

'Morgawse?' He still did not look towards me, but he nodded. His face was intensely expressionless. 'But why?'

He gave a shrug. 'I think she feared that Agravain would cause difficulties in her affair with Maelgwn. And also, Agravain was a rival to Medraut in winning the loyalty of the warband and the succession to the kingship of Orcade. But I am as certain that she blotted out my father's life as I am certain that the sun sets to rise. If I had thought sooner, when Medraut left the hall! But he was dead. We laid him on a bier to mourn him, and raised the coronach – that is an Irish dirge – by torchlight, most of the night. Agravain was wild: he flung himself beside the corpse and swore ... what is the matter?'

'Nothing,' I said. 'Just a dream. Go on.'

He gave me a steady, serious look. 'I remember that your father also has dreams. I would be grateful if you could tell it me.'

'Only that the day after your father died I dreamed that I saw the Queen casting a spell, and then a funeral procession with a covered body on a bier and Agravain as a mourner. I thought the body was yours. But go on.'

He nodded, apparently calmer about it than I was. 'Agravain swore that any person who had any part in killing Lot should die by his sword, and that Lot was the greatest king in all Erin, and all Britain, and all the Islands.'

'What about Arthur?'

'Arthur is not a king; he is High King,' my lord replied, a very faint smile touching his lips and vanishing again. 'Well, we stayed up all the night. When the first sun made the world breathe again, Agravain took me aside. That was yesterday morning. I felt as though the day were made of fine, bright, brittle glass and might shatter at any instant. I could tell from Agravain's eyes that it was the same to him if the sun rose or if it was swallowed by the earth for ever. 'Mother did this,' he said. I shook my head. 'Do not seek to deny it or explain it away; you know as surely as I that she killed him, she and that white-haired bastard half-brother of ours ...'

I was a bit shocked. 'Can't he accept that Lot was

Medraut's father as well?' I asked.

Gwalchmai gave me a very startled look. 'But he wasn't. Everyone knows that.'

I felt stupid and confused. 'I didn't know that. Why do you say so?'

'Everyone always knew. Medraut was born in Britain. My father came down to do some fighting in the north, and he left my mother at the court of her father, the Pendragon Uther. My father was gone from May until December, and Medraut was born in the next June. And besides that . . .' He stopped himself sharply.

'You know who his father is?' I asked, even more astonished.

He said nothing, shaking his head. 'But you do,' I insisted.

'Yes, I know. But let it rest there, Rhys *mo chara*. Ach, it is not that I do not trust you, but that secret is not mine to give away.'

'But who . . . does Medraut's father know?'

'He knows. But there is nothing he can do. Morgawse always had plans for Medraut. I do not think that Medraut knows, though, and he is happier so. Let it rest.'

We rode on silently for a little while. I tried to adjust the fact that everyone had always known Medraut to be a bastard into my picture of him; and then, for some strange reason, I thought of the Emperor Arthur, his straight fair hair and wide-set grey eyes. But no, Arthur was Morgawse's half-brother, and it was impossible.

'So, Agravain spoke very wildly,' Gwalchmai continued. 'He made me afraid for him. Our mother never liked him, and he is defenceless in too many ways to defy her openly. The rest of our father's warband knew it. It is strange: I could have sworn that Medraut held that warband to command it as he pleased, but it was plain to me that most of the men would follow Agravain, if Morgawse were not there. They never liked Morgawse, but they feared her greatly. Enough men have defied her only to disappear from the green earth for any of them to disobey her. But they hated to be ruled by a foreign woman and a witch, and Medraut was too near her and too close to her for their tastes. Many of the men had fought beside Agravain many years ago, and they wanted to be loyal; but they would not dare to support him against Morgawse.

'Maelgwn Gwynedd came to see Lot's corpse, and ordered the rest of Degannwy into mourning, from sympathy, but it was clear that he was pleased that our father was dead, and expected to have the warband and my father's possessions freely his. Agravain wanted to kill him at once. It is a good thing that Maelgwn speaks no Irish, or there would have been a fight between the warbands on the spot. As it was, I had to calm Agravain, and stay with him for hours. Finally I promised him that I would go and talk to our mother, and I made him promise not to act until I was done with that.

'I had been intending to see her since I first realized that Medraut and Rhuawn would give me no information about what had happened to you, but I'd looked for a public place to catch her in. Now, I knew, I had to speak with her privately. Medraut had vanished – I suppose he was off fetching you. I did not know what to do.

'Then, in the middle of the afternoon, Rhuawn came and sought me out. I left Agravain for a little and talked with him instead. He gave me a very strange look and said, 'So you have care for some of your family.' I replied, 'I have care for all of them, as far as I may for each, but some are my enemies. Medraut has hated me since I left the islands, and hated our lord Arthur even longer. Why have you listened to him?' He grew cold again. 'Medraut is not your enemy nor mine,' he said. 'He left Degannwy out of trouble over your father's death. But he sent me a message to say that he has found Rhys.' 'Where?' I asked. 'At a shepherd's hut, up in the mountains. He is hurt. Medraut says he wants you to come. I can show you the way there, this evening.'

'I almost agreed. I was tired, and my father's death made me want to see Medraut again. It is true, that much of what he told you, that we were close once. That is probably why he hates me so deeply now, because he truly feels that I have betrayed him. And Rhuawn was asking me to come with him, and I had already resolved to face my mother, so why should I fear Medraut alone? But as I was about to say that I would go then, I suddenly felt that Rhuawn was too quiet, and I recalled your message. I looked at his face, and it was as though I glimpsed another's face reflected there, like the bottom of a pond glimpsed through the bright mirror of its waters. So, instead of agreeing, I said, 'Perhaps. Speak to

224

me again this evening.' Rhuawn gave me a cold look and left without another word, and I went back to Agravain. You have told me that Rhuawn was not as guilty as I first thought, and now I do not know how much he understood when he made that suggestion, and how much he believed Medraut. I had said some most bitter things to him the day before, and I do not know how far my anger may have driven him. He is not a wicked man.'

'He knew better than to betray you,' I said. 'He knew you for years, and by your life and actions, and he knew Medraut only by his words, and that for a few weeks only. A man may be deluded by another's eloquence, but, by all the saints in Heaven, anyone with any sense ought to know better than to accuse a sane friend of madness.'

Gwalchmai only shook his head. 'Rhuawn is a good man . . . At any rate, when he had left, I thought for a time, and decided that I wished to see for myself what was happening. As you know, I have done a good amount of riding, and I knew of several shepherds' huts which Rhuawn might have meant. But they had earlier said that you left the fortress. That meant that it was probable the place they thought of was to the north, towards the main road. I gave it some more thought, then told Agravain what I intended, and prepared myself for as long a journey as might be necessary. And the second shepherd's hut I found had my mother's horse tied up before it. The rest you know. But, cousin . . .' He reined in Ceincaled suddenly and caught my forearm with his sword hand, so that I had to stop too. He met my eyes very seriously, and spoke deliberately, very quietly, 'I owe you a very great debt. My mother's shadow has lain across my whole life, but now I am free of it. Yet, if you had not stopped me from killing her, she would have bound me in it for ever. That alone would give me gratitude enough for a lifetime, but you have taken this whole struggle when it was not by nature yours, and you have fought and suffered to hold the faith when . . .'

'My lord Gwalchmai, for God's sake no more of that! When it comes to people being saved, you saved me a good deal more than I saved you. And if the conflict between Light and Darkness is not my struggle, whose is it? I have never heard that only warriors are allowed to serve God. I've done no more than I should have.' And I looked down at the spot on the saddle leather to avoid his eyes. Ronan, or Ronan's servant, really should have cleaned that.

Gwalchmai gave my arm a slight pressure, then released it. 'Indeed?' I looked back up, matter-of-fact as I was able to be, and he smiled, then suddenly touched Ceincaled, and the horse leapt to a canter. I kicked my rather bad-tempered warhorse into following. Gwalchmai called back, 'How much further is it to this St Elena's? That beast of Ronan's is supposedly a warhorse: we ought to be making better time.'

We made good time, actually, and reached St Elena's shortly after noon. I nearly missed the turning, but managed to remember a tall ash tree, and we picked our way down the path used by Father Gilla and his mare.

We had to rap repeatedly on the high wooden gate before the little window in the top of it opened and a thin, brown-eyed face peered out. 'We've no room for travellers,' said the woman.

'We're not seeking hospitality,' I said. 'But my friend Eivlin is sick and staying with you, as I did myself until yesterday afternoon . . .'

'Sanctam Mariam Matrem! You're the one they dragged off yesterday, those terrible warriors. How is it that you're here?'

'My lord here rescued me. He's come now to help heal my friend: you can ask Sister Teleri if you doubt me.'

The face vanished and the window closed. We waited a while, me standing by the gate, Gwalchmai on Ceincaled, leaning forward with one arm across his knees. Eventually the window was flung open again and the sharp dark face of Teleri peered out.

'Rhys. It is you then.'

'It is me, returned and in one piece. And I have brought my lord here.' Teleri looked behind me for the first time, and her stare fixed. Gwalchmai leapt from his horse, paused an instant to catch his balance, then gave a slight bow.

The gate opened. 'Come in, then.' Teleri surveyed Gwalchmai with intent interest, but spoke to me. 'Your Eivlin is no better, which is what you were gaping your mouth to ask, I suppose. Ach, man. I am glad to see you whole, and to know that you gave the slip to those wild Irish devils. Can your lord help the girl?'

I shrugged. Gwalchmai, just entered through the gate

and looking about himself, answered for me. 'It is possible, though not certain. I will try.' He paused, then earnestly asked his own question, 'My servant Rhys has told me that my lady Elidan, daughter of Caw, is of your sisterhood.'

'She is,' said Teleri flatly. 'Will you see this Eivlin lass now?'

He nodded. 'Yes. Where may I leave my horse?'

With Ceincaled and my warhorse left standing in the yard, we followed Teleri into the low-roofed building. A number of nuns had already gathered about to see, and they all stared very hard at Gwalchmai. His crimson cloak and war gear marked him out very plainly. But he only gave a courteous nod to those he passed and ignored the stares. He was probably used to it.

Eivlin had been brought to one of the nun's cells, and she lay on the bed, wrapped in blankets, looking very pale and lifeless. Only her hair lay over the mattress, and one sunbeam touched it, bringing out its ripe wheat colour. It cut me to the bone to see her so, and I stopped in the doorway, so that Gwalchmai nearly bumped into me. I stared at Eivlin.

Teleri, already by the bed, looked about impatiently. 'Well, stop staring like an ox and come in,' she snapped, 'if indeed you wish to see if your lord can help her.' I started and came in, standing aside. Gwalchmai entered and walked over to the bed. He dropped to one knee, caught her wrist and laid the back of his other hand against her forehead. He frowned.

'There is no fever,' he told Teleri.

'Truly? That I found out at once.' Teleri put her hands on her hips. 'No, there is nothing wrong to be found with her, except that, for all we do, she will not wake or stir. Now, Rhys says that he baptized her, and I've heard tell that baptism is death to sin; but if so, she's been rather thorough about it.'

'Did you try giving her hot mead with mint?' asked Gwalchmai.

She looked startled and dropped her hands. 'We did. A fine shock that, to wake sleepers. But she can't swallow, and didn't stir.'

'Her heart beats very faintly.'

'And grows fainter. You have some knowledge of medicine, I think.'

'A little. Mostly the care of wounds.' Gwalchmai took his hand from Eivlin's wrist and knelt, looking at her. 'I have worked with Gruffydd ap Cynan after my lord Arthur's battles – except when I was wounded myself, of course.'

'Indeed?' asked Teleri, a different note in her voice, one perilously like respect. 'Now there is a physician I have heard much about.'

'He is very skilled.' Gwalchmai brushed a strand of hair from Eivlin's face and shifted his hand to his sword. He frowned again.

Teleri took a step closer, then knelt beside him, straightening her gown. 'Your servant Rhys ap Sion believes this sleep to be the result of a curse. I have no knowledge of curses and less liking for them as causes of sickness, but if it is not, I do not know why she does not wake.'

'It is a curse. But now – the force of the curse is gone, and only the sleep is left. The Darkness struck her very hard and deep before it vanished, and life has gone very far away from her. And yet . . .' He chewed his lower lip, then deliberately drew his sword.

Teleri looked at him sharply, one hand ready to seize his sword hand. He smiled a little, apologetically. 'I wish to try something. I do not know whether it will help or not. This sword is no common weapon, so it may.' Teleri lowered her hand, still watching him suspiciously.

Gwalchmai laid the flat of the sword across Eivlin's forehead. She did not move or stir. He shifted his grip on the hilt, settling it, nervously rubbing his mouth with his other hand. I took another step nearer to see, looking at Eivlin's pale face under the cold steel. Gwalchmai bowed his head, his shoulders hunched.

Slowly, the sword began to glow. I heard Teleri's gasp loud in the small room, but I only looked at Eivlin. The wavering, submarine light flickered down the edge of the steel, traced a sinuous line along the centre of the blade, and focused in the hilt to a deep rose shade.

Gwalchmai dropped his free hand to his thigh, bracing himself. 'Dulce Lux,' he said clearly, but almost to himself, 'Care Domine, miserere . . .' and, changing his languages, 'O Ard Rígh Mor . . .' He straightened his shoulders, and the light shot down the sword, flaming into white brilliance. 'Lighten our darkness, we pray you, Lord . . .'

'Amen,' said Teleri, wondering. I barely heard her, for at that moment Eivlin drew a deep breath. I dropped down behind the other two and reached between them to catch her hand. Her fingers were cold, but I had a shock from them like the shock one gets in cold, dry weather. Gwalchmai caught the sword's hilt in both hands, sweat streaming into his beard, and threw his head back, eyes focused on nothing. He said something in Irish, poetry I think, his voice almost singing it. Eivlin's breast heaved, and I thought the colour was returning to her cheeks.

'Eivlin!' I said, and she opened her eyes, looked over the sword and the other two, and saw me.

'Rhys!' she answered, and pushed away the sword to sit up. The light flashed out, and Gwalchmai bowed his head, letting the blade drop to the floor. He held the hilt limply with both hands.

'Rhys,' repeated Eivlin, and got out of the bed. 'What is all this? You should not be up like this, with your head. What have you done with the pony?'

'Eivlin.' It was all I could say.

'Eivlin, Eivlin, he says. But what has happened? Where are we? I have had a nightmare and a sweet dream, and then you wake me from the second with your "Eivlin", and we are nowhere. Ach, how is your poor head?'

Teleri laughed, and Eivlin looked at her for the first time, then let her eyes slip to Gwalchmai. They widened, very blue, and she looked back to me. 'It was not a nightmare, was it?' she said. She began to shake a little, and I got up and put my arm around her. 'My lady sent a . . . but I am alive! We are alive, and it is gone! Did you work that Christian sorcery of yours?'

'Well, I did,' I replied.

Teleri gave me a very dubious look, and stood up briskly. 'The man says that he baptized you. In a most irregular fashion, near drowning the both of you, which is not required. And you have slept for two days, and would have slept for ever, if this lord had not woken you.'

Eivlin looked to Gwalchmai again and turned crimson. 'I thank you, lord Gwalchmai ap Lot.'

Gwalchmai looked up, then slowly stood, sheathing his

229

sword. 'Any service I have rendered you is slight in comparison with the great gift you have given to me and to my servant Rhys, in risking your life to oppose the Queen my mother.'

She flushed an even deeper red. 'I did not save him for you, but for myself.'

'I know. He has already told me that you plan to marry.'

She whirled on me, and I felt my face grow hot. 'Indeed, Rhys ap Sean? And when did you ask me if I would marry you?'

'I . . . well, it merely came out so, when I was speaking to my lord.'

'You should not be saying such things without asking first. It is I that you would marry, not your lord.'

'I – I . . . does that mean you won't?'

'Now, did I say that?' She looked proudly at the wall, crossing her arms. 'Think yourself, though, how it is to be told that you are going to be married, and not knowing it. Indeed!'

'Forgive me. Will you, then?' I had not meant to ask her so bluntly, but I had to, to appease her.

She gave me a very bright look. 'It may be so.' And then she threw her arms around me and said, 'Och, Rhys, Rhys *mo chroidh ban*, I am alive!' She began to cry. I stroked her hair and patted her on the back, carefully not looking at Teleri or Gwalchmai.

Teleri coughed. 'The girl should have something to eat.' Eivlin did not move. I didn't want her to, either. Teleri sighed. 'Well, then, I will find Elidan, and we will bring her something.'

'Elidan,' said Gwalchmai. Without looking up, I could sense how his eyes fixed on Teleri.

'Yes, your lady, Elidan,' Teleri said, then, rather sadly, 'you may speak to her, but I do not think she will wish to speak long.'

'If all she will give me is a short while, it will be enough.'

Teleri's light steps lingered in the doorway, and I knew she nodded; and then they passed on down the passageway. I glanced up. Gwalchmai moved over to the doorway and leaned there, looking out, and I could turn my attention back to Eivlin.

Eivlin stopped crying and began to demand to know

230

where we were and what had happened. I got as far as telling her about Medraut, when Gwalchmai stiffened, moved aside, and Teleri returned with a tray of food. Elidan entered, slowly, behind her.

Teleri set the food down by the bed. Elidan merely stood, calm, straight, looking at Gwalchmai.

He dropped sweepingly to one knee. 'My lady.'

She faced him, eyes narrowing a trifle. 'Lord Gwalchmai.' She glanced over to us. 'I am glad you succeeded in healing this girl.'

'It is cause enough for gladness. But, my lady, I have searched for you over all Britain. Allow me the favour of speaking what I have long desired to say to you.'

Her face did not change. 'You wish to ask my forgiveness – or so your servant says.'

'Yes.' He bowed his head, his hand tightening on his sword hilt.

Eivlin, staring in astonishment, glanced quickly at me. I shook my head. I did not want to stir; we were quite outside any of this, and I think all of us sensed it.

'Lady,' Gwalchmai began, when Elidan's silence became too heavy to bear, 'I know that I wronged you. I treated your love, which was beyond price, as a thing of little value, and I brought dishonour upon you before your clan and your kingdom. I swore you an oath, and broke it, and I killed your brother, disregarding both you and my own lord's command. These things are true, and surely they give me need of repentance. They have grieved me, since first I realized what I had done, more bitterly than any wound. And because you did not know this, I felt I must say it to you, that I know it was wrong, and that . . .' he stopped.

'You would say?' asked Elidan.

'That I loved you then, and love you now, and I beg that you, of your own nobility, pardon the wrong.'

'That is not nobility,' said Elidan. Her voice was even, but rough with strain. She clenched her hands by her sides, unclenched them, drew a deep breath. 'I never thought to see you again, after you left Caer Ebrauc. I never believed you regretted your crime. I believe you now, that you regret it, and . . . it helps. And yet . . .' She turned from him, braced herself against the wall. 'When first I knew that you had betrayed me, I thought I would go to my brother

231

Hueil and ask him for vengeance. But I knew that that request would destroy him, as the desire for vengeance had destroyed Bran; and I could not do that. Against my own desire, I bore the wrong without striking back, accepted dishonour, and left Caer Ebrauc. Slowly I came to accept the shame as my own penance for assenting to sleep with my brother's murderer, and I accepted the helplessness. You must accept the same.'

'My lady . . .'

'No!' she turned back to him, and there were tears on her face now. 'No! I once said I would kill myself before I would let you come near me again; and though I have bent that oath for this, I have not broken it, nor will I break it. I am not your lady; I am Elidan of St Elena's Abbey, and nothing to do with you.'

He looked up at her then, and her face did move. She bit her lip, as in pain, jerking her hands up as though she would press them against her face, forcing them down again. 'No,' she repeated, in a whisper this time. 'The sight of you is like a knife to my heart, and makes me remember things I would rather forget: love, too much love; and betrayal and callousness and murder and dishonour. Go away.'

'I know the truth of my own will in this,' Gwalchmai replied in a low voice. 'I will go, if you desire it. But can you not be merciful?'

She shook her head. 'I cannot be weak. I will not believe you and accept you again. I trusted you once, and was betrayed, and I will not be made a fool of again. It is a lie. The world is a lie, its beauty a deceit. I trusted it once, and I will not do so again. Such honour as I have, I will keep, here, and so let the rest perish, miserably as it is evil. I must be strong; I am the sister of a king, daughter of kings . . .' She gave a long sob, looking at him desperately. 'For God's sake, go!'

Gwalchmai bowed his head once more. 'As you will.' He stood, and said quietly, 'Rhys, I will wait for you by the horses. When you and Eivlin have decided when you wish to leave, come and tell me, and we will arrange the travelling. Elidan . . .' He lifted one hand towards her, then dropped it. 'I wish you joy.' He gave a bow which included all in the room, and left. The quiet was heavier than a tombstone.

Elidan sat on the bed and buried her face in her hands, shoulders shaking again.

'You're a fool,' said Teleri.

The other shook her head.

'Child, you love him yet, and he loves you to doting. What are you wanting, to refuse to forgive him?'

'I love him,' Elidan said in a muffled voice. 'I had not thought I did. I thought it was all dead within me and yet . . . but oh God, God, how can one trust the world? What would my clan say?'

'Your clan!' That brought an edge of contempt in Teleri's voice. 'What does that matter?'

Elidan looked up, her face wet, eyes terribly steady. 'They would be right. One cannot make peace with the world.'

'If one cannot forgive evils, how is anyone to live?'

'I must be strong,' Elidan said to herself, ignoring Teleri. 'Thank God I was strong . . . The world's evils are the truth of the world. Let it fall back into the night it came from!'

Her words suddenly recalled another voice, a thin, cold, inhuman voice saying 'All must fall back to the Darkness . . . Light is illusion, Darkness is true and strong.' The memory made me shake. 'Lady,' I said, slowly, 'that is not a very Christian thing to say.'

She stood, eyes chilling, still wet with tears. 'Be quiet!' she said, her tone that of a king's daughter. 'Let me alone!' And she fled the room, slamming the door behind her.

Teleri looked at the closed door, her face worn and old and very sad. 'And what have you shut yourself away from in honour, I wonder,' she whispered, to herself. 'You know, poor lady, but you will not yield for all that. You want to shut it all out, but you've only shut yourself in, and oh, child, will you ever get out again?' She shook her head, then turned to Eivlin with a shadow of her usual briskness. 'Come. I've brought you some sausages, and oat cakes with honey. You must eat them all, for you're sadly in need of food and drink.'

Eivlin shook her head, still staring at the closed door.

'Eat your oat cakes, and have some of this milk,' Teleri ordered. 'There's no point in talking about it.'

The milk was drunk and the oat cakes consumed in

silence. Once she had begun eating, Eivlin discovered that she was hungry. Teleri noticed me eyeing the food, sighed, and departed to return with more, and with a little package. 'For your lord,' she said, handing the latter to me. I thanked her, wanting to say more to her than I was able, and started eating. For all the strong feelings and high commitments on earth, one still has to eat, and that bread and cheese at day-break seemed a long way off.

When Eivlin was scraping the last of the honey off the plate with a fragment of oat cake, I finally asked her when she wanted to leave.

'Now.' She popped the crumb into her mouth and dusted her hands off.

'Ach, don't be silly,' said Teleri. 'You were near to death an hour ago.'

'Indeed, and perhaps I was, but now, thanks to your god and Rhys's lord Gwalchmai, I am fine again and ready to leave.'

Teleri shook her head. 'You would faint on the road.'

'I will not. I have just eaten, and I will ride a horse, and there is nothing the matter with me, since the curse is done with. I feel better than I have for long and long, and Rhys wants to leave now.'

'I didn't say anything,' I objected.

'And why should you need to, what with mooning at the door like a cow about to bellow for her calf? You've no wish to stay here with me and see your lord ride off alone.'

'I'm concerned for him,' I admitted. 'He deserved better than that.'

Eivlin looked at me evenly a moment, then shrugged. 'I think he did. He must be a fine man.'

I bit my lip and stood up. 'Eivlin, it's only for a while. If you want it, in a month or so we can go back to my clan's farm and settle there. You will have my whole clan there, and the finest holding near the Mor Hafren, and all manner of things will be well.'

Her eyes lit up. 'A sweet thing, that, to have a clan, to be no outcast and have no curse. But now. To be sure, I do not know all that has happened yet: you say it has been days, you say he freed you from Medraut and defeated my lady – a great thing that! – and now he will ride off on an unknown course. But I know enough to know that you will follow him, the more so because he has been hurt. And I will not be left behind. If I must steal a horse and ride after secretly, I will. If you are going to travel into a hostile land, with no certainty of coming back alive and whole, I swear by the sun and the wind – no, I swear by Christ – I am coming with you. We will leave now.'

Teleri shook her head. 'Neither of you should leave. Rhys ap Sion, I have not forgotten your head injury. You need the rest as much as she.'

'And Gwalchmai?' I asked. 'And if I stay here, what must I say to Elidan?'

Teleri frowned. 'There is that.'

'I do not think I am likely to be tactful to her; I think she is being a fool.'

'I do not think you are a great one for tact,' she agreed drily. 'Well, but this girl?'

'I am coming. I am not to be got rid of so easily.'

Teleri crossed her arms and frowned at Eivlin. Eivlin stared insolently back, and crossed her arms with an identical air. Teleri's lips quivered, and she fought for a moment to stop herself, but finally yielded and smiled. She sat down on the bed beside Eivlin and patted her arm. 'Less sick by far than you are wilful, my girl. But ach, I was wilful myself at your age, joining the sisters with my whole family howling at me no; and there's no harm to wilfulness in the right place. Go then, and when you've married this man of yours, be sure that the two of you aren't stubborn at the same time, for I think you and he could make the North Sea in February look like a quiet lake. Rhys, go tell your lord that we'll be out when I've found some things for Eivlin.' When I gaped, she snorted and snapped, 'Go along.'

I left, wondering. If I had looked at Teleri that way, I felt sure, I would not have convinced her of anything, but all Eivlin did was look insolent, and all was smooth sailing. The North Sea in February?

Gwalchmai was, as he had promised, waiting by the horses. He stood leaning against the abbey wall, idly stroking Ceincaled's neck while the stallion nibbled at his hair. When he saw me coming, though, he straightened, gave the horse a slap on the withers, and limped across to meet me.

'We can all leave together now – or as soon as Eivlin

comes out with Teleri,' I told him.

'But she was near to death. She cannot be ready to travel.'

'She will leave now, she says, if she must steal a horse to do so. I think she will be well enough. Any weakness she had was from hunger and weariness, and the hunger should be much better now. And, since we speak of hunger, Teleri gave me this for you.' I held out the package.

He blinked at it vaguely and made no move to take it. 'But you should wait here a few days. I can go back to Degannwy alone, and rejoin you later.'

'To Degannwy?' I stared at him. 'I thought we decided that that would be too dangerous.'

'And it would have been, arriving on the tail of Ronan's friends. Considerations of policy matter little to warbands when some of their number are newly dead. But it should be calmer now. Maelgwn should have less reason to wish for my death, with my mother defeated, and Agravain is there to calm down the warriors. I must go back to see Agravain. He knew I might be a few days, but he will not be peaceful until I am back, and I fear what he might say to Maelgwn.'

It was reasonable. Degannwy sounded safe enough. In fact ... 'Very well then, we can all go to Degannwy,' I said.

He looked dubious.

'My lord, it is not far, and Eivlin can ride with me. If your elder brother has a following in Degannwy, it's safer than St Elena's here. Medraut knows where this place is, and, if he's still alive, he might track us here again.'

Gwalchmai shook his head. 'He wouldn't. I doubt he will care for anything for long and long. The image of his god was broken with my mother's power.'

'As you say, then. But we will leave, regardless. Eivlin and Teleri will be out in a minute.'

Gwalchmai shook his head tiredly, tried to object again, then suddenly smiled a slight, almost apologetic smile and threw up his hands in surrender. I wanted to clasp his shoulder, talk to him as I would have talked to my brother or my cousins, and get him to talk the pain out. But I knew he wouldn't, that he would only retreat into attentive courtesy; so I nodded and went to put Teleri's package of oat cakes into the saddle-bags of Ronan's warhorse.

Teleri and Eivlin took their time. I had an uneasy feeling that Teleri was supplying provisions for any conditions of weather or the roads, and I could picture Eivlin cheerfully packing it all. Well, Gwalchmai certainly wouldn't want to stay at Degannwy very long, and if we travelled with him we'd need anything Teleri could think of to give. Eventually the two emerged from the building carrying, as I had anticipated, a huge pack. After some struggle, Gwalchmai managed to tie this onto Ceincaled in such a way that it did not render it impossible for him to pull out his spears.

Teleri watched him check those spears, then snapped her fingers and turned to me. 'We still have that spear you brought when you first came here,' she said. 'Do you want it back now?'

I looked at her blankly.

'Come, the spear you gave Gwyn to carry!'

'Oh! That is his spear. He didn't want anyone to know he owned one, though, and so said it was mine. Perhaps you could give it back to him – secretly.'

Teleri compressed her lips, but her eyes glinted, and she nodded. I explained to Gwalchmai, carefully casual, 'Gwyn is the boy who showed me the path here. He's one of the children the abbey raises out of charity. He's marked out to be a priest, so naturally they don't want him to play with spears.'

Gwalchmai nodded and rechecked the fastenings of the pack. Teleri shot me a slantwise look, but said nothing. She understood what I was doing, and why.

Everything tied in its place, Gwalchmai turned to Teleri and bowed. 'Sister Teleri, I think the three of us owe you much.'

She snorted. 'For healing this girl and her ox of a man? What else is a woman who purports to be a healer supposed to do? But I think you intend to thank me for it.'

He smiled. 'I do so intend, if you will permit it. Most persons in your place would consider our loyalties once and immediately become enemies, and I have hurt a friend of yours. The debt we owe is the greater because of this. I cannot speak of payment, and yet . . .' he tore the gold armlets from his arm and offered them to her. 'If you would take these, as a token of my gratitude and your worth, I would be honoured.'

Her eyebrows went up, and she stared at the armlets, as well she might, for they were heavy and worth a good deal. She put out her hand slowly and took one. 'This I'll keep,' she said, and then, taking another, 'and this goes to satisfy the other sisters for the things I have given you. Keep the rest, Lord. You may need money. So: go, and God's blessing be upon you, with a smooth journey.'

Gwalchmai slid the remaining armlet back over his wrist, gave another bow, and mounted. I caught Teleri's arms, told her thank you, kissed her – which surprised her – and scrambled onto Ronan's horse. Teleri embraced Eivlin and helped her onto the saddle in front of me. Then she opened the gate, and we rode out from St Elena's.

We had not reached the main road when we had to make another farewell. Gwyn burst from the wood carrying a sword made of two sticks, and shouted delightedly, 'Rhys! You're safe!'

Gwalchmai reined in Ceincaled hastily as the horse shied from the movement. 'Is this the boy that led you to St Elena's?' he asked me.

'Yes, my lord,' I said, not looking at him. If only Gwyn made no mention of his mother.

'You escaped?' asked Gwyn eagerly. 'Was there a fight?'

Gwalchmai sat, tall and graceful on his splendid stallion, smiling at the dirty and enthusiastic boy. 'There was a fight,' he said. 'And Rhys and I escaped. Your name, I think, is Gwyn.'

The boy looked at Gwalchmai fully for the first time, and his dark eyes widened. I could tell that he felt, as once I had felt, that here was a song come alive. He gave a deep and extraordinarily clumsy bow. 'Y-yes, Great Lord. Are you Rhys's lord, a great warrior, in the Family?'

'I am Rhys's lord, Gwalchmai ap Lot. I think I must thank you for showing my servant the way to St Elena's.'

Gwyn's face lit like a torch. 'It was no matter, Lord Gwalchmai.' In an undertone, 'Rhys, you didn't tell me that you served *him*.' He edged closer to me, then looked at Eivlin. 'And your friend is better, too, and everything's come out well, then!' He caught my foot and smiled radiantly at me. 'Rhys, did your lord rescue you, and kill all those evil warriors, like in the songs, with a fiery sword?'

I shook my head. 'Not all of them. Only some of them.'

The thought delighted him. 'I wish I had been there. I can throw spears. I would have fought them when they came, only . . .' His face fell. I remembered Elidan falling under the blow from the flat of Medraut's sword.

'Perhaps when you're older,' I said.

'I would have fought them,' Gwyn said fiercely. 'I wish they had let me. I had nightmares last night. I dreamt they were doing terrible things to you, and to Mama.'

'I'm sorry,' I said, awkwardly.

He smiled again. 'It was all right. I screamed so that I woke everyone up, and Mama gave me warm milk and sang to me until I went back to sleep; she hasn't done that since I was little.'

Gwalchmai laughed, and Gwyn remembered him, and went awkward again. 'I am glad you rescued him, Lord Gwalchmai.'

'You may be glad that he rescued me, as well, for he did that.' Gwyn gave me a highly impressed look, fastened his eyes back on Gwalchmai. My lord leaned forward, resting one arm across his knees. 'I think you lost a spear in helping Rhys.'

Gwyn nodded regretfully. 'A good one. Hywel gave it to me. I can make other ones, but I don't know how to make the points properly.'

'Perhaps you will get it back when you go home.' Gwalchmai drew one of his throwing spears from its strap and extended it towards Gwyn, butt end first. 'But in case you do not, take this.'

Gwyn took it slowly, scarcely daring to breathe. He clutched it tightly. 'Thank you, Lord Gwalchmai.' He made another attempt at a bow.

'You keep it carefully,' I said. My voice was too harsh; well, better that than to have it shaking. 'Practise with it. Become a good warrior, and then come to Camlann. The Emperor Arthur himself was a bastard raised in a monastery. It can be done.'

Gwalchmai gave me a surprised look. 'Study well, too,' he advised Gwyn. 'To be a priest is a noble thing, and I've heard that you're to be one.'

Gwyn shrugged off the notion, stroking the spear. 'I'm going to be a warrior. Do you really think I can be?' – earnestly, and to me.

239

'Yes,' I said firmly, 'If you work at it.'

Gwalchmai smiled, gathering up his reins. 'Well, the best of fortunes to you, then, and a welcome to Camlann, if you come there. Again, my thanks.' He touched Ceincaled's sides, and the horse started off at a trot. I followed, riding past Gwyn, who watched us with an exalted face, clutching his spear. When we had gone up the path a short way, I heard a triumphant whoop behind us and looked back to see him dashing down the path.

Gwalchmai was still smiling. 'He is a brave and spirited lad, that one. But you cannot think, Rhys, that he will come to Camlann.'

'He might.' I did not look at my lord. I could sense his curious glance, so I added, 'I like the boy, from what I've seen of him. I think he's being wasted at St Elena's. It makes me angry.'

Gwalchmai nodded again. From the way his smile faded as we rode on I could see that he was again thinking of Elidan. It made me bitter sick to think of him carrying that burden all his life, and sicker to think of Gwyn. But there was no answer for it. The world's a mixture, and something always goes wrong. And, on the whole, something at the back of my mind insisted, I would rather be Gwalchmai than Elidan. I did not think she would forget now, and, as Teleri had said, she was shutting herself in to shut the world out, and her spirit was too fierce to be content with that darkness.

Thirteen

The second time we entered Degannwy was like the first in that it was again dark by the time we arrived, and Maelgwn's guards again made us wait at the gates. Eivlin jeered at the one who was sent to Maelgwn, which made him walk off stiffly but in more of a hurry. I tightened the arm I had round her waist. There should be no reason for them to talk to Maelgwn. Perhaps they were only doing it to annoy us. Eivlin leaned back a little into my arms, comfortably smiling. She at least seemed unweakened by the journey. After I had managed to make Gwalchmai eat some of Teleri's provisions, I had given Eivlin the rest, so she'd no cause to go fainting from hunger.

Maelgwn's guard returned, another warrior with him. The guard nodded, and we were allowed through the gate, but the other warrior caught Ceincaled's bridle as soon as we entered. He addressed Gwalchmai in Irish.

'What is he saying?' I asked, whispering into Eivlin's ear.

She tilted her head back, looking at me. 'He's asking whether your lord will come at once to see the lord Agravain . . . he says that Agravain locked himself into his room last night, and has spoken to no one since.'

Gwalchmai questioned the other, and he responded. Eivlin continued to translate: 'Your lord says he will come at once, but asks if my lady, or his other brother, are also there. Brenaínn – that's the warrior – says that Medraut is here, but that he also has locked himself into his room, since last night. My lady has not returned. Brenaínn is afraid, and he says he mistrusts Maelgwn.'

I didn't like the sound of it. Agravain, little as I liked him, was still a security for us when he held control, but it did not sound as though his control extended very far at the moment. I had thought Morgawse soundly defeated, but what if she'd recovered? And I did not like the sound of Medraut shutting himself into his room and doing God alone knew what. And that fox Maelgwn Gwynedd still held Degannwy and all the lands about, and all his men still hated Arthur and the Family. It might be better to exercise discretion and investigate before we entered the stronghold.

Gwalchmai, however, thanked the warrior and trotted Ceincaled up the hill, head held high. I sighed and followed.

Agravain had apparently been given one of the anterooms of the feast hall, a more honourable location than our hut, though probably less comfortable. We had to pass through the hall itself to reach it. There was no proper feast that night, but Maelgwn and some of his warriors sat morosely about the high table, drinking. Gwalchmai paused to go up the hall and greet the king.

Maelgwn smiled unpleasantly. 'So, you are back then, just as my guard reported. With your servant, too. Well, well, some here are going to lose money.' Someone snickered, and Maelgwn eyed his warriors viciously. 'Myself included, then. There was high wagering that you would not return. Where is the lady, your mother the Queen?'

Gwalchmai shook his head. 'That I do not know. I last saw her yesterday. Ask of my brother Medraut.'

Maelgwn chuckled. I realized that he was drunk. 'I would have done that very thing, but no one can ask anything of your brother Medraut, any more than of your brother Agravain – or of your father Lot, though he may be in a different category. A most silent family. Do your affairs prosper? Tell me, is it true that you are a sorcerer?'

'It is not true,' Gwalchmai nearly snapped.

'Ah. I wondered, you see. You and your mother, at odds, and both . . . you ought to be a sorcerer. You look so much like her, and I think your family's bespelled. But if you see your mother, tell her I am waiting, hm? – but now you wish to talk to your brother, to your elder brother, since you will not speak to the younger. Go ahead.'

Gwalchmai bowed, freezingly courteous, and strode off to find Agravain.

The door, round the side of the feast hall, was certainly locked. My lord rapped on it, knocked again. No reply. He called, 'Agravain?' Silence. I shuffled my feet, about to suggest that Eivlin and I go off somewhere else, when I remembered that we were not safe in Degannwy. A pity. I had no wish to meet Agravain if he was in one of his rages.

Gwalchmai called again. After a moment came a sound of movement, then a short, cold command, in Irish.

'"Go away,"' Eivlin translated. I nodded. I had guessed.

'Agravain. It is me. What is the trouble?'

'Gwalchmai?' came from behind the door.

'Who else?'

An oath, footsteps; the door was flung open and Agravain stood in it staring at us. He was not a pleasant sight. He wore a mail-shirt over a badly crumpled tunic, and carried a naked sword. His bright hair and beard were matted and filthy, his eyes blood-shot and darkly circled. He had bitten through his lower lip, and the blood was smeared across his chin and cheek. He stared at Gwalchmai as though he couldn't recognize him.

'Agravain!' My lord stepped into the room, catching his brother's arms. 'God in Heaven, what has happened?'

'I killed her,' said Agravain in a horse, flat voice. 'I killed her, Gwalchmai. But she deserved it. She ... she ... och ochone, where have you been?'

'Never mind that, man, sit down. Rhys, find some mead.' Gwalchmai guided his brother into the room. I stood a moment before the door, then ran to find the mead. Eivlin looked at the other two, at me, then picked up her skirts and followed me, shouting, 'Rhys! Wait!' I stopped, waited until she caught up, and we went on together. We said nothing to each other.

Saidi ap Sugyn in the kitchens was not pleased to see either of us, but he had learned better than to argue with us. He gave us the mead, with some bread and ham I requested. If Agravain had locked himself in since the previous night, he ought to be hungry. But my brain kept repeating the words, 'I killed her'. No one needed to tell me whom he meant, and yet ... I looked at Eivlin, who was frowning deeply and carrying the bread. Her father had been under a curse for killing his brother, but this was something worse.

When we got back to the room, Gwalchmai had persuaded his brother to sit down and put the sword away, and had himself sat down beside him. He was talking, quietly and smoothly, in Irish. Agravain replied with a few incoherent words in British. My lord glanced up and nodded when I came in, so I found some goblets and poured the mead. Agravain drained his cup at once, while Gwalchmai set his down untouched. I thought Agravain had the better idea.

Agravain glared at me savagely, glanced down at the sword. Gwalchmai caught his arm again and shook him, saying, 'It is fine. Rhys is our servant; he will do no harm.'

The other shuddered and put his head in his hands. I edged over, picked up his empty cup and refilled it. When I gave it to him he drained it as quickly as he had the first, then sat staring at the bottom, clutching the empty vessel with both hands. I was afraid to disturb him. Gwalchmai signalled, so I handed him the flask of mead, and he poured more for his brother.

Agravain took only two swallows of his third cup before looking up at Gwalchmai. 'Why did you take so long coming back?'

'There were some matters of importance to me. And I had killed Ronan, you know. I could not come back at once. But you must tell me what has happened.'

Agravain began to shudder again. 'I told you. I killed her.'

'You killed our mother.' Gwalchmai's voice was clear and calm as he named the act.

'Yes. Yes. She . . . I . . . she killed Father. You know she did. She was playing the whore with that fox-haired bastard Maelgwn, so she killed Father.'

'Agravain.' Gwalchmai's hand clasped his brother's wrist, steadying, but his voice was raw with pain. 'You promised me that you would wait, that you would not act until after I had seen her.'

'Well, you went away to see her.'

'Till I'd come back, till you knew! There was no need, what have you done?'

'I killed her. She deserved it.'

'You've destroyed yourself. No, no, be still. Have some more mead.'

'I have been here, waiting for you to come back. I thought I would kill myself, at first, then I said, no, wait for Gwalchmai. Do you think they will kin-wreck me?'

Gwalchmai shook his head. 'That . . . oh. No, I think not. They may even make you king yet, and say that she was not of the blood of the clan, so that you have not murdered any kin. But *ochone, ochon, mo brathair* . . .'

'Speak British! If I try to talk of it in Irish I will go mad. It's too close to think about in Irish.' He took a deep swallow of mead and looked at his brother, more evenly now. 'I have called down the curse, haven't I? They say it is a terrible curse to kill your mother. But she deserved it.'

'But you did not, Agravain. Why did you act?'

He threw the nearly empty cup of mead across the room. 'You went out to find her. And I said, "Here am I, too cowardly to dare what my brother dares, afraid even to think of her." And then I realized, "Well, I have been afraid to think of her for years, afraid to look at her, much less fight her. But she has murdered my own father, used him up and tossed him aside and murdered him." So I got my horse and rode out. I found your tracks leaving the main road. When it was dark I found a shepherd's hut, and she was there. So was Medraut, but he was asleep. She looked very strange, as though age had touched her or her magic failed. She screamed and begged and wept and screamed. And I killed her. Medraut started waking before I could, could . . . bring down the sword; so then I had to, or he would have stopped me. So I killed her, and ran out, and came back here to wait for you. But she deserved it.'

Gwalchmai said nothing, merely embraced his brother. Agravain put his head down on the other's shoulder, clutching his arms. His shoulders shook as he began to weep. I knew that, whether or not it was dangerous to wander about Degannwy, the room was not a place for Eivlin or me. I touched her arm, and we slipped out, closing the door.

By the time I realized that I was not sure where to go, habit had brought me to the hut Maelgwn had first given us. Well, it was as good a place as any. I opened the door. Rhuawn was not there and the place needed cleaning. I went over to the hearth and built the fire up, while Eivlin sat on the bed and sliced the half loaf of bread which she'd kept. The day was too warm to warrant the fire, but the flames and the soft sound of it were comforting. When it was burning well I went and sat beside Eivlin, putting my arm about her, and we watched the smoke go up. I tried not to think of Agravain's face.

'What sort of a man was this Agravain?' Eivlin asked, after a little while.

I took a piece of the bread, thinking it over. 'A true warrior, of the sort you once told me you hated. Violent, moody, bad-tempered, though cheerful and generous enough with his equals. A fierce fighter, a fiercer feaster, and a great believer in thrashing servants to keep them in their place. God forgive me! I never liked him.'

'And now he has killed my lady, his own mother. And the thought of that act will eat into his heart, like rot eating into a wound.'

I nodded. 'My lord was right: Agravain has destroyed himself. Eivlin, my heart, it is a bitter cold thing to think of. He did not deserve it. He had enough that was noble in him: courage, honesty, great loyalty towards those he loved. You know the royal clan and the warband of the islands; do you think he will be kin-wrecked?'

'Och no. The warriors always wanted Agravain back, and spoke of him whenever they were frightened by Morgawse. King Lot had already named him as his successor. And the royal clan always hated Morgawse, though they feared her more than they hated her. They will be quick to find excuses for this lord now that my lady is dead.'

Good. He could go home and be with his clan, honoured by the warband, and perhaps even be king for a few years. But something of that mad misery in his eyes gave me a cold certainty that it would be no more than a few years. A curse? Not, I thought; in the sense of some black spell like the one that had nearly killed Eivlin. But the woman had been his mother, and he had never come to terms with her, and now he had murdered her and never could. Morgawse, dead. I remembered her terrible eyes and soft voice. Darkness, still present, threatened no less savagely with Morgawse of Orcade dead.

The door of the hut was flung open, and I started out of my brooding to see Rhuawn. He stared back, astonished, then grinned.

'Rhys! You are safe, then. I am glad. And you are the Queen's servant, Eivlin . . .'

I stood, carefully dusting off the bread crumbs. Eivlin also stood, eyeing Rhuawn suspiciously. 'Much health, Rhuawn,' I said.

He nodded briskly. 'But what has happened to you? How have you come back? I tell you, Rhys, these past few days have been as confused as some nightmare. I heard that Gwalchmai had come back. I told Medraut, through the door – he has locked himself into the Queen's room, and he will not speak to anyone. He said a few days ago that you had had trouble with Maelgwn's men . . .'

'Rhuawn . . .' I interrupted.

He frowned. 'Come. I know. I gave you a blow and some hard words when you were insolent. But do not hold that against me still.' He dropped onto the other bed, waving a loose hand for us to sit as well. Leaning forward, hands locked together between his knees, he went on, 'You were insolent, but, God knows, you spoke from loyalty. You are not to blame for misunderstanding the situation, and I lost my temper, and went further than I meant to. Is it well?' He put out a hand, smiling a little. After an instant's hesitation, I took it. Deluded still or not, Rhuawn's apology, such as it was, was sincere.

'It is well, if well with you, Lord. Though I think I did understand the situation.'

His smile vanished, but he shrugged. 'As you say. But come, tell me what has happened. I do not know whether I stand on firm earth or on ocean. Medraut said he fought some of Maelgwn's men, who were a bit over-hasty when they tried to prevent you from leaving. Did you escape from them?'

I shook my head. 'There is no way that I could escape from them, seeing that they were never there. I did escape, though, but from Medraut, the Queen Morgawse, and a warrior they had with them to guard the horses. That was Eivlin's doing.'

Rhuawn frowned, and began tapping his knee with his sword hand. 'Are you still unreasonable about Medraut?' he asked.

'Lord, I am saying nothing more than the truth. Medraut is a sorcerer and a liar. He charmed you, and nearly charmed me, into believing him honest. He and the Queen had some plan against your lord the Emperor which involved getting my lord Gwalchmai out of the way first. That was why he chose us to practise his lies on . . .'

But Rhuawn was shaking his head. 'This makes no sense. I like Medraut ap Lot. I have known for years, too, that Gwalchmai has a kind of madness in him.'

'You have also known that Morgawse was a witch.'

'So it has been said. But it is much more reasonable to believe that she has merely excited envious rumours.'

'Lord, you cannot believe that! Think of her a moment.'

He paused, uneasily, then shook his head again. 'This makes no sense. Why should I listen to a runaway servant?'

'Because I am speaking the truth. And I'll swear to it by any oath you choose.'

He studied me, and looked at Eivlin. She nodded her support. He stood abruptly, walked over to the fire. Not a stupid man, I thought, and basically a good man. Caught in his own confusions.

'If I believe you, Medraut is a subtle, treacherous, dangerous schemer.' He found a stick and prodded the fire savagely. 'While I am a fool.'

I wanted to agree, but it would be better to let him keep his place, that carefully won position of important warrior. 'Not a fool, Lord. Just a man who is honest enough to believe others honest, and experienced enough to know about court manoeuvrings and think of men's words and policies rather than their actions and characters. That is no dishonour.'

'In other words, Rhys, a fool.' His stick had caught fire, and he raised the tip out of the flames, watching the end burn. 'But there are good, arguable reasons for believing both sides here.'

'You have known Gwalchmai for years. Think about actions and personality instead of reasons.'

He shook his head. 'But I like Medraut. He is less . . . less unwordly than Gwalchmai, more careful of his clan and position. Or so he has seemed. You have never struck me as a liar, Rhys, and yet – you could be mistaken. Gwalchmai . . . yes, he is as generous, as noble and courteous a man as any I know, and yet . . .'

'Gwalchmai has murdered our mother.' The voice broke in like a sword stroke, and we all spun about. Medraut stood in the door, watching us. I had not heard him come.

There was nothing wild about him, as there had been about Agravain's appearance. He was too calm, almost, well dressed in a purple-bordered cloak, gold-studded baldric at a precise and elegant angle. But his eyes were too bright, and very, very cold.

'Well?' he asked, addressing no one. 'A fine madness, isn't it, Rhuawn, to bring a sword down into your mother's neck, and sheath it again all bloody with the source of your own life.'

'What are you saying?' asked Rhuawn, horrified at the words.

He smiled, brightly, mockingly. 'I think I was plain enough.' Dropping his hand from the door frame he strolled into the room. 'Gwalchmai and Agravain between them have murdered Morgawse of Orcade, daughter of the Pendragon Uther, their mother and mine. They killed her because they thought she was having an affair with Maelgwn.'

'Agravain killed her,' I said. Rhuawn stared at me, shocked. Medraut's clear grey eyes also fixed on me, and looking at him was as chilling as looking at Morgawse. 'Agravain killed her because she murdered Lot by sorcery.'

Medraut laughed. 'Agravain! A whimpering puppy, a cur that should have been drowned at birth! If she had been herself she could have blotted him off the face of the earth with one snap of her fingers. Oh, he may have held the sword, but the heart that forged the deed and the mind that framed it belong to Gwalchmai, may the hounds of Yffern devour his heart and mind down all the eternities we can dream of, asleep or waking. He killed her.'

Rhuawn was shaking his head in confusion. 'Rhys,' quietly. 'Rhys, is this true?'

'Agravain killed the Queen,' I insisted. 'He did it to revenge his father. Gwalchmai was there before Agravain arrived, but he only talked to her, and left again. I was there, and left with him. Medraut was there too. My lord did not kill her, though it would have been easy and desirable for him to have done so.'

'No.' Medraut laid one palm flat against the wall, looking at me with a fixed bright stare. 'No. He merely crushed her, kicked her aside, and left. He killed some men from his father's warband, his cousins, and left. With you. Why should I dispute it with you? I came to ask you where he is.'

'He is talking to Agravain.'

'And together they wash their hands in her blood and gloat, saying how well done it was, how now the earth is free of a great sorceress. Rhuawn!' Medraut whirled to him, face pale, but eyes even brighter. 'I told you he was mad. Do you see what has happened, now that he has gone unchecked? Murder, murder of his kin, murder of his own mother, my mother, who made all the world look pale

249

beside her beauty. She who commanded, and the stars bowed in heaven! She is dead. Oh by the sun, the blood, and the sword, and ... but it is better. He would have done worse things. She talked to him, and he would have done worse things to her. But ahhh...' the words died into a cry of pain, and he stood motionless, blinking. He was not pretending the pain for Rhuawn's sake. It was real enough, and more convincing than even his best acting had been. It called Rhuawn over to him, to catch his arm.

'Come, sit down,' Rhuawn said. 'The thing is appalling, I know, to lose both parents within three days' time; and yet, cousin, one must live on. Rhys, get him something to drink.' When I did not move, Rhuawn jerked his head up and glared. 'Do you still believe Gwalchmai, after this?'

'I was there,' I said. 'Gwalchmai did not kill her. And I'm certain she would have killed him – or killed Medraut, for that matter, if she thought it would help.'

'You lie!' Medraut jumped up again. 'She would never have killed me. She told me so. Not me! She, she ... God, but I will kill you, and Gwalchmai, and Arthur. Especially Arthur...'

'Hush. My lord Arthur has nothing to do with it.' Rhuawn was confused. 'Rhys, fetch him something to drink. Medraut, my lord Arthur is not your enemy.'

Medraut looked at him and began to laugh. I left to fetch some mead, and Eivlin left with me.

Saidi ap Sugyn was even less pleased to see us this time, but gave us another flask of mead. I took the flask and two more cups and started back to the hut, but I told Eivlin to find Gwalchmai and tell him what had happened. Agravain ought to be calm enough now to go to sleep, if he were not dead drunk, and I did not trust Medraut. He might do anything at all.

Except for the hissing of the fire, the hut was completely silent when I got back. Medraut, apparently, had no wish to be consoled. Rhuawn again crouched before the fire, prodding at it with his stick, while Medraut sat on the bed, looking relaxed and controlled again, eyes fixed on the door, fingers curled loosely about the hilt of his sword. When I came in, Rhuawn threw his stick into the fire, took the flask of mead from me, and poured a cup for himself and for Medraut. Medraut barely glanced at the offered drink, so

Rhuawn set the cup down beside him and went to the fire.

Gwalchmai came only a few minutes later, Eivlin trailing in behind him. He stopped in the door, waiting.

Medraut stood slowly, hand still on his sword, eyes unwavering. Gwalchmai met the stare evenly, though his hand also drifted to the gold of his sword hilt. 'Medraut.' He spoke the name very gently. 'You wished to see me.'

'Rhuawn.' Medraut still did not look away. 'I wish to speak to my brother privately.'

'Of course.' Rhuawn stepped towards the door, then stopped. 'Cousin, if you wish to come to Camlann with us, my lord Arthur offers rich hospitality to all. There would be a place for you. And friends, myself among them. It might be good for you to see another land, and to forget the past . . . . I will be waiting down the hill. Shout if you need help.'

Medraut nodded, not looking at him, and Rhuawn slipped past Gwalchmai out the door. Eivlin looked at me, pale-faced, and, when I nodded, followed him out, closing the door behind her. I stayed. Perhaps there was little I could do, but to wait down the hill seemed too far away.

Gwalchmai glanced at me and frowned a little. 'It is not necessary, Rhys.'

I crossed my arms and leaned against the wall by the fire.

'Let your mastiff stay and guard you, then,' said Medraut. 'It is unimportant whether he or anyone else hears what we say.' He took a deep breath, and the gold glittered on his baldric and collar. 'I wanted to see what you would say to the truth, the simple truth. You killed Mother.'

'I?'

'You. Oh, I know, Agravain carried the sword. But if you had not broken her with that other sword, your sword, she would be alive. Is it sweet to you, to have destroyed the most splendid thing the world ever held?'

'Medraut. It is not sweet, but very bitter – and yet I did not kill her.'

'Death and defeat are the same, especially for her. And the guilt is yours, evade it as you will, yours. And I know it. That is what I wished to tell you.' He was infinitely cool, elegantly calm.

Gwalchmai approached him slowly, stopping when they were only a foot or so apart. He too was completely calm, but with the kind of calmness the sick man has when the pain is so great, so wearing, that he ceases to struggle with it. His voice was entirely steady. 'Before God, I swear that when I left, my heart held no malice towards her. Earlier I might have killed her, but you yourself saw what became of that. Medraut, she is dead. And you saw, before we fought her at the last, how little you meant to her. Leave her be. It was a long, dark dream, brother, but it is ended now. If you will waken, the night is over.'

'The night is real, and your day is a delusion. What I told Rhuawn is true: you are mad, brother, chasing after an illusion and destroying the reality. One day I will take your Camlann, your lord Arthur, your beloved Family, and break them all to fragments, and the night will have its own.'

'Then you will break the most splendid and lovely thing in this dark West. Forget the Darkness, Medraut. You cared about other things once. I know, once you loved other things than power and her. Medraut, I have cared. I have thought of you, since I left, again and again, wondered what she did to you, prayed that you would break free. Can't you wake even now?'

'I have woken. She is dead. As for love, brother, I loved you once, and it makes me hate you the more now.' Medraut's mouth began to curl into his mocking smile again, and his eyes glittered. His hair shone in the lamplight. Facing him, Gwalchmai looked like a shadow. 'But perhaps I should go and see your sweet dream of light, brother. I think I will. I will accept Rhuawn's offer. I will go to Camlann, to visit my father.'

Gwalchmai's eyes widened only a fraction, but a jewel flashed on his collar as he drew in his breath too quickly. Medraut noticed and laughed.

'Yes, my father. I know now, you see. Mother told me. After Agravain used that sword of his.' He struck the hilt of his own sword abruptly, hard enough to hurt his hand, but no pain showed in his face, only an intensity near to desperation. 'Agravain was frightened, you see, and did it badly; and then he was more frightened, and ran out. I had just woken from the half-death your sorceries sent me to, but I came to her. He had cut her deeply, from the base of the neck through the collar bone, down towards her heart. But she was still alive. And she spoke to me. She said she had always loved me, only me, and never anyone else – she said that, do you hear.' Gwalchmai was shaking his head sadly in denial. 'She said that. But then she said, "So now, fulfil our plans, if you love me. Go to your father." And I said, "The man they called my father is dead; who do you mean?" And she smiled.' For the first time, Medraut's eyes left his brother's face, and stared out the door into the night. 'She smiled that smile of hers that made your heart stop, the smile that no one will ever see again. But when she spoke, her voice bubbled over the blood. She said, 'Your true father, who begot you in Britain, that summer when Uther was Pendragon. Go to my brother Arthur at Camlann. Go to your father.' At first I didn't see what she meant. Then I did see, and she knew that I saw it, and she died, still smiling. Then . . . then I put wood about the hut and fired it, and watched it burn until it was only ashes. She is dead, my mother. Shall I go to my father?' He smiled again, but the smile twisted into a grimace of pain. His shoulders were shaking, hands clenched, but the unwavering cold eyes were fixed on Gwalchmai again. I felt sick.

'Medraut!' Gwalchmai raised one hand in a helpless compassion.

'Death to you all!' Medraut whispered, then, his voice rising to a shriek of agony and fury, 'Death and ruin to you all, you traitors, you murdering, raping, unsurping . . .' The cry trailed into a scream of frenzy, and he turned, rushed out of the room into the night. The door slammed shut behind him.

Gwalchmai looked at the door, hand still lifted. 'Medraut,' he whispered, then slowly lowered his hand, fingers curling, straightening. 'Medraut.' I couldn't move. The fire hissed loudly in the silence, and the shadows flickered about the hearth.

After a minute, Gwalchmai sat down on the bed. He looked at me. After another moment, 'It is true,' very quietly.

'Arthur is his father?'

'Yes.'

'Incest? And Arthur her great enemy, as well as her brother?'

'Yes.' Gwalchmai nodded tiredly, rubbed one hand down his thigh. He looked at the fire. 'My lord did not know at the time that he was Uther's son. It was a month or so later that he led some raid for the Pendragon, and did it so well that he attracted Uther's attention. When Uther sought him out, it was discovered that my lord was his own son. My mother knew it beforehand. That was why she seduced him.' He looked back to me and said calmly, simply, 'You will say nothing of this to anyone. It would do harm to my lord.'

'They will guess, if he goes to Camlann. He looks like Arthur.'

'If they only guess, it will do no harm. Rumours can be ignored.'

'But will Medraut go to Camlann? Can he? You know, and can tell Arthur, that he means to destroy us all.'

'The High King must give hospitality to any noble who comes. He certainly can't refuse it to the son, or the brother, of the king of the Orcades. Arthur wanted to send me home when I first came, but he couldn't. Medraut will go to Camlann. And he will find many friends there, though he will still in himself be friendless.' Gwalchmai rested his elbows on his knees, rubbed his hands across his forehead. 'Maelgwn will let us go now, but he will continue to scheme on his own. Agravain will go home to Dun Fionn in the Orcades. We agreed that this would be best. The warband will probably name him king in the next few days, and the rest of the clan will doubtless confirm it when he gets back. We will visit Arthur first, of course, and he will swear loyalty. But he will die, Rhys. This thing will kill him. And . . .' He pressed his hands against his eyes. 'And . . .' His shoulders began to shake, as though something within him were breaking, and he gave one quiet, racking sob.

I stood against the wall a moment, looking at him. 'We can go home to my clan,' I had told Eivlin. And if I left him to ride out his own grief, we could. He had managed without me before, and doubtless he could manage without me again.

But to walk away from suffering is the act of a coward, and a selfish coward, and it is following Darkness instead of Light. I could not close the door behind me. I had only one choice to make, and I had already made that one.

I crossed the room, dropped to my knees beside him and

254

caught his arm. 'My lord.'

He looked up, mouth set with pain, eyes dark and exhausted.

'My lord,' I repeated, holding his shoulder. He caught my wrist, looking away, and began to weep with quiet, hopeless, tearing sobs, half-choked off, as though he feared to tear up his own heart. I held his shoulder. There was nothing at all to say.

In the end I could not do much except convince him to drink some of the mead and go to sleep. He could not talk the pain out, or cry loudly or shed numerous tears. I knew that the next day would find him courteous, rather remote, attentive to Agravain, ready to fence eloquently with Maelgwn about the journey back to Camlann or the tribute due to the Emperor.

When he was asleep I took the mead and went out to look for Eivlin.

She was still waiting down the hill, though Rhuawn was gone. She sat with her knees pulled up, looking at the moon. I came up behind her, then stopped, looking at the moonlight in her hair.

'Eivlin?' I said.

She turned, the light gliding over her face and shining on her eyes, and her smile made her wondrously beautiful. 'Rhys.' She patted the grass beside her, and I came and sat down.

'Isn't the moonlight lovely on the mountains?' she asked. 'Though on the sea it is even more beautiful. At Dun Fionn you can look out from the cliffs and see the crests of the waves all silver and traced with foam, and the hollows of the waves all black and shifting.' She stared up at the moon itself, a waxing moon in a deeply blue sky. 'How far away the moon is, the gem of the night. I wonder if she can see us.'

I shook my head. 'Would you like some mead?'

She smiled, tossed her head. 'Ach, everyone else has been having some. Yes.'

I poured it, and we drank it together, looking at the moon. 'Eivlin,' I said, when the cups were empty.

She looked at me, her lips half parted, eyes gentle. 'You are going to say that you cannot go back to your family and your farm,' she stated calmly.

I blinked. 'No. I can't now.'

'Because you love him?'

'That too. But because he needs me now.' I pulled a blade of grass and studied it by the moonlight. I could see the crease down its centre, and all the delicate little lines of its growth. 'You see, he never used to have a servant, until I came and asked him to take me to Camlann. He has a damnably proud humility which makes him always be at someone's service – Arthur's, Agravain's, Elidan's, whoever's. He could always be depended on, but depended on no one. So I began to do things for him without waiting for him to ask me, and because he is courteous and gentle he made room for me, until now he has come to depend on me. And, now, he needs me. Now especially. Dear God, he's suffered enough to break any man. I can't go. I've committed myself to him, and to what's happening at Camlann, too far to pull back. Rightly or wrongly, the only thing I can do now is to live for the Light, and pray God that Camlann survives Medraut and the things ahead. But whether or not we succeed, whether or not we actually keep the Light burning, the only choice I have now is to stay with it.' I let the blade of grass drop, thinking of what I was tying myself to and thinking of Morgawse's words.

Eivlin reached over and took my hand, cradling it in both of hers. 'If that is the only choice, my heart, at least it is a good one. And he's a good lord.'

I caught her hands in turn, with both of mine, turning to her. This was the thing that made it hard. 'But I still want you to come. Perhaps it's no world to marry into, to raise children in, but if you could . . .'

'"If I could!" Listen to the man! Do you think I am so easily put off, Rhys? Let your clan farm all the land on both sides of the Mor Hafren and let them root in it: I am coming with you. Always. Without asking me, you said you would marry me; and now, without being asked, I say I will. For ever.' She paused, then added briskly, 'But you must be sure we get our own house in Camlann, and be sure it is a good one. Your lord should be able to manage that, at the very least. And I will be the mistress of my own house, and it will be a very fine thing.'

'Yes,' I told her, grinning at her. 'Yes. A very fine thing indeed.'

'Well, sorcerer,' he said, 'Your sword isn't burning now. Does the magic fail before human courage?'

I was mad, but it was not my accustomed madness; nothing was clear, there was a red mist over my eyes and a salt taste in my mouth. I cried out howling like a dog, and rushed at him.

By Heaven, he fought bravely, and never dropped his savage grin. 'I . . . am not afraid . . . of your magic,' he told me, working hard to get the words out. He must have wanted very badly to say them. 'I am king, a king, may Yffern . . . take you . . .' His shield drooped a little and I saw my chance and thrust forward driving the sword through his ribs to the heart . . . I stepped back and let him fall to the earth . . . I kicked the body twice, hard, then left it for the plunderers and went back to Arthur and the Family. And that was how I committed murder . . .'